The Dragonlover's Guide to Pern

THE DRAGONLOVER'S GUIDE TO PERN

SECOND EDITION

Jody Lynn Nye
with
Anne McCaffrey

Illustrated by Todd Cameron Hamilton

Maps and additional illustrations by James Clouse

DEL REY

BALLANTINE BOOKS • NEW YORK

A Del Rey® Book
Published by Ballantine Books

Copyright © 1989, 1997 by Bill Fawcett and Associates

All rights reserved under International and Pan-American Copyright Conventions.
Published in the United States by Ballantine Books, a division of Random House, Inc., New York,
and simultaneously in Canada by Random House of Canada Limited, Toronto.

http://www.randomhouse.com

Library of Congress Catalog Card Number: 97-92989

ISBN: 0-345-41274-5

Cover design by Min Choi
Cover illustration by Todd Cameron Hamilton

Design by Holly Johnson

Manufactured in the United States of America

First Ballantine Books Trade Paperback Edition: December 1992

Second Ballantine Books Trade Paperback Edition: March 1997

10 9 8 7 6 5 4

To my grandmother,
Estelle S. Nye,
in whose costume shop I spent
some of the best times of my life.

Contents

Acknowledgments

My sincere thanks and appreciation to all the following people for their many contributions: Marilyn and Harry Alm of Ista Weyr, New Orleans, for their kind help and awe-inspiring mathematics; Dr. Jack Cohen; Ed at the Adler Planetarium; Derval Diamond for inspiration; Robin Wood and her lovely portraiture; Sarah "Sis" Brooks for wonderful meals and information on weaving and wholistic healing; Jay Katz, who helped to make the guide possible; Todd Hamilton and Jim Clouse for extraordinary artwork; Lila and Cassandra for walking on the computer keys; Barbara Young, editrix; Chris Power for responding to an emergency cry for spinning wheel data; Terri Beckett and my mother for supportiveness; Julia Eckler for setting Anne's words to music so beautifully; Todd and Gigi Johnson; and Anne McCaffrey (of course!), for whose patience, kindness, and encouragement I am forever grateful.

Introduction

In the fall of 1987, Bill Fawcett, Todd Hamilton, Todd Johnson, and I spent ten days in Anne McCaffrey's living room in Dragonhold in Ireland, asking questions—and, in Todd Hamilton's case, making sketches under her direction. There was so much to learn. Pern is richly textured and convincingly three-dimensional.

While I was finishing up the last touches on this guide to Pern, I was tempted to add to it. There was so much more I could have included. In the end, I decided to leave it as it is. I can't say enough in the space of one book about the heroic men and women who unite against the common menace of Thread; or dragons, the gentle giants of Pern; or fire lizards, the Pernese answer to kittens. Anne McCaffrey's wonderful books, the same ones that drew me to her world, will have to fill you in further on the things I could only touch on. This is a companion volume to her work, intended to help you visualize the setting and background for her chronicles. Todd and Jim Clouse have contributed over a hundred pieces of art, and Todd Johnson, Anne's son and a pilot, has included a well-researched, definitive article on the Fighting Wings.

Just what kind of a place is Pern? It is a world where you can make of a *dragon* an intelligent, endlessly sympathetic friend who will share your every thought and hope, and on whose back you can really *fly*. It is a place where technology has lost its toehold and pollution never existed. To be sure, it suffers a terrifying menace in Thread, but between incursions, Pern is still a world for explorers. The frontiers haven't yet all been crossed. And the coffee there tastes as good as it smells. It's almost too good to be true.

Jody Lynn Nye
Lake Zurich, Illinois

I.

Overview

In the constellation known as Sagittarius the Archer, positioned at -41° right ascendancy 19'25" two hundred light-years from the Sol system, there is a fourth-magnitude blue-white star designated as Alpha Sagittarius. The Arab astronomers who discovered it called it Rukbat Al-Rami, or "the Archer's Knee." Throughout Earth's history, it has also been called Al Rami, Ruchbar ur Ranich, Rucba, Rukbah, and Rukbar, all referring to the ancient Arabic tale that gave the constellation its name.

Sagittarius and Rukbat

Circling the star Rukbat are five planets, two asteroid belts, a rogue planet on an eccentric orbit captured by the gravity well in recent millennia, and an Oort cloud at the perimeter of the stellar system.

The Oort cloud is composed of smaller particles than expected of such a body, as Oort clouds are usually nebulous collections of stone and ice chunks—comets.

The first and second planets are too small to sustain human life. The fourth, which has a cluster of little moons, and the fifth planet, a dark world, are too far away from Rukbat for comfortable existence; they are separated from the sun and from each other by the two asteroid belts, which significantly cuts down on the sunlight they receive.

On the third planet, among seas of liquid water, heavy volcanic and plate-tectonic activity caused the earliest single land mass to re-form into three continents over the last hundred million years. One continent is gigantic, taking up more than half of the available landmass. The second, somewhat smaller and resembling a dragon in flight looking back over its shoulder, is approximately the size of Earth's Eurasian landmass. The last, very small, barren continent is isolated on the

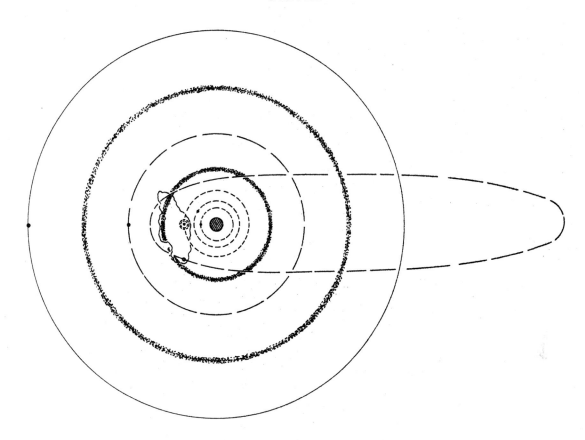

Orbit of the Red Star Through the Oort Cloud

other side of the world in the middle of an ocean five thousand miles wide. The planet's diameter is approximately sixty-five hundred miles.

A single revolution around Rukbat takes this world 366 Earth days. (A Pern day is a little over twenty-four hours long; the Pernese count 362 days to their year, with a leap year every sixth year.) The world has an axial tilt of fifteen degrees, giving it distinct seasons and climate belts ranging from snowy at both poles to hot summers at the tropical equator. It remains actively volcanic. New cones form in the sea bed near both large continents and in volcanic sea islands arrayed in long barrier ranges enclosing the two like giant parentheses. The southern continent shows considerable volcanic and tectonic activity. A deep trench, probably a subsidence center, lies in the ocean near the Eastern Barrier Range. The northern is more stable, having basement rock as its pedestal.

Two moons revolve around the planet. Timor, the more distant moon, is about the size of Luna, while the closer moon, Belior, is somewhat smaller, so Pern has tides. There is a constant thirty-mile-an-hour head wind, driven by the pattern of tides and thermals from the volcanoes.

Pern from Space

3

II.

Fit for Human Habitation

THE EEC EXPLORATION

In order to designate a planet as a potential site for colonization, the Exploration and Evaluation Corps was required to locate at least five identifiable landing sites, potable water, breathable air devoid of methanes or cyanides, and ensure that no sentient life form already existed there. The Rukbat system was at the extreme reach of the exploration circuit, but it seemed promising.

The EEC team that discovered the system consisted of four men and women. Ben Turnien was a top-flight geologist and chemist. Captain Castor, the pilot, was also an accomplished chemist. Shavva bint Faroud, a biologist, shared the duties of nexialist with botanist Mo Tan Liu. Unfortunately, the team was short-handed; they had lost four of their original eight to ill luck and carelessness on planets visited earlier, and Castor was unable to join the landing party due to a broken ankle.

The remaining three were forced to double up on jobs planetside. Even allowing five days for the survey, the small team was unable to give the world more than a cursory examination.

They found the third planet circling Rukbat to have a breathable atmosphere with slightly above normal oxygen content, and gravity only ninety percent of Earth normal. Through the atmosphere, the star Rukbat shone golden with a cast of green. The planet's soil appeared to be arable, fostering plant growth that, although its green hue tended to range more toward blue or yellow than did that of Earth vegetation, appeared to utilize photosynthesis to live.

Fossils showed animal life to have existed on the third planet as early as 100 million planetary years before. The most interesting casts were of a large creature with four limbs and two wings, big lizardlike creatures, and some gigantic snakes taken from a site north of the body of water on the southern continent that would one day be called Drake's Lake, At the thirty-five-million-year mark, widespread evidence of tree-fern fossils suggested a carboniferous landscape.

An extensive tar pit revealed fifty-thousand-year-old fossils of ruminants, flat-toothed cattlelike creatures that ate only vegetation. The "grass" those extinct creatures chewed contained no silicates and was visibly triangular in cross section, like most of the modern vegetation. The ruminants appeared to be extinct, which bothered the exploration team but, in fact, eased the way for a potential colony to bring in its own herbivorous meat animals.

More fossils, this time in a core sample taken offshore, showed a marine shell-colony system similar to coral that had existed for some 500 million years.

Life on the planet—marine, plant, animal, and fungoid—displayed considerable variation, suggesting to the landing party that the process of evolution was ongoing here, and not stagnant. The nexialist Liu reported finding litoral fungi that showed visible independent movement. Only one unexplained phenomenon was discovered: a large number of circular bare patches scattered all over the planet's surface. The team assumed a local fungus or vegetable plague was to blame, although they had no idea why the strong winds would not have reseeded those spots.

The mycota that proved to be the most interesting to the botanist/nexialist Liu was first discovered in a cave on the biggest island. He identified the luminous fungus as a mycelium that glowed when exposed to oxygen. It retained its light for an unusually long time, suggesting its usefulness as a light source. The spores were tiny, but there were enormous quantities in the caves.

Specimens were taken of seaweeds, trees, grassoids, beach-walking insectoids and crustacepoids, red and green algae, and of the soil itself. Ferns grew in abundance in the tropical regions of the planet. Flying insectoid pollinators attracted to flame had double sets of wings. Reptiloids, some as big as seven meters long and ten centimeters thick, inhabited the jungles. Big six-limbed avians which resembled English river barges, or "wherries," were named for them in the EEC report. Two identifiable types of the "wherry" avians, both predatory, were cataloged, as were numerous brilliantly plumed smaller avians.

A thousand types of the local insectoids, inland, shoregoing, and seagoing, were identified and cataloged. A brief survey uncovered 150 kinds of bacteria, fungi, and mycorrhizae within a fairly small area. Of the lower chordata, nematoda, "earthworms," sandworms, and ground mites abounded. Tunneling creatures that the team believed were not reptiloid managed to avoid the team's snares and had to be implied in the landing report. Fish and larger creatures fed along the shores at planetary dusk.

Large herpetoids existed in the jungles and in the warmer mixed terrain. One mottled monster seven centimeters broad and five high, with tentacles and claws and no discernable eyes or mouth, was described by Shavva in the report. The creature lured its prey with a terrible stench, an odor unpalatable to the human landing team but no doubt attractive to its food, and trapped the victims

Glows

on its sticky back. One of the scientists suggested that the sticky back was an external digestive system.

This creature led them to the discovery of another plant, a spine-throwing bush that shot its barrage toward anything that touched it.

Needlethorn Plant

Flying creatures with hides of green, blue, brown, bronze, or gold, four limbs, wings, heads, and forked tails, were spotted, and the landing party suspected them to be the egg layers who produced the shells lying in the beach sands along every tropical coast. The fliers were considered to be at least potentially intelligent, though limited. If the creatures laid their eggs on shorelines close enough to be washed away during storms, the team felt that they lacked reasoning capacity. And yet they were capable of organized play, which suggested they were aware of their environment. No more was noted about those graceful creatures in the report.

The planet was rich in minerals, though ore, which existed in quantities too small to be of interest to the Federated Sentient Planets as a mining concern, was not easily accessible. Near a small chain of lakes in the Southern Continent west of a vast lake feeding three rivers, investigation revealed deposits of iron, copper, vanadium, platinum, and gold. More minerals, including tin, bauxite, and nickel, were found farther to the west in dense, sulfurous mud flats. Gem-quality minerals existed in plenty, including diamonds, rubies, quartzes, beryls, and an entire range of precious stones. Three landing sites were identified in the South.

The big islands in the bay to the north were largely basaltic. The largest was a puzzle of geological samples. The western half was limestone overlying schist, with granite outcropping on the southwest coast. Gold-bearing quartz and all the corundum minerals appeared on that island, as well as black dia-

Mug of Klah

mond crystals. The sites produced enormous high-quality rough jewels, some of which were taken back by the landing team for further study.

Two potential landing sites were identified on the Northern Continent. One lay at the top of a chain of small lakes near what would one day be Telgar Hold. The other lay at the source of the river flowing near what is now Benden Weyr.

A hearty plant with delicious pungent-smelling bark passed the scientists' toxicity test. An infusion of the bark proved to taste as good as it smelled, like a cross between coffee and chocolate with a spicy aftertaste. To produce a strong enough infusion to drink, they ground up some of the bark and brewed it like coffee. In time, both the tree and the drink came to be known as klah.

COLONIAL LANDING, THE SHIPS AND COMMANDERS

A Charter was drawn up between the group of colonists and the Council of the Federated Sentient Planets. Six thousand twenty-three people signed the Pern Charter, giving them rights to certain numbers of stake acres. Three ships, under the command of Admiral Paul Benden, a hero of the Nathi War, spent fifteen years crossing from Earth to the Rukbat system. The *Yokohama* held the same number of people, both awake and in deepsleep, as the *Buenos Aires* and the smaller *Bahrain* combined.

One more sentient life-form joined the humans' exodus to Pern: Twenty-five dolphins, all volunteers, slept in the cryogenic

---

Approximate composition of groups of settlers:

YOKOHAMA
Flagship of Pern Colony, Admiral Paul Benden commanding. 2,900 people, of which 2,500 remained in deepsleep; the other 400 took turns alternating five-year watches.

BUENOS AIRES
Captain Ezra Keroon
1,733 people, of which 1,500 remained in deepsleep; the other 233 stayed awake or alternated watches.

BAHRAIN
Captain James Tillek
1,390 people, of which 1,200 remained in deepsleep; the other 190 alternated watches.
25 dolphins

Demographics
2,000 unattached
2,020 married (1,010 couples)
120 single parents
223 over bearing age
721 nomads
939 children
_____
Total 6,023

Dolphin

chambers. Like the humans, they were eager to explore new seas, and they had no objection to be put to work rounding up specimens of native creatures for the human marine biologists.

Each ship was constructed on long metal vanes interposed between the engines at the rear and a spherical living-and-cargo pod at the forward end. Cargo that did not need atmosphere or special care was lashed between the vanes to save interior space. Access to the engines was through a narrow passage that led through the core of the vanes but could be shut off from atmosphere.

The journey took fifteen Earth years. The crew aboard each ship alternated five-year shifts out of cryogenic sleep. Only vital personnel, among them Admiral Paul Benden and his two captains, Ezra Keroon and James Tillek, along with astrogator Avril Bitra, spent the entire trip awake. Benden had been the commander of the Purple Sector Fleet and led the FSP victory at Cygnus, which turned the tide of war against the Nathis. He was in his eighth decade when the colonists departed Earth. Humans of his day could expect to live up to eleven decades, so

Yokohama

he was considered to be in late middle age.

Six months before they reached Pern, the landing specialists were awakened to give them time to adjust before their services were needed. Emily Boll, co-leader of the colony, began final organization of the first landing personnel. The ships entered Pern's system at the end of the winter season in the Southern Continent, late autumn in the North.

Charter members of the colony, mostly veterans or surviving dependents of parents killed in the Nathi War, were allowed to purchase "stake" acres on Pern. Specialists could buy stake acres, too, by contracting their services, so many acres per contract year. There were approximately the same number of specialists as charterers. The third group was made up of 721 nomads—Jensche, Tuareg, gypsies, and Irish traveling folk—who, having resisted every assimilation or indoctrination program of Earth's increasingly high-tech society, were no longer welcome on their home planet. Taking the nomads along to Pern had been a requisite of the FSP-colonist Charter. All the two groups had in common was the wish to escape the over-technicized, impersonal society of the FSP worlds or the memory-filled remains of the war.

The chosen landing site, named Landing, was on the volcanic plateau in the Southern Continent behind an extinct cone of enormous size with three small cones in a line pointing away from it to the southwest. The large volcano was named Mount Garben, in honor of a senator who had been of service in expediting the FSP's approval of the colony.

After all the cargo had been brought down, the two smaller ships were completely gutted. Everything usable was taken, from bolts to the fuel tanks strapped alongside the

Path of Landing from Orbit Point

Shuttle

cargo bulk. In time, the *Yokohama* was the only ship with functional machinery left aboard. The communications receiver and the voice-activated computer which had guided the ships to Pern were not taken down to the surface. Nothing was left of the Dawn Sisters, as the orbiting ships came to be called in later centuries, but the spheres and vanes.

NATIVE FLORA, NATIVE FAUNA

The leaves of the local flora were predominantly acuminate or ovate at the apexes, and many had sagittate, truncate, or cordate bases, giving them the appearance of arrowheads or dragon-tails. Pernese leaves were angular and sharp, unlike most Terran plants, which had rounder outlines.

On Pern, shrubs grew in plenty, but there were disturbingly few old trees. All those discovered by the colonists seemed to be no older than two to four hundred years. The nonforested areas or plains were covered by the blue-green triangular grassoid described by the EEC team. This proved to be heavy in boron as well as containing the expected trace minerals of copper, magnesium, and sodium, but curiously, no silicates. The internal bacteria in Earth herd animals would need to be adapted to process native vegetation.

In the marshy lands thick-stemmed brushes the size and color of sage plants were discovered. Their arrowhead-shaped leaves, bruised and rubbed on injuries, provided relief from pain. Another native plant, with sharp spearhead leaves, proved to have a nar-

10

Bamboo Grass

generation of trees, creepers, and grasses. In general, the greenery was much thicker than the colonists had cause to expect from the report of the original exploratory team which had visited this world only twenty years after the rogue planet had passed by.

Parasites were rife. Pern had numerous types of insects, most of which had been noted in the EEC report. Buzzing flies, fireflies, and some types which the entymologists called VTOLS (for "Vertical Take-Off and Landing") were caught in large numbers around the settlement. Stinging pests like bedbugs and "crawlies"—tiny creatures like six-legged geckos with suction cup feet—quickly started making nuisances of themselves in the humans' new habitations. "Rollers" were a type of wood louse. "Springs" were insects that hung in spiral loops until they found something or someone to cling to; their irritating, prickly bite had to be treated with an antihistamine cream. Milli-

cotic sap, which the physicians studied for future use.

Weavers found native flax and sisals among the fibrous plants brought in by the searchers. Some textile makers experimented with weaving thread made of a pounded fiber produced from the inner sheath of a triangular native bamboo grass.

As the plant life was new to the FSP-trained botanists, they created their own names for the local plants. Among the first to be named were the sungazers, the flowers of a little plant that grew mostly underground, showing just the bloom in the grass, very much like an Earth strawflower or windflower.

The rain forests around the Landing plateau appeared to behave very much like those on Earth. The first plants, such as the local bamboo, grew up very quickly, then died and rotted to provide humus for the next

VTOL

Crawlers

pedes and flat, segmented worms scavenged among the seaweed or fallen leaves in the forests. There were also sandworms and earthworms, two related species of burrowers that the botanists observed filling the same niche as the Terran worm.

The biologists found flying pollinators that warred with their imported bees (and won), but the most active pollinator was the trundlebug. It was found to eat parasites, as well as to carry pollen and turn the soil, combining in one creature bee, earthworm, and ladybug. The botanists encouraged it to frequent the new Earth crops. Trundlebugs had the most elaborate color camouflage of all the insects; varieties of black, brown, sand, blue-green, and crystal-clear were found.

Trundle Bugs

All noninsectoid fauna on Pern was warm-blooded and based on a boron-silicon system, rather than the iron-calcium bond of earth animals.

Snakes with turtlelike faces existed in the jungles. Most of these were poisonous and left track marks from the toe teeth along their length on those creatures unlucky enough to be caught in their coils. Similar snakes that grew up to elephantine size lived in the rivers and seas.

The so-called tunnel snakes, which actually had legs, were the most numerous pests, appearing in caves and stony outcroppings. There were numerous varieties of the six-limbed beast. Most averaged two to four feet in length. Some had scales; some had skin. One type had very long legs, but most of them had short, stubby limbs for creeping low against the ground. Many varieties of tunnel snakes had sharp, powerful front claws for gripping and rending. The rear legs pushed the tunnel snakes' skinny bodies through the smallest openings in the rock. The middle pair of limbs served as stabilizers in land-bound varieties and as pseudoflippers with vestigial claws in those species that were water dwellers.

Most tunnel snakes had hearing organs in their chests, close to the ground, but there existed one variety of deep-tunnel beast that had no less than six ear-spots, to make up for the fact that it was nearly blind.

The water-dwelling tunnel snake's bite was venomous and could be dangerous if not treated promptly. The flesh of a victim would swell up painfully. All tunnel snakes had the ungulate jaw that allowed them to ingest small creatures whole. They could go for long periods without feeding, which helped them survive during Threadfall. Some hibernated during the cold seasons when prey was scarce.

Packtails, a tasty but dangerously barbed fish, resembled Terran monkfish.

Tunnel Snake

Fingertails, also edible, were a small carplike fish with a whippy tail. Spiderclaws resembled crabs with many pairs of jointed legs.

The first colonists trapped wherries as a source of meat. These predatory avians were the major hunter/scavengers on the planet and killed large numbers of the smaller imported animals during the first months of settlement.

Wherries had no feathers. Their bodies

Wherry

were covered with thick proto-feathers, multiple tufts like marabou. Their wings were cartilaginous and membranous under the thick down. Like the other native animals of Pern, wherries had six limbs: two wings, two front feet, and two back feet. The front feet, which were much smaller than the back two, had one mobile claw that locked into two rigid claws like pincers, which were used to grab and rend. The back legs were well-muscled and could be employed to kick powerfully, as well as to help the bird leap into the air. Their three toes canted backward when they flew, to keep from being caught by animals on the ground or other wherries. The big avians

turned cannibal when one of their numbers was wounded or killed.

Wherries nested in caves or rocky outcroppings, much as Earth seabirds do. They ate fish, carrion, tunnel snakes, insects, offal, or garbage.

DRAGONETS

The "graceful flying creatures" of the EEC report were spotted first by children out searching for biological specimens. Through luck and good timing, the children discov-

Dragonet Fishing

ered that the creatures' hatchlings would, not unlike Terran ducklings, Impress on the first being that fed them, human or dragonet. Soon many of the colonists had bonded with baby dragonets.

The dragonets were self-sufficient. They could fly almost from the moment of hatching, and they hunted for themselves after accepting the first meal offered by the impressor.

A fair of dragonets would begin humming when a hatching was imminent (and experience proved that the creatures could predict human and animal births, as well). They surrounded the eggs with a ring of seaweed and filled it with small fish and crawling creatures that would provide the hatchlings with their first meal. As soon as the newborns broke shell, they were greeted with cries of joy and offered food. A hatchling had a fierce birth hunger, and the first being—dragonet, human, or otherwise—that offered it food would Impress it.

IMPORTED FLORA

The botanist raised seedlings of all Earth trees in the hydroponics labs. The gingko and cottonwood trees did well in the open plains, breaking the ground and providing shelter for the oak and pine seedlings planted in their shade. Ash, rowan, and scrub pine went into the higher reaches, and willow trees grew on the wet riverbanks.

Earth-type grass was adapted for the animals to eat until they were sufficiently used to Pernese grassoid. In the Ninth Pass, isolated patches of grass still survive on the Southern Continent. Many types of Earth and First Centauri trees reseeded themselves

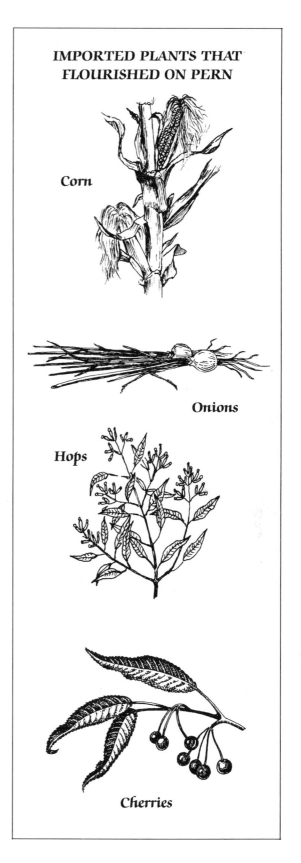

IMPORTED PLANTS THAT FLOURISHED ON PERN

Corn

Onions

Hops

Cherries

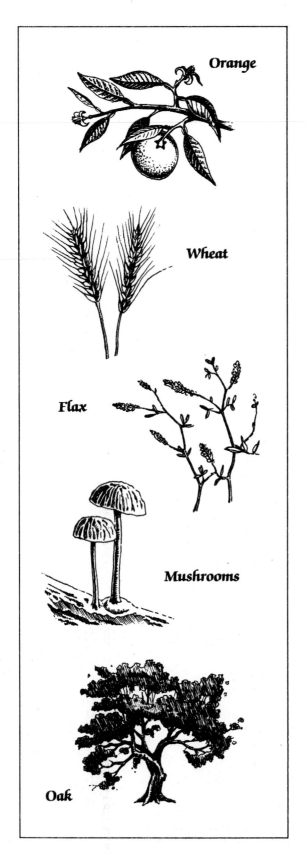

Orange

Wheat

Flax

Mushrooms

Oak

on grubbed ground and can still be found scattered among the Pernese types.

All of the types of Terran grains and legumes did well in the rich native soil. The first crops planted were fodder for the newly bred herds of imported grazers. Packaged organisms that would react symbiotically with the local bacteria were introduced to the soil to make native grasses palatable to the imported animals. The concentrations of boron, rendered inactive, simply passed through their digestive systems.

Mushrooms were raised by the colonists side by side with edible native fungi in the caves that riddled the palisade overlooking the Jordan River. Apples, pears, wine grapes, and numerous other fruits adapted easily to the Pernese soil.

All the medicinal and cooking herbs, among them tarragon, rosemary, lovage (for coughs), borage, thyme, coriander, nutmegoid bark from First Centauri (Earth nutmeg did not translate well), willow for headaches, and hazel for the skin, were grown from seed drawn from the agronomy stores, and thrived in Pernese soil.

Though treats were rare as the supplies began to dwindle, the bakers created little hand-sized one-crust pies for the children from bits of sweet dough and berries, as the brambles matured. Survivor species such as blueberries (which make the most popular bubblies), blackberries, raspberries, and gooseberries still exist in the Present Pass.

It was a spacer tradition to begin distilling liquor as soon as possible when reaching a new planet. It became the measure of every holder or each expedition to make "quikal" almost immediately. The administration trusted the colonists not to use plants that had not been checked for toxicity, but those fruits that had tested safe went promptly into the stills. Some of the imported fruits had a very high sugar content and made enormously powerful quikal. The local fruit made potable drinks, and everyone traded crocks of his or her particular brew.

IMPORTED FAUNA

The stores of ova and sperm aboard the ships were extensive. Any variety of any species that the biogeneticists had thought would prosper on the new world was included. Animal host mothers, some cows and goats of small but sturdy genotypes, were shipped frozen from Earth to Pern and revived to bear fertilized ova of nearly all the larger animals brought from the Animal Reproduction Banks of Terra.

The bearing techniques had been perfected on First Centauri. A host mother did not need to be of the same species as the fetuses she bore. With help, a goat could carry and bear calves or lambs, and a cow was capable of bringing colts and young llamas to term as easily as it could bear its own calves. The cattle of choice were long-haired Scotch cattle with short, curled horns, a small but very tough breed. Ova implanted in them were of every type of cattle suitable for milk, meat, or hide. The sheep were of various kinds, both long- and short-fleeced. With the exception of the Kashmir, all the goats bred survived.

Strong but fairly small horses were bred, blending Connemara and Welsh strains for riding. Shire horses were bred as draft animals and for the gypsy wagons. Llamas served as beasts of burden and to provide hair for spinning.

Goats

Cows

A S I M P O R T E D

A D A P T E D

Pigs were genetically adapted for survival on Pern

The first Earth creature to be born on Pern were chickens. Geese and ducks were next to be hatched out. The fertilized turkey ova failed to mature, but the other types of barnyard fowl were doing well enough that the veterinarians were not displeased to have lost only one species. Doves and pigeons hatched out, but between the wherries and tunnel snakes, neither species lasted long enough to mate.

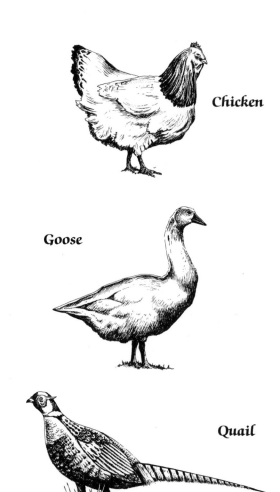

Chicken

Goose

Quail

The pigs were useful as disposal systems, transforming slops into protein-rich meat. Since not as many pigs were bred as other herd animals, pork came to be regarded as a special treat.

The chosen breed of dog was a ferret-dog, a Jack Russell terrier type that would kill the snakes that were attacking the nomad folk who slept in the open air. Later, the dogs were employed to chase and kill tunnel snakes. Felines were also useful against the vermin. Tabby cats were thawed out and began to produce litters within weeks.

Dogs were bred from original genetic stock

Chickens and geese exist on modern-day Pern only in the warmest Holds and in batteries where they are protected from wherries. Very few ducks have survived to the present.

Spiders were successfully hatched out to kill parasites that invaded the human habitations. Spiders survive in the Present Pass but are now known as "gossamer spinners." Ladybugs and other insects brought along to help propagate crops were mostly eaten by the much more numerous indigenous insect population, and few survive.

Grubs

ADAPTATIONS

Permission had been obtained by the bioengineers to use the techniques of the Eridani to adapt animals to Pern. The most important of these methods were gene paring, mentasynth, and chromosome enhancements.

Fish and other marine life from Earth were introduced to the waters of Pern with a minimum of adaptational changes. There was protein-rich plankton in the seas, and the many indigenous fish were pronounced edible by the mariners and their dolphins.

Horses were improved somewhat by genetic tinkering. A number of genotypes coexisted and interbred for sixteen hundreds years, until the plague. During the plague all of the remaining true horses died out, leaving only the "runnerbeasts."

The "grubs," which rendered a piece of protected ground inimical to Thread, were engineered by a renegade biologist/botanist of the original colony. Unfortunately, he left no records of the research that generated these useful insects. He calculated that it would take four hundred years—or until the middle of the Second Interval—for the grubs to multiply enough to protect all of the Southern Continent. Twenty-five hundred years after Landing, the Southern Continent had become unchecked jungle because of the grubs' protection.

Forests of adaptable trees were grown during the Intervals from seeds saved in vacuum packs and cryogenic flasks. They had to be protected during the Falls, so only those species that would continue to be useful to humans were consciously preserved. Any sports that remained in the Southern Continent after the First and Second Passes managed to avoid being destroyed by Thread until the grubs had spread.

The creator of the grubs also experimented with cheetah fetuses, trying to

Evolution of the Pern Feline from Terran Housecat

produce a mentasynth-enhanced feline that would kill tunnel snakes and other dangerous creatures. He was familiar enough with the Eridani equations to know that cats reacted poorly to mentasynth, but he recklessly ignored that knowledge. His bioengineered animals killed him and escaped before he could call for help. They bred in the wild, unseen by man until the Sixth Pass.

Deer and other forest-loving animals did not survive the transition to Pern

When the population moved to the Northern Continent, herds of dogs, goats, sheep, and cattle were left behind to go wild. Some of the dogs and goats still thrive in the wild, but the other breeds have been wiped out by predators.

THE FIRST STAKEHOLDS

Stores were made available by requisition to all who needed them, ostensibly for the purpose of working toward the day when they would claim their stake acres somewhere on Pern and become independent and self-reliant. Each colonist, adult and child alike, understood that when the supplies were gone, they were gone, but until then everyone had an equal claim to the goods. There would be no monetary system instituted.

The colony administration treated all the people like adults, assuming that they would rely upon good sense and maturity to settle matters. Each man, woman, and child was expected to accept responsibility for his or her own actions, and not fall back on a deity to solve problems—an outlook that was a side effect of the crippling Nathi war. Hysterical religions had been debunked. To the colonists, heroes were better than gods. Strong role models of both sexes were encouraged.

Within a year the colonists had spread to their chosen homes. As the planet had no sentient species, the settlers had the privilege of naming the landmarks and provinces of their new home. Some of the names they chose were fanciful, like Xanadu and Paradise River, but some reflected the stakeholders' pride in their background or former homes. The result was a curious reshuffling of Earth geography. Seminole, Roma, Milan, and Thessaly were a few such names.

The plateau behind Mount Garben was simply called Landing, but upriver from it was Cambridge-on-Jordan, the stakehold of the chief legist, Cabot Francis Carter, who had been raised a Boston Brahmin on Earth. Drake Bonneau won a vigorous campaign to have the great lake he had discovered named for him. Three rivers led north from Drake's Lake, a stakehold he shared with several other miners and metallurgists.

Karachi Camp, named for an ancient city in Pakistan on Earth, was the chief min-

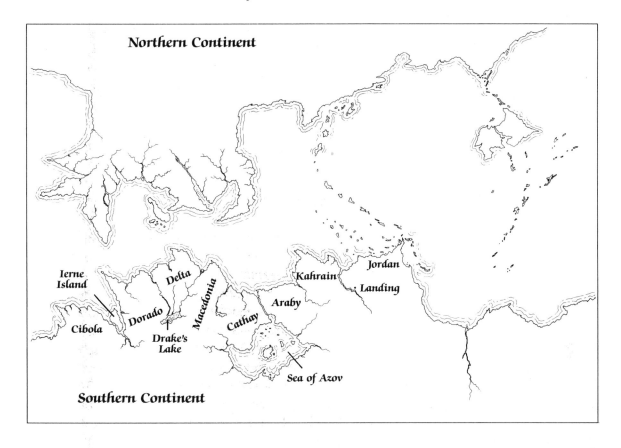

ing stake, which yielded high-grade iron, copper, silver, mercury, lead, and vanadium ore. Key Largo, Monaco Bay, and Oslo Harbor were fishing centers. The dolphineers set up operations in Monaco Bay, near the main fishery and cannery. The seagoing ships, carried in numbered pieces aboard the *Yokohama* and reconstructed in the new harbors, were made of siliplex, a light, almost indestructible compound. As it emptied of personnel, Landing still remained the administrative center and supply depot. The main animal-breeding labs were there, as were the hospital, training center, and school.

The nomads were assigned lands, though none of them intended to settle under roofs. Their lands were warm enough to allow them to sleep rough if they chose. Otherwise, natural shelter in the form of caves and cliff overhangs abounded throughout the varied landscape.

For a long time the wanderers were suspicious, expecting at every turn to be told to move on from their assigned territories. Although education was offered free to those who wanted to learn the trades, most of the traveling folk fought against even those loose conventions and vanished into the countryside, never to be seen again. Most of them were killed in the first Threadfall. Those who survived were brought to the north in the transports and, still defying conformity, became the nucleus of the Holdless people of Pern.

Until the eighth year of the colony, the stakeholds prospered.

III.

The Red Star

THREAD!

The Exploration and Evaluation Corps team had noticed the eccentric planet on its irregular circuit through the plane of the ecliptic. The team noted in its report that the planet must have been captured by the gravity well of Rukbat, and was unable to escape from the orbit. They judged that its period of revolution was somewhat over two hundred years.

The face of the rogue planet seemed to be made up of formations of heavy gases that changed only rarely under tornadic winds of lighter gases that ripped across the surface. The team assumed severe tectonic conditions underneath the gases because of the tremendous and irregular pull the rogue suffered from Rukbat.

Though they had seen other worlds stripped bare by unknown agencies thought to have to do with those systems' Oort clouds, the EEC team considered that they had too little time and data to determine the cause of the curious overlapping circles of denuded earth and stone on the third planet. One of the team cited the theory of "space viruses" propounded by Hoyle and Wickramansingh, a theory that some considered to be discredited by scientists on Ceti III. But the idea of a mass extinction seemed unlikely,

judging by the speed at which the ground vegetation was regenerating. Observing that where the circles touched one another, they stopped expanding, the team judged it to be the work of a local fungus. No blame was accorded to the wandering planet next out from the sun.

The tragedy of the events in the colony's eighth year was that the colonists knew that the rogue planet was dragging Oort material after it, and they knew that Pern would pass through the contrail again and again. If the Oort cloud had been composed of large particles and chunks, as was the case in other stellar systems with which the FSP were more familiar, it would have produced a showy meteor shower as the particles entered Pern's atmosphere, not the decimation by Thread that befell. It was not until the Pass began that the biologists understood why they found no plants older than a few centuries, and why those that existed grew up very quickly. The biosphere was not depauperate but survivalist.

As it was, the colony was completely taken by surprise. Hundreds of people died in the First Fall. Nothing was left of the hapless victims but whatever pieces of metal they had been wearing. Many victims were burned and scarred by Thread before their dragonets flamed the remains or drove the victims into the water to kill the mycorrhizoid.

The Fall began east of the Jordan River and continued southwest, striking seven stakeholds in Jordan and Kahrain provinces. The next wave hit Macedonia, and apparently doubled back to strike the as yet unoccupied Bordeaux stakehold.

Numerous animals, mostly sheep and cattle, were lost in the first Fall experienced by the humans, which was actually the fourth Fall of the Pass. Twenty-three precious mares and a stallion were consumed before the shocked settlers could get their stock under cover. Humans struck by the filaments appeared to dissolve as the Threads engorged, and died painfully.

When Thread began to fall, the dolphins alerted the mariners to the curious behavior of the ocean's inhabitants. Fish and sea creatures followed the Leading Edge, swarming to eat Thread as it fell in the water. Later investigations disclosed helpful variables: Hot thermals from forest fires often ignited falling Thread, preventing it from reaching the ground. Wet or extremely cold weather destroyed Thread in the air; rain and snow caused messy clumps of decayed Thread to fall from the sky. Cold froze the hot Threads into harmless black "crackdust." Since water, stone, and metal were unaffected by

Thread, caves and stone buildings, tin-roofed Quonset huts, lakes, and rivers were potential havens from a Fall. Not all the settlements were immediately affected, but Landing realized that if the attacks continued, no place on Pern would be safe. At first it was hoped that Thread was a sporadic or temporary occurrence, but reexamination of the EEC reports proved that the incursions were planetwide.

DEFENSE

Once the pattern of the attacks was determined, the colonists looked for defensive measures. Flamethrowers were mounted on either side of the transport sleds, and pilots pursued the Leading Edge of Fall until it was beyond vulnerable human habitations. In the beginning, there were a lot of midair accidents—although most of the pilots were expert at flying sleds, they were not accustomed to flying in such close formation or combating such a widespread menace. In order to avoid collision and maximize their efficiency, it was decided to maintain certain altitudes, fly static patterns to the edge of Fall, then turn and repeat the pattern at the same altitude across the deadly rain. Flying

Sled

into the Leading Edge, the rear openings of the sleds were protected unless someone missed too much Thread and the wind currents swept it under the canopy. The sleds flew toward the Thread, blazing away with both guns.

Thread that had not been destroyed burrowed deep into the soil and consumed all plant life for a considerable radius. Acid, specifically nitric acid, HNO_3, was poured on infestations. Where pumps were available, water was flushed down Thread burrows, but that brought the sticky dead mess up to swirl around the feet of the defenders.

The settler's pet dragonets had a more personal survival mechanism. By chewing phosphine-bearing rock, they produced an internal gas that ignited into flame upon contact with oxygen. They protected many homes that had been constructed of vegetable plastics or wood, neither of which could withstand Thread. Many observed their behavior, but few recognized their potential as protectors of the settlements.

APPEARANCE AND BEHAVIOR OF THREAD

Thread begins as a spore in the icy cometary trail following the Red Star. As it is captured by planetary gravity, it elongates into a slender filament heated by the friction of its fall through the atmosphere.

Observation of living Thread is difficult, since it seems to have no more than twenty minutes of life—unless it was fed carbon-based compounds. At risk of their own lives, volunteers brought samples of Thread to the biologists' laboratory.

Thread was discovered to be a network of mycorrhizoid fibers, similar to a harmless Earth mycota which was symbiotic with some plants. Carbon-based Thread contains very large, complex proteins that enable it to move and burrow or to digest any organic substance.

Not all Thread is dangerous. Some of the mycorrhiza die on the surface, without penetrating the ground or consuming nutrition. Thread leaves behind shells, which quickly deteriorate in the open air. Some Threads mature, though the further life cycles were never discovered by the colonial scientists.

Thread and Spores

25

Feeding Thread changes color, shifting from its normal hot silver to sickly green, gray, pink, and yellow tones. It appears to elongate from the center of the original strand outward toward both ends.

Threads hiss and struggle energetically when captured. The original strand was only 1/4 inch wide but 98 feet long. By the time one captured Thread replicated itself several thousand times, it had engorged to nearly 470 feet long and three feet thick.

When a Thread "dies," its cooling silver surface blackens and decays into a tarry substance within its tough shell. The shells quickly become putrid. When those are burned or dissolved with acid, they produce an incredible stench. Fire and water were the colonists' best weapons against Thread.

When F'nor of Benden and brown dragon Canth went *between* to the Red Star in the Ninth Pass, they encountered some Thread spores in the atmosphere, but it was the cyclonic dust clouds spinning through the atmosphere that sanded their skin and hide bare. Because of the conditions on the Red Star, F'nor could offer little firsthand observation of any use to the dragonriders who were eager to burn Thread at what they believed to be its source. All research on the Oort cloud had been long lost by that time.

The Red Star

IV.

From Dragonets
to Dragons

UNTAPPED POTENTIAL

"If only the dragonets were larger!"

For eight years, fire-dragonets had been thought of only as pets and useful watch-animals, protecting children from snakes and the chicken runs from wherries.

Perceptive eyes saw that the intelligent mustering of the dragonets during the first Threadfalls was a potential answer to protecting the settlements from danger. Adding heroism to the personality traits already ascribed to the little creatures, the colonists cheered the returning warriors, most of whom stank of sulfurous fumes.

The regurgitated mass of sand that the dragonets brought up after flaming the Threads suggested that their second stomachs had evolved for the purpose of containing and mixing phosphine-bearing rock with internal acids to produce flame. The rock itself was easily obtainable on the surface of volcanic terrain, and a dragonet's back teeth were certainly strong enough to masticate it.

Dragonets resemble the dragons of Terran mythology. They have four limbs and two wings and, with a little advance prepara-tion, are capable of breathing fire. Dragonets' wings are translucent membranes stretched out over the dragon's version of arm, hand, and finger bones, like those of a bat. The membrane looks fragile, but it is fairly dura-ble. Considering the size of the sails, the wing is remarkably light. The boron crystalline structure is lighter than a similar carbon-based wing. Around the bones and where it attaches to the muscles, the membrane is thicker.

The rear limbs have three real toes, not claws, on the feet. The front limbs are

Dragonet

Tridactyl Claw

mood is reflected in the changeable color of its eyes. Green or blue registers contentment, yellow signals alarm, and red means anger. Depending on a dragonet's state of wakefulness, one, two, or all three pairs of eyelids will close. When a dragonet goes hunting underwater, the transparent innermost lid protects the eye from harm. Dragonets have neither eyelashes nor ears. Their intercommunication has always been chiefly telepathic. The sensitive head knobs act as audio receptors for other sounds.

Dragonet Eye

equipped with pincers, a single toe that folds back against two which are rigid claws, used for hunting in the water. This caused the marine biologists to ascribe a plankton eater as the dragonets' ancestor.

On the back of a dragonet's neck is a line of ridges leading from just behind the head knobs down to the shoulder muscles of the wings. The ridges are not prominent between the wings and continue from just behind them to the forked end of the tail. Hidden in the fork is the creature's sphincter. The genitalia are concealed behind pouchlike flaps of skin under the junction of tail and body, and are only revealed during mating.

The multifaceted eyes in the little blunt faces are protected by protruding brow ridges and triple sets of eyelids. A dragonet's

Dragonets are warm-blooded, with an internal body temperature of 35 degrees Celsius. Their dark green ichor is based on copper, a characteristic they share with tunnel snakes and wherries. The skeletal system is based on light, flexible plates rather than more easily breakable bones. Their lung capacity, contained within a ribcage composed of a single piece, is surprisingly large. With dorsally placed lung sacs fully inflated, a dragonet's chest will swell to double its normal size. Between impressively sharp, tough teeth lies a forked tongue.

Unlike the tunnel snakes, which vary from smooth hide to scales, dragonets have a uniformly soft, hairless skin. Their hides are glossy but not metallic. Dragon skins vary in color, based on the amounts of nickel, cobalt, and iron in their makeup. The golds range from pale yellow to dark, antique gold. Bronzes all have a golden-green sheen, but occasionally a few can be found that are nearly as dark as a brown. The shimmering hides of the blues and greens show nearly the whole spectrum of those shades, while browns go from tan through to chocolate. A sick or ill-cared-for dragonet will have a dull skin. Healthy, happy ones have silky, resilient hides.

During an attempt to X-ray the first dragonet Impressed by a human, the colony's scientists learned another characteristic of these most graceful of Pernese natives: they could teleport. The distressed dragonet escaped from the examination room by disappearing, only to reappear in the antechamber on the other side of a closed door, where his mistress awaited him.

Dragonets are also capable of limited telepathy. No other suggestion explained to the first colonists how the little creatures always missed colliding in midair, or how they coordinated their silent attacks against wherries or herpetoids, or how they always knew where they were.

Any sunlit place or burrow above the high tide mark is suitable for a dragonet female to lay her eggs. Tunnel snakes get more of a green's eggs than a gold's, because the golden queens are much more protective, vigilant, and intelligent. Golds will also muster the other colors to help them protect their eggs. Bronzes, the next largest, who generally mate with the golden queen, lead the blues and browns in defense of the nest. In the wild, there are few green dragonets in the fair of a gold. The greens have their own nests elsewhere.

Curiously, once a dragonet has lived through its first moments, centuries might pass before it dies. Dragonets were not designed for "planned obsolescence," as humans were. A dragonet fifty years old looks the same as one just into maturity. Perhaps with Threadfall and other natural hazards, the dragonets' longevity became necessary to keep the race from becoming extinct. Over time, one fertile female could repopulate the planet. Unless trauma occurred, it would live on and on.

A newly hatched dragonet is only a few inches long. When one reaches full growth, it is the length of a woman's arm from nose tip to tail tip.

**Proportionate Size:
A Man and a Fully Grown Dragonet**

Dragon Egg

MENTASYNTH

The first alterations to the dragonets, accomplished in the early colony years, involved treating a clutch of eggs with mentasynth, the Eridani compound designed to enhance fetuses' empathy. Their pincer claws were also genetically altered to a pentadactyl arrangement. When the eggs hatched in an environment that closely duplicated a nest in the wild, the new dragonets were capable of more direct communication and empathy with the humans who Impressed them.

Over the next several dragonet generations, the improved dragonets grew to be larger adults than their wild counterparts did, probably a result of superior food and care. They also developed more pronounced head knobs.

FIVE TOES FROM THREE

The original dragonets had a single pincer that closed on a two-fixed-claw "hand." Examination showed that the forearm had two arm bones that rotated to produce the ambidactyl movement, which gave the biologists the potential to change the claw configuration for the better. The original dragonets' front feet were adequate for catching fish, which was their principal dietary staple, but not as efficient as a pentadactyl hand for catching land-bound creatures.

The genes were altered to produce four "fingers" and a "thumb." The bioengineered dragonets bred true; as they became more and more prevalent, people began to call them "fire-dragonets," and finally "fire lizards." These new fire lizards were also leaner than the old dragonets and had flatter noses.

By the time Thread fell, nearly everyone who was capable of Impressing had one or more fire-dragonets of the newly enhanced or the old, natural configurations.

Kitty Ping

Pentadactyl Claw

DRAGONS

Kit Ping Yung, the colony's chief geneticist, was a tiny, frail woman, already over a hundred years old at the time of Landing. Her skill at manipulating the Eridani techniques of genetic engineering was impressive, almost legendary throughout the FSP. After several attempts to alter the dragonets, she produced a batch of dragon embryos, which she was satisfied would do what the colony needed

them to do. Shortly thereafter, she died at the age of 110, without having seen the results of her work. Her assistants and her granddaughter were left to follow her program as it progressed.

Using the original success as a stepping-stone, Kitti Ping had given the experimental eggs the gene equation for five-digit claws. Her program also called for forelegs shortened to more modified "arms," and a stronger endoskeleton, so the dragon would be comfortable upright. The back legs would be massive with muscle, relying on the natural ball-and-socket joints to keep the knees from dislocating on takeoff and landing. She made no changes in the basic wing design.

The dragons would need a certain amount of boron to remain healthy, just as humans needed calcium for their skeletal systems. Fortunately, an earlier program of Kitti's allowed for this need: She had introduced into the colonists' carbon-based animals the ability to metabolize trace elements of boron—which they ingested as part of their diet on Pern—into muscle tissue, rather than excreting it. Thus the dragons would be able to fill their boron requirement from a diet of animal meat.

Dragon Musculature

Dragon Skeletal Structure

Kitti also used mentasynth to enhance the already strong empathy that the dragonets exhibited. Her tinkering did not interfere with the natural tendencies of the species. The new dragons would be able to teleport from place to place almost instantaneously, just as the dragonets did. They would Impress easily as permanent companions to creatures other than their own species, and would now grow large enough to carry a human being and protect human habitations from Thread.

THE FIRST HATCHING

When the time came for the Hatching of the meter-long eggs, hot sands took the place of the beach nest, and humans proffered food and feelings of love and welcome to the hatchlings, in place of the dragons' biological family. It took a day and a half for the eighteen successful eggs to Hatch and Impress on their young human companions.

Dragon's Eggs

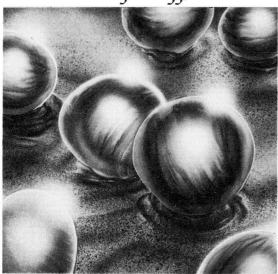

The first group of the bioengineered eggs yielded two gold dragon queens, three bronze dragons, and three browns. The second group yielded three gold queens. The third group brought five golds, one bronze, and one brown into the world. The fourth group, engineered after Kitti Ping's death, Hatched four golds, three bronzes, and two browns.

The greatest wonder of the first Hatching was the discovery that, at the moment of Impression, each new dragon-mate was suddenly aware of the dragon's mental touch and voice as it named itself to him or her. The dragons proved to have distinct personalities of their own, which appeared to be perfectly compatible with those of their Impressed humans.

The original dragons were ten to twelve feet long and about sixteen to eighteen hands high at the shoulder. Every successive generation grew larger than the one before, at first dramatically, then tapering off to small growth spurts. The gradual increase in size reached its culmination twenty-five centuries later, two Turns before the Ninth Pass, with Ramoth, who, at forty-five meters, was the largest dragon ever shelled.

The dragons had the ability to fly as soon as their wings dried, but as they did not have to hunt for their food or flee from predators, flight was not an immediate necessity. The veterinarians and biologists were reluctant to allow the new dragons to fly until they were fully mature, for fear of straining their wing muscles. The fire-dragons hunted fish and meat for the growing hatchlings and the humans found it was a full-time job to bathe, oil, and feed their charges.

Once the dragons were permitted to fly, the riders discovered that straps were needed for a secure seat on the neck ridges. It was possible during leisurely flight to remain on

One of the Original Eighteen Dragons and Rider

the back of one of these small dragons using only the knees for pressure, as on a horse, but it would take more than that to keep a rider from falling off when a dragon changed direction in pursuit of a clump of Thread. In order to allow his rider to mount, a dragon would crouch down and put out a forearm for use as a step-up. As the dragons got bigger, it became necessary to wait to mount until the fighting straps, which could double as handholds, were in place.

The wings of the fully evolved dragon are each approximately three-fourths the length of the entire dragon, who will run from twenty-five to forty meters long. The

Relative Size: A Bronze Rider, His Dragon, and a Queen Egg

tip-to-tip wingspan, including the breadth of the shoulders, is therefore one and two-thirds the length of a dragon.

What is usually thought of as a "dragon-length" as a measure of distance is equal to the average length of the most common dragons, the greens, who number the same as all the blues, browns, and bronzes put together. Modern green dragons grow to be-

tween twenty to twenty-five meters in length. Blues are the next largest at twenty-five to thirty, browns range from thirty to thirty-five meters, bronzes from thirty-five to thirty-eight and golds from thirty-eight to forty-two as a rule, though Ramoth was closer to forty-five meters long (or about the size of a jet plane).

Dragons' noses are more pointed than

Green

Blue

Brown

Gold

Bronze

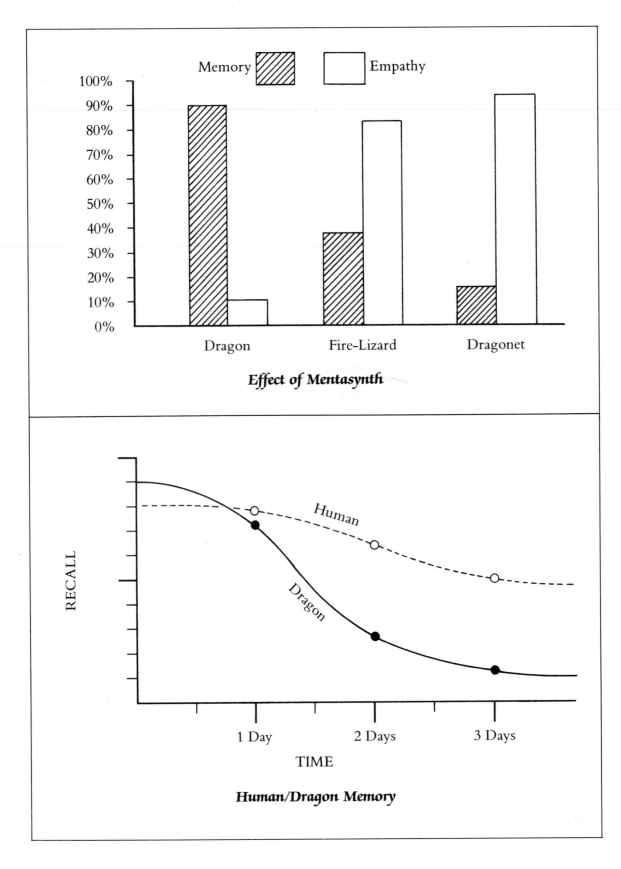

Effect of Mentasynth

Human/Dragon Memory

Ramoth and L 1011 Jet

those of fire-dragonets, and their head knobs are fully developed. Their manual dexterity is increased, as is their intelligence, but their memories are reduced to short-term retention, as Kitti Ping made use of that portion of the brain for a superior telepathic link with humans. Their human mates constantly need to remind them of important facts with repetition and reassurance.

The first dragons were too small to fly an entire Threadfall, but they were far more effective aerial protection than the slower, less agile airborne sleds. With their mounts' natural ability to avoid collision, the riders soon learned the patterns for fighting that the sled pilots used. As their numbers and their experience increased, the small dragons fought longer and over more locations. Many were lost *between* or to injuries. Indeed, the initial "Flight" riders were not far ahead

of the weyrlings they trained to follow them. It took the entire Pass of fifty years for Fort Hold to reach full strength in number of fighting dragons.

THE FIRST WEYRS

In the face of the colony's first experience with Thread, Landing became crowded with stakeholders who had fled from their ravaged settlements back to their deserted temporary dwellings. There was little room for the dragonfolk to live with their beasts, and they were already being set apart from their un-Impressed neighbors, some of whom saw dragons only as a means of removing strong backs from the work force.

The dragonriders and their families moved into the Catherine Caves around the edge of the plateau. The dragons were perfectly comfortable living underground, and the humans were pleased to have roomy quarters that were secure from Thread.

BETWEEN

Between is a *nonspace*, a postulatum. *Between* is the journey from one place to another without crossing the space in between. A dragon can move through time and space at will, depending on what he perceives as his rider's stated destination. Every rider is trained to be careful when he wishes to cross time zones. If he was in Fort in the morning and wished to go to Benden at the same time of day, he would actually be going back in time three hours because of the day's progression.

Going *between* times takes longer than going *between* places. If the dragon cannot find the time or place his rider has pictured, they will not come out of *between*. That was why it was so dangerous for Lessa of Benden to jump *between* four hundred Turns at the beginning of the Ninth Pass using only the Ruatha tapestry as a guideline. She intuited its significance as an actual record, but she could have misjudged its accuracy and lost herself and Pern's only remaining queen dragon in the cold void.

MATING

From the outset, dragon queens were encouraged to mate with as many of the males, both brown and bronze, as possible, to take maximum advantage of the available gene pool. Brown-gold matings produce few bronzes and no queens, but the resultant hatchlings are healthy. Each queen rises to mate two or three times a year, and produces clutches of ten to sixteen eggs at a time.

Except in certain mating situations, dragons are never aggressive with one another. When they are ready to rise, the queens become primitive, gorging on kills. The males turn competitive, their only goal to outmaneuver each other in mating flight to get to the queen. *(Illustrated on page 41.)*

Dragons have no territorial imperatives. Their riders make sure they lack for nothing, not love, nor food, nor shelter; and since dragons have no long-term memory, they quickly forget the unpleasant realities of Thread. Their mild personalities act as calming influences on their riders.

Because of the incredible emotional and physical effects dragons mating have on the humans bonded to them, the riders discourage outside involvement with anyone who is likely to be jealous. The resultant discord of such a situation interferes with the mental health of the riders and, through them, their dragons, It is loyalty to the whole of Pern, rather than to a single man or woman, that is encouraged.

WATCH-WHERS

In an effort to produce more dragons after her grandmother's death, Wind Blossom Ping also attempted to use the Eridani equations on dragonet genetic material. However, she did not have the same grasp of genetics as Kitti Ping, and the results of her tinkering were not totally successful.

What hatched from the eggs she engineered looked like ugly, malformed dragons, and were dubbed "whers." Their wings were stumpy pinions that looked functional but

Mating Flight

Wher

were not. They were smooth-skinned and colored like dragons, but that was almost the only point of resemblance.

When full-grown, whers weighed between six and eight hundred pounds, about the size of a small, low-slung horse. Their feet were arranged with two claws, and a single pad supported the body weight; in spite of such bad design, they could move with surprising speed.

Whers were Impressable, and they adored their human mates with the same devotion and empathy as dragons did. They were also very territorial and, if not properly introduced, would kill anyone they believed was invading their home. As a result of Wind Blossom's attempt to smooth out the natural faceting of the eyes, their eyes had malformed lenses with countless little facets that aimed light directly back into the fovea like a magnifying glass. Whers were photophobic and had poor focal length, but they were effective guardians at night, able to see even in total darkness. Their senses of smell and hearing were as keen as their night vision. They were not as intelligent as dragons, but they could serve a purpose. And they bred true.

Whers are solitary and antisocial. If a female hatches eggs away from a human habitation, the young return to the wild. They avoid encounters during the day, but they will kill if disturbed at night. Only a few eggs of each laying mature to hatch.

RUTH

The white dragon Ruth is a throwback to the original dragons in size and proportion. As he is only twenty feet long, his rider, Jaxom,

must take the same precautions not to overload or overfly him.

Ruth would be considered genetically flawed by those living during the Ninth Pass. Most similarly stunted eggs simply fail to Hatch, and most of them show no signs of life at all. The Tradition has always been that if an egg does not Hatch by itself, it is not helped. But Jaxom did interfere, and Ruth not only lived and prospered, but changed the outlook and history of Pern.

I think the nearest thing to being a dragonrider is a racehorse jockey.
—*Interview with Anne McCaffrey, Dragonhold, Ireland, 1987.*

Jaxom

V.

Weyrlings

THE IMPRESSION— A SHORT STORY

To Felessan's speculative eye, the eggs hardening on the Hatching Ground looked different. Well, maybe not very different. Maybe not different at all. Perhaps it was just his knowledge that this time, this Hatching, was to be his first try at Impression, and that put the eggs in an entirely new light. The idea that he was considered worthy to Impress one of Pern's great dragons delighted and scared him.

The sunlight shone through the high openings to the Weyr Bowl outside, refracting gloriously off the mottled eggshells. Since F'lar had taken him and two other boys in the Lower Caverns aside two nights earlier to tell them that they were eligible to be Candidates if they so chose—as if anybody with sense would turn down such a chance—Felessan had made several detours from his chores to pass through the great echoing cavern. Which egg held a bronze dragon, and which a blue? To Felessan's knowledge, no one had ever been able to work out a system to tell the smaller eggs apart. Of course, the queen egg was easy to pick out. It was mostly gold, like its occupant, it was bigger than all the rest, and it rested, lovingly protected, between the claws of its broody golden mother.

Ramoth opened one great jeweled eye about halfway and regarded the boy passively. To his relief, it showed the blue of sleepy contentment rather than the red or yellow of annoyance. Felessan was afraid that she was sizing him up and passing judgment on him: "Might make a *blue* rider, but no more than that," as the elders and senior weyrlings had been doing for two days now. He did not see where the others got off making remarks about him. Faranth only knew how they had tricked the dragons they rode into choosing them in the first place! He clapped a hand over his mouth, for fear of letting the unkind thoughts become words. What if Ramoth heard him? Who knew what affected Impression?

The sleeping chambers were crowded this last sevenday, with the addition of the new boys found on Search from Hold and Hall. Most of them were strangers, but Felessan recognized Borand, who was from Lemos Hold. Borand had once accompanied a supply train making its trip to the Weyr, and the two of them, along with many other boys from the caverns, had spent a long, hot after-

44

noon stacking cloth sacks of river grains in the storage caverns under Manora's watchful eye. He was glad Borand had come to Benden. Only two of the other boys his age in the Weyr were standing to the egg this time, and the others were eyeing the three chosen ones with an air of suspicion. He did not know why none of them had been picked as Candidates this time. He was hardly sure why he *had.*

How did one Impress a dragon? All they had heard from the senior riders were oblique warnings that meant nothing. "Don't do this . . . don't do that . . . mustn't ever do this . . ." And most enigmatic: "Don't let your dragon eat too much." "You must never be afraid of your dragon," F'nor had cautioned the boys before handing them over to Felena for the fitting of their robes. "He will never hurt you." That was all very well, but how did one attract a dragon in the first place?

There were nearly twice as many Candidates as there were eggs in the sand. F'lar liked to give the dragonets a wide choice, but it always meant that there were just that many disappointed boys left standing on the ground when the Hatching was finished. Felessan shrugged. Just so long as he was not one of them, he did not care. It was worse with the girls, of course. Anywhere from two to ten of them, and only one queen dragon to Impress.

The boys had all had a chance to touch the eggs. Felessan had shivered when he stroked one of the elongated ovals, and Ramoth had looked at him. He remembered the time he and Jaxom had sneaked in to have a look at the clutch from which Ruth had eventually Hatched. The boys' adventure had not hurt the dragonets, but Felessan had feared for sevendays that someone would know he had done it.

"Another day to go, they say," a boy from the Minecrafthall complained as Feles-san returned to the sleeping chamber to get his hunting snares and knife. "I'm to break up firestone till the noon meal. I could have done that at home."

"My duty is to hunt tunnel snakes in the storage tunnels below the kitchen cavern," Felessan offered. Hunting was his talent, and he was proud of it. "Want to come with me?"

"No, thanks," the boy said, patting his stomach. His name was Varon. He was a chunky lad with a head of black hair and dark freckles dusted across his cheeks. "I might get stuck where a wisp like you would fit through."

"I'll come," a red-haired boy said with a smile. Called Catrul, he came from a small hold in Bitra. He was built much like Felessan, with long legs and a skinny frame that spoke more of missed meals than hereditary slenderness. He took from his pack a two-tined hunting knife, which Felessan eyed with envy. It was just the right configuration to take the head off a tunnel snake with a single chop. "I'd rather do that than scrub pots. The scaled kind is good to eat."

"These are smooth-skinned," Felessan said apologetically. "May I try your knife?"

"If I can borrow one of your snares," Catrul countered, handing over the shining blade. "Let's go."

Catrul was as adept with snare as with knife, and Felessan was pleased that his new friend enjoyed hunting as much as he did. The trick of killing tunnel snakes was to avoid their sharp claws and teeth and strike at their unprotected backs and necks. The boys watched in silence as one of the beasts crept closer and closer to the place where Catrul had spread a snare. The snake, invisible in the darkness, passed cautiously over the single grains of glows dispersed along the corridor. The boys could measure its progress by how quickly the glows disappeared and reappeared. Another man-length, then another—

Anne McCaffrey's comments on Impression

"It's love at first sight across a crowded room—one of the most magical things that could possibly happen to anybody. To me, it's like getting up on a horse that's been schooled, and the minute you give him the aids, he knows exactly what you want, perfectly, only there's much more of a rapport. Impressing a dragon is the amalgam of everything you wanted in your pet as a child and couldn't have, because your pet wasn't up to it. It's suddenly having the whole candy store window *yours*.

"At the instant of Impression, part of the miracle is that you realize now you will never be alone, you will always be supported for the rest of your life—the feeling of total surrender to another mind which understands you totally. It is completely in rapport with you, and suddenly a great weight has been lifted from your shoulders, because you know that there is

"Pull, Catrul!" Felessan cried suddenly. With a whoop, the redheaded boy sprang to his knees and fell onto his back, yanking the cord taut.

From the side, Felessan dove over the flailing pair of stabilizers that were the tunnel snake's middle limbs and yanked the tail and hindquarters back and down. There was a snapping sound as the snake's neck broke. It twitched in a frenzy for a few seconds, then fell still.

"Whee-ooop!" Felessan picked up the carcass by the tail and shook it.

"Not so loud!" Catrul complained. "You'll scare all the rest off."

"I don't care," Felessan shouted, enjoying the way his voice echoed all the way into the depths of the Weyr. In the distance, it broke into two sounds, a shrill echo almost above the range of hearing, and a vibrato thrum that bounced off the solid stone walls around them.

"Ow!" Catrul said, pressing his hands over his ears and crouching against the dark floor. "That's loud!"

"Yow!" Felessan cried again. The echo sprang away, but the thrumming filled the cavern around them and continued long after the higher-pitched sound had died.

"How'd you do that?" Catrul asked, listening to the sound in wonder. He swept the glows together in a trembling palm and felt for the basket.

"*I'm* not doing it." Felessan looked around, big-eyed. "That humming sounds like it's coming from above. The Hatching! The eggs are Hatching!"

"Now? It couldn't be now! We're not ready!"

Felessan was already running through the dark passage toward the kitchens, coiling the snares up as he ran. "We'd better *get* ready. It's happening!"

They dashed through the Living Cavern and into the Inner Cavern. The humming was louder out there, and people were rushing back and forth, hurrying to make all ready for the guests who would be arriving to witness the Hatching. Felessan looked around for Manora, but he guessed that his foster mother was at the hearths, overseeing the preparations for the Impression feast.

"Come on," Felessan said, pulling Catrul toward the bathing pool. "Can't face the egg dirty."

"We'll be late!" Catrul cried, pulling off his clothing and climbing into the warm, swirling water. He and Felessan reached for the jar of sweetsand at the same time, and it fell between their hands into the pool. Both of them dove for it and came up sputtering. In their haste, they churned up the bathing pool until there was as much water out of it as in it.

"Better wet than dirty," Felessan assured his friend, leading him back to their sleeping chamber to change.

Felena was waiting with the pile of clean white Candidates' robes over her arm. As Felessan and Catrul appeared, clutching bathing sheets around them, she handed a robe to each of them and bade them hurry. "The bronzes are already on their ledge," she said.

"But it's too soon," one of the boys cried. "I don't know what to think yet."

"How will I know what to do?" another boy asked.

Felessan was worrying about the same things, but he said nothing. He just concentrated on pulling on the thin white cloth over his wet skin. With a nervous hand, he smoothed his shock of hair back on his head. Catrul and the Minecraft lad were white and solemn. The robes had been the final touch. The reality of the situation had dawned on the boys. No matter what they thought or hoped, the event was upon them, and it would be all over very soon. They would Impress now, or not, as the dragons pleased. In awed silence, the barefoot boys followed Felena through the stone corridor to the Hatching Ground.

that support system there. And with it comes a tremendous responsibility, because you know if something happens to you, that dragon will suicide.

"Now, the dragon will take care of you, so it's really up to you to take care of the dragon. You have the feeling of one mind suddenly encasing yours, and every ounce of your blood, every tissue in your body, is suddenly linked to another living creature. It cannot be but the most ecstatic moment. If the kids were old enough, they'd have orgasms.

"You feel pain through the link, and you would do anything to stop your dragon's pain. If you were happy or comfortable, the dragon would also share in the pleasure, but not necessarily the sensory feeling. Dragons would be peripherally aware of 'mechanical duties' *(such as eating, or sex, or sleeping)* and they'd know right away if you were sick. They would start to get worried, not knowing why. Unusual occurrences or sensations would come to the dragon's awareness."

Around them in the passage, drudges were hastening to refill the glowbaskets with fresh glows, the light throwing weird shadows across their faces. At the end of the tunnel there was a real blaze of light—the oblique

rays of the midday sun hitting the Hatching Grounds. The arena was filling up with people. Felessan was suddenly terrified. Practically all of Pern would be watching him. Borand caught his eye and made a brave thumbs-up sign, even though his face showed that he was nervous, too. The closer they got to the chamber, the warmer the floor became under their feet.

As instructed, once the boys reached the sands, they spread out, forming a loose semicircle around the rocking eggs. Ramoth coiled on the egg mound, protecting the queen egg, hissing and snarling, her forked tongue licking out at the air, her eyes awhirl with a red light. The four female Candidates stood at a respectful distance, but their eyes were on the big golden egg.

Felessan promptly forgot about them. Before him now was the biggest moment of his life. There was the clutch of eggs, all rocking back and forth on the hot sand. Which one would crack first? His impatience nearly strangled him, and he had to force himself to breathe. The hush of the great chamber made him feel both very important and very small; he felt as if every single person in the Hatching Ground were watching him. He did his best to look patient, though his feet felt as if they were burning up. Discreetly, he lifted first one scorched sole and then the other.

Why do they make us come out barefoot? he wondered. Does it make a difference to the dragon? Without moving his head, he slewed a glance over to the left, to see if anyone else was as uncomfortable as he was. Beside him, Catrul was shifting from foot to foot. How long would they have to stand there? The sand was growing hotter by the moment.

The hum went on and on, and the eggs twitched and jerked, as if the dragonets were as impatient as the Candidates. Felessan was hypnotized by their movement, and by the humming of the bronze dragons which was building slowly in power, like the sound of an approaching storm.

With a loud pop, a mottled egg with a pattern that looked like a river and waterfall burst open, and a young bronze dragonet fell to the sand, bawling a protest. There was a sigh of pleasure from the audience in the stands behind him. It was a good sign that the first hatchling was a bronze. Felessan wanted more than anything to look at the young dragon, to see if it was his, but he did not dare. What if it was not? Oh, but what if it *was* his? He would be so disappointed if it was not. He risked a glance at the little creature, whose glistening wet wings were unfurling and drying in the hot air. He was so beautiful! Felessan's heart felt as if it was about to explode in misery as the whirling jeweled eyes changed from blue to green and the little dragon moved decisively toward Varon.

"He says his name is Horoth!" the tall Minecraft lad cried in triumph as he knelt and touched the young dragon's upturned face. The hum grew louder, as if the senior dragons approved the match. Then V'ron, as the new dragonrider would now be known, led the staggering dragonet toward the ground-level exit where brown and green riders waited to escort the new weryings to their shared barracks.

Briefly Felessan watched V'ron and Horoth. The first Hatching was almost like a signal for things to begin happening. All of a sudden, several eggs broke open at once. Crooning piteously, the dragonets sought around them, searching the faces of the Candidates. A brown dragonet fell across Felessan's feet and lay bawling on the sand.

Is this the one I want? he asked himself as he helped the little creature to stand up.

The brown creeled and tottered away.

A tiny green dragon drew Felessan's attention, calling shrilly.

"Does she want me?" He started toward her. At the same time, two blue hatchlings made for one boy, then one of them turned away. The green went on by, still searching for the right Candidate. Felessan gave it a sidelong hopeful glance, but it ignored him.

Catrul was on his hands and knees on the sand, tears pouring down a face that smiled as wide as its narrow bones would allow. Staring lovingly up at him was a very small dragonet.

Felessan stared at the brown in astonishment. He did not know whether to rejoice for his friend or melt in frustration. Every dragon had to have a rider. He dared not risk a look at the Weyrleaders on the Tier. Then his eyes were drawn away by a blaze of greeny gold.

"Oh, a bronze," he breathed. Not an ordinary bronze, either, but a flawless combination of gold and green and tan that looked like the dappled sun through leaves, only more perfect. "Oh! Is he coming...to me?"

Felessan's heart pounded as he took a step forward to meet the dragonet, who was crooning in impatience to reach him. The boy's longer legs brought him close more quickly than the hatchling's wobbly short ones could. He completely forgot any recent twinge of disappointment.

This bronze was the handsomest, most perfectly formed, prettiest-colored, strongest hatchling in the clutch. Oops! He gasped as it tripped on its wing tip and its bulky hind legs kept on moving, plowing its sensitive nose farther into the hot sand. Felessan dropped to his knees to help the little beast right itself. Its glowing eyes focused on his.

Suddenly, some indefinable sensation surged through his body, followed by a consciousness that centered itself both in his head and a few feet in front of him, inside the body of the little bronze, making every breath echo, every movement repeat itself.

My name is Golanth, the bronze hatchling said.

Felessan reached out to stroke the dragonet's skin, knowing before he did how soft it would be, and how happy Golanth would be for the caress. He loved the little dragon with an astonishing sense of completion. He was overwhelmingly happy, happier than he had ever been in his life. All he wanted to do was to look at the little bronze dragon, just look at him. Felessan had the amazing feeling of being *together* with Golanth. No matter where he was, the rapport would remain between them. But he had no intention of ever being away from Golanth.

Golanth certainly had the softest skin Felessan had ever touched. Even though the little bronze was only a few minutes old, he was as steady on his feet as could be. And his wings! They were drying faster than any other hatchling on the Ground, even the ones who had broken shell before him. What transparent sails they were, and so perfect that they looked like they had been carved from glass. Felessan was so full of joy and pride that his chest hurt. His jaws ached, but he could not stop smiling.

I'm hungry, Golanth told him piteously, adding a croon to his plea.

"Hungry!" Felessan was abashed. He had stood there like a lump of coal while his dragon was hungry! *Terribly* hungry. His own guts were rumbling in sympathy, and he realized that the could feel the craving for food right through their precious link. His training flooded back to him, and he remembered there would be food out in the Weyr Bowl for them.

"Come on, we've got to get you some food! There's food right out here. Just come along with me now," he chattered on, reassuring Golanth, who tottered along beside him. The sand was hot, and the young dragon's claws were still soft and damp from being in the egg. "It's all right—here, I'll help you. Don't worry about it. It sure is hot here, isn't it? My feet hurt, too, but that's okay. We're just going outside. It's much cooler there. And the food!"

I'm very, very hungry, Golanth told him.

Other hatchlings were already being fed by their proud new weyrmates, with some guidance from the senior riders. One of the brown riders came over to F'lessan and handed him a big bowl of fresh red meat.

"Here you go, F'lessan."

Felessan dragged his eyes away from Golanth's and recognized T'gran; at the same moment he realized that the smiling older rider was the first to address him by his new name.

"What's his name?"

"Golanth." F'lessan grinned as he rolled the name around in his mouth for the first time. "This is my friend T'gran," he told Golanth. "And his dragon is Branth. He's a brown dragon."

The older rider smiled and clapped a hand to F'lessan's shoulder. "The Weyrleaders are mighty proud of you. F'lar just looked as pleased as can be, and the Weyrwoman—I think she was glowing as much as Ramoth was. You just see to Golanth now. He's a fine-looking little fellow, isn't he?" T'gran walked away, and Golanth opened his mouth for the meat.

The first pieces were swallowed promptly, and Golanth asked for more, rolling his jeweled eyes at F'lessan in appeal. His stomach hurt so much. It was so empty.

"It's all right!" F'lessan promised him. "It's all right. Your stomach will stop hurting, really. Here's more. And more. Boy, you are hungry, aren't you? No, wait, chew

it!" the boy pleaded as a large lump of meat disappeared down his weyrmate's throat. "You can have as much as you want, but you'll choke if you don't chew your food."

Chew? The mental tone was puzzled.

"Uh, . . . mash the meat between your teeth." F'lessan tried to demonstrate, pointing. "Those are teeth. You tear the meat with the front ones, and you chew with the back ones. Yes, you're all right now. Good."

As the edge of Golanth's hunger abated, F'lessan began to take in his surroundings more fully. Suddenly the Weyr Bowl seemed bigger than he remembered it, and the sky was more beautiful. Everything was *new.* "See? It's lovely out here. This is where we'll be living."

I like it. I like everything you like, Golanth told him, taking another chunk of meat. The bowl was nearly empty, and the dragonet's voracious eating was slowing down. The frantic spin of his eyes had abated to a placid whirl. Then the skin on Golanth's shoulder twitched and his eyes changed color.

"What's the matter?"

I itch came suddenly from the dragonet's mind.

F'lessan started at Golanth's emphatic tone. He set down the bowl and ran his hands over the shoulder joint. "You do? Here?"

No, further down. Yes, there.

"Yes, you feel very dry suddenly. I'll get some oil." He turned around and around, trying to recall where the oil was kept. A few of the senior riders looked up at him questioningly. "I need some oil!" he exclaimed. "He's itching. His skin is dry."

"Of course it is," one of the men said. With a smile, he handed F'lessan a pot of oil and a paddle.

"Oh, good!" F'lessan seized the oil and smeared some on Golanth's shoulder. Instantly he shared his dragon's relief. "I'd better do a good job. I'll oil you all over, to make sure you won't be uncomfortable." He spread paddlesful of oil all over the bronze dragonet, admiring the shimmer of his hide in the sun.

You are so considerate, Golanth said, his eyes glowing with love. The scent of the meat attracted him again, and he plunged his muzzle into the bowl while F'lessan worked. *You are so clever, and you make me very happy.*

F'lessan sighed with joy, caressing the soft, soft skin of his weyrmate and scratching above the dragon's sensitive eye ridges. "I'm happy, too."

Joyful creelings from a fair of Impressed fire lizards echoed overhead in the wide Weyr Bowl, as a very small green dragon joined the other hatchlings in the sun. F'lessan noted with one astonished glance that the weyrling with her was Mirrim. A *girl* impressing a green? Why she hadn't even been standing on the sands. Then Golanth nudged his arm again, and the boy turned back to spread more oil on his new friend.

When at last his dragon's skin was soothed, F'lessan helped Golanth make his way toward the Weyrling Barracks at the opposite end of the Bowl from the Hatching Grounds. Through their new bond, the boy could tell that Golanth was growing very tired. After all, he had only been Hatched that day. He needed to get some rest from the exertion of breaking shell and walking so far from the Hatching sands.

Somehow F'lessan managed to get the staggering bronze up the ramp, into the barracks, and over to the side of the room he had been assigned by the Weyrlingmaster. With a sigh of relief, Golanth collapsed onto the little stone couch. F'lessan discovered that he, too, was exhausted. He had been up practically all the night before, too nervous to sleep, not knowing what to expect and worrying what the other Candidates would say if the Weyrleader's son failed to Impress on his first try.

But it had all turned out just fine! And he had Impressed a bronze, too—the most beautiful, intelligent, wonderful bronze on Pern! The reality of the Hatching was more wonderful, more terrifying, and more rewarding than any description he had ever heard. He would never be alone again—and he had never realized how alone he had been until Golanth's presence filled his soul.

He sat down next to the small bronze hatchling, who was trying vainly to keep his glowing jeweled eyes open. As F'lessan smiled down at Golanth, the translucent lids slid closed one by one, then all Golanth's muscles relaxed at once. Suddenly F'lessan's eyelids became too heavy to hold up, and he leaned against Golanth's shoulder. With a little sigh, the boy slumped down next to the bronze dragonet. In a moment, their placid breathing joined that of the other new weyrmates.

With a soft step, the Werylingmaster made his way through the rows of stone couches, checking on each boy and dragonet. He lifted one of F'lessan's long, thin legs where it was dragging on the floor and settled it next to the other. Beaming paternally down at the young pair, he drew the woven coverlet up from the end of the couch and settled it over them. F'lessan was smiling in his sleep.

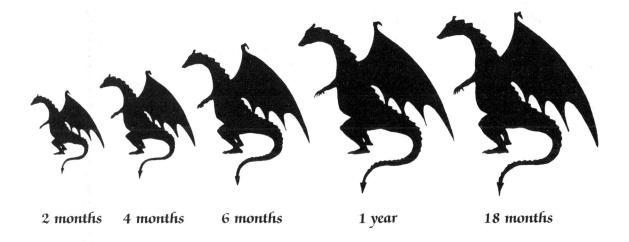

2 months   4 months   6 months   1 year   18 months

THE CARE AND FEEDING OF A YOUNG DRAGON

Dragon eggs are ovoid, with predominantly cream-colored shells marbled in soft colors. After a clutching all the folk in a Weyr join in the guessing game as to what color dragon will hatch out of each of the meter-long eggs. The gold eggs are easier to detect, as they are ten to twenty percent bigger than the others and tend to be more gold in hue. There is surprisingly little difference between most other types.

Dragons are born hungry. They consume the yolk before hatching, absorbing all the soft material in the thick, leathery shell of the egg until it is down to a thin, crackable layer.

A young dragon, called a dragonet, will always find someone suitable among those present in the Grounds during the Hatching, usually a Candidate, but occasionally some unsuspecting person off the sands. Though some riders may appear to other humans to be odd choices, each dragon unerringly chooses just the right rider.

Once the eggs have hatched, the baby dragons and their weyrmates fall into the care of the Weyrlingmaster, chosen from among the more senior riders. He is in charge of the weyrlings' physical well-being, training, and every facet of dragon care. He sees to it that the weyrlings clean and oil their dragons every day.

At first, the young dragons feed almost daily, and then once every three to five days, devouring one or two wherries or a small herdbeast from among the Weyr's flocks. As soon as the young pair are allowed to fly, they are taken out of the Weyr with a senior pair and taught to hunt wild wherries, fish, and other edibles.

Dragons remain in the Weyrling Barracks as long as they are small. At a year old, they will have reached seventy percent of their adult size. Once they can fly, they are transferred from the barracks to their own, larger quarters.

VI.
Training and Fighting Dragons

BY TODD JOHNSON

WEYRLING TRAINING

Dragon and rider start their destiny inauspiciously: as creeling, frightened dragonet and timorous, white-robed Candidate. Confused, dazed, and finally fused in the bonding of Impression, the pair are just barely capable of locomotion—often one has to carry the other off the Hatching Grounds. Yet in little more than a year the dragonpair can be expected to form part of a Fighting Wing. Preparing the weyrlings is the responsibility of the Weyrlingmaster.

The Weyrlingmaster's importance is awesome: At any time he may have up to ninety weyrlings in his charge. The Weyrlingmaster is chosen by the Weyrleader as the dragonrider best able to train new riders to fight Thread. Normally the Weyrleader consults with his Wingleaders before making his selection. Once chosen, a Weyrlingmaster remains in the position until he stands down or dies. Historically, Weyrlingmasters often stand down after only a few years of service, many returning to duty with the Wings.

The bemused, newly Impressed dragonpairs are led from the Hatching Grounds to the Weyrling Barracks, a place set off from the rest of the Weyr. Young dragons, and oc-casionally young riders, are given to excesses (emotional, culinary, even sexual) that often result in a distressed dragon and rider. Inflicting such emotions upon the rest of a Fighting Weyr could have disastrous consequences, so the young weyrlings live apart.

Confused, often overwhelmed by the intensity of the Impressment, and distressed by the ravenous hunger of their new partners, the human half of the dragonpairs look to the Weyrlingmaster and his helpers to provide them with food for their hungry dragons. Once they have eaten, the helpers then guide them into the Weyrling Barracks. Here, finally sated, the newly Hatched dragons promptly fall asleep. This common first surge of eating and sleeping is usually accompanied by the stretching and itching of the dragonets' skin. From then on the young humans must oil their dragon partners daily.

Each weyrling's name has already been shortened into the dragonrider's honorific, by which he will be known for the rest of his life: Felessan to F'lessan, Naton to N'ton. The shorter name is not only a signal that the boy has Impressed a dragon, but also a time-saver for the Wingleaders, who must shout orders across dragonlengths while the dragons fly Threadfall.

While their dragons are maturing, the Weyrlingmaster assigns duties and drills to the young riders. These duties include most of the standard duties that everyone in the Weyr must perform: making clothes, casting cookware, collecting medicinal herbs, tending Weyr flocks, or even cleaning latrines. The drills, while tiresome and boring, are designed to turn dragon and rider into a fighting team capable of becoming part of the larger team that is the Wing.

Many of the first and most arduous experiences a weyrling rider faces are drills combined with the chore of selecting, sizing, and bagging firestone. All weyrlings must have a good understanding of firestone. This includes knowing reflexively the standard issue for a fighting dragon and its rate of consumption in Threadfall. The Weyrlingmaster, while teaching the weyrlings how to bag the firestone, also points out the proper sizes and look of good firestone. It is not uncommon for a representative of the Minecrafthall to assist during this part of the weyrling's training.

During Threadfalls, young weyrlings are charged with the duty of bagging firestone and passing the bags on to older riders, who will take them to fighting dragons at the site of the Fall. The Weyrlingmaster forms the young riders into groups of "weyrling's chains." These are teams of weyrlings working to fill empty firestone bags and pass them through a chain of waiting team members to the supply dragons. It is here that the weyrlings learn the "dragon toss": how to toss (and catch) full bags of firestone the distance of one dragon to another. It is a technique that requires a lot of skill, practice, and well-developed muscles.

When Thread is not falling, and there is more than enough firestone bagged and ready, the Weyrlingmaster will exercise the young weyrlings in a Ground Drill. These are very precise, exacting marching drills requiring the young riders to perform intricate maneuvers in teams. During these drills, the Weyrlingmaster starts selecting those whom he thinks need special training and those whose potential merits their learning additional skills. The first group receive extra training in close drill; the second group receive extra training in conducting the close drills, as is befitting future Wingseconds and Wingleaders. The training lasts for all the daylight hours and is fatiguing.

As the weyrlings' first year progresses and their dragons grow large enough to carry them, the young riders make their first set of fighting straps and any other equipment necessary for the care of a dragon and for the job of fighting Thread.

Once or twice a year, fighting straps have to be replaced entirely. Some splicing is done on the leather gear, using sailor's palms and waxed gut, but it is safer to make a new set than to rely on old, stretched straps. The hide is always well oiled and worked supple so that it will not chafe the dragon's neck, and lined with a smooth piece of suede to pad the girth. The straps hold a rider in that space between those neck ridges better than one could ever be held by saddle and stirrups. When learning the thermals in the Bowl, weyrlings will convey passengers, who sit behind them in the dorsal fins and hang on. As the dragon gets older, the pair's duties change to the more serious adult pursuits.

Once the straps are made to the satisfaction of the Weyrlingmaster and his assistants, the weyrlings begin flight training. A dragon instinctively knows the principles of flight; young riders, few of whom have ever been dragonback more than once, have no understanding at all. During times when there is no Threadfall, lectures by the more experienced riders, often Wingleaders, teach the youngsters the rudiments. Ground Drill follows, with both dragon and rider anxious to get airborne. Finally, often reluctantly, the Weyrlingmaster announces the dates of the first flights.

Even formation flying on a dragon is a solitary experience, a feeling shared only by dragon and rider. There is also an understandable exuberance during those first flights. The rider, joined to his or her dragon, actually *is* flying: The air rushes over their wings; they fly through clouds.

A dragonrider must learn to fly alone; no one rides with him. The first flight is made under the watchful eye of the Weyrlingmaster and one of his assistants. Usually one is on the ground and the other is airborne. The first flight is no more impressive than that made at Kitty Hawk by the Wright brothers: a few wingbeats into the air and a shallow glide to the ground.

To the young rider the rush of air, the jolt of being flung upward by his dragon's strong hind legs, the beat of leathery dragonwings, and the shallow glide followed by an often jarring descent to the ground is a time of pure magic. The Weyrlingmaster now has the young dragonpair repeat the short flight three times.

"So you won't think it's a fluke!" he explains to the anxious weyrling.

The pace of flight training is very light for the first month, until all weyrlings of a particular Hatching have become familiarized with the sensations of flight. At this early stage in the relationship, it is possible for an overly compliant dragon to accede to his partner's dangerous whims—occasionally fatally.

After the first month's limited flights, the pace intensifies. At this time the weyrlings move out of barracks and into free weyrs. They start flying in teams of three. In these trios they begin the flying drills that they will need when fighting Thread. The firestone drills on the ground are transferred to the air, with riders flinging sacks from one to another while the Weyrlingmaster orders the trio to turn left, turn right, climb left, climb right, dive, and so on, until the riders are seasoned in all the standard maneuvers. Next the Weyrlingmaster combines groups and repeats the drills.

When all the weyrlings of a Hatching are flying well in formation, the Weyrlingmaster starts training the weyrlings to go *between*. This training starts with drilling of terrain recognition, as the Weyrlingmaster instructs the dragonriders on how best to visualize their destination. When he is satisfied with the progress of a particular dragonpair, the Weyrlingmaster flies with the pair and takes them *between*—the rider playing the role of passenger as his dragon takes visual reference from the Weyrlingmaster. The first jump *between* is always startling; the Weyrlingmaster will jump *between* with a pair several times before letting them visualize the destination and make the jump unaided.

Again, even with the greatest precautions, a few new weyrling pairs go *between* and never reappear. During the more hurried training that has to be conducted during a Threadfall, it is not uncommon at this point to lose one or more weyrling pairs per Hatching. This often occurs in bunches, with several Hatchings all passing through this training safely and then as many as a half dozen failing to reappear from one group.

As each weyrling pair progresses beyond this point, they join to form their threes into nines and to practice precision jumps *between* under the careful eye of the Weyrlingmaster or his assistants. The drill is the aerial version of the Ground Drills the young weyrlings practiced before their dragons could fly. Losses are rare at this point, though injuries (mostly from collisions) are common.

The final phase of the weyrlings' training begins when they are taught how to chew firestone to make flame. The introduction takes one long day and must be handled with extreme care. Again the Weyrlingmaster trains each dragonpair individually.

Although the ability to chew firestone is instinctive in dragons, the exercise must be supervised. The Weyrlingmaster normally starts the pair out on a soft stone (not firestone), to get the dragon used to the concept of thinking of its "other stomach" and the young rider familiar with the procedures. Once the dragon is used to chewing and processing the rock, the Weyrlingmaster gives the pair true firestone. At first this is low-grade ore, and the dragon produces only a small flame. By the end of the day, the pair will have trained up to producing full flame.

Once all weyrlings are able to flame, the Weyrlingmaster continues to train the new riders, using ever more challenging drills and recognition points farther from the Weyr.

At this point the weyrlings tend to spend as much time as possible with the "real" riders. They begin to join the more experienced dragons and riders on recreational flights and visits to Holds. During this period the experienced pairs and Wingleaders get to know the weyrlings.

Now the time approaches when the young riders will be drafted into Fighting Wings. Their first assignment is to the Weyrlings' Wing—the Wing of young dragonriders and older injured dragonriders who bring fresh sacks of firestone to riders as they fight Thread.

Flying firestone to riders in Threadfall is dangerous. In some ways this is more dangerous than flying in a Fighting Wing, because riders coming from *between* into the Threadfall area may not have a clear idea of the Leading Edge of the Fall. Also, the rider must depend more on his own initiative than he would if he were flying in formation with a group of his fellows. So the inexperienced pairs are more prone to extending themselves, and there is no one to cover for mistakes. But it is in flying firestone during Threadfall that new riders first get "blooded"—and often fatally.

There is no way around that expedient: There comes a time when a rider and his dragon must face Thread on Pern for the first time. Most riders prefer to face this alone rather than endanger others. In hard times, weyrlings have no choice but to be placed directly into understrength or overfatigued Fighting Wings; understandably, this course results in more injuries and fatalities.

It is the many losses that occur during this "blooding" that most often make a Weyrlingmaster resign. Too often in full Fall a Weyrlingmaster will have to watch a young weyrling emerge from *between* at the wrong time—to be engulfed in roiling Thread and,

Weyrling Scored by Thread

in screaming agony, wink back into *between* and out of existence.

"It's bad enough to see my wingmen and mates die, but to see a flock of my boys and dragons come back scored, dazed, and forever haunted, some never come back at all..." one ex-Weyrlingmaster said to explain his unexpected retirement.

THE FIGHTING WINGS

There is no real choice as to whether or not the Thread must be fought. Most young riders recover from their exposure to the first horrors of fighting Thread. Weyrlingmasters accept the price of their teachings or stand down. Weyrlings so blooded are marked as ready to move into the ranks of the Fighting Wings. The fighting strength of the Weyr varies, with the high being some 330 fighting dragons, not counting the queens, invalids, or weyrlings in training. Rarely is a Weyr able to boast of being at full strength (although in olden times, before the founding of the Benden Weyr and again before the founding of the remaining Weyrs, there were at least five hundred dragons in a Weyr). A

Weyrleader counts himself lucky to have nine good Wings of reasonable strength and some spare riders to make up for losses; his worries begin only when he reaches the inevitable point when he cannot make nine Wings with a scant twelve dragons each.

WING AND FLIGHTS

A Wing is the smallest cohesive group of riders. Each Wing is led by a Wingleader, who is aided by Wingseconds. Most often the Wingleader is a bronze rider, the Wingseconds riding browns, but circumstances may put any rider in any position. In good times a Wing contains thirty dragons. Twelve is the smallest working Wing a Weyrleader will normally permit to fly.

Three Wings are considered the smallest number that can successfully fight a Threadfall. This grouping of three Wings is referred to by some as a Flight. As three Wings (up to ninety dragons) forms a fairly large and cumbersome grouping of dragons, it is the largest unit treated as a permanent group, with the exception of the Weyr itself. The Weyrleader often uses the Flight as the administrative

Maximum Altitudes Attainable by Flying or Fighting Dragons

Maximum Flight

Maximum Fight

unit. This gives him additional flexibility when assigning new riders or promoting riders to new positions. The Wings are grouped into Flights on the basis of fitness and compatibility, which means that the groupings are not static: a Weyrleader may group two tired but veteran Wings with a young but enthusiastic Wing, or spread out his new riders into three Wings and use the resulting Flight sparingly until the Wings have settled in. It's a balancing act based upon intangible factors and in which each false judgment potentially means scored riders or dragons at least, and burrowed Thread at worst.

In addition to the simpler task of integrating a new green or blue dragonrider into the Fighting Wings, the Weyrleader must resolve the more difficult problem of bringing in new brown and bronze riders—the traditional Wingseconds and Wingleaders. Where misplacing a blue or green rider within a Wing could cause disaster for the Wing, misplacing an inexperienced brown or bronze rider could cause disaster for the Flight or Weyr. Most young bronze riders serve time first as regular Wing riders and then as Wingseconds before being permitted to lead a Wing against Thread. Brown riders receive similar treatment.

Riders who fail to win the Weyrleader's respect may continue to ride as Wing riders. A bronze rider has the recourse of flying the senior queen dragon and becoming Weyrleader himself; a brown rider can merely strive harder and hope for a change of leadership. In a society where cooperation is the highest value, voluntary transfers are rare and considered a sign of failure.

In placing brown and bronze riders within the Wings, whether as Wingleaders, Wingseconds, or mere Wing riders, the wise Weyrleader consults with his Wingleaders beforehand. One option the Weyrleaders often exercise is to allow certain riders to spend time as assistants to the Weyrlingmaster, allowing them as much as a full Turn to relax, giving the Weyrlingmaster an aide with a bright new perspective, and providing the Weyrleader with a ready pool of proven leaders in case of trouble. It is also a Weyrleader prerogative, in those rare cases of overstrength Flights, to assign riders as guides for the Weyrlings' Wing.

A weyrling becomes a true dragonrider when assigned to a Fighting Wing. Every weyrling yearns to hear the traditional "The Weyrleader has allowed me to ride with you" from some Wingleader and to move from the weyrling tables to the tables of his Fighting Wing. If the weyrling expects anything more or an aura to appear, he is sadly mistaken: The next day he finds himself sent on chores much like those he was given before. Only now everything is very much for real. When Thread is due to fall, no shirking is allowed—the dragonrider is up hours beforehand, stoking his dragon with firestone, checking his gear, and awaiting his Wingleader's call to fly.

Practice is conducted with greater fervor; mistakes that other weyrlings might have guffawed at now draw stern reproval from wingmates. Practice includes special drill for those duties that particular Wing might be called upon to perform: left Wing, right Wing, or forward Wing all have different maneuvers. The Wing maneuvers are worked out by the Weyrleader and the Wingleaders.

THREADFIGHTING TACTICS

Every Threadfall is different—there is always one best way to fly against it—and a Weyrleader is lax if he is not always striving to perfect his Weyr's ability to meet each Threadfall with as much flame and as few casualties as

possible. Wind and the time through the Pass have the greatest effects on Threadfall; rain has the next greatest effect.

"Rain! Let it rain thick and heavy and drown the Thread while we drink in the Weyr!" dragonriders often wish.

The severe winds and rain of a cold front are the dragonriders' greatest weather threat: With turbulent air low down and unknown up-and-down-drafts, only the most experienced of riders can hope to fight well, and only the foolhardy can expect to return unscathed. As the Pass of the Red Star comes closer, the frequency of Threadfalls increases until they occur at the rate of once every fourteen hours in bands across the planet, giving weary dragonriders no rest.

To meet the threat of Thread combined with foul weather, the Weyrleader must use planning, teamwork, and long-practiced formations. Casualties play a role in how a Weyr weathers the Pass, but training is decisive. Training is carried out at all times, by individual pairs, as Wings, as Flights, and by the full Weyr.

The individual rider trains best by flying his old trio and practicing with falling ropes soaked in colored dyes. The rope imitates Thread. Several riders throw more rope than a pair of dragons could hope to catch, and it is up to the training riders to make the best of the situation. Rope that falls uncharred to the ground is counted against them, while dye marks on their dragons or on themselves score double points in their favor. Riders trade off partners to learn techniques, as well as to invent new tactics. The rope drill is carried out in all weather, even pouring rain, when Thread would be drowned in its Fall.

As a Wing, the riders practice formation flying. A rider at the point of a flight must maintain an awareness of those on his left and right. They are guarding him from any Thread in those directions. So long as he maintains his position in the formation, he does not have the worry that he might be flamed from left or right.

The Wing may be arrayed in any number of different ways: in a straight line; stacked by Wingseconds into three lines; in a forward vee or backward vee; flying upward or downward or level. Each different position and angle of flight entails different advantages and dangers. Every rider is expected to know how to fly faultlessly in every possible Wing formation. The Wing drills until it can go *between*, while climbing or diving and turning in any direction, and come out of *between* in the same formation it started with.

A dragon must be allowed room in the Wing to enable him to maneuver. Because of this, the space left between the dragons is greater than a dragon's flame could cover. Wings take turns dropping dyed rope at each other, and the whole Wing practices flaming, drilling to ensure that each dragon and rider has an instinctive knowledge of his covered area. Great care is taken in training to avoid two dragons going after the same clump of Thread—it represents wasted effort and means that another section of the sky has been left uncovered.

After Wing training comes Flight training. The Flight is regarded as the least force required to fight a Threadfall unaided (but almost certainly with casualties). The Weyrleader organizes the training by Flights. When there is time for such training, it is an invaluable tool for the Weyrleader to try new riders in different positions, to juggle tired or understrength Wings to form Flights capable of meeting Threadfall, and to practice new tactics or hone old ones.

Only occasionally during a Pass does a Weyrleader find a great enough lull to allow the luxury of pitting one Flight against the dyed ropes of another, but it is these Great Drills which prove the most rewarding, both for the Weyrleader and the riders. Such Great Drills simulate Threadfall as closely as possible without actually getting Threadscored.

But the test and truth of a Weyrleader is in Threadfall. Weyrleaders have flown Threadfalls differently during each of the Passes of the Red Star. In the time of Moreta, it was considered best to array the entire Weyr in three levels and fly straight from Leading Edge to end of Threadfall. F'lar, encountering difficult times only seen before by the very first dragonriders, adopted a more chop-and-change attitude, throwing his scanty forces at Threadfall as best he could. As time went on, and the Oldtimers arrived from *between* through time, F'lar's tactics were modified both by acquired knowledge

Thread Fighting Formations

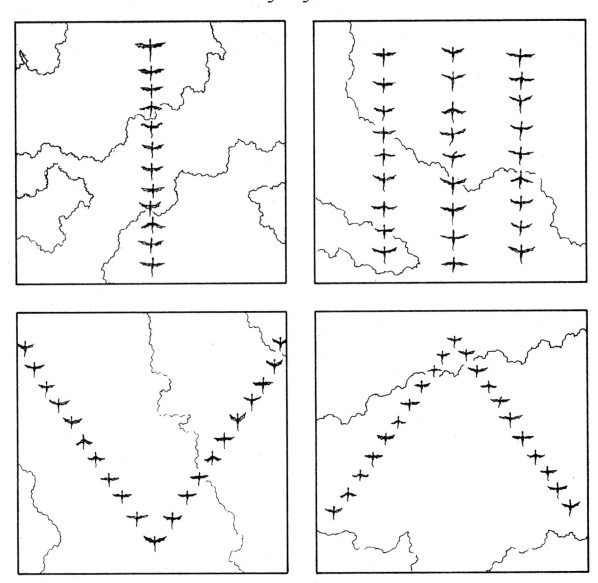

and by the availability of more dragons.

The consensus among modern dragonriders is that one must "gauge the Fall and gauge the wind." Thread can fall thickly, in sheets, or it can fall in splotches or in any combination of the above configurations. The wind influences the Threadfall, and worse, if there is severe turbulence, can fling Thread onto a dragon or throw a dragon into Thread. Dragons are fantastically strong, but a thirty- to forty-knot wind will keep a dragon straining hard just to stay on station. The blues and the greens are worked over the hardest by high winds, the browns and bronzes having more strength and stamina. However, all the dragons suffer in high winds.

In truly severe turbulence a dragon could be driven away from Thread in one instance and blown right into it in the next. In that case all that saves dragons and their riders from complete catastrophe is the ability to go *between*. In such Falls, many Weyrleaders choose to send up one Flight at a time, arrayed in three Wings flying upward or downward vee formations, and change Flights several times throughout the Fall.

Calmer weather allows the Weyrleader more latitude: he may choose to send two Flights to make a leisurely Fall, one Flight to rest his other Flights, or all Flights with the hope of minimizing casualties. Still, trick gusts and flutters may make Fall in a calm wind dangerous, and Thread must always be gauged separate of wind. Otherwise the Weyrleader may choose the wrong tactic, flying the tiring Wings on line formation above the looser three-vees formation.

F'lar's tactics, as a young, inexperienced, and hopelessly underdragoned Weyrleader, were those of desperation. He threw what he could, where he could, and when he could, and counted himself lucky for the casualties. Even so, had it not been for the timely arrival of the Oldtimers, there is little doubt of the fate of Pern. With six full Weyrs and spare loaned to his Weyr, F'lar could afford better tactics. Still, he was much influenced by the success of his chop-and-change tactics and much aided by the greater stamina of his modern dragons over those from the Ancient times.

In general, except when on exhibition to Lord Holder and other Weyrleaders, F'lar tended to send one Flight to feel out the Fall, and others as needed. Most often F'lar's Flights flew arrayed in keeping with the wind: an upward vee to meet downdrafts, or a downward vee to meet updrafts, and level for calm days. Most often F'lar's dragonriders would rise to meet Threadfall rather than try to descend upon it.

Sh'gall, of Moreta's time, was more stolid in his approach. Against every Fall, until the plague forced a change, Sh'gall would fly the full Weyr complete, with the Flights arrayed as stacked Wings, and all three Flights flying side by side. He maintained this position whenever possible, with only the wind forcing him to vary it slightly: stacked backward to meet downdrafts, forward to meet updrafts, and straight for calm air.

The doughty dragonriders of Ista Weyr are best trained in dealing with the sort of foul weather where Thread can still do damage. Their tactics are more varied than any other Weyr's, encompassing such odd formations as "Wing low, Wing high" and "Hollow Flight" to deal with the extremes of wind and weather they commonly face.

Backing up all of these tactics are the Queen's Wing, the Wing formed of all the queen dragons of the Weyr. Queens cannot digest firestone; however, by carrying agenothree (HNO_3—nitric acid) sprayers on their backs, the queen riders are exceedingly effective as the low-flying mop-up Flight. In bad weather the aid of the Queen's Wing, with the sturdier, stronger, steadier queens, is invaluable.

Flying Leathers

The final line of protection against Thread lies not in the hands of dragonriders but in the hands of individual holders. These carry agenothree tanks on their backs and follow behind the Leading Edge of Fall to incinerate any Thread before it can burrow.

For an individual rider fighting Thread, the large formations are important, and he must maintain his position; once the first Thread comes into view, nothing matters but the Thread in front of him or to his side. Life becomes a blur of weaving for this clump or rising to that clump; diving aside as a wingman's dragon flames inward to catch a clump that was missed; and going *between* to avoid that clump that suddenly rises into view or, much worse, to freeze the burning Thread that suddenly eats into human or dragon. In the "calmer" moments the rider is nabbing the hastily thrown sack of firestone and feeding the gaping maw of his dragon.

Finally it's over, and there is a flare of exultation, the joyful awareness that rider and dragon have survived. Then the memories creep back—memories of impossible moves, of incredibly near misses, of agonizing pain. When the sweep riding is over, and everyone is back at the Weyr and scores covered with numbweed, then the dragonriders remember the large formation their Weyrleader used and consider its effectiveness.

"What, only three scored? Good pattern, then."

After a Wing has flown, the Weyr will be filled with such sounds as the melancholy keening of injured dragons and the relieved laughter of those who survived unscored. There are riding straps to be inspected, food to eat, and children to rear. Even when no Thread falls, there are lessons to be learned, skills to be honed, and drills to be practiced.

After a big Threadfall there are too often dead to be honored. And always, always, there is going to be more Thread falling later.

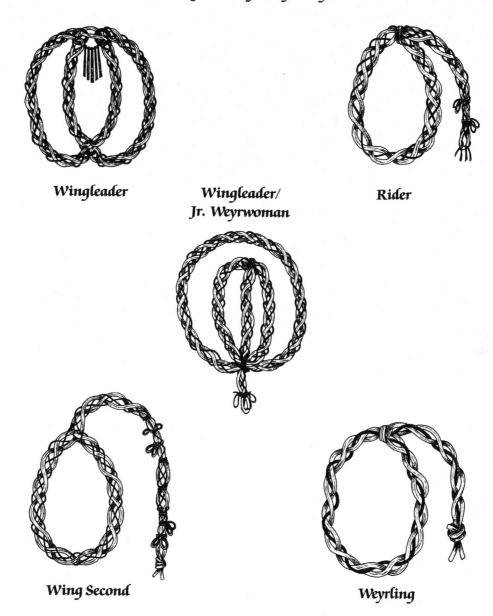

Wingleader

Wingleader/
Jr. Weyrwoman

Rider

Wing Second

Weyrling

SHOULDER KNOTS USED BY DRAGONRIDERS

Shoulder Knots

People on Pern display their rank by the elaborately woven and knotted cords they wear on their shoulders. Dragonriders indicate rank within the Weyr by design and complexity of their knots. The two colors of a dragonrider's shoulder knot indicate to which Weyr he belongs and the color of the dragon the rides. Riders can also wear badges with a dragon blazoned in the color of their mounts on a background of their Weyr color. The women and drudges of the Lower Caverns wear a simple cord of the dominant Weyr color only.

VII.

Threadfall

Charts

The first Fall the colonists experienced was actually the fourth Fall of the Pass. The other three had fallen in the sea, in the polar ice caps where the mycelia could do no damage, or onto unoccupied terrain.

An aerial survey of the areas attacked by Thread revealed that the Thread appeared at predictable intervals in predictable locations. It would traverse three time zones for a period of four hours, covering twenty degrees longitude northeast to southwest. In the Second Long Interval, much of this vital documentation was lost and had to be tediously reconstructed by F'lar of Benden Weyr in the Ninth Pass.

Thread always fell within five degrees north or south of the strip predicted. As the Pass went on, the attacks came more and more frequently but did not vary from this pattern, which spiraled from north to south, matching the rotation of the planet.

The colonists used the term "Leading Edge" to denote the wave of Thread advancing during a Fall, and "Following, or Trailing Edge," to refer to the line behind which no Thread fell. Once the Following Edge was in view, the fighters knew that the Fall was about to end. At sea level, Thread is visible on the horizon thirty minutes before it will be overhead.

PASSES AND INTERVALS

Year	Event
8–58	First Pass
58–258	First Interval
258–308	Second Pass
308–508	Second Interval
508–558	Third Pass
558–758	Third Interval
758–808	Fourth Pass
808–1258	First Long Interval (200 years plus 50 of no Threadfall plus 200 years)
1258–1308	Fifth Pass
1308–1508	Fifth Interval
1508–1558	Sixth Pass
1558–1758	Sixth Interval
1758–1808	Seventh Pass
1808–2008	Seventh Interval
2008–2058	Eighth Pass
2058–2508	Second Long Interval
2508–	Ninth Pass

First Threadfalls

Passes lasted fifty years as the Red Star dragged its trail of Oort matter through Pern's atmosphere. Thread would begin to fall in the first warm weather after the time in midwinter when the Red Star appeared bracketed by the Eye Rock and the sun balanced on the Star Stones, rock formations that were placed on the lip of every Weyr to provide eternal pointers.

The Red Star passes through and around the Rukbat system on a revolution of 250 years. For 50 of those years, it descends, intersecting the plane of the ecliptic like a chain link. During the remaining 200, the Red Star makes the rest of its journey outside Rukbat's solar system until it reaches the point of aphelion, where it begins its pass once more.

Because the planet has an eccentric orbit, it does not always drag its trail of Oort matter close enough to Pern to cause a Pass. Twice in human memory on Pern, the Red Star failed to come into contact with the third planet.

VIII.

Fort,

the First Hold

THE MOVE NORTH

Soon after the First Hatching, in the ninth year of the colony, it became evident that the Southern Continent was too unstable and dangerous to occupy. The earthquakes were increasing in frequency and intensity. Even though the stakeholds were gradually closed down as their inhabitants moved to safer quarters in the North, the colonists left behind much of their heavier equipment and other goods that they would not immediately need. They always meant to go back.

As the land grew more unstable, the agronomists examined the Northern Continent. It had only fifteen to twenty percent arable land, instead of the forty percent of the more fertile Southern Continent, but it was far less volcanic in character. The seismologists had underestimated how violent the reactions of the tectonic chains would be to the approach of the rogue planet. Until Mount Garben began to spew ash, they believed that any disruption would come from the three smaller cones along the great volcano's flank.

In the same year that the first dragons Hatched, one of the small mountains blew out ash toward the Jordan River, prompting the settlers to move personnel and irreplace-able equipment to Fort Hold immediately. Because of the paucity of transport, much of the machinery and supplies was sealed in the Catherine Caves for pickup later.

Curiously, the ever-helpful fire-dragonets absented themselves from the emergency moving preparations. At the time Mount Garben erupted, only the golds and a few of the bronzes were with their human friends. The others were warily observing the eruption of the mountain. Because the fire-dragonets were so long-lived, it is believed that the image projected to Lord Jaxom came from creatures who had actually seen the explosion, or their first- or second-generation descendants.

As construction of Fort Hold neared completion, the colonists found that they were running out of viable transport. The sleds and transports were wearing out. They might have lasted another twenty years under normal use, but the Pernese had to move people and things as quickly as possible. The original planners had never considered the need for a mass exodus.

There was some rivalry as to who would have use of the remaining power packs. Every task had to be judged for its importance to the settlement. The terraformers building the Hold and roads got first priority, because they were working toward the greatest good for the greatest number. What other packs remained were taken way from less vital projects, like Wind Blossom Ping's biogenetic experiments, and put to other, more immediate uses.

By the colony's thirtieth year, it was clear that there would be no response to the one homing capsule that had been launched during the first crisis. The last of the transports had worn out fighting Thread and bringing colonists to the safety of Fort Hold. By this time, the dragons had bred up to sufficient numbers to take the place of the shuttles, thereby saving what precious supplies of disposable materials still remained for construction of shelter for the migrating colonists.

FORT HOLD

Fort Hold: On a brown field, a yellow Lattice*

The immediate need to provide safe housing set on basement rock made the "fort" discovered in the Northern Continent an attractive solution, if it could be made ready before the ash-spewing volcanoes and attendant earth-

quakes did too much damage to the stakeholds in Southern.

In a valley formed by a fault, the right-angled face of a palisade three kilometers long was gashed nearly at its foot by a narrow horizontal slit four meters high, permitting entry to the caverns inside. Crawling up over the lip, explorers found a maze of small caverns linked together with a gigantic, vaulted bubble of rock too high for any torch beam to illuminate. A natural stair inside allowed them easy access to another cave on the inner side of the thin face.

The gigantic cavern was fifty-seven meters deep, tapering to forty-five meters and forty-two meters at either end. At the back of the "Great Hall," eighteen different openings led deep into further tunnel complexes. Springs of fresh water circulated in one of the tunnels.

Construction began after a secondary survey. Nothing of the natural face of the mountain, a rugged cliff with a hanging curtain of rock two meters thick, was changed. But the inside was transformed into a beautiful, opulent, and ornate, almost Byzantine, living space.

The lip of the cave was filled in with native rock, so that the addition would look natural, leaving a wide opening that would serve as a main entrance. The doors were made of a solid bronze-colored alloy obtained by melting down plates of the colony ships. A ramp was formed out of blocks and crushed rock and slagged solidly into place before the natural courtyard. Steps were cut into the sides of the ramp.

The space just inside the thin rock wall was chosen for offices and living quarters for the administrators. An inner wall was built up paralleling the natural curtain, and levels

*Badges and knots are noted and pictured individually, below the name of the Hold, Hall, or Weyr to which they pertain.)

Fort Hold

began to be floored in, their windows cut evenly into the rock face. Each Hold window was supplied with tight-fitting metal shutters of the same alloy as the doors so that none of the inhabitants would be threatened by the sight of falling Thread. Hallways were melted smooth, as were the walls in living quarters, but the rooms intended for storage just had the rough corners knocked off. The outer Hold was built almost right away from the rock quarried out during the construction of the inner Hold.

Natural chimneys leading from the interior caves to the clifftop provided ventilation ducts. Deep artesian wells and the surface water source in the tunnel allowed for water to be pumped right into the baths and sinks throughout the complex. The thermal layer under the ridge provided heat in the winter that could be diverted directly out of the complex during the summer with the flip of a lever.

Above the first five levels, the lines of windows became irregular, since the rooms onto which they opened were constructed not behind the curtain wall but from smaller, single caves.

Some tunnels found by the miners extended several hundred feet underground into large bubble caverns. The work to make them habitable was assisted by the watch-whers, who, though photophobic and by no means as intelligent as dragons, were able to find faults underground, saving many lives by pointing out pitfalls and loose rock before the miners could detect them.

The ground-level caves that eventually became the beasthold were originally intended as the veterinary surgery. Fort supported herds of ovines, porcines, bovines, varieties of Earth fowl and Pernese avians, and the two surviving types of canines. The breed that resembled a Jack Russell terrier proved to be first-class at pursuing and killing tunnel snakes. The other, a large German shepherd/boxer breed, was used for herding and hunting. Canines were also of use for pulling mill wheels and turning hearth spits. But not all of the dogs nor all the domestic cats, used for catching tunnel snakes and other pests, made the Second Crossing to the Northern Continent with their owners. Many of them bred in the wild on the now-deserted Southern Continent.

The communications "eyrie," built high on the outer cliff with a long, winding stair leading from inside ground level, in later years became the Harper Hall Drum Heights. The stairs were cut with stonecutters, puzzling later generations, who could not understand how those perfectly square steps were made.

Fort Hold was intended to house only the population of Landing, which because of Threadfall had grown back to between a thousand and twelve hundred. As Southern Continent grew more dangerous, Fort became crowded with refugees. Because Fort was unprepared to house such numbers, over five thousand had to sleep in three shifts wherever they could fit. Any area that was not positively uninhabitable by human beings was used as a dormitory at least one third of the day. People slept in corridors, in corners of rooms used for quiet occupations, and in storerooms that were not entirely full of containers and crates. Children slept in community crèches with child-care volunteers who mustered them to help out with the construction with light activities during the day.

Threadfall Shutters

It was such an immense complex that the builders could easily make more levels to house more people. It would have taken more than a single lifetime to learn all the ins and outs of the complex cave system. Several of the natural passageways were found to be dangerous, the stone of the floor and walls too crumbly and fragile to last under heavy traffic over the projected lifetime of the Hold. The builders blocked several of these corridors by slagging the entryways closed with the stonecutters, and opened new corridors between important chambers.

Ramps were made out of the native stone, but the metal spiral staircases throughout the warren came from the three colony ships. The smaller ships, the *Buenos Aires* and the *Bahrain,* donated twelve between them, and the larger *Yokohama* eight.

Most people stayed in their stakeholds in Southern throughout most of the First Pass, then began to migrate north. The population of Fort expanded until it was necessary for the growing young dragons and their riders to move into Fort Weyr, though the Weyr was not yet ready for habitation. The sheer press of humanity gave the Fort Holders impetus to found their own Holds as soon as it was safe to do so. Once the Pass was over, the crowded dormitories became large apartments for only a fraction of the people who had slept there during the crisis.

Ruatha was the first of the other Holds to be founded. People and dragons from Ruatha and Fort Weyr later flew east to found Benden. Gradually, the swollen populations of Fort and Benden spread out to other stakeholds and farmholds around the stable Northern Continent. The tradition of expansion continued through the years. The Lord Holders of Fort have always allowed their holders to build and seek new dwellings during Intervals.

Those who were working on Fort Hold needed somewhere to live safe and secure from Thread while the construction was going on. Out of the rubble being quarried from inside the caverns they built cotholds. The earliest ones lay in the shadow of the high cliff, but as Turns passed, more were built out near the grain fields where alfalfa was planted to feed the animals, and in the orchards that were started from carefully hoarded seeds of apples, plums, and pears in vita-packs. The present Hold contains 750 to 900 people, but more than 10,000 others in the countryside rely upon Fort for protection and the administration of resources.

Cotholds are made of local stone with slate roofs held in place with lead, an easily worked metal found in quantity in the area. The cotholds were all very much alike: little boxlike buildings of one to three stories with bronze window shutters, except for the decorative bands of color just under the eaves, out of danger from Threadfall. The colors were intended to show Craft affiliation, possibly with a picture or two, but not every cotholder changed the decoration when he moved in. A tanner might live in a cot that is called "Baker's Cot," for a noteworthy tenant who had lived there two or three generations before.

Dunca's cot, beholden for generations to the Harper Hall, has an unadorned strip of blue lining the eaves, as the plump cotholder is proud of her status but has neither the talent nor the imagination to personalize the decoration.

The roads leading through and out of Fort Hold are as good as any Roman road on Earth. The stonecutters melted rock down several feet in squared U-shaped trenches with drainage holes set at intervals. The trenches were filled in with layers of big broken stones, smaller stones, and then gravel. The roads nearest the Hold are cobbled to withstand more traffic than is seen on the ones leading to Fort Weyr or Ruatha.

The graveled span to the Weyr is so well maintained that it takes only one day on a fast runnerbeast to reach it. On foot, the trip takes two to three days, but the going is easy and well sheltered. Except for tithe trains, the road is rarely used in F'lar's day. If someone has an important message for the Weyr, he can bespeak a dragon, and helios or drums can transmit messages that are not strictly confidential.

Food

Foodstuffs for those who live in and by Fort Hold are handled by a central storage facility. Fort's cavern system includes a vast storehouse to which all the farmholders bring crops and withdraw enough to feed their families for a day, or a few days, depending on their own facilities. Fort Hold supports about ten thousand people who do not live in the Hold proper, but in the farmlands and beastfolds around it. Fort's food center is divided into caverns for each type of storage, and one large, high-ceilinged room for food preparation.

When Fort Hold was first occupied, the mass catering system used by Landing was already in place. The dieticians issued requirements for proper nutrition, and the cooks were highly skilled in making monotonous ingredients interesting. During the First Pass, a small amount of meat was served in a typical meal, and most likely, lentils or beans would supplement the settlers' need for protein. Bread, milk products, vegetables, and homemade liquor, wine, or beer rounded out the meal.

The hydroponics tanks that used to provide the Fort Holders with their vegetables were gradually turned to other uses, and some of the species died out between the First Pass and the Eighth. Mushrooms were propagated in the cool, dark chambers near the cold storage caves. Klahbark was popular not only infused as a drink but sprinkled into dishes as a spice. Competitions were held between Brewmasters, and Fort grew its own grapes on the warm slopes to the north beyond the beastholds.

The cooking facilities—and the cooks—in Fort Hold and Weyr are the best on Pern. Chefs and cooks have their own Craft, though it has no major Crafthall. Cooking is considered one of the Hold Crafts.

The cooks barter among themselves for recipes and special spices. An aspiring chef might foster at Fort to learn the best cooking. When he or she has learned the skill, the new cook returns home again. Holders and folk in the Lower Caverns of a Weyr learn to prepare food at an early age. Good cooking is considered an instinct, and good cooks are encouraged to fulfill their potential. Both men and women can hold the position of Head Cook in a Hold or Weyr.

Present-day Fort Holders eat a lot of stews and filling, hearty soups to make use of every edible part of a herdbeast. Roasts are served only infrequently, for special occasions. Salted fish is a frequent main dish, supplied to the storehouses by Fort Sea Hold in exchange for red meat and fruit for those who like a change from seafood. Fort makes salty cheddar, Stilton, and a few soft cheeses for spreading on bread. Mushrooms are popular, as are dishes made with peanuts, river grains (rice), and soybeans. Legumes are added to savory dishes to thicken them up.

The constraint as always is to grow the most food on the most land that can be protected during a Pass. Those who farm during Intervals can spread out and experiment.

Tubers are kept over the cold season in

Hearty Herdbeast Stew

For tastiest results, use either the meat of mature bovine or young ovine. If using bovine, the meat can be either raw or roasted rare to medium rare. To serve four, assemble the following ingredients:

1 to 1½ pounds herdbeast, cut into 1-inch pieces
3 tablespoons flour
3 tablespoons butter or margarine
1 garlic clove (if desired)
½ large onion, cut into bite-size pieces
1 pound peeled tomatoes (or 1 16-ounce can of tomatoes in their own juice)
2 cups water
4 small or 2 medium potatoes, peeled
2–4 small carrots, sliced
2 ribs celery, sliced into 1-inch pieces
bay leaf
1 cup corn kernels or baby corn cut into 1-inch pieces, drained
salt
pepper
¼ teaspoon dry mustard or cracked mustard seeds
garlic salt
parsley

Dredge the pieces of meat in flour. Melt the butter in a saucepan. When bubbly, add the meat. Brown the pieces on all sides. Sprinkle salt and pepper. Add the onion and garlic; cook until transparent. Add the tomatoes and two

sandpiles, along with swedes, parsnips, fingeroots, and turnips. One crop that is never neglected is the kitchen herb and spice garden. Clumps of herbs hanging overhead in the kitchens and corridors sweeten the air while they dry. At Fort and Nerat, the holders raise the whole range of herbs that the colonists brought with them to Pern.

Fort Hold grows sugar beets for sweetening, several varieties of berries, and wheat—all the ingredients needed for the bubbly pies its Bakercraft makes so well.

Clothing

Fort Holders have a keen eye for style. Since they are so close to the Weavercrafthall in Southern Boll, Fort Holders get the news first on what is fashionable for each season. The Hold lies in the temperate zone, so the styles of dress vary with the seasons. In the cold season, fur-lined cloth garments are necessary in the stone corridors of the Hold and the Weyr, even though the thermal heating keeps off most of the chill. The holders wear floor-length dresses and pants through most of the Turn, though the weather gets very hot in the height of summer, when someone may reinvent the bikini or weave clothing out of grasses, depending on how much attention he or she wants to attract.

Tastes in clothing tend toward the ornate in Fort Hold. In the evening, the holders design new clothes, using stones and hammered gold or silver leaf and interesting dyed designs for adornment. The Hold is famous for its complex brocades, knit or woven on multiple looms. The knit brocades are done on needles as thin as sewing needles, using ordinary thread of sisal or cotton, but there's nothing ordinary about the results. Brocade jackets cut to the ancient Chinese pattern turn up from time to time.

Many patterns of weaving and embroidery are peculiar to Fort Hold. The weavers can produce cotton velvet, terry cloth, and other slubbed fabrics. A common cloth similar to denim is made for work clothes. There are no zippers on Pern; trousers close with button flaps, drawstrings, or a two-sided substance like Velcro. Long-sleeved boat-necked sweaters and bush trousers are recommended wear for going outside the Hold, as there are many plants to beware of in the brush: needlethorn, itch-leaf, saw grass, and other plants too useful to medicine or cookery to wipe out.

cups of water. Break up the tomatoes with a spoon. Add potatoes, bay leaf, carrots, and celery. Bring the mixture to a boil, cover, reduce to a simmer, and let cook for 30 minutes, stirring occasionally.

Add corn, spices to taste. Bring the stew to a boil again, cover, and return to simmer. Cook for 15–30 minutes, stirring occasionally, until corn, potatoes, and meat are all tender. Uncover and cook for 15 or so minutes until stew is slightly thickened.

Example of Women's Garb in Fort Hold, Using Local Fabrics

Hold Decoration

The inside of the Great Hall is spectacular. The stone is decorated with etched and painted line patterns of great complexity. Knotwork designs of African, Celtic, or Indian extraction arch high over the doorways and surround niches cut into the rock where statues and works of art are on display. The color on the wall designs is reapplied from time to time, but no one has ever tried to clean or repaint the etchings on the wide, arched ceiling.

The Lady Holder of Fort oversees the placement of valuable works of art left behind by her ancestors. In the Archives are oil paintings hundreds of Turns old, and fax pictures far older are treasured as heirlooms that make contemporary artists sigh with envy of the skill.

The Lord and Lady Holders' apartments

75

are crammed with objets d'art, not unlike an eighteenth-century French salon. The rugs are very old and very fine. A small remnant of one of the first rugs to decorate the Hold is framed on the wall of the Lord Holder's apartment. Tapestries line the stone walls between the windows, lending vivid color to the otherwise unbroken gray.

Gathers and Celebrations

In the fortieth year of the colony, when everyone on Pern but those on Ierne Island had moved north, the calendar was reversed at winter solstice so that the months would coincide with the seasons, and their year begin as winter ended.

The most important Gather at Fort is the two-day celebration for Turnover, at the winter solstice. A Pernese Turn consists of 366 days, or 52 sevendays plus two days left over. Those two days of Turnover, called Turn's End and Turn's Beginning, are marked by special presentations by the Harper Hall.

Another festival is Crossing Day, which celebrates the anniversary of the Second Crossing.

There is a Harvest Gather every Turn, but the most important of these comes once every 250 Turns. The first Harvest Gather after a Pass ends is a major festival, held on the twenty-eighth (the last) day of the ninth month.

A celebration peculiar to Fort Hold and Weyr is the Firstday of the Weyr, the first day of the fifth month, dating from the fourteenth year of the colony. Each region has a celebration for the Weyr it is beholden to, but Fort's is special since it honors the first Weyr and the first of dragonkind.

Ruatha is the center for runnerbeast racing, but Fort, too, holds some race meets. Fort has no formal track. The races meet wherever there is a flat enough grassoid field lying fallow that season. The Fort Holders host many sailing races. Gaming meets are popular, too, such as board game tournaments or partnered chess on a big board, a Pernese variation of the Ancient game.

Fort Hold celebrates the Landing, but they have forgotten its real importance. Landing is considered to be the eighth day of the third month in Southern. After the plague, the celebration was remembered as Landing Day, but the reason for its name was lost. This day has come to be a planting festival for early crops.

The Gather stalls are stored in a back cavern until they are wanted. Each Craft has traditional places where they set up their pitches, unchanged in hundreds of Turns.

HOLDCRAFTS

Some of the Crafts practiced on Pern have no central Crafthalls because they are simply too widespread or too routine. Among such occupations are winecraft, hunting, cooking, trading, and art.

A child who shows artistic tendencies is encouraged to develop his skills. He can apply himself to portraiture, sculpture, or whatever his talents suggest. Art is a random ability. The artist can be steered toward employment in whichever Craft will best allow him to perfect his talent to Mastership.

If he chooses to apply for training by a Craft, there are places for artists in the Weavercrafthall as pattern or fabric designers, or pattern assemblers, working with fabric either woven, knit, or sewn. Tapestry weaving is a good way for an artist to express himself. In a land in which everyone lives within stone walls, even bad tapestries can find homes, so the novice weaving is never wasted.

The Harper Hall is always eager to find accurate copyists and artists for scores and archives. For those who are good at working with their hands, there may be a place as an instrument crafter or ornamenter. The Smithhall uses a more technical kind of artist, one who is more accurate than imaginative. The smiths need draftsmen to make their drawings for them, but there is also a place for artists in that Craft to make fine jewelry.

An artist may be able to find work in a big Hold as a supernumerary, depending on the Holder's inclination. A fellow good with color might have a job painting signs or murals on the gray stone walls. The Pernese like gaudy colors. Some artists travel from place to place painting barns and signs for farmers and crafters.

The most common materials for sketching are charcoal on slate or bark. Paper is still too much of a luxury item for such a profitless venture as artwork.

HARPERCRAFT

Harper: On a white field, a rich blue Harp

This section of the Fort Hold complex was once the ground-level living quarters for those who had claustrophobia or a fear of heights. The Hall ceilings were cut immensely high, because the colonists had no idea what the rooms would be used for in days to come. That has worked out to the Craft's advantage, giving superb acoustics to the chorus room. The Hall is constructed around a central courtyard entirely made of stone. The windows are flanked by jointed metal shut-

Harper Hall

DAILY LIFE ON PERN

Writing materials

Until recently, paper was unknown on Pern. The colonists wrote on plastic sheets extruded from their polymeric synthesizers. Later generations used slates, hide, and canvas for their message sheets. After all this time, there is rarely anything left in most writing desks but scraped and re-scraped hide used over and over again, which makes the ink run into indecipherability. There is a lot of hide available, but most often it is put to other uses, and only scraps are used for writing.

Message slates are written on using charcoal sticks, or painted with a water-soluble pigment, for ease in reuse. Other slates are coated with a vegetable lipid that resembles wax and can be melted smooth again and again for inscribing messages or practicing penmanship.

Klah

This spicy drink is generally served hot, possibly with milk and/or sweetening, sometimes with a splash of a warming liquor. It is brewed from the bark of a native tree. The flavor is something like cinnamony chocolate, with a touch of hazelnut and coffee. It can be drunk cold, but the preferred taste is warm. Klah contains a mild stimulant like caffeine and is used as the morning drink.

ters kept in good repair. The Great Hall has windows nearly three man-heights high.

The communications center high above the plain has continued in its function, exchanging radio sets for drums, right into the present day.

Unlike any other Craft or guild on Pern, harpers do not have any other official Crafthall except for the one in Fort Hold. The Harper Hall holds a great responsibility beyond those of simple education and entertainment: It is the receptacle and the preserver of Pern's history. Not only does a harper learn the Traditions, but he learns also how to teach them to others.

In order to maintain an atmosphere that is conducive to learning, the founder of the Harper Hall, Rudi Schwartz, established classes in a hall of the residence chambers specifically for teaching children during the day. The high ceilings made it an ideal room for scratch bands of musical enthusiasts to rehearse in the evenings.

The Harper Hall started out as a small Craft and ended up as the propaganda point and communications center for Pern. It has become the clearing point for information, as well as a Craft, responsible for the job of sorting out rumor from real news.

The harpers began as the teachers who gave children their basic instruction before sending them on to other assignments for which they showed aptitude, and as the musicians who entertained the Hold in the evenings after the day's work. Gradually the Craft evolved in a similar direction to the druidic tradition on ancient Earth: prognosticator, judge, and bard.

The Harper Hall's purpose is the dissemination of information. The network of journeymen and Masters across Pern keeps all the Holds, Halls, and Weyrs in touch with one another. Musically skilled people can begin their apprenticeships in distant Halls, though the Harper Hall does not recruit outside students for its information-gathering service. Masterharpers prefer to study likely candidates at close range. A single misplaced or indiscreet message can badly damage the Hall's credibility as an unbiased judge.

Apprentices sponsored to the Craft by their local Masters are forwarded to the Harper Hall for further evaluation. If an apprentice is accepted by the Hall, he or she is given exhaustive instruction in voice, instrument making, composition and writing, and chorale singing, and must demonstrate proficiency in playing at least one instrument besides percussion. If, after his initial instruction, he shows talent in one branch of the Craft, the student may become apprenticed to the specific Master in charge of that specialty.

Not all apprentices are promoted to journeyman. Those who are take on new responsibilities, such as administrative duties. If they remain in the Harper Hall, they may be put in charge of some of their Master's apprentices. Chorale journeymen learn to arrange music and conduct a group of singers. Those who play instruments or sing well may be asked to pass those skills on to paying students and must learn to teach.

If a journeyman leaves the Hall, he may go to a large or major Hold, where he might be one of several harpers hired by the Holder. Telgar, Benden, High Reaches, Tillek, and Ista each have one or two Masters and a number of journeymen, depending on the number of children and elderly. In addition to teaching the children, the harpers entertain those too old to work.

A Hold may be without harpers if the Lord Holder is too stingy to pay a reasonable wage and no one will work for what he is willing to pay. In some small holds, a harper may be assigned to work for room and

An Earth equivalent to klah

Mix together:

2 tablespoons sweet ground chocolate
½ cup dark cocoa
⅜ teaspoon cinnamon
1 teaspoon dark instant coffee crystals, ground to powder
small pinch of nutmeg

Use two to four teaspoons of the mixture per cup of boiling water. Stir well. The klah should be thick, much like hot cocoa.

Sweetening

Sweetening comes from sweet cane or sugar beets. No bees survive on Pern, so beeswax and honey are unknown. The Pern colonists brought sugarcane cuttings and beet seeds with them, which they adapted to living in Pernese soil.

Most of the cane come from Nerat, Boll, and Ista. Recipes in which honey is a traditional ingredient use cane syrup or molasses instead.

The Bakercraft specializes in producing decorative sugars and icings. In the northern Holds, the Craft grows enormous crops of beets over the warm season, and barters extra sweetening with Holds and Crafts for other needed supplies.

Cleanliness

On Pern, soap made of lye and fat is a very rare item. Instead, the Pernese rely on fuller's earth, lanolin, saponin root, oils, and sweetsand.

Sweetsand, a naturally foaming fine sand, can get out the stench of firestone and works also on any other strong smell or heavy soil. Everyone bathes with it.

Saponin root and lanolin are used for sensitive skin and fine hair. Fuller's earth, a rare clay, is good for the complexion and for cleaning certain kinds of fabrics. Oils and vegetable waxes are good for cleaning floors, and still other herbal oils make do for skin treatments.

The recipe for soap still exists, but the chief ingredient, lye, is difficult to get. In order to make lye, water is run through hardwood ash. Hardwoods are so precious that to burn up a valuable supply of wood for soap is considered absurd. Toward the end of an Interval, when hardwood is in greater supply, someone to whom the recipe was passed down through the generations may save up all the scraps and sawdust and make a small quantity of scented bars as a luxury item.

Now that hardwoods are being cultivated in Lemos and elsewhere, the Woodcrafthall intends to make soap a sideline.

board, depending on the hold's importance to the Harper Hall.

A harper negotiates his own contract with the Holder seeking to employ him. He may choose privileges rather than marks, or a combination of perquisites and money, such as a few marks, a runner beast, a choice apartment, and certain edible (or drinkable) delicacies. Haggling for services can go just as smartly as any dicker at a Gather. If a harper is permanently assigned to a post, he is expected to settle down and marry a local girl. If he is temporary, he will probably make himself popular with the ladies, not limiting his attentions to a single one who will be broken-hearted when he leaves. One of his duties is to help arrange marriages for young men and women both inside and outside the Hold.

Journeyman harpers, known as "route riders," teach at some of the lesser cotholds as they drop by each in turn, staying overnight and going on the next day, so they can cover an entire territory at least once a month. It is a strenuous position. Their job is to sing one or two songs, pick up any information, and pass the news from hold to hold.

A tactful journeyman may also be asked to dispense justice and officiate at weddings. If the disputers who requested his services are not satisfied with his decision, they can appeal to the Masterharper. Beyond him, they may go to the local Lord Holder or still higher, to a conclave of Lord Holders.

If a Lord Holder reverses a harper's decision, it is only courtesy to let the harper know why. The Lords need the Harper Hall as much as the Hall needs the goodwill of the Lord Holders.

Because of their position as justiciars and information bearers, harpers enjoy a sort of invulnerability that forbids anyone to hurt or mistreat them. It is the depth of bad manners to injure a harper. If a Holder is stingy or dishonest, the Hall withdraws its harpers from his Hold and blackballs him until he changes his mind, but if a Holder is actively brutal, all the other Crafts will join in the boycott and withdraw their Masters from the Hold. Traders might cease to stop there as word of the boycott spreads. The Crafthalls pride themselves on their autonomy, and they stick together when threatened. An economic sanction is a powerful coercion on Pern, as the sources for commodities are limited.

However, if a harper feels that a Holder is in dire need of a lesson, he may spread a satirical song about him. It is often a greater punishment to be laughed at than to have one's pockets pinched by a boycott.

Scriber:
Quill on Hold,
Craft, or Weyr badge

Literacy and education are handled on the apprentice system all over Pern. From the colony days forward, everyone has been taught by rote the fundamentals of reading, writing, and basic accountancies by his fosterer or Craftsmaster. The Hold harper takes over and teaches history and more specific subjects. From him children learn the Traditional songs and how to sing them. The songs are more than just musical entertainment—they embody the history of Pern, advice, warn-ings, and listings too tedious to learn without music.

Women in the Holds do not always learn to read, nor do some farmholders. Drudges are rarely taught to read. They are usually the mental defectives, given what tasks they can easily handle, most of which do not include the written word.

The harper's job of prognosticator altered somewhat to teaching the Pernese how to determine when to expect Thread and to prepare for it. The Sagas and Traditional songs instruct them what to look for and what to do.

> Seas boil and mountains move,
> Sands heat, dragons prove
> Red Star passes.
> Stones pile and fires burn
> Green withers, arm Pern.
> Guard all passes.
> Star Stone watch, scan sky.
> Ready the Weyrs, all riders fly;
> Red Star passes.
>
> *(Dragonflight)*

The harper's job is to maintain the history of a place so that men will know their background and be able to learn from their ancestors' actions. He learns from the extensive Archives kept at the Hall by the Master Archivist, and passes along Traditions to the new generations who need to learn the perspective that history gives.

Children who live in outside holds learn from their parents in the warm season, and winter in a large or major Hold, where a harper teaches them. Children who live too far away or in a hold too poor to afford its own harper or to have many books and records are taught by a woman or elder of the family. They are further educated by roving journeymen harpers who cover a route, going from small hold to small hold all year round.

A child's education continues until he is fourteen, which is considered the age of reason and responsibility. At that time he begins full-time work. Unless he shows particular promise for music, he will attend no more classes with the harper. Holders marry around age sixteen, and the girls have their children as soon as possible. By this age they will have absorbed as much education as they are going to get.

Under the Masterharper in the Harper Hall, there are administrators and music Masters, journeymen, apprentices, students, and, provided by the Hall's headwoman, cooks, stewards, and drudges. Outside the Hall, the Masterharper has charge of the Masters and journeymen who work in Holds and Weyrs, and oversees their judgments in cases of law, of which records are sent to him as soon as possible. Information gathered by the journeymen and Masters out of the Hall travels from Hold to Hall, or directly to the Harper Hall if it is sufficiently important.

At present, the Healercrafthall, too, occupies part of the Harper Hall. Over the long history of Pern, it has occupied several different locations as need dictated. It made the greatest sense, as Pernese became more spread out over the smaller Northern Continent, to base the healers where requests for their assistance could be relayed the most quickly. Apprentice or journeyman harpers act as messengers, translating the beaten measures and bringing news from the Drum Heights at greater speed than by any other means than dragonback or fire-lizard message tube.

The Masterharper has his own apprentices and journeymen, who report directly to him at all times, whose talents run beyond those of simple musical proficiency. He makes use of those who can make quick and reasonable decisions on their own. An ap-

prentice cannot always report to his journeyman or Master in a sticky situation, and needs to be able to think on his feet. The Harper Hall "plays more than one tune" for Pern. Not only does it provide entertainment for every occasion, it effects important social change by helping people to accept new ideas.

Robinton, the most famous Masterharper of Pern, has technically retired, but his opinion, his expertise, and his good humor will be sought until he dies. He is a rueful, self-directed man who has a total understanding of his world and is just a little disappointed in those people in it who do not live up to their potential. He has a keen eye for human foibles and has the knack for expressing complicated concepts so that anyone can understand them. Robinton is a natural actor, a merciless imitator of other people's voices and mannerisms. This trait got him in trouble frequently during his youth but became useful when he was asked to fill roles on behalf of the information-gathering branch of the Harper Hall. It was this side of him, as well as his musical talents, that eventually saw him elected Masterharper. His musical skills do encompass a great range; he composes and arranges instrumental pieces, as well as singable ditties.

Robinton has never married but has enjoyed a warm relationship with Silvina, the headwoman of the Harper Hall. They produced one son, Camo, who turned out to be retarded. Robinton could not bring himself to father any more children, lest they all turn out to be like the first. His misfortune is a source of melancholy to him.

It takes a man with a strong mind and a commanding personality to be the Masterharper. The Long Interval robbed the Hall of much of its purpose. If there was no need for dragons or Threadfall procedures, what need was there for harpers, except as teachers of the young and as evening entertainers?

Masterharper's Pin

Instruments and Tools

Composition Masters rarely waste hide and ink on apprentices. Most composition and design work in the Harper Hall (and in the Smithcrafthall) is done on sandtables. These tables are long, rectangular boxes divided widthwise into two compartments and set on raised trestles. The boxes are filled with very fine sand, almost powdered stone. The sand is dampened down with hand sprayers filled with water, which are kept on the dividers or in a bracket attached to the side of the table. Using a stylus, the composer or designer presses characters into the sand. A brush or the blunt end of the stylus is used to fill in errors. When the work is finished, the sand is allowed to dry, and then the surface is sprayed with liquid clay, a substance like plaster, to preserve the score or design. If the table is needed by another composer, the casting can be removed and brushed clean. When done carefully to a very specific depth, the casting can be daubed with ink and "printed" on hide. The clays are dissolved and reused over and over.

Songs are composed for all occasions: births, deaths, Lord Holder accessions and confirmations, weddings, and festivals; and to spread news.

The Instrument Maker's Workshop

Part of the harper's trade is the making and repairing of instruments. A harper can better understand the tonal qualities of the music he plays if he knows how to put together the instrument that produces it. A poorly joined gitar is more likely to produce false tones, thereby reducing the credibility of its player; a harp with an incorrectly made frame cannot stay in tune.

With Robinton's assistance and faithful support, Benden Weyr was able to reestablish its authority on the eve of Threadfall. Privately, he has always had a mad crush on the Weyrwoman, partly because she is unattainable, and partly because she is unconsciously sexy. Publicly, he swears a greater allegiance to Benden wine, the finest pressings on Pern. He is not a classic alcoholic—he suffers none of the behavior changes or the physical marking of that disease—but he is a dedicated and consummate tippler with a virtually unmatched capacity. (Only the two Winecraftmasters of Benden and Tillek, and Mastersmith Fandarel, can boast greater tolerances.)

When Robinton retired, due to ill health, Master Sebell ascended to the position, though not the title, of Masterharper. Robinton moved to Cove Hold, where he instructs apprentices and journeymen sent to him from the Hall, and assists Lord Lytol in the excavation of the archaeological sites discovered by Lord Jaxom and the white dragon Ruth of Ruatha.

Master Jerint's Workshop

In the Harper Hall, apprentices begin their education in the crafting of instruments by learning about the tools they will use. All the traditional woodworker's tools are here: knives; saws; drafting equipment; oil, water, and glue tubs; brushes; awls; vises; forge and anvil; plus many designed especially for making musical instruments. The apprentice begins by making only the simplest ones: pipes, tabors and sticks, tamborines. When these are adjudged by the Instrument-Craftmaster to be fashioned correctly, the apprentice moves on to more complex joinery.

Journeymen should know how to make any instrument from frames, skins, metals, and lengths of wood. Masters who specialize in instrument crafting must know not only how to make the instruments and cases from scratch, but how to make the tools, and choose and prepare the raw materials, as

well. Legend has it that the Instrument-Craftmaster can glance at a herdbeast in a field and judge how well its hide will sound stretched over a drum frame.

The Instrument-Crafthall is laid out in a large, L-shaped stone room. Heavy, smooth stone floor tiles are fitted together with scarcely a crack between them. The walls are lined to the ceiling beams with instruments in all conditions: partially made, ill made, and Mastercrafted. Sandtables stand here and there around the room for use by the students and teachers when working on their designs. At his own worktable, the Master keeps piles of cured record hides showing how instruments were crafted throughout Pern's history, telling which designs were favored and why, citing regional preference, and so on. There are also tomes written by past Masters discussing which woods and metals are best for specific uses. Journeymen are encouraged to use one of these traditional designs when crafting their personal gitars, as these will usually be the standard by which their skill is judged.

Instrument players in the Harper Hall have a wide choice of instruments. The instrument makers are allowed, even encouraged, to experiment in style. There are varieties of gitars, some with the traditional bell, some with big, curved bells like lutes or mandolins. There may even be a sort of banjo made by a talented journeyman. Students are taught to make many different kinds of flutes from reed, wood, or metal, or combinations of the three. They learn to make all kinds of percussion instruments—tambourines, tabors, conga, and bongos—and the full range of orchestral drums: snare, trap drums, kettle and bass.

Kettle drums, big-bellied frames made of copper or bronze, are used in the Drum Heights for sending messages. Ceramic, wooden, or brass-tongued xylophones and thumb-pianos make good accompaniment for certain kinds of songs. Menolly demonstrated her prowess to Master Jerint by constructing a bodhran, a shallow hand drum formed by stretching skin across a round frame with a crosspiece beneath for the player to hold. The bodhran is played with a knucklebone or two-ended stick. It is one of the most versatile of drums, and a skilled player can get many different sounds out of it.

Brass horns are of antique design because the Pernese cannot make anything more sophisticated at their level of mechanical development. They have coronets and trumpets, straight horns, a form of trombone, and bugles, but no flügel or French horns, or any other that need complicated valves. The technology does not exist to duplicate the synthesizers that came with the Landing group. Those wore out long ago or

are still sealed in the Catherine Caves in the Southern Continent.

Harps exist in many styles. A wealthy Hold might have a floor harp, but even a lap harp is rare because of the lack of valuable hardwoods. Lyres or dulcimers, which are economical in size, are much more common. A journeyman in the Instrument-Craft will learn what to look for in suitable metals and woods. The newly formed Woodcraft in Lemos exchanges information and techniques with the Harpercrafthall. It is at Master Robinton's urging that such information not be so tightly held as craft secrets so that one man's death cannot throw a whole world into confusion, as it has in the past.

HEALERCRAFT

Healer: On a white field, a purple Caduceus

The Healercraft is one of the oldest Crafts on Pern. The colonists brought with them many different medical specialists, and medicine was one of the first programs for which they started apprenticing boys and girls. Once the children had the basic training in first aid, those who showed particular aptitude were encouraged to go on to further study.

Children and adults had to learn what plants and which animal bites or scratches

MEDICINAL HERBS AND THEIR USES

Numbweed

Very early on, it was noticed that injured dragonets bruised the leaves of a twiggy, sagelike shrub with their snouts or claws and rubbed their wounds against the sap that oozed out of the plump, sagittate leaves. Touching the sap caused total numbness at the contact site. The colonists quickly learned to imitate their dragonets and use the sap to deaden the pain of Threadscore.

The gray-green plants sprout tufts of blossoms like statice, and grow in plenty in jungle areas.

were toxic on their new world. The ships brought many medicinal plants from Earth and First Centauri, which the colonists were able to adapt to Pernese soil. All the seasoning herbs and spices from the two worlds grew in the soil or in hydroponics tanks. Native herbs and shrubs underwent thorough tests to determine their uses in healing or cookery. Some discoveries were made by accident, such as that of numbweed.

The Healercraft doesn't have the technology to sustain defective humans. After twenty-five centuries on Pern, the race has been bred clean of most defects. The humans may have mutated somewhat over the years. Pernese humans live long lives and are still active in their eighth decade. Most of their ailments are a result of their environment.

Threadscore is a severe burn. The mycorrhizoid becomes tremendously hot during the fall through atmosphere and, if given the chance, will eat its way right through skin. The edges of a Threadscore are blackened and burned.

One of the most common treatments for Threadscore, like any other burn, is cold water. The wounds are immediately coated with numbweed to deaden the pain, but they are left otherwise uncovered to promote healing.

Most of the medical emergencies among the colonists were broken bones and births. The doctors taught field surgery to their apprentices who showed the most aptitude and had the strongest stomachs. Obstetricians got plenty of practice at their specialty. Pern grew from a population of 6,023 humans to thousands more within a few years. Since man had been living more healthfully, there were no terrible wasting diseases to decimate their numbers. The causes of cancer had been pinpointed and largely wiped out. Other degenerative conditions had been bred out of the race over the centuries. For those who still smoked before the colony embarked, a nonnicotine smoking substitute was distributed to help them break the habit. Tobacco was not considered important enough to grow in the newly tilled fields when foodstuffs were so much more desperately needed.

The main diagnostic center and surgical hospital was in Landing, until, partway through the ninth year of the colony, all the main hospital functions were moved up to Fort Hold. (Benden Hold, too, had hospital facilities when it started out, but those shrank down to a few healers who sent their difficult cases, and their apprentices, back to Fort.) A doctor and at least a couple of nurses were assigned to each of the southern stakeholds, but each of these had other jobs, as well. Anyone who suffered from a condition that his local doctor could not handle was sledded in to Landing. All the training facilities were maintained in the centers.

The Healer Hall is administered by the Masterhealer, at present Master Oldive. Under him are Masters of the different disciplines of healing, whose specialties and ranks can be read by the rank cords on their shoulders. Oldive also oversees stewards who take care of stocking supplies, keeping the Hall clean, and preparing food. Another of his assistants is the Nursing Master, a nurse with teaching skill and administrative ability. There are doctors and nurses and apprentices of diagnostics, pediatrics, geriatrics, obstetrics, urology, pharmacy, dentistry, surgery, and respiratory ailments. Gifted Masterhealers become specialists in one of these facets of the craft. Some remain at the Hall to teach; others find posts where such a specialty is needed. Each Weyr has at least one urologist and a surgeon.

Not all trained healers have specialties. Some, especially those who are sent to remote holds, are general practitioners. Because of the difficulty of moving seriously ill

Fellis

Fellis trees are branchy and small and have easily recognizable yellow blossoms with pointed petals. The juice boiled from the leaves and stems is a narcotic painkiller. An herb that commonly grows nearby is used as a cure for the addiction that can result from the constant use of fellis, but the healers are aware of the tendency and keep an eye open for overdosing.

Redwort

Redwort grows in clumps low to the ground. The thick stem has reddish veins running through it and produces flat-topped purple or rose flowers.

This clean-smelling herb is used as an antiseptic wash and protects the skin from being affected by numbweed salve. Redwort wash leaves a characteristic red stain on the skin.

Needlethorn

This succulent bush will shoot its hollow, toxic spines at anything that disturbs it during its growing season. When the flowers of the *ging* tree open (needlethorn and ging are always found growing together), the plant has fallen into its dormant stage, and the needles can be gathered without danger. The barbless needles are strong enough to be used with a syringe for giving intravenous and subcutaneous injections or for drawing blood.

Mosstea

An herb used to pack wounds against infection. It can also be infused to make a soothing tea.

Citron

A citrus fruit that contains vitamin C.

---

forming the Lord Holder, who will see that word is sent back.

When a medical emergency arises, the Healer Hall studies the problem and publishes or distributes the means for curing or controlling it. In the case of the Great Plague that wiped out half the population of Pern, Masterhealer Capiam, who was a Master diagnostician, was forced to treat the symptoms empirically at first instead of suggesting a cure. Many medical techniques have been lost or have fallen out of favor over the centuries.

Healers learn new techniques by returning to the Healer Hall for refresher courses. As in any Craft, a healer "walks the tables" to advance in grade. One may train all the way up to journeyman rank in one of the other Healer Halls on Pern, such as that in Southern Hold or in South Telgar, but must still return to the main Healer Hall to attain mastery. It is common for apprentices to learn their basic skills in the Hall and be sent out to other Holds as journeymen under masters who are specialists in certain fields. Unlike all other Crafts but the Beastcraft, Healercraft must rely on on-the-job training for its students.

Midwifery is a specialty that many apprentices take up, since the skill is needed in every hold on Pern. Most healers get at least basic instruction in delivering babies.

Nursing is the journeyman stage of a healer's education. Some remain nurses, and some who attain mastery of their Craft go on to become doctors known throughout Pern for their expertise. There is no guarantee of a healer's competency just because he had his training in the Healer Hall of Pern, but the noncompetitive atmosphere means that a candidate stands or falls on his own skills.

The head nurse has responsibility for a stated number of beds or wards in the great Healer Hall complexes. He or she is in charge of journeymen and journeywomen nurses and dressers. There are Master Nurses in the

patients, a specialist is generally brought in by the Masterhealer of a hold instead of risking losing the patient on the journey. On occasion, a healer may call in a dragon to do an emergency ambulance run if there is sufficient cause. It is a very serious matter to summon a dragon, and no healer will do it lightly twice, since the dragons have duties elsewhere. Most emergencies can be handled on a local level.

A healer will pass news of anything new or unusual back to the Hall through the journeyman harpers who pass through, or by in-craft, but every healer needs to be exposed to all facets of his occupation to have a thorough grasp of it.

Healers control most chronic ailments with the help of maintenance dosages of cordials and home remedies. A wine cup of distilled hyssop every day keeps off respiratory problems such as croup. Willow tea keeps arthritis under control. A glass of wine is thought to keep the blood thin. Alfalfa tea is good for the stomach and acts as a diuretic. A preparation of yarrow is good against acne. The archives are full of herbal and homeopathic cures that can be made with the plants that grow throughout Pern.

The Pernese do not attach any social stigma to suicide. In the case of a terminally ill patient, the decision whether to employ euthanasia is in the hands of the healer, his Master, and the patient, if he is conscious and in his right mind. A Lord Holder does not get involved when a man makes the decision to take a "mercy draught." A person's death is considered to be a private matter. If a patient is suffering from a terminal ailment, he or she can choose to die—there is no question of whether or not a man is responsible for his own continued existence. Suicide is expected (though not encouraged) behavior in the Weyrs when a fighter loses his dragon to injuries or illness. When riders die, their dragons suicide by going *between.*

Anyone who is unhappy is encouraged to seek out someone with whom he can discuss his problems. Healers who help soothe troubled minds follow in the footsteps of the Ancient psychologists and psychiatrists who came to Pern in the colony ships. If a holder disagrees with everybody and everything, he can leave his Hold of birth and start afresh somewhere else. He is not trapped in one place until the end of his life. Even during the

Barley

This cereal grain can also be brewed as a tea to combat the symptoms of cystitis, which is a common complaint of female dragonriders.

Other Herbs and Their Uses

Analgesic: red willow salic, meadowsweet

Anodyne: aconite, whitethorn, adonis, glovecap, hops

Antispasmodic: parsley, basil

Burns: aloe, dragon's tongue (Pern aloe), comfrey, cucumber, witch hazel

Cough medicine: tussilago, comfrey, hyssop, thymus, borrago

Diaphoretic: box, ezob

Diuretic: ash bark

Febrifuge: sweatroot, spearleek, whitebulb

Tonic: featherfern, nettleweed, tansy

Present Pass, there is still a lot of untenanted land and unused space to pioneer.

The bodies of the dead are rarely buried in the ground without some sort of protection from the sky. There is a dislike of leaving the body of a loved one where it might get Threadseared. Instead, the dead are interred in stone cairns or under stone tablets. Cremations are not uncommon, but in poor or woodless holds, cave burials are more accepted. Fisherfolk have elaborate and solemn ceremonies for burial at sea.

FORT WEYR

Fort Weyr: On a brown field, a black Fort

The medium-sized caldera that Fort Weyr occupies was found during flyovers to Fort Hold. Within five years at Fort Hold, the dragons and riders had begun to outgrow their quarters; they moved over to Fort Weyr in the fourteenth year of the colony, under Weyrleader Sean Connell and bronze Carenath, with his wife Sorka, senior queen rider for Faranth.

The Weyr was built to hold a maximum of five hundred dragons. The architectural style is a fairly simple one. Because the Weyr was occupied in a hurry, the rough edges were knocked off the walls and floors to make it livable. But many modifications were made over the next fifty Turns.

Stonecutters were employed to join individual underground caverns into a single complex. There was enough fuel to cut any configuration the architects wished. The corridors twist on for quite a way into the mountain, though not all of the passages are still in use. The Weyr Bowl was left untouched, but the Living Caverns were thoroughly redone.

The Hatching Ground at Fort Weyr is very showy. The upper deck, where spectators sit, is supported by natural columns. The caverns in Fort Weyr are all very high and rounded, left behind by bubbles in the volcanic flow. The Star Stones and Eye Rock high on Fort Weyr's rim are the largest on Pern.

Behind natural small cliffs dotting the walls of the volcanic crater, the individual weyrs were made large, taking into consideration the size into which dragons were intended to evolve eventually. At first the original dragons, who numbered only ninety-two, rattled around in the large chambers like clappers in a bell, a situation very unlike the cramped arrangement they had left behind in Fort Hold. Very quickly, Kitti Ping's formula for increased size began to manifest itself in successive generations of dragons until, by the Second Pass, dragons had reached the size they would remain until late in the Second Long interval.

The other four northern Weyrs are not as carefully made as Fort or Benden. Dragonriders with a talent for stonemasonry in Igen, Ista, High Reaches, and Telgar spend their spare time chipping out new corridors and smoothing the walls in frequently used chambers. Because it is such hard work, and accomplishing anything major takes such a long time, there is little perceptible style to these Weyrs. Fort was able to assume a grandeur suitable to the first Weyr on Pern.

The Fort Weyr kitchen is up an imposing flight of steps and lies under an elaborate vaulted ceiling. The hearths run along the outside kitchen wall, with room to feed not only the 450 dragonriders but the 1,200 support staffers who live in the Weyr. The night hearth, which always has a pot of soup or stew and a kettle of klah heating, is in a separate room just off the kitchen, where runners coming into the Weyr from *between* or by the Fort Hold road are fed.

Copper utensils ranging from immense soup cauldrons to tiny saucepans hang from the ceiling in rows, shined by drudges until the head cook can see his face in every one of them. Some of these copper pots were made here, but many predate the Second Crossing. They are the Head Cook's pride and joy, and reputed to be a finer collection than that in the Fort Hold kitchens, where his grandfather is the Head Cook.

Hectar is a tall, thin, sad-looking man who came from Fort Hold when his great-grandmother Agatha reported that the Weyr needed a new Head Cook. His assistants are all much shorter than he is, so he does not understand their need to get the steps to take down pots from the hooks, which he can reach without effort. Hectar is never satisfied with anything he cooks and is forever moaning that his stew does not taste right, or that he has burned the bread. He complains that the flour did not arrive premilled, and that it was badly ground by the kitchen drudges. The dogs did not move evenly around the spits, and the meat is undercooked. All of his complaints bemoan his imaginary inadequacies. The headwoman of the Lower Caverns is accustomed to soothing him, assuring him that the food tastes magnificent, which it does, and that he did not leave out a single ingredient.

Hectar lives on tastings from his recipes. He does not eat much otherwise and never touches sweets. The stews and soups never taste the same way twice because he is always experimenting, varying the amounts of spices and the proportions of vegetables. His anxiety is doubled by his great-grandmother Agatha's insistence that his grandfather is a better cook than poor Hectar ever will be. Hectar is the exception to the rule that you can never trust a thin cook.

Agatha retired from the headwoman's job a few Turns ago, but she still keeps a finger in every pie. Like all the aunties, she is honored for her age but teased for her arrogant and overbearing airs. Her strength of purpose was needed to hold her own with the Oldtimer women, who felt she was taking a job that rightfully belonged to one of them when they came forward. Her approval is and was respected. She held the job of headwoman for a long time and was still keeping the Weyr caverns in perfect order when she was persuaded to retire for her health's sake. Agatha's "Hmph! Not bad" is high praise.

Now that she is retired, she gets too little exercise to keep the joint ailment from which she suffers at bay. She takes fish oil for the vitamin E to ease her stiffness. She has more time on her hands than she needs and spends much of it bickering with a crony of hers, a gifted tanner who can make wherry hide as smooth as fabric. He has high blood pressure, which he treats with garlic. Anyone in the caverns can find either one of them just by following the stench of fish or garlic.

Garlic is popular as a cold remedy. The sandy soil in the Weyr Bowl is good for raising all the bulb and root families of vegetables. Moreta used it as a palliative when the plague was starting its ravages. It serves as a medicinal herb, as well as a condiment.

The new headwoman, Margetta, is so young and full of energy that she runs at full speed until she collapses. She came from the Old Time, but she hardly seems to be like the others who came forward with her. Everyone knows when she is awake, because then she seems to be everywhere at once, overseeing the drudges, measuring out spices from the locked stores, or counting heads in the dining cavern. Everyone knows when Margetta falls asleep, too, because her snores are as loud as a roaring dragon.

Margetta is the one to whom the duty falls to inform the Senior Weyrwoman of shortages in the stores. She and her stewards oversee the repair of furniture, rugs, and tapestries. They also see to the replacement of riders' clothing, sleeping furs, and boots, and

provide hide for repair of riding gear. Margetta is also the liaison with the Craftmasters who work inside Fort Weyr.

The extensive Lower Caverns and Hatching Grounds are much the same size as the ones at Benden Weyr. Some corridors in the back of the caverns end in blind walls. The blocked-off area in back of the Weyr dates from the end of the First Pass, when those living in the caverns cleared out to other Holds and Benden Weyr. In these back rooms are remnants of the move from South to North. With the decline in Weyr population, most of these rooms have been turned over to storage. Empty plastic packing cases are used for contemporary supplies. Bits and pieces make their way to the workshops of the Weyr's smith: screws, fasteners, engine parts, coils of electrical cord, wires of rainbow colors, and connectors. No one has uses for some of the parts. Sixteen-pin chips are turned over to the children as toys.

Behind a fall of earth, there are further corridors, closed during an avalanche, that no one has been in for millennia. Records on plas-film are stacked everywhere. Some are indistinguishable from the dirt in which they are buried. The inhabitants of Fort Weyr always meant to rescue the contents of these rooms, but they never got around to it. Now there is not even a memory of the existence of the rooms themselves.

Margetta also has the task of clearing out a weyr when a dragonrider dies. If he has designated no one to have his belongings, they either go into the common storerooms or are thrown away. Anyone who wants them can have the discarded possessions, and the headwoman is happy to get a little space emptied out. The storerooms are chockfull of twenty-five hundred years' worth of dragonriders' impedimenta.

A weyr has little furniture. Beyond the dragon's stone couch and its weyrmate's bed, there may be a garment chest. There are closets in a few of the principal chambers, such as those of the Weyrleaders and Weyrwomen, but as the power tools began to wear out, closets ceased to be priority construction items. A rider will have rugs and tapestries to keep out the cold of the stone, and perhaps a small table and chair, especially if he practices a handicraft, but generally dragonriders do not keep many personal possessions.

Dragonriders have spare-time occupations, which they fit in between taking care of their dragons and their duties within the Weyr. Most riders make their own riding straps, because they need to be able to trust the leathers to the last tug. Some riders have a talent for tannery and make more goods than they need, to barter with or gift to other Weyrfolk. Those with a bent toward tailoring or barbering are sought after in the evenings. Fur-lined clothing is a must in the stone weyrs, especially in Fort Hold's cold winters.

All the Weyrwomen keep their hair cropped close, with the exception of Lessa, who takes pride in her thick, dark tresses and keeps them plaited closely under her flying helmet, and Mirrim, who admires Lessa enough to copy her. Moreta was looking forward to the day when she would be able to let her blond hair grow out. As mirrors are rare, no one tries to cut his or her own hair. Anybody in the Weyr with a deft touch at cutting hair is much in demand during restdays or in the evening. The men tend to be cleanshaven: Due to genetic drift, Pernese males have very little body or facial hair. Some Lord Holders allow their hair to grow longer than dragonriders do as a mark that they are of the leisure class, but they, too, tend not to cultivate facial hair. Drudges, who need to keep their hair out of the way, have it clipped under a bowl by a headwoman.

Most riders prefer short hair for safety. There is a risk in keeping one's hair long during Threadfighting. The first time a longer-haired rider gets threaded across the back of the neck, or has a fragment of Thread tangled in his hair, he is usually first in line for the barber.

Dragonriders enjoy gambling. Fort dragonriders like a good dice game and have reinvented craps and other games of chance. Like all the Weyrs, they play dragon poker. Since this is an Old Time Weyr, there are some decks still in use whose face cards bear the likenesses of riders so long dead that no one remembers who they were. Fort Hold plays board games, some of which have made their way into the Weyr. Chess is often played in the evenings. Before the fire lizards came, a game could be left set up on a table for days until the players got back to it. Now players are well advised to finish before they leave, lest when they return they find the pieces rearranged or missing.

When the Weyrs are all in harmony, the Weyrleaders meet at Fort. There is a beautifully appointed chamber known as the Council Room. It is dominated by a table in the shape of a half oval with seats for each of the six original Weyrleaders at the top, and seats for visitors and others of less consequence arranged at the curve opposite. The Weyrwomen sit at the sides near the Weyrleaders.

The wall decorations, brought forward from the Old Time, are tapestries pertaining to each Weyr. They are very lavish and beautifully made, showing Masterwork of needlecraft. The ones depicting Benden Weyr were left behind when Fort Weyr was abandoned, and have four hundred Turns more wear on them.

The tabletop is a magnificent mosaic done in chips of semiprecious and precious stones, the work of a lifetime from the Minecraft lapidaries. Each of the chairs is ornately decorated, with fancy chair arms and seatback. The padded seat pads are sumptuously embroidered.

Because of the frequent change of Weyrleaders, the seat pads are newly made for each man. The Senior Weyrwoman of each Weyr is usually the only one to attend these conferences, and her chair decoration is of a more permanent character.

The Weyr trains its own dragon healers, mostly from riders who show an aptitude and an interest in healing, though anyone with training and knowledge can help heal injured and burned dragons. Dragonriding takes up most, but not all, of a rider's time. The Healer Hall instructs all healers in basic techniques of first aid, but apprentice dragon healers learn from others in their Weyr. Moreta, for example, was a dragon surgeon. A dragon healer needs dispassion, skill, and dexterity to be effective. It does the dragon no good if a healer is afraid to perform a painful operation to save a wing or a leg. In case of emergency, a beastcrafter may be called in to assist a dragon surgeon.

All weyrlings physic their own dragons. If a young dragon's tail is too thick, denoting constipation, his weyrmate must administer the purge. If he has bitten his tongue learning to chew firestone, the rider applies numbweed salve until the bleeding stops and the ichor has clotted. Fortunately dragons are a healthy breed, but dragonriders are always encouraged to learn more about caring for them.

IX.

Benden, the Second Weyr

BENDEN WEYR

Benden Weyr: On a red field, a Roman Numeral Two in black

Benden Weyr was founded during the First Interval by Michael Connell, also called Mihall or M'hall, eldest son of Sean and Sorka Connell, and his wife, Torene. Pern needed more dragons, and Fort was at last up to full strength. Though he was only in his twenties when he led his force of dragons and humans eastward, he was the one allowed to establish the new Weyr because the administrators in Fort realized he was a canny leader who inspired trust in those who followed him and would lead them responsibly. Mihall Connell was the first to bear the title of Benden Weyrleader.

The Weyr was named to honor Admiral Paul Benden, over his objections. It was established in the eighteenth year of the colony.

Mihall grew up in the Lower Caverns of Fort Weyr under the care of a foster mother. Sorka loved her children, but she had little time to look after them, as most of her time went to taking care of Faranth. Would-be dragonriders had to make the same decision to give up the care of their children into someone else's hands. A young dragon required too much attention to allow a man or woman to spend adequate time and love raising well-adjusted children. Extending the family to include fosterers and the half brothers and half sisters who sometimes resulted from mating flights between riders married to other people was the first wedge to break into monogamous relationships in the Weyr.

Mihall Connell grew up wanting to ride dragons. He spent as much time in the Weyr as he could, learning about the care of dragons and helping out in the Lower Caverns. The records are unclear, but it is believed that his bronze came from the fourth Hatching of Faranth's eggs.

Torene, brought up in Ruatha, showed

an aptitude for anticipating the needs of sick creatures. As a child, she began to spend more and more time at the Weyr, encouraged, like other empathic children and adults, to start getting to know dragons as early as possible. Young Torene exhibited extraordinary empathy, which made her a natural candidate for a queen egg. Once she Impressed, it was discovered that her ability to hear other dragons' telepathic voices did not fade as the bonds between weyrmates grew stronger. Torene's strength of purpose was one of the key elements in forming a second group of dragonriders that was independent from the first.

M'hall and Torene chose Benden Weyr's location because they saw the potential of the natural cavern which would become the Hatching Ground. The upper deck was terraformed, but the rest he left unaltered. At his urging, the miners who helped construct Benden Weyr opened up and smoothed out caverns and corridors that already existed in the volcanic matrix, rather than chopping whole rooms out with the steadily depleting resource of the stonecutters. Thus Benden Weyr has a more natural feel to it than Fort.

Benden's architecture may not be as elaborate as that of Fort Weyr, but the style is the same. These two Weyrs and Holds, and Ruatha, their contemporary, feel old. The rooms are of irregular shapes but have smooth walls. Closet niches are cut at intervals in the walls of corridors and large storage chambers. Colored cement is used for accent and for filling in broken places in the stone.

The Bowl is full of light sand. The lake, which covers a good quarter of the bottom of

Benden Weyr

The Bowl

the Bowl, is of sweet water kept clear by water plants, snails, algae, and grasses. Indigenous water lilies float on the surface. Like the Earth flower of the same name, these flowers' petals are white, but the leaves are triangular in shape, much like those of the herb woad. Their edible roots, which also have a triangular cross-section, taste like water chestnuts. The herdbeasts live near the lake and are kept away from the place where the dragons bathe.

Benden's Lower Caverns are not as high-vaulted as Fort's, and they are more spread out. The separate levels are tiered, making use of the myriad bubbles in the strata. The passages between the deepest side caverns are very narrow, but they are ventilated to the upper air. Massive passageways lie between the largest caverns at ground and first level. The firepits scored at the top of this and every other domicile on Pern are intend-

ed to be set ablaze during Threadfall to prevent Thread from falling down the ventilation shafts and infiltrating the Living Caverns.

The ventilation system uses fans run by water from the upper reservoirs dripping slowly into a bucket weighting the chain that moves the props. Geothermal energy runs the service shafts by use of thermal sinks. Twin tubes run down through the rock to red-hot stone—water is pumped down one, and the steam comes up the other. Steam is used to heat the higher weyrs, as well as to provide hydraulic assist for the heavy trays in the service chutes.

By the end of the First Pass, there were over twenty thousand people in the Northern Continent. Benden Weyr was swelling as Fort had. Most of the Ancient Timers' rooms were sealed as the holders moved out to stakeholds across the continent. The only folk left in Benden Weyr beside the dragonfolk were those who worked in the Lower Caverns as support staff for the Weyr. Vegetables were originally raised in the hydroponics tanks, and grain grew in carefully protected fields near the Weyr. When the Pass ended, Benden Hold was constructed.

Benden Weyr, though less fancy on the inside than Fort and built on a smaller scale, has a warmer ambiance. Benden's original portion was built when there was still fuel to run the stonecutters. The hallways were cut high and square, and walls were slagged to perfect smoothness. But when supplies began to run out, the inhabitants of Benden Weyr merely knocked the rough corners off natural caverns and cavelets, smoothing only the floor of corridors. All six Weyrs were treated with stonecutters to provide ventilation and thermal heat. The sites for the last four were chosen during the first Interval and carved out somewhat while the stonecutters lasted.

Triple Helix: The Genetic Code of Dragons

The stonecutters were put to use in other places, too. Ventilation grilles cover air shafts drilled through the heart of the mountain, bringing fresh air through the fire pits into the deepest caves in the Weyr. The Star Stones and Eye Rock are smaller than those at Fort, but they are of a higher quality. The Stones in the other Weyrs were made with hammer and chisel and have a more rustic look; the Eye Rocks are more like the eyes of needles than of beasts or men.

Benden Weyr is bigger now than it was even at the height of its human population. Rooms that were once occupied by the Ancient Timers are used for storage or just sealed off. Very large weyrs that originally were shaped by two dragons now have only one, but there are more weyrs.

The labs and hydroponics tanks in the rear corridors of Benden Weyr are only now being rediscovered. The knowledge to use the devices sealed in these rooms has long disappeared. A design printed on the wall is a reproduction of Kitti Ping's genetic code of the dragons, which the current Weyrfolk cannot translate.

The Queen's Weyr

Once the Present Pass began, Manora, the headwoman, was delighted to be rid of the Turns of penury into which the Weyr had fallen. Mustering her work force, she turned to refurbishing the Weyr from the inside out. Lessa's apartments were the first project tackled by the women of the Lower Caverns. As soon as Lessa Impressed Ramoth, Manora went to work and had the Weyrwoman's rooms in fine shape by the time of the first Threadfall.

The room off the side of the queen's weyr is decorated in tapestries of warm colors dyed and spun in Manora's spare moments: green, clear yellow, orange, lavender, and red. Only the best furs are on the bed in the Weyrwoman's chamber. Benden Hold is famous for patchwork quilts. Lessa was given a few that are sewn in intricate geometric patterns and creative variations on traditional designs.

Even Ramoth's couch has a fancy coverlet. To keep the cold out, the great couch is covered with straw and rushes, then covered over with a padded quilt. Lessa's is the most elaborate weyr. She has both a bathing room and a service shaft, and the ventilation ducts carry warm air up into the room. All is kept spotlessly clean, and the tapestries are beaten or refurbished often to keep the dust down.

The Support Structure of the Weyr

The Weyrs get their food and other goods from tithe trains that come in from the Holds that they protect. Manora is the overall manager of the Lower Caverns of Benden. She keeps in close accord with the Head Cook, who is in charge of arranging meals from the time the food arrives at the Weyr to the moment it is set on the table. She has stewards and bookkeepers to look after each detail. Several workers are needed just to keep track of supplies. Men, women, and children work at tasks assigned to them by Manora, who keeps master lists of their talents and responsibilities.

Manora and her well-trained assistants can gear up for emergencies or births very quickly. There is a step-by-step set of instructions to follow for each situation.

Girls who are found on Search who do not immediately Impress wait for their chance but continue to live a normal life in the Weyr. They might fall in love and have babies, and find other functions to fulfill. Even if they never Impress, they are not sent away. Once a girl has been chosen on Search, it means that she is found to have superior empathy and strength of character, two traits the Weyr wishes to perpetuate in its bloodlines.

Not all women who live in the Lower Caverns were found on Search. The Weyr's lifestyle calls to young, adventurous folk, as well as those so desperate to leave the place in which they were born that they would rather go Holdless than stay. Women who are unhappy in their home Holds frequently seek a place in the Weyr. If they can provide a good reason for being taken in , such as possessing a necessary skill, they will be allowed to stay for life. If they were abused in their Holds, they are often placed in other Holds, away from their abuser. Women in the Weyrs need not marry if they do not want to, nor have child after child until they are old and worn-out, as they might be expected to in the Holds.

Weyrwomen often welcomed these empathic or talented women to the Lower Caverns. A great attempt has always been made by the Weyrwoman to find exactly the right person to foster her children, not only because a queen dragon requires so much care, but because a Weyrwoman has other responsibilities as well. As a foster mother, Manora is one of the most sought after women in Benden Weyr. She has had as many as eleven or twelve fosterlings at a time.

When a child begins to develop a strong individual personality, its mother will get together with the available foster mothers and the Weyrwoman to decide who would be the best person to raise it. No rivalry is involved in the decision. The importance of such a decision is to find who will be best suited to raising a happy child from a baby of its particular temperament.

The Weyr's firm belief is that there is no reason for a child to be unhappy. Fostering brings out the best talents and joy in a youngster who would otherwise be neglected by his rider parents and grow up hating dragons for taking them away, to the detriment of the entire Weyr. The whole system of dragonriders was established as total support and care for dragons. The support system for the dragonriders, the Lower Caverns, must also be well run for the benefit of all those who rely upon it.

Children of the Weyr learn early to develop their most outstanding talents, which become their *second* jobs if they Impress. A child's natural talent is optimized through training and direction, but he has to learn to demonstrate it. Each child has many opportunities, from the time he shows a talent through the time he grows up. From the time he is old enough to take on responsibilities, he is sent on chores. Gradually the child's aptitude is revealed and encouraged.

If there is no need in the Weyr at that moment for that particular talent, he is placed outside the Weyr in an appropriate Hold beholden to the Weyr, or farther afield if the Lord of a Hold should know of a need elsewhere. Crafthalls do allow recognition for apprentice training in the Weyr.

A Weyrbred man or woman who fails Impression can always fall back on the job for which he was trained. If he or she has no specific talent, the dragonriders' women put their heads together to decide what the non-rider person can do. Men who grow up in the Weyr who do not Impress or do not want to Impress can easily work in the Weyr as support personnel, providing they can get along with those who live there.

Each night Manora receives from the Head Cook a list of what he needs, so that the supplies can be brought in from the remote storage caves by drudges and children. Major events like Hatchings are planned more than a sevenday in advance, using supplies kept in a reserve cavern and set aside for special occasions. Spices and wines are seen to by Manora personally.

Under the Head Cook are chefs who are in charge of certain parts of meal preparation. The baker takes care of all breads and rolls on a daily basis, assisted by a light pastry chef, whose duties are limited except on special occasions, when he is put in charge of desserts and fancy, filled entrées. The salad and vegetable cook employs aunties and uncles to clean and chop greens and peel roots for the pot. The hearth chef sears roasts and whole fowl on the spit hearths in the open air outside the main cavern.

A long range of solid fuel cookers in the kitchen is where most of the cooking is done. Some are set aside specifically for stovetop, bakery, or simmering areas.

The kitchen in Benden Weyr has a lower roof than the one in Fort, and the chamber opens right out into the Weyr Bowl. The night hearth is in a sheltered alcove rather than a separate room. The night hearth cook is usually a baker, with the task of making rolls and cereal for the morning, but he also needs to have an expert hand with stews and casseroles.

Food is served at regular hours, but the night hearth always has a pot of stew or soup simmering, a kettle of fresh klah, bowls of dried fruit, and a basket of bread rolls. After the Present Pass began, there was always fresh fruit, the gift of grateful holders.

A steward, male or female, supervises the preparation of the meals, and another sees to its serving by a host of helpers of all ages. Meals are served in the big refectory, which is a broad, low chamber with uneven ceilings like a rathskeller, with a couple of drudges or assistants in charge of serving each long table. The Lord Holders' table, where guests of honor are seated when dining with the Weyr, is farther away from the hearthfire, to avoid unpleasant odors and smoke from the cooking. The other tables are closer to the fires. They're warmer, but not necessarily more comfortable.

The watch-rider generally alerts those in the Weyr that a tithe train is on its way. Children without pressing duties gather around the caravan as the train enters the Weyr. The beastdrivers and wagoneers are often kindly to children, bringing candy and fruits especially for them.

As the sacks and baskets are unloaded, stewards working under Manora sort the shipments into the various food groups, depending on the peculiarities of storage for each item. Bulk items that need dry storerooms—milled flour, grains, lentils, legumes, dried meat and fish, and sweetening—are carried to caverns that lie just down the corridor from the drying hearths.

Cattle are driven down to the beastfolds near the lake in the Weyr Bowl, where the Weyr's herder notes their number and type. The beasts are kept separate from the Weyr's flocks and herds until it is clear that they are without disease. This precaution is automatic since the plague in Moreta's day.

The beastherds at Benden Weyr are just big enough at any time to give every dragon in the Weyr a meal. The Lord Holders send the scrag ends of their own herds for the dragons' herds. The Weyrfolk hunt for most of their meat, supplementing with the odd herdbeast, the younger stock sent by the Lord Holders, domestic wherry herds, and meat animals.

Root vegetables go into a cavern with an immense heap of sand for drainage to keep the roots from rotting. The northern farms raise many kinds: sweet potatoes, swedes, parsnips, turnips, fingerroots, redroots, and several strains of tubers.

Leafy vegetables, cheeses, and fruits go into cold storerooms with running water that are stocked with ice brought in every two or three days from the snowy wastes to keep them fresh. These items and all fresh meat are used up first.

Meat is fresh-killed when it is needed. A hunting dragon can bring back many carcasses slung across its body behind the rider or dangling over its neck behind the forepaws.

Before the Pass began, fresh food was in sparse supply. Dragonriders had to go out hunting for meat and gather vegetables and herbs themselves. Only the loyal three, Benden, Bitra, and Lemos Holds, sent tithe trains to the Weyr, but their goods were far from being the best produced in those Holds. Fresh vegetables and tender meat were rare treats. Dragonriders would bring the women of the Lower Caverns out to the forests and shorelines to gather what they could themselves. They had to go all the way into Nerat for numbweed and wild fruit. The Holds were not generous to the gleaners.

Once Thread began to fall, the Weyr was inundated with donations, not only of food but of other commodities. Nerat sent numbweed and delicacies of fresh fruit, such as berry preserves, apples, and pears, as well as Pernese fruits and fruit ale, a popular drink in that Hold. The Tannercraft in Igen included first-class hides of all grades, from that used for riding straps to glove leather.

The Weyr employs a number of crafters full-time. The Hold tanner is needed to treat hides for clothing and riding gear. He teaches riders to choose hide and make their own riding straps, but his biggest job is making shoes and boots for the hundreds of dragonriders and thousands of support staff who live in Benden.

Clothes are made by tailors and leathercrafters, but, especially during an Interval, clothes making is a spare-time occupation of dragonriders. Evenings will often be spent discussing types of stitching and how to get the most out of pieces of fabric and hide. The best thread is made from the guts of a certain kind of wild wherry.

Those without sufficient skill to make their own garments barter other skills with those who have. A man might trade fifteen yards of ribbon to a tanner for a pair of shoes. Another may exchange his fine embroidery for a dress tunic. The Weyr encourages every talent needed to survive. It has had to be self-sufficient every Interval since it was founded.

Hunting is a spare-time occupation of extreme importance to Weyr survival. Riders bring in feral cattle, big fish, whersports, and wherries to supplement the meat brought into the Weyr by supply trains.

Wherries taste rather like turkey. No part of the big avian is wasted: The offal provides food for fire lizards; the guts are used in sewing and for bowstrings and bolos; the ichor is good for polishing furniture and treating leather; and a wherry carcass is likely to be found in the soup kettle the morning after the roast is eaten.

Dragons need a certain amount of boron to survive, the way that animals bred from Earth prototypes need calcium. Boron occurs in the skeletal structure of all Pernese animals, like wherries, and those whom the biogeneticists adjusted to synthesize it. Without boron, dragons and other native creatures die of a form of scurvy.

Benden Weyr's herds are large enough at any given time to feed all the dragons one square meal, but dragons frequently hunt wild wherries or a herdbeast from a neighboring farmhold. Permission is always sought before a rider lets his beast hunt, in order that the Weyr may keep good relations with those outside of it.

F'lessan is a hunter of wild wherries by training. He hunts on foot, as a rule, using snares or a form of crossbow to bring the big avians down. He also hunts tunnel snakes with snares and lances, since one of those weapons is not enough by itself to kill the clawed and sharp-toothed menaces.

Longbows and crossbows are used almost exclusively in forests, where there is the wood to make them and no room to employ other hunting implements. Bolos and slings are also popular for hunting.

Crossbow

The Weyrs do a lot of their own knitting and spinning. They shear their own ovines for fleece, and more comes on the supply trains. The Weavercraftmaster sends a teacher to the Weyr to demonstrate the basic skills for treating fleece. Everyone knits, usually using the hair of adapted ovines as yarn. The Weavercrafthall has tailors and dyers permanently assigned to Weyrs with which it is on good terms.

A very special spare-time occupation is brewing. The competition is fierce among dragonriders to make the best beer, which vies with klah for the most commonly quaffed beverage in Benden Weyr. Fortunately for the rivals, there is more than one kind of beer. One dragonrider will make the best stout, another will produce the best lager. Some of the deepest, coolest caverns are ideal for storing kegs and bottles.

During a Pass of the Red Star, dragonriders have little time to do anything for themselves. Holders and Craftmasters, nervous about protection from Threadfall, become very willing to give the dragonriders anything they want, including supplying some of the things that the Weyr has been accustomed to creating for itself. After Turns of being ignored, suddenly the dragonriders are the most important people on Pern, and they are human enough to take advantage of the situation. There are some abuses, but the give and take quickly levels out.

The Weyr harper or Weyrsinger is a journeyman or Master from the Harper Hall whose job is to educate the children of the Weyr, provide entertainment, and keep records of Hatchings and other special events. Just like in a Hold, the harper will give musical instruction to children who show aptitude for playing or singing.

C'gan was an exception among Weyr harpers in that he Impressed blue Tagath. None of the others have ever Impressed dragons in the pursuit of their duties, although some have offered themselves as Candidates.

OATHS AND MALEDICTA

The Pernese of the Present Pass have forgotten the meaning of such expressions as "Jays," short for Jesus, and "by all that's holy," among others brought to the planet by the settlers. One oath whose meaning was lost when the last dolphineer died was "Go for a blow," loosely translated as "Go soak your head." Some of the others have remained intact, such as "by heaven" (meaning the sky), or "fardles," a useful expletive.

Pernese swear words do not pertain to sex or religion, since the former is not considered to be dirty, or concealed as unnatural, and the latter simply does not exist in the society. Instead, exclamations denote danger, the Red Star, oaths of binding, excretory functions, and inconveniences.

Maledicta

Wherry teeth: nonsense; I don't believe you

Crackdust, shards: expletives indicating annoyance or disbelief

That's well dusted: It's nasty or unpleasant

He was born under the Red Star: someone evil or generally disliked or unlucky

Bend a tail: defecate

A hunk of firestone; all gas and ash: a braggart or a blowhard

Has a dragon's two stomachs: a "hollow leg," endless appetite

Duties

A weyrling will be assigned to make sure glowbaskets are filled with fresh handfuls of glows, to help clean rooms or to carry out waste. Common rooms get cleaned by the headwoman's staff, though sometimes that chore is assigned as a punitive duty to a dragonrider who has committed some small peccadillo. Each individual weyr is supposed to be cleaned on non-Thread days by its inhabitants. A rider is expected to keep his own room clean, but not all do. Sometimes a rider's non-Impressed weyrmate, male or female, takes over the domestic duties. The assigned jobs are usually tedious but not difficult. Hard labor is assigned only as punishment for malfeasance.

Another unloved duty is cleaning the latrines and filing the water supply. The lavatory facilities inside Benden were made while Mihall's men still had probes and stonecutters to mold rock. Long chimneys leading down to sewers were topped by seats with holes. A reservoir at the top traps water to clear the chimney.

Usually an individual weyr will consist of a big room with a stone couch worn smooth by centuries of dragon hide. Access to a sun parlor just behind the ledge on the Bowl is through a natural or constructed baffle to keep the wind out. The air is warm in the dragon's chamber. Dragons have slower circulation than humans and sometimes need a thin rug on their couches to protect them from cold, but once they are asleep, they do not care.

In most Weyrs a rider sleeps in a small chamber just off the dragon's weyr. Benden Weyr uses rope-frame beds, spread with strong bags for reeds, grasses, straw, or down. Sometimes this is no more than an alcove, but in the fancier, earlier Weyrs, it is a separate room, sometimes with a sliding door and even a bathing chamber.

Occasionally a Wingleader's chamber will have a lounge attached where the leaders can meet. If a rider knows of a vacant weyr he'd rather occupy, he can discuss the possibility of relocating with the headwoman.

Not all of the individual weyrs have sanitary facilities. The Weyr continued to grow long beyond the day that the stonecutters ran out of fuel. When Benden reached its full complement of 350 dragons, the masons, who were then working with simpler tools, broke through behind natural ridges into volcanic air pockets to form rudimentary weyrs. Junior riders who hoped for better quarters worked to clean up the rough walls and floors on their own, or traded up to new quarters when a weyr fell vacant.

Dragons who are over a Turn in age excrete while *between*. The excretal opening is concealed in the spade-shaped end of the tail, pressed closed by the forked end. Before the dragonets learn to fly *between* to evacuate, the weyrlings on punishment duty have the job of mucking out the Weyrling Barracks.

Weyrlings are also assigned to sack the firestone that the junior dragonriders bring in from the mines or from surface scars in the volcanic rock of the mountain range. It is a hard, dusty job, but it is vital to Threadfighting to have enough sacks prepared to last the Fall.

As an aid to help them practice flying, weyrlings are put on "elevator duty," riding the thermal currents up and down in the Bowl. The young dragons and riders provide lifts for people from the floor of the Bowl or another weyr to wherever they want to go. The women of the Lower Caverns make use of the service when they are carrying food to or intending to clean weyr. The service shafts in Lessa's and the other Weyrwomens' chambers exist only there and in another few weyrs.

Apprentice healers in the Weyr are given basic first-aid training by other healers. If

Tail fork first: backward

Wherry hunt: "wild-goose chase," a fruitless, foolish quest

Like trying to draw an inside straight in Bitra: an impossibility

Hatching fire lizards: building castles in the air

Shaffit!: irritation expletive

Chew it raw and swallow: accept the inevitable

A dragon among the wherries: cat among the pigeons

Smokeless weyrling: a disparagement meaning useless

Oaths

By the first shell: The first Hatching is of noteworthy importance to those who revere dragonkind. They swear by the beasts and men who protect them from the danger of Threadfall. Many Pernese oaths are of a similar character, in which a rider will pledge his behavior (or his disbelief) by the first Egg of Faranth's clutch (the first of the fertile queens) or the egg of his own dragon. Expletives in the same vein depict broken or damaged eggs ("shards," "scorch the shell and sear the skin," or "shells").

"Through Fog, Fall, and Fire" is reminiscent of the vow of the American postman, who promises to deliver the mail "through rain and sleet and dark of night." Like a good Celtic triad, it names three disasters or trials through which one must pass to prove faith.

they show special aptitude for human medicine, those young healers who emerge during the Interval are sent to the Crafthall in Fort Hold for instruction. During the Pass, there is plenty of on-the-job training. Most dragonriders of any length of service have scars on face, hands, shoulders, and upper body. The onerous, smelly job of gathering and boiling numbweed is usually done by the women of the Lower Caverns and the Weyrwomen, but any idle pair of hands is likely to get drafted to help.

Healers who are also dragonriders are often asked to perform litter duty if there is an accident on the mountains outside the Weyr in one of the Holds. Telgar Hold frequently calls on Telgar Weyr or Benden for help during the heavy snows. Dragons can carry medical litters with straps thrown across the rump just above the base of the tail. Generally one of the smaller dragons, blue or green, draws this duty. The procedure is dangerous and requires considerable flying skill from the weyrling. Unless it is absolutely necessary to move a wounded human, temporary accommodations are established wherever the accident occurred. It is easier to bring a healer to an injury than the other way around.

Dragonriders suffer from a host of kidney and back problems brought on by the cold of *between*. Weyrwomen and other females who fly frequently often have bouts with cystitis. The healers have effective remedies that have been used for centuries for these ailments.

Those who Impress dragons tend to live longer than those who do not, but during a Pass the chances of a fighting dragonrider outliving his career are limited. During Intervals, they live very long lives.

The availability of good beer and the occasional bottle of wine gives rise to the next necessity: the morning draught. Inveterate tipplers make use of concoctions to stave off drunkenness, including tincture of asparagus. For those who have overindulged and cannot carry it or had not had the forethought to take something ahead of time, Manora or her assistant Felena will administer the morning draught, also known as the "killer cure." It is an herbal brew, made with asparagus and willow and a handful of other items, and it tastes terrible. But it works every time.

Dragonrider

Teas and tisanes exist for every small ailment a person might suffer. Purges are dispensed as a handful of herbs in the morning klah of someone who has been suffering from blockage. Headache teas are made of sage, wintergreen, and willow in varying proportions according to taste. Everyone drinks klah, which is brewed from the bark of local shrubs. The best teas come from Upper Nerat, upper Southern Boll, and the highlands of Ista. Mint, lemongrass, and verbena are grown in the Weyr Bowl. Nerat and upper Southern Boll supply citrus. The headwoman of one Weyr will trade its local herbs with another to fill her stock of medicinals.

Dragons are rarely ill. If for some reason a dragon is not flying, whether from illness or injury, a dragon healer will keep a close eye on the dragon's color and skin tone. Frequently a grounded dragon will save up his excreta for five days or so and go *between* as soon as he can. Sometimes a younger dragon will misjudge how long he can wait and will need to be helped out with a purge, which affects both dragon and rider. The weyrling will then learn to watch how thick his beast's tail is getting.

A badly injured dragon is treated just like a weyrling; his rider will need to bathe him and muck out his quarters.

Gambling followed man into the stars. The dragonriders amuse themselves at odd moments in the evening by practicing gambling tricks and sharping each other at games of skill.

Prestidigitation, or sleight of hand, is the special trick of Bendenites. The secrets are jealously guarded and revealed to no one outside the Weyr. The practitioners are forbidden to exercise their skill to turn a profit for fear of alienating holders, but they amuse and befuddle those who cannot see the trick. Benden Holders, on the other hand, have not been issued any warnings not to run games and tricks for profit, often to the detriment of the greener riders.

Dragonriders will bet for money on practically anything, especially complicated wagers on the outcome of Hatchings. Such things are winked at, because the Leaders know their men have to have some outlet.

Jugglers trained in the Harper Hall for amusement pass their skills on to any rider who cares to try. Benden riders pride themselves in having more dextrous hands than any other Weyr on Pern.

BENDEN HOLD

Benden Hold: On a violet field, three red Bends Sinister

The inviting eastern sweep of the mountainside drew the founders of Benden Hold to this valley from the Weyr and the abandoned stakes of Thessaly and Roma in the year 22 after Landing. They found that there was an impressive warren running through the cliffs that needed little additional excavation to create a large and well-proportioned Hold.

The stonecutters were brought in to smooth out the walls and to create partitions and steps between chambers. The roadway between the Hold and the Weyr was slagged down on three sides at bedrock level and the trench filled in with layers of flagstone, then broken rock, then gravel, making it self-draining and easily maintained.

Benden's face is far less forbidding than that of Fort Hold, with a smaller main entrance. The Hold was built to house about seven hundred people initially, but some of the less accessible caverns were redesignated as storerooms. Benden now has a population between five and six hundred, and serves as the central hub for eight to ten thousand more in smaller holds around it and over the chain of mountains along the coast.

Benden Hold supports itself by demanding that holders spend a certain amount

Benden Hold

of time working in the Hold fields or caverns, unless they supply food directly to Hold stores. The Crafthalls tithe time or craft-works in exchange for support from the Hold. During an Intervals, this form of tax-ation is not strictly enforced. Benden's fields are fertile, and the Hold can trade for what it needs. Toward the beginning of a Pass, how-ever, there is a scramble among holders and crafters to get the Lord Holder well disposed toward them so that they will get preferred accommodation in the Hold during Threadfall.

Benden was one of only three Holds that remained loyal to its Weyr during the Second Long Interval, as Lord Raid contin-ued the Tradition without questioning or un-derstanding. He coerced Bitra and Lemos, the other major settlements beholden to the Weyr, into following his lead. In the Council

of Lords before the attack on Benden Weyr, Raid also managed to sway Nerat to his side.

Benden has carefully guarded treasured patterns for patchwork, which it uses for clothing as well as for quilts. Ornate sleeve-less padded vests in patchwork worn over shirts are a trademark of the fashionable Ben-denite. Embroidery is a skill many take up to pass the long evenings.

Benden cultivates nut trees in specially protected orchards on the slope below the Hold. The soil is rich enough and has suffi-cient drainage to raise the walnuts for which Benden is known, and also almonds and hazelnuts. Wedgenuts (Brazil nuts) and pe-cans come from Nerat. Benden raises a lot of tubers, which make a fine-grained bread when the holders want a change from breads made of wheat flour.

The Bakecraft in Benden makes sweet breads for which they are justly renowned. The Winecraft trades grape yeast with them for baked goods. Journeymen bring in quite a few marks at Gathers for their fingerroot loaf, soda-rising bread with raisins, citrus cake frosted with soft, sweetened cheese, and crumbly nut bread. Another delicacy is a puffy oil pastry with layers of nuts and sweetening.

The Hold raises its own klah trees. Everyone but infants drinks klah. Children frequently mix theirs with sweetening and milk until they get used to the pungent infusion. Beer is always available, but the wines are kept locked up, and the Steward keeps the key. Ordinary wines are available in the evenings, but the good wines are kept for special occasions.

BENDEN WINE

Vintner:
On a white field,
a dark red Wineskin

In one of the oldest sections of the Hold lies the Benden Winecrafthall. It announces its presence even in the dark with the reek of

centuries worth of yeast and spoiled grape juice. Here, as in Tillek, the craft of viniculture has been practiced for over two millennia. The wine caverns are believed to be one of the reasons this particular system of caves was chosen for the new Hold.

To the unpracticed eye, this cavern resembles the Winecrafthall in Tillek. Racks upon racks of crocks and bottles lie in shadowed corners out of the way of clumsy feet. The air is always cool and moist, circulating with the open air through ventilation shafts many dragonlengths high.

The winepresses in which the grapes are squeezed are stone tuns fifteen inches thick, cut from the very rock of the Hold with the same amazing precision as the corridors and floors. Wood has always been so scarce that traditional wooden "stomping vats" were never viable.

Apprentices hurry in and out of the storage caverns carrying withy baskets of grapes held high over their heads, and others (frequently as punitive duty) press out the juice in the traditional manner in the stone winepresses. The atmosphere is heady and rich with yeast. Many winecrafters wear cloth masks over their noses and mouths to keep from inhaling too much yeast and sneezing.

Journeymen oversee rows of apprentices at the stone tables, who sort the grapes and discard the unsuitable ones into overflowing, stinking bins that are hauled out and washed by other wrinkle-nosed apprentices (another punitive duty). Still other journeymen follow the Winecraftmaster from vat to vat, tasting when invited and listening carefully as he expounds upon secrets of the craft.

Mastervintner Gorton holds court here. He is a garrulous, fleshy man in a leather apron who bears the marks of his profession: a nose with a bulbous end and a tracery of burst capillaries, and a complexion like a sunrise. Gorton likes his wine. His consumption is formidable, and he appears always to be

BENDEN BAKLAVA

12 ounces melted clarified butter
   or fat
 4 ounces oil
32 ounces pulverized Benden nuts
   powdered bark spice (optional)
40 leaves of flour-and-water
   dough stretched to paper
   thinness
12 ounces granulated sweetening
¼ ounce strained citrus juice
 6 ounces water
¼ ounce sweet syrup

Mix butter and oil. Cut dough to shape of the baking pan by laying the pan on top of stacked leaves. Butter the inside of the baking dish. Gently place one leaf of dough into pan, fitting carefully along the bottom of the pan. The leaves are very fragile, so fold to pick them up, and unfold when in place in the pan. Brush with butter-and-oil mixture. Repeat with nine more sheets. Sprinkle 3 tablespoons of powdered nuts

Gorton, who can heave a barrel or stomp grapes with the best of them, starts the picking every harvest. Crying encouragement to his apprentices, he works furiously to set a good example, then steps back to watch everyone else work.

Benden produces the whole range of wines, from the finest white to fruit wines and ice wines, and even a small quantity of retsina.

Everywhere in the caverns are the one- and two-liter glass bottles and ceramic gallon crocks sealed with wooden stoppers covered over with lead foils or solid seals made of vegetable lipids. Pern has no beeswax or cork

**Secret Benden Wine Vats
and Mastervintner Gorton**

slightly inebriated, but never enough to reveal the secrets of his Craft.

Gorton has been in the Benden Winecrafthall for many Turns. He is not so much an artist as a scientist. He keeps close track of what he does to a new vintage so he can duplicate the results later on. He carries in a case slung from his belt a rock crystal cup with silver chasing made especially for tasting wine. The crystal will not pick up any flavor from the wine, nor add any to it.

trees to seal bottles in the Earth fashion. Huge wooden barrels and knee-high kegs line the low end of the airless secondary cavern just off the corridor from the alcove that serves Gorton as an office. Not all of the barrels contain wine. Benden makes a fairly good beer of its own and trades with Telgar for the best of their brewing.

The barrels are made on strakes manufactured from ancient patterns of the original barrels brought to Pern by the colonists. These odd contraptions force wood into the right shape with springs and shave the lengths to bend in the right direction. Now that hardwoods are becoming more available, Gorton can replace some of the ceramic and glass barrels that his craft has been using for so long to eke out the supply.

In order to keep his palate pure, Gorton never touches sweets. He claims they spoil his ability to distinguish between vintages. His figure attests to his other weakness; he cannot resist fresh bread. But there is always a handful of sweets in his pocket for children. Gorton has a soft spot for youngsters, though he and his wife, Warra, have none of their own.

Gorton always looks forward to attending the Fort Hold festivities where the Winecraft sells or barters wines. He has a jocular animosity for Tillek Winecraftmaster Dikson. They have carried on the traditional friendly rivalry between Benden and Tillek that has gone on as long as both Holds have been producing wine. Dikson tries to improve the range of Tillek wines, while Gordon experiments with fruit wines and cordials. There is a fair competition between Gorton and the Tillek Winecraftmaster every year to formulate the tastiest, smoothest spring wine, a delicate drink that is spiced with woodruff herb.

Gorton knows that Dikson has planted craft spies in his Hall from time to time, but

(with optional spice to taste) on tenth leaf. Open two more leaves of dough on top of nut mixture, buttering each in turn. Repeat with the nut mixture and two more leaves until all are used up. As soon as the last two leaves are used, brush the top with butter and oil.

With a very sharp knife, score the top of the pastry lightly lengthwise into four, and then draw the knife diagonally to make lozenge-shaped portions. Bake in a 325° oven for 90 minutes.

Combine the next three ingredients in a saucepan. Cook until the sweetening dissolves. Boil for five minutes, or until a drop of it forms a soft ball when dropped into cold water. Remove from heat; stir in syrup. Cool. As soon as the pastry is baked, remove from oven and pour the sweet mixture over it. Cool the pastry to room temperature. Serve.

there has never been a successful one. He has kept Benden's mystique intact. The secret of Benden wine is in the glass-lined, pressurized air seal tanks from the three gutted colony ships, brought to Benden by Rene Mallibeau, the man honored as the first Winecraftmaster. The perfect hermetic seal of the tanks ensures that maturing wine never loses the "angel hair" of a quality vintage, and they can be siphoned without effort.

Robinton is an old friend of Gorton,

who keeps a supply of "specials" to send to the Masterharper for his personal enjoyment. The "specials" need not have been of Gorton's own pressing. The wine caverns are huge, and there is plenty of storage room. Gorton knows where there are secreted wines two to four hundred Turns old. The Winecraft releases good aged wines for accessions of Lord Holders, celebrations, Hatchings, births of heirs, and other important occasions. The wines are indicated by the name of the Winecraftmaster and the number of the Turn in his career that it was pressed, such as Gorton 7, Gorton 11, Gorton 14 (reputed to be the best white wine ever), Darvik 17, Darvik 12, Anneke 5, and so on.

Naturally, there is tremendous rivalry among the Winecraftmasters as to who gets to be the Benden Master. As each Master lives a fairly long time, many a young apprentice has grown old in frustrated anticipation. The chosen candidate comes into office with the facility for tasting inbred, then trained to the highest standard.

Not all of Benden's Winecraftmasters have been men. The accolade has been passed to talented daughters, too. Anneke, the Master two before Gorton, was named to the office by her father on his deathbed.

Because the secrets of the Benden winecraft are passed along at the last possible moment, some secrets have been lost because the Master died untimely and did not have a chance to reveal them to anyone. Many Masters, as they lay dying, have whispered to their successors, "...Never let them have the vats..."

X.

Holds, Crafthalls, and Weyrs

INTRODUCTION

Pern's population of four to five million is divided among several major Holds and hundreds of smaller holds and isolated cotholds across the southern two-thirds of the Northern Continent and in smaller, more isolated clumps in the Southern Continent. Of five climate zones (two polar, two temperate, and one tropical), only three are inhabited. Benden, in the temperate zone, has weather much like New York. Igen and Keroon, though half in the temperate and half in the tropical zone, are mostly desert. Ista, Southern Boll, and Nerat are tropical. The climate has a major effect on the organization of each Hold.

HOLD STRUCTURE

The largest Holds have a population of no more than a thousand, forming a support system for the Lord Holder's administration and a central hub for trading and education. Many more thousands look to each of the major Holds from tiny holds and cotholds scattered throughout the countryside. The social structure is similar to that of any agrarian society. Most of the smaller holders are farmers. The typical size of a Pernese farm is ten to twenty acres. The cots are built of stone or hollowed out of the volcanic rock in a mountainside. Miners and prospectors tend also to live in isolation, bringing their discoveries to the major Hold during Gathers and festivals, or to their Crafthalls.

To save manpower hours on the larger farms, the fields are often burned off after harvest instead of being plowed under. What extra time the holders have is spent in building and repairing shelters. Burned fields are allowed to stand fallow for a Turn or so to replenish the soil. More land is farmed in Intervals than during Passes, because there is no longer a fear of losing precious crops to the sky-borne threat.

It is ironic that during the Passes, when there are more herdbeasts needed to support more dragons than are Hatched during Intervals, the crops needed to feed them are reduced to what can be easily protected by the Weyrs. The surface of the Northern Continent is approximately the size of Eurasia on Earth, and as the population grows, the farmers are running out of arable land to till. The Southern Continent is regaining its importance as the northerners, fleeing overcrowding in their home Holds, go south to open new farmholds.

Depending on availability of building stone or natural caves, a Hold may be established anywhere there is arable land. The population has grown and diminished in cycles over the Turns, growing when harvests were good and declining because of fire, starvation, disease, and Threadfall. Viruses and bacteria brought by the original colonists in their intestines surface occasionally, causing epidemic and plague.

During Threadfall, most of the population takes shelter in the isolated holds, which for that reason need to be self-sufficient. Their ancestors, the settlers who came to Pern, preferred autonomy, and it has become inbred. To them, the best form of government is no government at all, though it is difficult to form a cohesive society with no overlying rules of conduct and nowhere to take grievances. Over the centuries, in times when Thread has fallen, "people clung to the safety of stone walls, stout doors, and to the traditional leadership of their Lord Holders" (The Girl Who Heard Dragons). They form survival units to stay alive, and when the crisis is over, go about their business again.

The lack of centralization is directly attributable to the original philosophic foundation of the colony, though it had to mobilize under central authority in order to protect itself and its resources when Thread started falling in the eighth year of the colony's history. Even during the Pass, they continued promoting disjointure by establishing new Holds in the Northern Continent that would thereafter enjoy the autonomy that the original Pernese colonists sought.

For the former city dwellers among them, returning to a monolithic structure such as a Hold was not so severe as it was to the surviving nomads. Most of the nomads' numbers were wiped out during the first few Falls. The survivors gradually and reluctantly threw in their lot with the stakeholders. Under such trusted leaders as Admiral Benden and Governor Boll, the Pernese mobilized to combat the menace of Thread to the best of their ability.

People gain status on Pern by doing what they do best. They merit honor from their activities, not from any innate nobility. The mark of a good Holder is his ability to exercise control of a Hold in times of crisis and to administer Hold business wisely at all other times. When a Lord Holder dies or retires, his heir or successor may be of no relation to him at all. What matters is that the man is able to fulfill the responsibilites he owes to the many hundreds or thousands who will look to him. Most frequently, though, an heir will be of the Blood, or a fosterling who has lived in the Hold sufficiently long to be familiar with its operation and to have gained the trust of its folk.

Older members of society are venerated for their accumulated knowledge and age and are considered to have made their contributions already. A prudent Holder will keep their needs in mind and ask their advice when he requires it. A Holder's family is his greatest administrative asset. In the major Holds, aunties and uncles, as the elderlies are called, live in separate floors devoted especially to their care. When the Holder can afford it, healers are retained to look after the aunties and uncles, but in the smaller and poorer Holds, it falls to the daughters of the Holder and others with caring and skill to tend them.

A man born on Pern will probably live

anywhere from eight to eleven decades, unless something befalls him in the meantime. Normally, the oldsters are assigned to non-stress duties that will not strain them unduly.

Each of the three parts of the societal structure, Hold, Hall, and Weyr, are independent from and interdependent upon one another. A Holder cannot command a Craftmaster against his will, or deny the products of a Crafthall to other Holds. The two are considered to be of equal rank. The Master of an entire craft is equivalent to a Weyrleader or a Lord Holder. They owe one another respect.

In a major Hold, a Lord Holder will employ a staff of craftmasters to oversee their specialties in his demesne. He hires what masters and journeymen he can afford to pay or board, depending on the level of skill he requires and the level of persuasiveness he can bring to bear against his prospective employee. A wealthy major Hold will have one or two Masterharpers and a couple of journeymen to oversee the teaching, organize interhold communications, and provide entertainment. The Holder will employ at least one Masterhealer and some apprentice healers to look after those under his care. The more elderly and infirm people in a Hold, the greater number of healers needed. Smiths of various specialties will be persuaded to set up Crafthalls in the Hold or nearby, but whether or not the Lord Holder uses their services exclusively depends on His Hold's needs.

If at any time a Holder runs short on marks, he may dismiss his Craftmasters. If a Craftmaster is dissatisfied with his position, he may resign. Crafters, like Weyrfolk, are autonomous and are not subject to the Holder's pleasure. If any man finds he is unable to tolerate his Holder, he has the option of moving elsewhere without hindrance. There is no stigma attached to disaffection.

Hold Insignia

A Holder will indicate his Hold of origin by wearing a round badge displaying the heraldry of his Hold, or a shoulder knot woven with the appropriate colors and a combination of silver or gold thread to designate whether it is a major or minor Hold.

Penal system

The individual holders can appeal to the Lord Holder for justice. If a man commits a crime, the Lord Holder will most likely determine punishment to be restitution and service to the wronged party. Imprisonment is the next severest penalty, and death can be decreed for heinous crimes such as murder.

The greatest penalty a man can suffer is to be made Holdless. During an Interval, deprival of shelter does not put a man at risk as it does during a Pass, but it cuts him off from the societal structure. For an honest man to be Holdless is a severe punishment. Even death is not as frightening to a man as being without shelter during a Pass.

Psychopathy is rare on Pern. Careful screening of the original colonists made sure that any maladjusted individuals received care, and individuals diagnosed as severely maladjusted, considered incurable, were refused space in the convoy. As it was to be a small, intelligently constructed society, those with psychological needs were attended to, so problems did not feed on themselves. The authors of the Charter wanted to create as perfect a colony as possible.

CRAFT STRUCTURE

The development of specialized crafthalls as teaching units progressed naturally from the gathered population. An active program of apprenticeship based on those used on Earth and First Centauri began immediately once the children of the colonists made landfall.

The first Craft in Landing to begin formal apprenticeship was the Healercraft, since that skill was the most vital to prolonged survival of a new colony. Such skills as first aid, midwifery, and herbcraft were needed every day. Minecraft, Smithcraft, and Beastcraft followed closely. Fishing, weaving, and viniculture all had long-held secrets and skills that were preserved over the ages by passing them down to new generations. Life in a colony has its dangers. The new Pernese recognized that and knew they could not risk being deprived of skilled men and women in every discipline. As rewards for diligence, an apprentice could earn stake acres upon reaching maturity.

A craft is established by its inventors or best proponents in each Hold, who appoint Craftmasters, the recognized experts. He or she trains interested apprentices; when an apprentice reaches journeyman status, he or she is considered competent to practice the Craft independently. Thereafter, journeymen study on their own or with other Masters and journeymen to achieve mastery, while teaching new apprentices the Craft they have learned. A Mastercrafthall is established to maintain standards among the scattered Halls and to provide a school of instruction for apprentices.

Most apprenticeships last five to seven years. By that time, an apprentice will have all the on-the-job experience he needs. If he chooses to persevere in his studies, he will follow his own path, his chosen specialty, to Mastership. There are also all-around masters, but those are rare (and in time generally become the Craftmaster).

To his journeyman or master, an apprentice owes obedience. In return the master owes qualified teaching and sufficient experience for the apprentice or journeyman to pass the oral and practical proficiency exams and advance in his Craft. The student is given ample opportunity to demonstrate what he knows. Advancement in grade is called "walking the tables," from the practice of seating each rank at a separate table in the common dining hall. When an apprentice or journeyman is advanced a rank, the ceremony often occurs at a meal or other assembly, at which time the honoree takes his place at his new table.

Crafthall Insignia

A crafter shows his rank by the use of shoulder cords. The most elaborate design is worn by the Craftmaster, knotted from the craft colors. Those below him wear simpler knots that will also indicate by which Hold they are employed (if they work outside the Mastercrafthall). A crafter will wear a roundel badge that shows by its symbol to which Craft he or she belongs.

Journeyman

Apprentice

Craftmaster

SHOULDER KNOTS WORN BY CRAFTERS

Women in the Crafts

Women in the Crafts are accorded respect equal to that given men of equal ability. Opportunities for them are not as limited as in a Hold, where they are expected to bear as many children as possible while keeping up with their other duties.

The simple fact that women have to bear the babies, because men cannot, led naturally to the establishment of a fostering system to keep trained women in the work force. Women and men who had the knack of child care were given the duties of seeing to the daily needs of the children of others as well as their own in Weyr, Hold, and Hall. A mother could have her baby and, after the first three months of primary care, turn it over to a foster mother whom she trusted.

Such a practice left women free to pursue their craft without having to worry about their offspring.

Menolly, of the Harper Hall, has four children whom she fosters with Silvina, the Hall's headwoman. Menolly's talents are needed elsewhere, and her inclination has never been toward child rearing.

The gradual decline in the number of female apprentices and journeywomen stemmed from the Great Plague. As women had to produce more and more babies to replenish the population, females fell away from the Crafts, until it was forgotten except in the record hides that they had ever been equal members. The push to increase the population got out of hand, and some Crafts had no women in them for nearly four hundred Turns. Menolly is merely the first journeywoman in the Harper Hall after a long

ONE MARK WILL BUY:	
A plain leather belt with bronze buckle	Tannercraft
A full sack of fine-milled pastry flour	Bakercraft
Sixteen small (1-pound) loaves of bread	Bakercraft
Half a sack of sweetening	Bakercraft
192 bubbly pies	Bakercraft
Two sacks of nuts in the shell	Benden Hold
A plain shirt	Weavercraft
A child's frock	Weavercraft
A small knife	Smithcraft
One young ovine or four fowl	Beastcraft
A keg of ale	Winecraft
Two bottles of wine (undistinguished vintage)	Winecraft
A pair of moccasins	Tannercraft
A hand-sized hardwood box with hinges, hasp	Woodcraft
An apprentice-made pipe	Harpercraft
Two sacks of Cromcoal	Minecraft
A whetstone	Minecraft
A graduated-bead necklace, agate or quartz	Minecraft
A bangle bracelet, jade	Lemos Minecrafthall
⅛ of a bovine herdbeast	Keroon Hold

time, not the first ever. A Historical Saga tells the story of a journeywoman who married a Lord Holder of Ista, who was so proud of his wife's prowess that he built a Harpercrafthall for her in his Hold.

The reinstitution of women has been as gradual as the decline. As those with strong wills and skilled hands showed that they were as adept as the men, they began to join the Healercraft, the Weavercraft, the Smithcraft, and the Minecraft. Ironically, it is the Harpercraft, the Craft that deals with communication and fresh ideas, that has had the most protracted absence of female crafters.

MEANS OF EXCHANGE

The usual method of exchanging goods or services is barter. A man will trade his skill or merchandise for that of another, usually at a Gather. Gathers, Hold-sponsored fairs, are held as frequently as once every seven days in major Holds, or as infrequently as two to three times a Turn in smaller, more isolated holds.

The unit of monetary exchange is the mark. These are disks made of wood, supplied as blanks by Lemos Hold and stamped with special dies that denote value and source. The value of the mark fluctuates with supply of barterable goods. After a bad harvest, a mark is worth more because the goods it represents are harder to obtain; after a good harvest, the situation is reversed. This fiscal autonomy is set by a group of traders, Craftmasters, and Lord Holders that meet every year at harvest time to fix what a mark will buy for the next Turn. In a good Turn, an ornamental belt will cost two marks.

Each major Hall and Hold has its own die stamps for impressing marks. The denominations are 1/32 of a mark, 1/16, 1/8, 1/4, 1/2, 1, 2, 5, 10 marks, and a few 100 mark pieces for very large transactions. For fractional marks, only one number is stamped on the blank. A horizontal line above the number shows that it is worth less than one mark. If the line is below the number, the piece is worth that number of whole marks. The designs on marks are very complex and hard to duplicate without the correct tools, which the Smithcraft provides. An imperfection is consciously added to every imprinting to make them even harder to counterfeit.

Only so many marks are issued per Turn, to balance the supply of goods or to replace old, worn-out mark pieces.

Musical instruments sell for prices from two marks and up. Runnerbeasts can be had from nine marks up, and their riding gear from three marks for used leathers to more than twelve for custom gear for a Lord Holder's steed.

Marks

HIGH REACHES HOLD

High Reaches Hold: Per Pale, dark blue and tan

High Reaches Hold is windy and bleak, though it is saved from the worst weather by a neighboring ocean current, even if that current is cold. The traveling gulf stream, which makes its way around the entire northern hemisphere of the great ocean of Pern, begins its southward journey just north of High Reaches.

High Reaches merits the dubious distinction of having spawned Fax. Fax was a younger son of a cadet branch of the Blood, born in the last decades before the Ninth Pass. He considered the main bloodline too effeminate, too dilute, and began to take over where and when he could. With his host of dissatisfied jolly boys, he slew the Lord Holder and his family. Numb with shock, no one put up a fight or otherwise tried to stop him. A Holder had only a ceremonial guard on hand, not a standing army. The family was defenseless. In any case, he had blocked off their every escape route. In his own twisted way he was a top military strategist.

Every move in his conquest was unspeakable by civilized standards. To keep his actions secret, he sequestered the Hold harpers and refused to allow itinerant singers to enter the Hold. Harpers were in a precarious position in Fax's day. It was still twenty

Turns before the end of the Long Interval, and their duty was to teach Hold children what they owed to dragons and dragonriders, whom most holders would as soon have forgotten as useless parasites. Because they served as a reminder of the Weyr, harpers themselves were often considered useless parasites. It was actually the tradition of immunity that kept a harper safe much of the time. Their Craft was still needed after the 250 Turns since Thread should have fallen, because the harpers were the best communication system the Holds had.

Once he was in complete control of the Hold, Fax released the High Reaches harpers but left them so terrified that they could not tell anyone else what was going on. He took pleasure in his knowledge that whoever they did manage to tell would not believe them, since what he was doing had never happened in all of the history of Pern.

After conquering High Reaches, he married Gemma of Crom, adding that Hold to his territory. He conquered Nabol in much the same way as his home Hold and murdered the Holders of three lesser holds. His host of strongarm men, now swelled to an army, knocked holders about as they pleased. Fax's final acquisition was Ruatha. He craved it because it was rich and had the finest bloodstock of runnerbeasts on Pern. He had the runnerbeasts moved from Ruatha after Lord Holder Micawl's family was dead—all but Lessa of Ruatha, who was warned of the impending invasion and fled to the watchwher's den for safety.

When Fax was killed, his army was quickly disbanded and went back to being hunters, fishermen, and farmers. There is no doubt that a strong arm can be useful in settling a brawl, but a force such as Fax commanded went against everything the people of Pern believed in. Having the autonomous Holds united under a tyrant was precisely

what the colonists had set out to avoid when they came to Pern in the first place.

Since Fax's death, High Reaches Hold has been in the capable hands of Lord Holder Bargen. Because of the extremely cold weather, the folk in High Reaches learn survival techniques early and drill their children until they follow the rules without thinking.

The Hold is burrowed deep into the mountain, with only a few shuttered windows overlooking the rows of cotholds that line the river road. But for a few smaller holds, High Reaches is well isolated on its westward-jutting peninsula. Its Weavercrafthall is unusually skilled. The weavers shear the llamas that High Reaches uses as pack animals; the hair is woven into an unusually fine and soft, warm cloth. Lord Lytol of Ruatha spent many Turns here as a Masterweaver between the time he left the Weyr

High Reaches Winter Garb

after his dragon's death and when he moved to Ruatha to care for the infant Lord Jaxom. High Reaches has several minor Crafthalls, including a glass-smith's shop, which, besides the usual custom necessary for a Hold's operation, does quite a good business in bottles and jugs.

Fortified wines are a popular drink here, more so than in Holds farther south. Fruit brandies such as pear, apple, and blackberry are prepared against the long, cold season. High Reaches imports a lot of spices for preserving meat and fish, and for mulling wines.

The knitters in High Reaches practice the art of felting, a Craft they share with Southern Boll, though anyone can tell the difference between holder-made and Craft-made goods. As a rule, High Reaches holders use their skill for gloves, sweaters, heavy skirts, and trousers to go under weatherproof hide. The tropical Weavercraft puts its skill to lighter work, such as felt hats and decorative slippers for ladies. Felting obscures the careful knit stitches of the heavy fleece sweaters, but renders the fabric much warmer and less likely to catch hook or barb casually. Being less permeable, felted knits also last longer. In order that a High Reaches "gansie," or seaman's sweater, can be easily distinguished, the knitters use the old star-and-egg Fair Isle pattern brought from Earth by the colonists. The sweaters are often brilliantly colored, predominantly made in tan and blue, the Hold colors, but banded with bright gold and red dyes made from lichen for greater visibility.

High Reaches is also well-known for its skill at shipbuilding, second only to Tillek Hold. The holders bend timbers and dress wood in the waters north of the Hold and ship numbered and measured lengths of seasoned wood from the flat oval caverns under the Hold intended for assembly elsewhere. During much of the year, the bay is scoured clean of sand and weed by the icy northern waters, leaving it deep and clear, safe for any ship that comes so far north.

HIGH REACHES WEYR

High Reaches Weyr: On a dark blue field, a Mountain Range in black

High Reaches was the third Weyr, founded entirely by dragons and riders from Fort Weyr. After the First Pass ended, the queens kept laying good-sized clutches for a while. There were no deaths from Threadscore or misadventure, so the population quickly rose to a squeeze in the available living space. The volcanic caldera in High Reaches was handy.

High Reaches is one of the most striking of all the Weyrs. The north rim of the Bowl is called the Seven Spindles for the high, crownlike points arrayed around that end, formed of old flow from the volcano and clipped to sharp spikes when the caldera blew up in ages past. The Hatching Ground is in a wide, high, oval cavern at the northernmost edge of the Bowl next to the queens' weyrs.

Like Fort and Benden, High Reaches was hollowed out with stonecutters. Some thermal baths were put in in the queens' caverns and the Weyrleader's chamber, but most sanitary and bathing facilities in this and all later Weyrs were supplied with exterior pipes of ceramics or metal.

Most of the Oldtimers who came forward to High Reaches left for Southern Weyr after the death of Weyrleader T'kul, leaving Kylara and T'bor, formerly of Southern, as the new Weyrleaders. When the two queen dragons died, Pilgra became Weyrwoman for Segrith. T'bor, though brash and occasionally thoughtless, is entirely behind the Benden Weyr leadership.

BALEN HOLD

Balen Hold: On a pine-green field, three peridot-green Bends

Balen is a small sea hold on the north side of the peninsula west of High Reaches. Balen is famous for its lumber mills, which saw timbers from High Reaches and its own pine forests into boards. Balen, too, has numerous caverns in which wood is seasoned for building. Skilled woodsmiths here make furniture, as well as fixtures for ships.

TILLEK HOLD

Tillek Hold: On a white field, a dark blue Reversed Lattice

Named for James Tillek, captain of the colony ship *Bahrain,* this is the most westerly major Hold in the Northern Continent. Tillek and the dolphineers founded this Hold with their stake acres after the Second Crossing. With the aid of the dolphins, the seagoing population of this stakehold charted the currents and coasts. Tillek is known for its conifer forests (which have grown up in the Long Interval), its terraced farms, the Fishercrafthall, shipbuilding, and its wine.

Tillek's population is seasonal, depending on how many ships are in harbor. As most of the men tend to be involved in shipboard activities, Lord Oterel places many women in positions of authority. The hardiness of Tillek Hold women is legendary. Having himself done a fair number of Turns on the sea, Lord Oterel understands the needs of administration both on ship and on land. His Lady Steward is his wife's sister, Bronwen. She is a good organizer and sees that the Hold runs well and on schedule. Timeliness, particularly with regard to meals, is a crucial issue when so many need to leave the Hold in the predawn hours to catch the tides. Bronwen's husband, Captain Ekito, is away much

High Reaches Weyr

of the year on fishing trips, and her many children are fostered with other women in the Hold, as Bronwen has much to do.

Bronwen works closely with Cytor, Portmaster of Tillek Sea Hold. Cytor is a retired sea captain who knows the ropes and can handle the rough seamen who use the Sea Hold as their base. The wharf is built of great heavy blocks, right into the harbor, which is good and deep but sheltered from the elements. From the Sea Hold, a ship can pick up the southern current and move with surprising speed down the west coast of the continent toward Southern Boll and east beyond it to Ista.

There was little flat land for farming when the first holders came here, since the primary interest in Tillek was its sheltered harbor to the northwest of what is now the Hold. The holders gradually built terraces into the mountain that held the Hold, giving the broad farms a northeastern exposure. The roads leading to the Hold proper were also terraced, with ramps built for wagons along either side.

The Tillek Gather meadow occupies the steppe nearest the entrance to the Hold. This allows the traders to take best advantage of the roads when hauling or driving their goods to the pitches arranged at the meadow's perimeter.

Tillek harvests lumber from its extensive conifer forests during the warm weather, and lays it down in dry caverns to season, often for a full Turn. Much of this wood is shipped to other ports, but some of it stays in the Hold for the shipwrights' use.

During the cold season, the woodsmiths of Tillek preassemble aged wood for

KNITTING PATTERNS

By tradition, each Hold has an exclusive knit pattern. The styles vary considerably between Holds. Also by tradition, the patterns are knit with plain yarn, or dyed in each Hold's dominant color. The dyes are made from plants, roots, mosses, fish, or whatever is most available. Ista's color, bright orange, comes from a shellfish that lives in the tropical waters.

ISTA: The need for warm garments is almost unknown here, but the seaholders have sweaters and warm trousers for faring into cold seas. The knit pattern traditional to Ista Sea Hold is the embossed or raised leaf decoratively rendered in bright shades of orange and white, the Hold colors.

This style is also made in fine cool fabrics of cotton and sisal, and is popular for ladies' shawls.

LEWIS HOLD: crossover rib

HALF CIRCLE: Twisted V stitch, which looks like endless rows of half circles, alternating with cable stitch and bobbles

shipment and dress wood to be used by the shipwrights as soon as the weather breaks. The shipbuilders' cavern is high and wide, suitable for bending timbers with complete disregard for the weather outside.

A much-practiced skill in Tillek during storms and bad weather is knitting. Mothers teach their fosterlings the skill from the time they can hold the needles, and gradually introduce them to stitches and patterns of greater complexity and intricacy. On a typical evening, the men will gather to mend nets or knit, using the same skills for different applications. Beginners make socks and caps, which are frequently unraveled later to save precious yarn. Skilled knitters may use multiple pairs of needles and several strands of yarn at once.

Like all the Sea Holds, Tillek fishermen use a specific stitch pattern to denote port of origin. Tillek seaholders wear a trellis stitch in which the Hold symbol can be easily rendered. It is often dyed in the Hold colors: white and blue from the fields of meadowsweet flowers that grow in the nearby mountain valleys. But it shows up as frequently in the distinctive single-colored raised knit pattern, combined with a traveling cable and double moss stitch. The sturdy, nearly waterproof sweaters and jerseys serve to protect the man wearing them from the elements, but also to identify him if his body is washed ashore. The seamen are very matter-of-fact about the dangers of their craft. They may make jokes about other unlucky fishermen, but they respect the seas of Pern.

Traders compete to get the most skilled work of the knitters to take with them on their travel routes to the temperate Holds, especially those closest to the snowy wastes. These are done in colors other than those reserved for the Hold fishermen. *Nålbindning* mittens, incredibly warm, harder-wearing than knit, and more flexible in cold and wet than hide, fetch a handsome price. The ancient secrets of their making are not for sale. Some brocade knitting is done here, but it cannot compete with the delicate brocades of Fort Hold.

Tillek Goblet

Anyone who has tasted the products of either Hold has heard of the rivalry between the Benden and Tillek wine caverns. Benden wines continue to be the most sought after on Pern, with Tillek's running a distant second. The current Tillek Winecraftmaster's name is Dikson, a rangy, redheaded fellow with a nose and cheeks the same color as his best red wines. Tillek's wines are considered to be a bit foxy, and tend to have a harsh aftertaste. Some attribute this to the acidity of the soil. Even after hundreds of Turns, and improvements made in the Craft, Tillek has been unable to equal Benden's reputation for smoothness. Dikson, like his predecessors, uses the finest wood casks, which have been improved by the incorporation of the new hardwoods growing in Lemos and Igen; only

RUATHA AND RUATHA RIVER HOLD: a very distinctive smocked rib pattern

BIG BAY (IGEN SEA HOLD): cable alternating with double cable

SEA CLIFF: moire stitch

MISTY HOLD: lattice cable

TILLEK: raised knit pattern

combined with traveling cable and double moss stitch.

SATTLE: chain and moss cable

ROCKY HOLD: star stitch

HOLD GAR: shell stitch

FORT SEA HOLD: triple twisted rib

VALLEY HOLD: reversed arrowhead cable, in deference to their hold badge

GREYSTONES: twisted columns, for the sarsenlike rock spurs that appear here

BAY HEAD: twisted diamond

NERAT: scallop shell stitch

the finest woven cloth is used for straining. Lime, to sweeten the soil, has been carefully dug in around the roots of ancient vines as thick as a man's body, but all to no avail. Dikson has sent spies to Bender Hold's Wine-craftmaster as apprentices, but he has never received any information that helps him.

Dikson initiated a dry red wine that has evolved quite a following among seamen, who like a hearty drink they can taste through the salt water. His white wines are only fair compared to those of some of his predecessors, like Vilbrian, his own master. A Vilbrian 12 (indicating the twelfth Turn of Vilbrian's pressings) is considered to be "...*almost,* almost as good as a Benden white." Though loyalists always add, "of an inferior Turn."

FISHERCRAFTHALL

Fisher/Seacrafter: On a white field, a sea-blue Fish

This Tillek-based craft comprises several specialties under the aegis of Idarolan, the Masterfisher. Under Idarolan there are Master captains and Mastercraftsmen; and under them are the captains, who rate their journeyman seamen according to tradition: seaman, able-bodied, second mate, first mate. Apprentices act as cabin boys and lure tiers.

Shipbuilding includes construction and maintenance of boats, improvements on lines and sheets, and learning to choose materials for sails. Seamanship also involves basic navigation, understanding of the wind and sea currents, and the study of individual coastlines, underwater reefs in southern waters, and navigable rivers. Journeymen are taught to make maps of the generally accepted trade routes and the locations of the moorings best sheltered from the wind. Chart making is a precise craft, and only those who have fair hands as copyists are trusted to make charts, since many men's lives will depend on them.

Very accurate charts have been handed down to the Fishercraft from their remote ancestors. Modern seamen have ceased to wonder how the Archive charts of the coastal waters are so incredibly accurate and detailed, and are just grateful that they are so. The knowledge that these are original fax pictures taken by the atmospheric probes has been lost since Moreta's day, when the Masterfisher succumbed to the plague, as did so many of his crafters. All that an apprentice today knows is that he had better copy those charts correctly.

Any sea captain will want to have charts with him of his own copying, and keeps archives of sailing dates and cargo carried on board his ship. In the Seacrafthold, a treasured artifact is an antique map reputed to have been drawn by the first Craftmaster (Jim Tillek) and dates from before the Crossing. (The fact that the journey from Earth to Pern over twenty-eight hundred Turns before was also called the Crossing has long since been forgotten.)

The Seacrafthold's archives helped to solve the mystery of Threadfall after the Long Interval as Weyrleader F'lar was able to study the number of clear sailing days the sea captains had reported during the previous Pass.

It is easy to learn the basics of fishing. Apprentices start off tying lures, coiling ropes, scrubbing and polishing ship's wood and brass, and repairing nets. The journeymen do most of the actual work of fishing aboard a boat. They set the nets and haul in the catch, and both journeymen and their apprentices have the messy job of cleaning the fish. A Masterfisher knows how to judge where and when a good run of fish will appear, and will captain a crew to go and bring in the catch. All year round the women, children, and apprentices dry fish to store for use over the long, cold winter.

In a skiff, a journeyman teaches an apprentice how to work with the equipment, tend sail, and use cast nets and drag nets. The rocky coasts abound with shore-hugging fish that are easily caught from small boats.

Master Mactavis, the shipcraftmaster of Tillek, is a perfectionist. He prides himself that every man in every crew he oversees is an unexcelled specialist. If they do not live up to expectation, he gives them the sharp edge of his tongue while pointing out their mistakes. "The lives of men depend on you" is his favorite reminder. "Who knows what storms she'll be in?" is another.

The personality of each man working on a ship needs to dovetail as well with his mates' as his skill does, for the crew that builds a ship usually sails her as well. This way, the crew know the ship, every ring, spar, and board of her, before she hits the water, saving precious sevendays that would otherwise be spent learning the vessel and her quirks. Their own lives thus depend upon their own work.

The wood is chosen carefully from available stores. Sailmakers, sheet makers, and chandlers custom-outfit new ships or make replacement goods for existing craft. Tar and pitch come either from Tillek's or nearby High Reaches' conifer forests.

Tillek Hold Three-Master

During an Interval they can make ships on the beach, but when Thread falls, they move indoors. The cavern in which they build ships is high, with a slip for sliding the finished ship into water. Prior to a Pass, all ships that are not prepared are brought into drydock for refitting. Pumps already exist in a ship's belly for bailing the hull, but during a Pass, the pumps are used for flooding the deck during Threadfall. Ceramic joints are used instead of wooden ones, which would be eaten off by Thread. A thin layer of lead is hammered around the mast and spars, and a canopy of metal is kept aboard to be drawn over the exposed parts of the ship as it passes through the Leading Edge of the Fall. Standard procedure is to unship the sails, draw the canopy and flood the deck, and sail straight into the Fall toward Following Edge. A ship is not vulnerable for long in the midst of the sea, but it is terrifying even for brave men.

Dolphins, which are respected as another intelligent species, still exist in the seas of Pern, but no one seeks them out. The seacrafters are taught not to bother them, and if ever a fishing crew catches a dolphin by accident, they let it go with apologies. They know that the dolphins have always been allowed the freedom of the seas, and they never eat them. Over the generations dolphins have tried to reestablish communication with humans, but the dolphineers are all long dead. No one else knows the language, though the dolphins still occasionally help becalmed or wrecked seamen. Most of the original dolphineers in the crossing came to Tillek or Ista, but they had very few apprentices—during that first Pass, not many had the time free to take up that kind of skill. The last trained dolphineer died less than a hundred years after the Landing.

NABOL HOLD

Nabol Hold: On a brown field, a Narrow Fretty in white

The name Nabol has long been associated with greed. "As grasping as a Nabolese," a trader will say about a man who drives an unpleasantly sharp bargain. The man for whom the Hold was named, Nabhi Nabol, was one of the pilots who made a daring attempt to retrieve samples of Thread spores from outside the atmosphere—but for a price.

In exchange for a stakehold of the whole Big Island, which Avril Bitra had proved to him was rich in gem minerals, Nabol volunteered to pilot a gig into the cometlike Oort trail following the plutonic Red Star. He and Bart Lemos were killed when making atmospheric reentry. The samples and data were lost, and with them the colony's last hope of destroying the spores at the source. Other needs were more pressing, and the project to study Threadspores was set aside.

The road to Nabol Hold ends at a ramp that leads up to a gate; the corner gatehouse was built by Fax to repel attacks from any other force, though none existed in Pern but his own. The courtyard is large and paved with a pattern of flagstones. A watch-wher lives in a den in the corner farthest from the Hold's entrance. The Hold is carved into a mountain face that has under it a low, hollow overhang that is used as an entryway. It was first used for sheltering beasts in times of Threadfall.

The Gather meadow in the Hold's shadow shares the same source of pure mountain water. There are few stalls to be had, as if the Crafthalls and others with goods to sell prefer to go elsewhere, and the Hold does not care whether or not they come. The wine usually comes from Tillek or Southern Boll, so drinkers cannot be too choosy in their tippling.

Nabol has a three-cornered courtyard with the main entrance at one end and a kitchen courtyard surrounded by walls carved out of the cliff face at the other. The main entrance leads into the Great Hall. At the south end of the huge chamber are stairs leading up to the Lord Holder's apartment and into the Inner Hold.

The Lord Holder's apartment consists of four large rooms, each with tall shuttered windows facing obliquely toward the east. Each pane of glass is clear, a sample of expert glasscrafting; the choice of clear glass suggests that the Lord Holder who installed them mistrusted his people too much to obscure any part of his view with colored panes. A wide, curving stone hearth between the windows in the sleeping room helps retain the heat in the cold mountain air.

Narrow ramps carved into bubbles in the volcanic rock join the lower chambers with the entryway and the refectory hall, and a steep stairway on the north side of the Great Hall allows access to the Lord Holder's chambers. The kitchen is large, with two sets of ovens and five spit-runs for roasting whole herdbeasts.

Along the main hallway past the kitchen are the stairs to the lower level and the glow room. An ancillary hallway leads off to a row of locked storerooms. Out the kitchen door to the left is the ashpit, set as far as possible from the main Hold door.

The current Lord Holder is a man named Deckter, a remote relative of the last Lord and one believed to break the pattern of dishonest and grasping leaders in Nabol's history.

Meron of Nabol, the unlamented Lord who preceded Deckter, managed in only a few Turns to make himself nearly as notorious as Fax. He was not of Lord Holder's Blood, but served as Fax's steward and was quick enough to step into his dead Master's place. The other Lord Holders took their time confirming him in his rank, but they let him pass when other concerns required their attention. Thread had begun to fall, and the Weyr was again rising to prominence.

Meron was responsible in part for the deaths of two queen dragons, Prideth and Wirenth, in High Reaches Weyr. Both queen riders survived, but Kylara, Meron's mistress, was left mindless. Wirenth's rider,

Brekke, was prevented from suicide through the efforts of Manora and F'nor of Benden.

Meron further demonstrated his contempt for dragonkind by trying to coerce his Impressed bronze fire lizard to go *between* to the Red Star even before the Weyrleaders had had a chance to decide if it safe to do so. Against the better interests of the northern Lords and Weyrleaders, he continued illicit trading with the Oldtimers in the South, and traded green fire lizard eggs for valuable goods, thereby tricking his vendors, whom he considered gullible enough to believe they were getting good value.

His last act of malicious interference, on his deathbed, was to refuse to name an heir to Nabol, hoping to throw the Hold into confusion after he died. However, under coercion he named Deckter, a grand-nephew, who he believed would displease his tormentors. Lord Deckter was, in fact, the choice hoped for by the other Lord Holders and the Harper Hall.

Nabol has rich grasslands, on which the Nabolese raise ovines and domestic wherries. Like Lemos and upper Telgar, Nabol is experimenting in forestry to propagate the valuable and sought-after pine, ash, and other softwoods for furniture. Willow trees grow along the river flowing through the Esvay Valley, and lavender and mustard do well on the slopes nearby. The sandy soil is also suitable for tubers and root vegetables, and salad vegetables of all kinds: celery, brassicae, greens, and fingerroots (carrots). Some wine grapes grow on the slopes, but Nabolese also have a taste for pressed cider, which they make from their own apples, an innovation begun by the Holder whom Fax deposed. That Lord had cultivated the orchards planted by a Nabol Lord many generations back, in an effort to create another marketable product.

RUATHA HOLD

Ruatha Hold: Chequy, bright red and dark brown

Ruatha, the second oldest Hold in the Northern Continent, has given Pern many of its most famous Weyrwomen. It is also the breeding place of the finest runnerbeasts on Pern.

At the time Ruatha was first inhabited, Fort Hold had reached the bursting point with all the former inhabitants of the Southern Continent. Ruatha's lovely valley and cave system was only two days' ride on horseback from Fort Hold, and its grass flats and portageable river were suitable for raising food animals and transporting them elsewhere easily. Red Hanrahan, who first called the stakehold Redsford Hold for the fast-flowing river between it and Fort, elected to move into the new Hold with his family. In time, the Hold's name was translated to the Irish for Red's Ford, "Rua Atha." The saying came to be known that "Fort Hold just happened, but Ruatha was planned." It was designed to be expanded as need arose.

Red Hanrahan was a veterinarian with an uncanny way with animals. Between the dragons and the herd beasts, Fort Hold had become too crowded for the breeding of healthy beasts, Red moved his half of the problem to Ruatha, where he was able to allow the beasts to multiply rapidly, some-times producing three lambs at a time out of a single ewe. The meat was desperately needed by the Fort Holders. With the help of the dragonriders, the beasts were rounded up and herded into the caverns. Refrigeration was still possible, so the meat was frozen as soon as it was slaughtered. Dressed meat went downstream past what is now Ruatha River Hold, south to the Fort Hold water, and upstream. Vegetables and fruit raised in the hydroponics tanks at Fort Hold went back to Ruatha, balancing out the beast-holders' diet.

Red and his family loved horses. Though they were of little value as a meat animal or as a beast of burden until the roads could be finished, he still spent time raising them. With the sperm and ova available, he could breed for strength, speed, and beauty in riding stock. He raised heavy horses, too. The mechanical plows would run out of fuel soon enough, and Red had in mind Clydesdale-Shire stock, as well as oxen, to take their place.

Ruatha was much larger in its earliest days than in later Turns, when many of the inhabitants moved out to smaller holds after the end of the First Pass. When the rooms were no longer in use, the rear corridors were blocked off. Most of the additions had been built on the outside of the Hold rather than the inside.

Descendants of Red and Brian Hanrahan continued to Hold in Ruatha. In the Sixth Pass, Lord Alessan's family still maintained the tradition of raising runnerbeasts, the genetically adapted equines. Alessan had the empathy for both runner and dragon that caused dragonriders on Search to ask for him, but his father, Lord Leef, refused to let him go, as he was to be heir to Ruatha.

Alessan's father wanted his son to breed strong beasts of burden that could work hard on little food, but Alessan did just the opposite, and he created a supreme stock of racing runnerbeasts. These, tragically, became almost the only remnant of the glorious history of Ruathan horseflesh after the plague. Alessan's descendants held Ruatha until shortly before the Present Pass, when Lessa, last of the Ruathan Blood, went to Benden Weyr.

Except for an interruption of Turns during which Fax broke Ruatha into the ruin it was when Jaxom and his regent, Lord Lytol, took Hold, Ruatha was the site of the most prestigious runnerbeast Gathers on Pern. To be asked to race one's beasts at Ruatha was to receive an honor much sought after among breeders. Lord Jaxom has been striving to re-create Ruatha's former greatness.

In Lord Leef's day, Ruatha was much smaller and less ornate than it is now. Alessan himself began the new construction that increased the Hold's size and utility. The courtyard wall was a simple one, and the tower and gates that now block entrance from the causeway road were added over the Turns. Over the next thousand Turns new stables were built out from the southern end of the old one. Women's quarters were constructed over the kitchen complex, and many small crafholds grew in the shelter of the cliffs and the ramp. The watch-wher den in which Lessa took shelter did not exist in Moreta's and Alessan's day. But Alessan's precious racetrack is still where it was a thousand Turns ago.

The stables were converted within the last ten Turns into a combination weyr and sleeping room for Lord Jaxom and the white dragon Ruth.

Lessa herself is the last full-blooded descendant of the Ruathan house. Through a curious discovery that had been lost over four hundred Turns, she was able to go back *between* times thirteen Turns to save herself from Fax's slaughter of her family. (That the

process was known in Moreta's day is evident to modern dragonriders; no single dragonrider merely going *between* places could have covered all the stops necessary to deliver the life-giving serum in the course of a single day.) Another jump in time verified Lessa's discovery. She went forward ten Turns from her childhood to the day on which F'lar came to Ruatha on Search and killed Fax.

Benden Weyr, during the beginning of the Ninth (current) Pass, was becoming desperate. It was evident that the number of dragons and riders was too small to combat Thread adequately. No solution had yet been found either to the haunting "Question Song," which held the clue to the reason for the five empty Weyrs. Once Lessa had learned to go *between* times, she became convinced that the five Weyrs had come forward in time to her era, to fight Thread in the new Pass. No one else believed her, so she took it upon herself to prove it and save Pern. There had once hung in the main Hall a tapestry, a

Lessa

treasured family heirloom of the House of Ruatha, which Lessa believed depicted the Hold as it had been four hundred Turns before. When the tapestry was woven, the carven door cap and lintels had not yet been added, nor had the Tower, gate, or second courtyard.

Once she had returned the tapestry to Ruatha, Lessa used it as a focus for Ramoth to travel *between* four hundred Turns into the past. The effort nearly killed both of them, but Lessa's solution to the "Question Song" was the correct one. In fact, it was her urging that had prompted it to be written, so that through the temporal anomaly, she could later solve it. Lessa returned to her Turn with eighteen hundred fighting dragons and seventeen queens to fight the next Fall.

The Oldtimers, as they came to be known, were a mixed blessing. Their Pass had been over just long enough that they were bored with peace. In the Weyr there is not much to do during Interval. The Oldtimers had developed an adrenaline addiction from being under constant tension for fifty Turns that made it impossible to slow down. The younger Oldtimers had an easier time adjusting to the end of the Pass, but the condition was permanent in the longtime fighters. It takes only four Turns to make it irreversible. Providing them with the challenge of a new Pass probably saved the sanity of many.

SOUTHERN BOLL HOLD

Southern Boll Hold: On a white field, bright red Chevrons

A Hold was established by Emily Boll and Pierre de Courcis to the south of Fort Hold amidst the tropical lushness of the peninsula, after Emily recovered from the injuries suffered in a shuttle crash during the ninth year of the colony. The stonecutters were employed to cut roads down to the chosen site and to help the holders start making their home habitable. It was called Southern at first, for its position south of Fort. After Governor Emily Boll's death in 33, the stakeholders decided to honor her by naming their home for her. They simply appended her name and called it Southern-Boll. After a brief time, the hyphen was dropped from use.

Pack animals travel the long, terraced road to Southern Boll. The road is good but steep in places, so travelers prefer not to try to maneuver wagons all the way south. The Hold has no port of its own, so traders call in at Hold Gar, two days ride to the north, for the many goods produced in Southern Boll.

Surrounded as it is on three sides by the cool end of the oceanic current, the Hold boasts hot, balmy weather in all seasons. Hats will not stay on in the constant wind, so those who live in Southern Boll tend toward veils, head scarves, and turbans. For those who do not mind the sun, muumuus, sarongs, bikinis, and daishikis are not uncommon wear; there is even the occasional grass skirt.

Boll also uses furniture made of twisted vines like wicker wound around metal supports. Instead of heavy padding, chairs are made with slings in light, flexible frames, or with caned backs and seats.

Southern Boll, Ista, and Nerat have very large populations, as do most tropical zones, where a person does not have to work hard merely to exist. Occasional occupation will help eke out a satisfactory living for a family that can gather most of what it needs to feed itself from the countryside. Telgar and Keroon also have a large indolent population in the southern reaches. Boll brings in a lot of fish, and the heavy jungle is full of fruit trees and wild melon vines. Soft fruits, like bananas, kiwi, and mangoes, are cultivated alongside goru pear, wedgenut, and peach trees. The more delicate cooking and medicinal herbs and hot-climate spices provide trade goods and season light dishes served in the heat of the day.

Some of the few remaining flocks of chickens live in the Hold. Southern Boll makes up for its isolation by having many goods for trade with the North that cannot be found in any other Hold.

Southern Boll also raises numerous herbs used to make tea. The Earth genus *Camellia* from which tea came did not survive, but tasty, stimulating, soothing substitutes were found among native herbs and blends of imported ones. Fruit liquors as well as grape wines are popular here, and many bottles are exported to other Holds for special occasions.

The Hold boasts the presence of the secondary Glasscrafthall. The Mastersmith, to whom Glassmaster Arkeli looks, lauds the high quality of the fine sands that line Southern Boll's beaches. Glassblowing and ceram-

Swimming at Southern Boll

ics are taught here. Apprentice jars and bottles can be distinguished from those journeyman-made by the concentration of pale green tint, showing impurities in the glass. Well-blown glass is perfectly clear. Colored sand is sometimes used to produce tinted glass, as are certain metals, to create what Terrans refer to as cobalt, cranberry, and ruby glass. Carnival glass is made on occasion, as are leaded crystal and plate glass.

The original plate glass is still in the windows of the main Hold. One handsome window ringed with a stained-glass mosaic looks in upon the Lord Holder's chamber, spilling rainbows across the floor.

Southern Boll is full of color. The range of tropical trees and plants produces a riot of bright flowers and shoots. Even the products of the small Minecrafthold here are especially colorful. Ruby, all the varieties of garnet, green malachite, copper, and blue copper sulfate come out of the mines in the mountains behind the Hold.

WEAVERCRAFTHALL

Weaver:
On a white field, a lavender Bolt of Cloth

Tailor:
On a white field, a lavender Needle and Spool

The presence of a major Crafthall has an effect on what crops are raised in the Hold. Unlike most Holds, in which food crops take almost absolute precedence over all others during a Pass, Southern Boll raises Earth flax and a Pernese fiber similar to it, sisal, and cotton to trade with the Weavercrafthall. The natural abundance of other food allows the holders to make the choice to grow a fiber crop. The Hall provides employment for a number of Southern Boll's men and women.

Flax produces an elegant, crisp cloth that stands up well Turn after Turn. Though it is difficult to make smooth, sisal, when beaten and pulped, makes a silky fabric easy to print or dye that is light enough to be worn in the hottest weather. It can also be woven into nearly invisible sheers. But it is cotton which is in the greatest demand and which is in the shortest supply by the end of every Pass. Cotton, for its tremendous flexibility, is a luxury fiber on Pern. Cotton seed lasts nearly forever in dry climates. The plant likes sand-and-clay soil, so Southern Boll is a very good choice for a source.

The colonists kept cotton alive as a species because nothing served so well for wearing against the skin to soak up perspiration, and in layers for warmth. By the first Interval, every scrap of cotton they had with them was in shreds. They grew all they could during the Interval and kept up the custom of stockpiling it throughout the cycles. Silk quickly became a memory, for though the colonists' ova banks contained silkworms, the mulberry bushes that are the worms' only food were not viable on Pern.

The Weavercraft trades their goods with High Reaches, Lemos, Bitra, Nabol, and Igen for the long fleece from mountain ovines, as their own ovines, evolved for the warm climate, do not grow thick coats. High Reaches also provides them with llama hair. Holders frequently make use of drop-spindles or spinning wheels in the evening while listening to music or sharing a chat with friends. Part of a dragonrider's evening occupation might be spinning or weaving. Everyone who can is always making thread, as so much of it is needed. During the Intervals, the Masterweaver has a number of students from the Weyrs in his Hall. There are small looms in every Hall, Hold, and Weyr, either for hobby or serious employment. Cloth goods are useful in every occupation. Because the Weavercraft cannot possibly supply every Hold, each makes its own hand looms, crochet hooks, spindles, and shuttles.

Since the Weavercraft's goods are not perishable, tremendous stocks can be kept in dry caverns until called for. For every type of fiber, there are different wheels and looms: flax wheels, wool wheels, sisal wheels (very delicate), and cotton wheels of every size and strength, and looms from the very simple to the infinitely complex. As a spinner finishes drawing a spool of thread half as big and fully as heavy as himself, he passes it on to the dyers, who tint and dry it. The Weavercrafthall is famous for certain special dyes whose compositions are considered a deep, dark craft secret. Master Zurg's signature is evident in thread of rich golden, brilliant orange, or special purple hues. Most of the rainbow dyes come from shellfish found off the coast.

Once the thread is colored or bleached, it is either covered and stored or passed on to the weavers or knitters. Weavers receive training in making looms and devices for working yarn. A bit of cloth is reserved for very skilled Weavercraft artists who paint the dye directly onto cloth by hand, for one-of-a-kind lengths of fancy fabric.

Some of the looms here can be used only by the most talented of weavers. A Masterweaver might make slubbed fabrics like velour, or cotton velvet, or brocades. The skill that produced the brocade looms used to

make the famous Fort Hold brocades came from here. Flax, polished cotton, and metal-wrapped threads simulate Earth-made patterned fabrics of silk, examples of which are in the Weavercrafthall museum. Every large Hold has an upright tapestry loom or two, on which are made wall hangings and floor coverings to break up the endless gray of the stone walls.

As hardwood for shuttles and spindles was difficult to come by, the weavers first used plastic substitutes until the plastics wore out and the extrusion machines broke down. Then they turned to soapstone and agate, both light enough and easily smoothed into the right shapes.

The technology for building the equipment came to Pern with the colonists, who blended together two worlds worth of ancient home crafts. Patterns are simply copied over and over, with pieces being replaced as they wear out. Amerind standing looms, Swedish knitting belts, spindles, embroidery hoops, Centauri braiding trees, frames for slit-work tapestries—all have found favor at different times. The Craft patterns themselves have been passed down, too, from the minds of the dextrous and Craft-minded colonists and the data banks of the ships. Weaving, embroidery, and knitting, significant parts of many Earth cultures' identities, are now forged together as one. Afghans, granny circle blankets, flannels, burlap, and cambric are all the province of the Weavercrafthall. Silk-screening and dye patterns are recorded in the Hall's Archives for students to attempt to copy or to admire for their difficulty.

Decorative gloves are made of tatted lace, and even knit lace, made painstakingly from flax or cotton thread, but most everyday gloves are sewn of fine, soft fabrics woven from the neck fleece of young ovines.

The Weavercrafthall has an ongoing rivalry with the Tannercrafthall as the fashion

Loom

center on Pern. The Mastertailors evolve styles which the cognoscenti copy eagerly, but at which more conservative holders turn up their noses, and individualists ignore. What is "in" this season will be "out" again quickly enough. A native of Southern Boll, Masterweaver Zurg naturally favors the bright colors for which his home Hold is famous.

CROM HOLD

Crom Hold: On a yellow-gold field, three light blue Bends

Crom was one of the seven holds held by the conqueror Fax. It is perhaps the only one he came by legitimately, through his marriage to Gemma, Lady of Crom, daughter of the old Lord Holder. She died giving birth to Jaxom, named Lord Holder of Ruatha by his father shortly before his death. Lord Nessel, the man who took the Hold after Fax was killed, had much to do to repair Crom's impoverished condition. Like High Reaches and Ruatha in Fax's day, Crom had a reputation for being a stronghold for bullyboys and mercenaries.

The principal Hold lies near a tumbling river that threads its way southwest along the Western Mountain Range. The fields that feed the Hold lie to the south. The window embrasures and door lintels are without ornamental carving, as if the Lord Holder who commissioned them did not wish to take advantage of the Minecrafthold's masons so nearby. Some say the Hold has changed little under Nessel's hand. He does coerce his holders to buy blackstone to heat their houses; the holders consider Cromcoal an unnecessary expense when the southern part of the Hold provides so much pine and softwood, which burns cleaner and is free for the chopping.

There is not enough grass to sustain many herdbeasts in the north mountain reaches. Crom raises mostly ovines for meat and trades with neighboring Telgar for river grains and bovines. With the onset of the cold season, numerous animals are slaughtered, and the remaining beasts are brought into sheltered pens to weather out the snows. The Lady Holder and her steward see to the salting and preservation of hides, fleece, and meat. Crom raises the hardier of the medicinal and cooking herbs, such as sage, all the mints, rue against fleas, cinquefoil for bowel problems, and mugwort for gout.

Crom is beholden to Telgar Weyr, with which it has little direct contact, especially during the hard winters. They are divided by a spur of the Central Mountain Range beyond the Mastersmithhall. Weyrleader R'mart keeps in contact mainly through the watchdragon posted on the fireheights.

MINECRAFTHALL

Miner: On a white field, a black Pick and Shovel in Saltire

In Crom itself, the mines produce firestone, blackstone (also called Cromcoal), and sapphires, all of which are handy to the much-respected Minecrafthall. Like the Farmcraft, with which it has an ongoing rivalry, the Minecraft has many minor halls all over Pern. The skill of the Masterminer must extend not only to the excavation and shaping of minerals, but also to the knowledge of ecology of the land. The Minecraft is considered to be solid, honest, and reliable, as well as discreet. Its influence on Pern is deliberately underplayed by Masterminer Nicat, who would rather get on with his job and leave bickering to those with less to do.

Complaints fostered by the Masterfarmer, presently Andemon, usually have to do with disputed fields in which the Masterminer wants to dig and which the Farmcrafter wishes to plant. They each recognize the necessity for the other; without both of them, ecology would quickly break down, and life on Pern would be much less comfortable.

The Minecraft works hand in hand with the Smithcraft, for whom it digs ore and minerals in exchange for new and more efficient tools. Their functions frequently dovetail. Not only must the Masterminer be premier in his Craft, but he must also be able to coordinate with the Mastersmith. In effect, they are two halves of the same whole. The smith refines ore and puts it to its final uses. There are dozens of mines all over the planet, and Masterminer Nicat is in charge of them all.

He has in his service a huge number of harper journeymen who act as the communication system between him and his Masterminers. With the Harper Hall's aid, he keeps in close touch with what is happening in the world, both specific to his craft and of general interest. Nicat occasionally makes use of fire lizards as messengers, but he also uses the little dragon cousins in the mines for killing tunnel snakes and detecting gas leaks.

A miner may practice a specialty of his Craft. Some mine only gems, a science in itself. It takes a special skill to get the crystals out of matrix intact. Others seek liquid minerals, such as rock oil and natural gas, both useful to the Smithcraft. Geology and petrography are specialties of the Minecraft, though they are not known by those names. The minecraft also trains interested students in lapidary, spelunking, and mountain climbing, all of which require the study of the stress and structure of stone formations. The lapidary classes are especially popular in both Hold and Weyr. Gems have no specific value on Pern except as ornamentation and in limited functions within the Smithcraft. For example, the black diamonds found off the shore of Ista are not terribly sought after by amateur jewelers since they are not very pretty, but the stones make useful tools to the smiths.

Women in the Crafthall cut and polish stones to make their own jewelry, which they wear or barter freely. Agate and other pretty stones are traded around or given as gifts. Any stone that a man or woman considers attractive is used for making into a necklace or brooch. Most non-Craft students seek only to learn enough to polish the stones and to bore holes in them to put them on a necklace. The Smithcraft sells or barters tools for ladies to make jewelry, and sells some settings ready-made for the insertion of gems. Most stones come from the Minecraft, either in trade or as gifts.

Jewelry crafting employs shells, bone, and pretty bits of wood as well as cut and polished stones to make scrimshaw, pins, brooches, necklaces, and rings.

There are distinct regional tastes in Pernese jewelry. Pern has much the same range of precious and semiprecious stones as does Earth: the full range of colors of garnet and sapphire; tourmalines; agates of every kind including lace agate and moonstone; the full range of quartz crystals; and all the corundums, including beryl. Some untapped diamond pipes still exist in the Southern Hold in the Ninth Pass.

Far from being stagnant, the Minecraft seeks to expand its skills and to discover more of the Ancient knowledge that has been lost over thousands of Turns. Its many Halls Pernwide work to improve techniques and safety procedures in bringing out the ore efficiently.

GREENFIELDS HOLD

Greenfields Hold: On an aqua field, medium blue Bends

This huge farmcrafthold lies across the estuary on the same latitude as Nabol. Greenfields is a major grain producer and exporter. Its cliffhold caverns house only three hundred people, but many cotholds lie scattered in the fertile countryside around it.

TELGAR HOLD

Telgar Hold: Per Pale, bright red, white, and medium blue

The Hold was named for Sallah Telgar, pilot of Admiral Paul Benden's ship *Yokohama*, who is believed to have suffered from the architects were able to spend time. The corridors in each of the seven levels (five of living quarters, one for the Lower Caverns and kitchens, and one for the Drum Heights) are fairly even, slagged smooth with the stone-cutters. Each window is fitted with heavy bronze shutters.

A wide main entrance leads into the Great Hall. The hallway at the left rear of this huge, high chamber leads to the refectory, in which there are long rows of stone-topped tables and wooden-topped benches. In a storeroom just off the kitchen are even more tables and benches with their metal trestles, for use during the seasons of the year in which Telgar's population swells. The Lord Holder's chambers are directly above the main entrance. They are most ornate, lined with colorful tapestries and objets d'art from every part of Pern. In Larad's study, there are large maps of his Holdings on the wall, with colored markers depicting where each type of crop and beast is raised.

Telgar is one of the wealthiest, if not *the* wealthiest, of the major Holds. It houses the prestigious Smithcraft; contrary to current belief, the Craft and *not* the Hold was the reason for settling this rich valley. The water-driven wheels that spin in the swift current of the Telgar River to the northeast of the Hold have curiously shaped parts which are older than anyone can remember. Other minor industrial Crafts have their home here as well. Farriers and blacksmiths are sent here from all over Pern to learn skills to take back home. Telgar is famous for its etching and engraving, and its skill at producing all types of printed fabric, silk screen, and batik. Until recently, the Woodcraft was here, but it was moved to Lemos, nearest the best supply of wood, after the Mastersmith and the Lord Holder of Lemos gave their approval.

The vast fields in Telgar produce most of the grain consumed throughout the north. And for those looking for a good pint, the

Telgar Hold

treachery of Avril Bitra and her associates, but historians from Bitra and Lemos bitterly dispute that interpretation.

This is the largest Hold in present-day Pern. The stone palisade in which it is situated looks like the prow of a ship, with one great flat face turned west and the other east, as is considered proper for a major hold. (All holds are expected to have an eastern face, to watch out for Thread.) From the Great Court, the Hold commands a tremendous vista of the valley to the south. A thousand people live in the Hold complex, and the Hold supports some fifteen thousand others in the immediate area.

Upon the gate are twin watchtowers overlooking the ramp down to the road. With all of the activities centered in Telgar, it is not unreasonable for the Steward to want to keep a close watch on the comings and goings.

Telgar is another Hold upon which the

best beer on Pern comes from Telgar, brewed from that very grain.

Much of a Hold's character comes from its Lord Holder. Lord Larad is young but considered to be strong, a fine organizer, and an amiable man. His holders and stewards value his simple approval more than copious words of praise from any other man.

Telgar often has some rough weather over the course of a Turn. The main Hold tends to get snowed in during the cold season, so it must be self-sufficient. It needs to care for more than its own permanent population, since traders and their families commonly winter over in Telgar, where they are welcomed by Larad, a willing host.

Trader:
On a white field, a steel-gray Four-Spoke Cartwheel

In the spring, the traders leave Telgar for their annual circuit of the Northern Continent. Most follow the traditional road, traveling west to Crom, Nabol, the High Reaches, Tillek, down to Southern Boll, up to Ruatha, then to Fort Hold, where they take ship for Ista. The traders debark in Nerat, travel north and west to Greystones and Valley Hold or Half Circle, and finally converge in Benden Hold. As the weather begins to turn cool, they follow the river road down into Keroon and Igen, and travel up the Great Dunto River back to Telgar before the weather traps them elsewhere.

Sea Traders begin their routes in Tillek or Fort Sea Hold and stop in at Ista, Big Bay, Igen, Keroon, and Nerat. Telgar sends its goods downriver to Big Bay by means of shore luggers, heavy haulers something like river barges; not very fast but very safe, the shore luggers can carry a considerable amount of goods.

As quarters are very cramped in the winter, Larad needs to keep a close eye on organization to prevent some of his temporary population from starting brawls out of boredom. The best harpers are in his employ to lead singing and provide entertainment. Some of the most complicated dances are devised in Telgar over the long winter season.

Telgar sends out patrols in the winter to make sure those living in small outlying holds are all right. In the mild spring and summer, itinerant harpers can bring the alarm back to Telgar if help is needed in a small hold, but in winter the snow is usually too deep for a single man to make the circuit safely. The Telgar Weyrleader will lend a support system of weyrlings if he is in a good mood, and normally provides rescue riders in the case of an avalanche.

Besides the traders, Telgar also occasionally hosts other wanderers, some who pride themselves on their independence, and others who are merely eccentric.

A very rare talent is known as a "nose," a person whose olfactory sense is so finely developed that he is able to determine the components of an aromatic solution, or to compile one. Such people are vital to the design and production of perfumes. A woman named Mariko wanders between Telgar and Ista throughout the Turn, gathering fragrant herbs and mosses. She started out in the Winecraft, but found she was more interested in scents than tastes and retired to pursue her own Craft.

She prefers to travel by herself, but lately she has been shadowed by a companion, a young woman who follows her, eager to learn Mariko's secrets. The old woman is too crafty for her young companion and eludes her when gathering certain ingredients for her inimitable perfumes. Mariko is not sure how she gets her results, and she is not ready to tell anyone her methods yet.

MEASUREMENTS

fingertip—½ inch wide

hand—4 inches

hand-span—extended thumb to little fingertip; 8–9 inches

man-height—varies; over 5 feet 2 inches, under 6 feet 2 inches

dragonlength—size of a green; 40 feet

weaver's-length—from nosetip to extended arm fingertip; approximately 1 yard

Various crafts, such as the Smithcraft, have their own special sets of measurements. Fandarel has evolved descriptions of the sizes of microscopic objects seen through his magnifying device. In Leathercraft and Woodcraft, necessary calibrations for the thickness of hide or wood are established by the use of metal calipers and rules provided by the Smithcraft. In the Weavercraft, cloth grades are established by the Masterweaver based on how many threads lie in a square fingertip of cloth.

Mariko blends the herbs into a base of rendered fat or pure alcohol saved for her by friends who remained in the Winecraft. With only a runnerbeast and a pack animal, she travels far in the warm seasons, compiling new perfumes and soothing herbals, which she barters in the cold seasons for food, shelter, and clothing.

Mariko is a throwback to the Japanese racial type, with wide cheekbones, a delicate nose and chin, and epicanthic folds. No one knows exactly how old she is. She is allowed to stay in the Smithcraft any time she appears, because Fandarel likes her, understanding her single-minded devotion to her Craft.

SMITHCRAFTHALL

Smith:
On a white field,
a bright red Anvil

Fandarel represents the Smithcraft as only a man of his bulk and competence can. The endless search for efficiency makes the Smithcraft one of the most progressive of the crafts. Techniques are in constant flux with new technology to create the best and the fastest with the most sparing use of precious raw materials. Neatness counts.

The Smithcraft and the Minecraft work

closely together. One supplies raw materials while the other supplies the tools with which the first can do its job.

The Crafthall was set up here, north of what came to be Telgar Hold, because of its proximity to the necessary ore and raw materials and to the Telgar River, which flows swiftly and deep down from the Northern Barrier Range all the way to the Big Bay. The earliest smiths set water-driven wheels in the Telgar to run their machinery. The great wheeled barges follow Telgar's riverbank from the iron mines north of the Hold and continue their runs taking refined materials and finished goods down to the Sea Hold.

Processes that were lost to the colonists over the Turns are tackled with enthusiasm by journeymen and masters of this craft. The smith's motto is "If it has been done, it can be done again." As equipment that the colonists brought with them wore out, facile minds in the Smithcraft had to find other ways of doing the same things.

Under Fandarel's direction, the Smithcraft has re-created distance viewers, invented the distance writer by combining litmus paper oscillographs with telegraphy, copied the Oldtimers' flamethrowers, and done chemical research that resulted in the use of agenothree (HNO_3, nitric acid) as a combination Threadbane and airborne fertilizer. The smith's more ordinary occupations include overseeing his many Craftmasters, who are engaged in a variety of specialties.

The Smithcraft embraces a number of occupations. The masons who construct a building may come from the Minecraft, but the stress analyses of the stone and foundation are done by the Smithcraft. Some Masters concentrate on making tools and doing practical metalwork. The Craft makes cooking vessels of all sizes, some with a nonstick coating to ease cleanup. Other Master metalsmiths do fancy metal crafting, such as casting jewelry.

Journeymen work up to mastery in their choice of specialties, doing the uncomplicated and heavy work so the various masters are free to practice their skills. Apprentices may begin by sorting ore and working the bellows for metalsmiths, or extruding wire through wire plates for Master Fandarel's distance-writer project.

Among the newest projects on which Fandarel is setting loose his brainstormers are some of the artifacts coming out of the caves around the Ancient Timers' Plateau. Disassembled machinery of all kinds has been found coated in grease or transparent hidelike material. Some of the machines use magnetics, which the Smithcraft understands. Some use nickel oxide batteries, which are similar in function if not appearance to the acid batteries and Leyden jars which the Smithcraft is currently using for metal plating and running the distance writer.

The Glasscraft and the Woodcraft are offshoots of the Smithcrafthall, each in its own building in the complex. Journeyman smiths interested in the Glasscraft will be immersed in work in everything from ceramics to lead crystal to porcelain. This branch practices glassblowing that ranges in complexity from flasks to bottles to windowpanes to lenses for the distance viewer and microscope. Wansor, the starsmith, came from this discipline, where he specialized in optics.

Woodcrafters begin with whittling and go on to working with chisel and saw, creating furniture, toys, jewelry, and a new invention, paper, from the slowly increasing supply of that precious commodity of wood. Smiths who have a knack for chemistry formulate stains, dyes, varnishes, and cleaning compounds in their own building, which is at far remove from the others. (Among the other compounds they create are explosives.) In these disciplines, the apprentices spend a great deal of their time washing pots and retorts, sifting sand, and sweeping.

A Smithcraft apprenticeship is one of the longest, but at its end the graduate journeyman is a practicing member of one of the most respected Crafts on Pern.

Distance Viewer

STARCRAFT

Starsmith:
On a white field,
a bright red
Eight-Pointed Star

This is an offshoot of the Smithcraft, personified by Wansor. Wansor was a glass-smith who was assigned to study the new distance-viewer and small-seer that were brought back from Benden Weyr by Fandarel. He discovered the practical applications of the distance-viewer and began the important work of charting the skies around Pern. With his aid, Lord Jaxom and the Benden Weyrleaders were able to understand the maps found in the shuttle buried in the Ship Meadow. Wansor also trained the viewer on the Red Star. Studies of that wandering world are still ongoing, and little of use is yet known to dragonriders, who would like to put an end to the menace of Thread at what they believe to be its source.

TELGAR WEYR

Telgar Weyr:
On a white field,
a Field of Grain
in black

Telgar was one of the earliest Weyr sites chosen, but it was the last of the Ancient Weyrs to be occupied.

Tremendous ore deposits of iron, copper, lead, zinc, vanadium, and coal were found above the place where the Hold was founded. Rock oil was discovered, too, but its applications were limited to industrial use. Also noticed was the broad crater, not unlike the one near the eastern shore of the Northern Continent and the one to the southwest near the great Fort cavern.

Because Telgar was a mininghold first, there was little need to protect the vegetation. What protection was needed was flown by the riders from Igen Weyr. It was easier for the miners and smiths if the bare rock was exposed. The men in the mines had little to fear from a threat that could not eat stone, metal, or water. Gradually, as the demand increased to expand farms to include the fertile fields below the Hold, the Weyr was established. Telgar quickly grew in prominence as a Hold rich in natural resources and good grain.

Telgar's Weyr Bowl lies in a huge volcano at the top of the Central Mountain Range just south of its junction with the Northern Barrier. It protects the woodlands of Lemos to its east and the grainlands to the west.

This Weyr shamed itself during the Great Plague by refusing to lend dragonriders to aid Moreta and the others who volunteered to carry serum to the runnerbeast Holds, which needed it to prevent a second outbreak. Because of their insult to the Weyrwoman, she vowed to ignore them in their need and brought the serum herself to the parts of Keroon they would have covered, exhausting the elderly queendragon carrying her and sending her *between* forever.

The current Weyrleader enjoys a mutual respect with the Benden Weyrleaders. The show of unity at Lord Asgenar's wedding in Telgar Hold cemented the relationship between the Oldtimers and the modern dragonweyr.

SOUTH TELGAR HOLD

South Telgar Hold: Per Pale, bright red and medium blue

South Telgar lies at the same latitude as Igen Weyr. It is situated on the south bank of the river flowing west across the Telgar plain. The Hold was constructed especially for the denizens of Telgar who could not tolerate the hard winter weather in the main Hold. Many of the older folk come here when they retire from their duties in Telgar. The site was chosen for the Hold because a mineral spring bubbles to the surface not far from the bank of the river. The high limestone content makes the spring water spas naturally effervescent.

The daring soul who founded South Telgar broke with many Traditions (and common sense, some say) by constructing a stone complex in the shelter of the cliffs—not inside the cliff itself, which faces west. The main Hold faces east.

South Telgar has a Healer Hall almost as big as the main Hall in Fort Hold. It is in a separate building near the Hold. The Masterhealer oversees a broad training program in pediatrics and geriatrics. Apprentice healers and nurses can begin their instruction here before taking their journeymen's examinations in Fort. The climate is warm enough to make use of the mineral springs all year round, for the relief of joint ailments suffered by many of the Hall's elderly patients.

ISTA HOLD

Ista Hold: Per Pale, bright orange and white

The name "Ista" is an acronym for the four families of colonists who settled the Big Island. The island seemed to be unlucky for those who claimed it as their stakehold: first Avril Bitra, then Nabhi Nabol, both of whom died before the Second Crossing. Those who came to stay on the island afterward kept its reputation in mind, but if Ista had once had any malice toward the settlers, it appeared to have been spent.

Joel Lilienkamp spent his last years here after the last of the mechanized transports wore out. One of his children helped establish Ista Weyr in the forty-second year of the colony.

Ista is well into the tropical zone. Its temperature throughout a Turn never goes below 55 degrees during the day, and is often very hot indeed. Like the people of Southern Boll, Istans sleep on hammocks instead of rope beds, and wear either many layers of thin fabric or very little at all, depending on how each person chooses to deal with the heat.

All the seagoing traders stop at Ista coming and going along their routes. Ista exports native fish and spider claws, fine handiwork, gems, and herbs. Fiber plants of all kinds grow huge here. Ista occasionally supplies Southern Boll with sisal. Healers come

from the Healer Hall in Fort Hold to gather needlethorn. Mariko, the wandering "nose," spends a few months every Turn here, purchasing essences from certain Ancient suppliers who claim they are even older than she—but they decline to say how old that is.

A past Lord Holder with a green thumb managed to propagate citrus trees in Ista. The fruit is popular, especially in the coldest Holds, where the juice is used to help stave off colds. The groves of orange, yellow, and green fruit with mottled rinds are a particular treasure of the Istan Lord Holders. Sweetcane, the source of sweetening in the South as sweet-roots are in the north, is grown in Ista and Nerat. For those who like spicy dishes, the farmcrafters also raise endless varieties of peppers, ranging from very mild to dragonfire.

Shell jewelry is popular here. Mother-of-pearl, scrimshaw, and cameos, not to mention strung lengths of tiny, pretty shells, are common adornments for both men and women. Ista is also known for the emeralds of a clear, deep blue-green that are still found occasionally in its mines. The official badge of a Lord Holder requires one of these marvelous emeralds, as a Craftmaster's makes use of a sapphire, which also can be found in Ista.

An intermittent crater peak that surfaces occasionally off the southwest coast of the island is believed to be the source of the black stone beach, which the local stonecutters from Ista's Minecrafthold say is made up of granulated black diamonds. The Smithcrafthall in Telgar appreciates an occasional sack of the dust, which has numerous applications in toolmaking.

Ista is very well populated, though its people are spread out over a wide area. Ista island is very large. In every cove where there is access to the sea, a few hundred people live by taking what they need off the land, and by

Upper Level

Main Level

Lower Level

HARPER HALL

fishing. As all along Nerat and Southern Boll, the Istan coastline is dense with humanity. It is possible, in fact comfortable, to live in a thatched cottage during an interval. Holds in the tropics have more access to fruit, which they barter to other Holds for goods they need, especially in seasons when the harvests were bad elsewhere.

The Island is the site of the great harpers' enclave at Turnover Gather. One of the Lord Holders had a huge Harper Hall built in Ista for the sake of his Lady wife, a journeywoman harper with whom he fell in love. For her sake, he determined to make their Hall "the next center of the Harpercraft," a rival center for music. Ista only has two or three harpers at a time, who rattle around like beans in the big, echoing, empty Hall. There is rarely need for more than a voice Master, an instrument Master, and their apprentices. In all its history, it was never packed to the brim until the idea was proposed to hold Turnover Gather in it.

For those from the temperate climate, celebrating Turnover in Ista is a treat. Because there is no need to sleep under a roof when Thread is not falling, Ista can host many more harpers and guests than almost any other Hold. The Gather has grown in size since its inception and is now a major event in the Northern Continent.

ISTA WEYR

Ista Weyr: On a bright orange field, a Smoking Mountain in black

Ista, the fifth Weyr, is one of the most curiously constructed. Situated on the bay at the southwest corner of the Big Island, the black half volcano thrusts four fingers and a thumb into the tropical sky. The mountain must have been formed by an eruption that knocked the bay half of its caldera into the sea, letting lava flow in a gradual drop-off, which the pounding of the current has worn away into a plateau. For all its tiny size, Ista has a mind-boggling, mazelike warren of narrow tunnels that double back and run into one another.

Just offshore, a small mountain surfaces once in a while when there are earthshakes or upheaveals. The beach under Ista Weyr is sand that, when inspected, proves to be black diamond dust.

Ista supplements the lack of dragonrider weyrs with "forest weyrs," cliffside dwellings on the *outer* face of the Bowl. It attained its full population shortly before the Second Pass in the year 258. Fresh water flows into the caverns from the northeast through underground streams. The corral where the herdbeasts graze has an artificial pool filled from pipes coming through the Weyr. With

Ista Weyr

the sea so near at hand, there is no need for a bathing pool for dragons, though the dragonets who have not yet learned to fly like to bathe under the cataract of the artificial waterfall created by Ista Weyr's architects in the north wall of the Bowl.

The Old Time Weyrleader of Ista, D'ram, declared the mating flight of his junior queen Caylith open after the death of his Weyrwoman. The current Ista Weyrleader, G'dened, is a son of D'ram.

D'ram removed to Southern, where he drew attention to the handsome bay in which Cove Hold was later constructed. In time, he assumed the Weyrleadership at Southern, holding his own with Lord Toric. D'ram has shown interest in the archaeological excavations in the Landing plateau and elsewhere, lending the aid of his younger riders and dragons to dig and sort artifacts.

IGEN HOLD

Igen Hold: Per Pale, bright red and golden yellow

Igen Hold lies above the marshy flats on the eastern edge of the great desert that stretches all the way southwest to Keroon Bay. Igenites are hardy folk. Their chief items of trade are river grains (rice), ovines, runnerbeasts, and the opals and turquoises that the local Minecrafthall digs out of caves and gorges that were once seabed. Though they cannot compete with Lemos for the lushness of Lord Holder Asgenar's hardwood and fruitwood forests, Lord Laudey has taken advantage of the Weyrs' new attitude on wood and is allowing Igen's forests to burgeon.

Igen lies south of the imaginary line of demarcation between the temperate and tropical climate belts.

There are few holders in the bleak expanse of the desert, so most of the population is to be found along the coastlines. Those who have vast herds live with them to the northwest of the Hold in the grassy plains east of Igen Weyr, and the Hold's farmlands lie to the South along the river. The Hold itself overlooks a shelf of rock high above the Igen River, a broad, shallow, muddy stream that flows south dividing Igen from Keroon.

Igen Garb

Family holds are chiseled and chipped into the windswept cliff faces south of the Hold entrance. There are no cotholds at the foot of the Hold because the river tends to flood frequently, submerging the sandy, clay-based banks, and also because the natural caverns are large and plentiful. Igen has no fire-heights, but there is no green within dragon-lengths of the Hold or family dwellings. During the dry season, the thick red mud of the river is revealed, driving what is left of the shallow, fast-running stream into braided channels.

Because of the hot, dry climate, the holders adopt styles of dress unique to Igen. Burnoose robes are common, as are broad-brimmed hats, high-crowned to provide plenty of room to cool the scalp underneath during the long days. Under the wide hats protecting their faces from the sun, Igen women wear veils and snoods over their hair to keep out the dust. They favor bright colors and resemble fantastic insects in the shimmering landscape of the desert.

Other concessions to comfort include the use of the hammock. Rush bags and furs are too warm in any season, and are reserved for the sick—and for those from Holds hotter than Igen. Deep sandstone caverns under the Hold are filled with ice and snow brought in at night by dragons and stored in straw to keep food from spoiling. Food that will not keep any other way is dried and later reconstituted. Sorbets, ices, fools, and ice creams are special treats, and workers keep pitchers of cold drinks handy inside straw-padded boxes to prevent heat exhaustion.

Igen is a big trade center. Traders whose warehouses are in Big Bay, and the runner-beast breeders of Katz Field, find Igen a convenient jumping-off point for sending shipments on to Keroon, Nerat, Benden, and the rest of eastern Pern.

Gathers at Igen Hold would appear to be sleepy and dull during the day. Everyone moves slowly in the heat, and the dances are slow and graceful. At night, Igen awakens as the air begins to cool. The Gather square is open to the sky only in the dancing square. The rest of it is covered with sheltering cloth or hide canopies with tentlike sides that divide walkway from Gather stalls, and the stalls from each other. Folk take naps in the hottest part of the day, preparing for the lively evening. At dusk, the dances speed up, and conversation becomes lively.

Drinks are served in long tubes that "sweat," keeping the liquid inside them cool the way that botas do. Igen raises plenty of tropical fruit: melons, berries, rind-fruit, redfruit, and genetically altered descendants of pineapple and kiwi berries, two very juicy fruits popular with the holders.

Lord Laudey of Igen allows the Holdless folk to shelter without charge in the great cavern complexes near the Igen River, providing they break no laws or bother any holder. The wanderers suffer the greatest hardship during Threadfall. Those who were not rendered Holdless as a matter of justice for wrongdoing, but simply prefer the road under their feet to a roof over their heads, are not welcome in Holds already crowded by those who have a right to be there. In many places, for the privilege of safety during a Fall, the Holdless may be cheated of their marks of forced to work many hours for mere shelter.

The Holdless are not necessarily a criminal element. Among the complement of passengers aboard the three colony ships were nearly a thousand men, women, and children from several tribes of Gypsies and other wanderers who once lived in many nations on Earth. The brands of thief and vandal were not applied to them when they awoke on Pern. Instead, it was the wanderers who were disconcerted. They were used to doing odd jobs and stealing to make their way, but on

Pern, they found that they could ask for what they wanted; what the colony had was free to all. In present-day Pern, the difficulty most Pernese have with the wanderers has less to do with the old Gypsy reputation than with their acute discomfort that anyone would be willing to live without the security of a stone roof against the menace from the sky.

Most Holdless, however, are *not* comfortable without access to shelter. Thus many flock to Igen, particularly when Threadfall is imminent. The vast system of caves echo with whispers from all over Pern. Information of every kind finds its way eventually to the ears of the Holdless of Igen. It is available to any comer—for a price, which is more likely to be a favor than a mark.

TANNERCRAFTHALL

Tanner: On a white field, an outstretched Hide in sienna-brown

Handy to the central trade routes, the main Tannercrafthall in Igen is able to stay on top of fashions and trends in boots and other leatherwear.

The main Hall teaches the basics of tannery to any interested student; in fact, the Tannercraft has one of the most active Craft schools for nonapprentices, since the needs and applications for cured hides are many. Most people have some knowledge of the basics, whether they learn them here or from the tanners back in their home Holds.

Apprentices cure all the hides they can in their own holds. Salt is used for curing when it is available. Curing done with creatures' brains produce glove-soft leather that is much prized for garments. The Crafthall is well downwind of the Hold, protecting the population from the natural effluence of smells that accompany the preservation of hides. Hanging from the rafters and beams are sheaves of drying thongs, and stretching racks hang or are propped against any unoccupied surface. Because of the noxious air, the bronze shutters of the many windows are flung wide most of the time. The stone floors are swept and scrubbed regularly, but scraps of leather and scattered drops of cure or dye are constantly underfoot.

The more sure-handed apprentices are expected to regrind knives and tools to the customary razor-edged sharpness as part of their duties. Every tanner's hands are covered with cuts and blots—the marks of his profession. The Mastertanner's own hands are a rainbow of dyes.

Every major Hold has a tanner-trained cobbler working full-time. He keeps lasts of everyone important to make shoes or boots in their size. Each Weyr has at least one tanner or hide specialist whose job it is to produce the leathers needed for riding gear.

The Tannercraftmaster is really not as important as many of the other Craftmasters. Like cooking, Winecraft, and masonry, tannery is considered a hold craft. The rougher work, such as the fashioning of harness, riding garments, and furniture covering, is easily learned and passed on. To maintain crafthold prestige, Mastertanner Belesdan has reserved as craft secrets some special processes and chemicals, techniques, and compounds to make finer leathers, such as glove

and boot leather. He personally oversees the continuation of some Ancient techniques, which he keeps very secret. He considers it good business to have as barterable goods or services for trade some things that only the Tannercraft can provide.

Belesdan will often send specialists to various Holds known for their herdbeasts, to go through the hides that have accumulated over the winter. He provides certification of quality of hides for traders who will be carrying them to Gathers in Holds all over Pern in the course of a Turn. Buyers know that if a hide bears the stamp of the Tannerhall, it has been prepared properly and will not rot.

Since Pernese floors are all stone or earthen, the people need heavy shoes or boots to protect their feet from the cold, and they tend to be very gaudy in their footwear. Some of Master Belesdan's special dyes are intended solely for boot leather. He dabbles in color and experiments with new designs for his eager customers. Since leather is easily obtainable—almost more easily than cloth—fashion-minded folk will have many pairs of shoes. Leather gloves and caps also make fashion statements.

There is an ongoing rivalry between the Tannercraftmaster and Masterweaver Zurg in the Weavercrafthall in Southern Boll. Each is always trying to outdo the other in outrageousness and popularity.

IGEN WEYR

Igen Weyr: On a golden yellow field, black Sand Dunes

Igen is one of the smaller Weyrs, but at one time it had one of the largest territories to patrol. Founded after High Reaches Weyr in the First Interval, Igen Weyr protected the Keroon and Igen River Holds on the braided streams of the river and the inhabited lands around Telgar. Most of what lay between was desert or mountain. A small force could pursue Thread into those regions where it could do no more harm. As the population expanded eastward from Fort and westward from Benden, more protection was seen to be needed for the Second Pass.

The rim of the extinct volcano that houses Igen Weyr has been eroded into sharp and interesting patterns by the constant wind across the desert. As at the Hold, most of the activity takes place in the cool evening. During the day, even the lake acts like a mirror to reflect the merciless sun back in the eyes of bathers.

The Oldtimer who leads Igen is G'narish, a relatively young man. His support of Benden during the incident in which Wingleader F'nor was nearly killed over a belt knife, and afterward, when the dissident Oldtimers were banished to Southern, showed he was willing to change as Pern had changed over the four hundred Turns since

his day. He was surprised but happy to be able to call on other Weyrs freely for assistance. His young energy is a good foil to the elderly Lord Holder Laudey.

BIG BAY (IGEN SEA HOLD)

Big Bay Hold: Paly, beet-red on golden yellow

Big Bay Hold is a chief trading center for beasts and good of all kinds. It is a small sea hold that grew out of a cluster of storehouses built by traders in this sheltered cover in the curve of Igen's Claw. The dry air serves to keep goods from spoiling or mildewing.

Every trader has his own warehouse or beastfold, depending on the nature of his goods. Holder Jivan is an utterly fair man who keeps track of the comings and goings of beasts and goods on lengths of hide in his own shorthand, which no one else can read. He has copies of all the brands and hallmarks that the holders and crafters use, and adjudicates all disputes between traders in the calm voice that no one has ever heard him raise.

Adjuncts from every crafthall live in Big Bay. Their job is quality control, to see that those products which are represented as being of a certain value and skill level are of that quality. The Beastcrafthall is the second largest on Pern, and several animal healers are in Jivan's employ.

Some disputes solve themselves when all the facts are brought out. If, for example, a trader claims that a herd of white-faced black bovines is his, but that it was moved in the night to another trader's fold, it is easy to check the manifests to discover the stops along both traders' routes to see which one of them was latest in northern Telgar, where that type of beast is raised. Dishonest traders get the word that they and their goods are no longer welcome to use the facilities of Big Bay Hold.

only half a day's ride to the west of Katz Field, so all of western Pern can participate in the heats.

Katz Field is the chief testing point for distance runners. Its central location makes it a good place to hold prize fairs for farmcrafters during Intervals. They always hold hauling matches, plowing competitions, and tests to see which runnerbeasts can break and pull so much weight. Betting is rife during the long racing season, with always a promise for turnovers at the next meet. A man who wishes to lay a wager will either find his own action or look up the bet makers, distinguished only by their badges, which depict a crested blue avian. The badge is a rueful joke the bet makers crack on themselves. That avian, a native bird like the wherry, has a reputation for being a skillful thief.

KATZ FIELD HOLD

Katz Field Hold: Palet, beet-red on light green

Katz Field is located in the tropical peninsula south of Igen. Its flat downs and fine grasses are perfect for racing, and this is the southern meeting place for runnerbeast races. With Keroon so close by across the bay, and the Telgar plain only two or three days easy ride to the north, Katz Field is lively during most seasons of the Turn. Racers are shipped from Fort and Ruatha to Big Bay Hold, which is

KEROON HOLD

Keroon Hold: Per Fess, golden yellow, white, and peridot-green

Named for Captain Ezra Keroon, master of the colony ship *Buenos Aires,* this is also the home Hold of Moreta, heroine of *The Ballad of Moreta's Ride,* a saga taught to all children as a part of their Traditional education. The miners uncovered quantities of iron, vanadium, copper, tin, and lead here—plenty for their colony's needs but not enough to have made the planet viable as a mining venture.

Most of the Hold is plains lands, and enormous herds of runnerbeasts and herdbeasts graze on the triangular-stemmed grassoids. This is a major marketing center for all of the breeds of herdbeast. Traders and breeders can take their purchases home on big, flat shore-huggers from the Sea Hold. Runners have been adapted to the long, sloping plains, and riders keep the numbers of little holds in Keroon in close touch. The Lord Holder, at present Corman, is the central authority in what is one of the five largest Holds in the North and one of the three most productive.

The land is grassy and nearly treeless, descending from hills to the warm, sandy beaches of Keroon Bay to the southwest and Nerat Bay to the southeast.

Keroon Hold itself lies in a mountainous outcropping just northeast of the tip of land that points south toward Igen's Toe. Moreta came from a small runnerbeast hold halfway down the river that flows into the Igen River from the Keroon Heights. In her day the Hold was more populous than it is now, and some of the cotholds have disappeared. The plague all but destroyed the economy of Keroon, as it did that of Ruatha.

The chief geographic feature of interest in this Hold is the Red Butte, an igneous, ridged lacolithic dome a hundred dragon-lengths (seventy-five-hundred feet) across at its widest point. This distinctive granite mound is an important landmark in Pernese history. It was the site of the historic meeting of the six Weyrleaders to decide how to combat the plague described in *The Ballad of Moreta's Ride*.

The Red Butte does serve a purpose, which is possibly why it was used as a meeting place by the Weyrs. It has been a flight-training point for weyrlings throughout the ages. One of the very first visualization points a young rider and dragon learn is the Red Butte. Once the pair can get here from *between*, they can get almost anywhere else. It is a matter for celebration to know that a young dragonrider has reached and returned safely from the Red Butte in Keroon.

Even the smaller holds in Keroon have enough livestock herds to be considered medium-sized beastholds. Keroon specializes in bovines and porcines, important trade commodities. The terrain is excellent for bovines and the bigger grazers, as well as for the runnerbeasts. The compact, long-haired ovines are found right up into the lower ranges of the mountains that resemble those in Switzerland on Earth. Most northern Holds raise ovines for their all-around utility.

BEASTCRAFTHALL

Herder: On a white field, a yellow Bull's Head

The Masterherder, who is usually a skilled veterinarian, covers all breed propagation. His craft is in charge of the care of stud beasts and breeding dams, and keeping track of the best bloodlines. His goal is to breed stronger animals suitable to their uses and locations. Mountain ovines and bovines are different from the types best off in fields and plains. He and his crafters keep stud beasts of each variety to breed stronger crosses in Holds that find their breeds are weakening.

Artificial insemination has survived as a skill from the earliest days of beastcrafting. The present-day Craftmasters do not know the source of their knowledge, but the process works and continues to work, so they continue to employ it. During the First and Second Passes, the veterinarians used embryo transplant as well, but those techniques are long lost.

Part of the Masterherder's job is to keep holders from producing monstrosities. The Beastcraft steps in to prevent runners from being overbred for size or strength, and instead encourages the cultivation of appropriate breeds. A female racing runnerbeast will not easily produce a plow animal, as Lord Alessan of Ruatha discovered when he tried to breed hardy animals for carting that could get along on little fodder. Heavy draft animals exist already for those jobs, and the

Beastcraft would rather have encouraged trade than taxing the strain of one line to produce traits already present in another. To Alessan's good fortune as a racing enthusiast, his combination did produce fleet sprint runners, as well as massive draft beasts. Unfortunately the plague caused many good bloodlines, as well as knowledge and technique, to be lost forever.

The Beastcrafthall has nothing to do with dragons, fire lizards, or watch-whers. Generally, a dragon healer from one of the Weyrs, such as Moreta, cares for one of these when need arises.

The beastcrafters are involved mainly with the study of the animals that once came from Earth: runnerbeasts, bovines, llamas, porcines, caprines, ovines, and canines. They also look after avians, domestic wherries, and the rare chickens and geese, improving egg yield and size of roasting fowl. Some journeymen make a particular study of tunnel snakes, not as they do of breeding stock, but more as an investigation of their habits so that holders may more easily rid themselves of these destructive and dangerous pests.

Herder with Runnerbeast

The Plague

Seamen from the ship *Windtoss* out of Igen Sea Hold brought a curious beast they had discovered to the Beastcrafthall at Keroon for identification. The disease that the large spotted feline was carrying spread quickly through the beasthold, infecting runners that were later shipped to Southern Boll, Telgar, and the Gather at Ruatha. Four days later, the seamen brought the beast to the Gather at Ista, where it was destroyed. From those Holds the plague spread, unidentified and unchecked, until it decimated the Northern Continent.

THE DRAGONLOVER'S GUIDE TO PERN

Without any clues on how to treat the disease, healers were instructed instead to proceed empirically, treating the symptoms as they appeared: headache, fever, chills, a dry cough, and heart palpitations. Quarantine was declared, and an effort was made to trace the exposed beasts that had been shipped from Keroon.

The trick to surviving the plague was to avoid secondary infection, and the cure was within those who survived it. Uninfected people were immunized with a vaccine made from the blood serum of those who had had the plague and recovered.

But the solution was only temporary. The plague mutated and would have recurred if every human and beast who had been exposed was not inoculated a second time after the first dose of serum wore off. Many were near death from dehydration and starvation because they were too weak to care for themselves, even though they had lived through the first attack. Those people were the most likely to die of a second outbreak.

The Weyrs, led by Moreta, Weyrwoman at Fort Weyr, took it upon themselves to deliver the serum. Moreta's heroic efforts saved the lives of countless holders and runnerbeasts at the cost of her own. Through *The Ballad of Moreta's Ride,* her story has lived on down the generations.

LEMOS HOLD

Lemos Hold: On a medium blue field, four white Eight-Pointed Stars

When the population of the Northern Continent grew outward from the two original Holds after the Second Crossing, Fort spread east and Benden spread west, Lemos was formed as an offshoot of Benden Hold. Stakeholders from the Southern Continent sailed north to Nerat from Seminole Hold and traveled on to Benden. Those who lived on Ierne Island held out the longest in Southern, but at last they, too, had to admit that they were not safe from the combined threats of Thread and earthquakes. Even the tinkers and the Romanies came north with the last of the stakeholders because they realized they could not survive if they stayed in the South. Some of the stakeholders went on to Tillek for the privacy of its remote peninsula, and still others founded Lemos. The wanderers, now called the Holdless, stayed for a while in Benden, then moved on to the new Hold and vanished into the landscape.

The Hold was named for Bart Lemos, a miner who staked out the Yukon territory. Like Avril Bitra and Nabhi Nabol, he was believed by some to be an unsung hero. His children were instrumental in founding the Hold and insisted on naming it for him.

Lord Asgenar

During the Intervals, the Lord Holders of Lemos experimented in forestry, knowing that once Thread fell again, the expanses of woodland would probably be sacrificed. To Lord Asgenar's delight, Weyrleader F'lar believed that wood could be an asset rather than otherwise, and helped the Lord Holder to preserve his precious hardwood stands. F'lar also played a strong role in persuading the Oldtimer Weyrleaders to appreciate trees for their commercial value rather than as nuisances.

Once the forests were considered safe, the Smithcraft approved Craftmaster Bendarek's move to Lemos to establish the Woodcrafthall. Those Lord Holders who had no major Crafthalls in their Holds tried to block the move, partly out of jealousy and partly to keep Lemos from gaining a trading advantage, but as the crafts are autonomous from the Lord Holders, the Hall eventually came into being. Asgenar is deservedly proud of the honor of hosting the new Craft.

Lemos is one of the few places on Pern where one can learn how to make and use the longbow, a woodsman's weapon. It is used primarily for hunting wild wherries and other avians among the trees, where there is not enough room to use sling or bolo, two more favored weapons. On occasion, bows have been used for pursuing dangerous fugitives through the forests.

"Hard wood and hard stone, a way by which Lemos is known." It makes the Hold sound inhospitable, but it is in fact a friendly, well-aspected place. The expression refers instead to Lemos's most profitable exports. Lemos ships not only logs and boards to other Holds, but finished furniture and other wooden goods, which are shipped to Igen Sea Hold or Keroon for distribution. Their other chief trading goods are fleeces and ovines from the upper Hold meadows, and jade. Lemos also has a small Winecrafthall, which make a decent table wine from its own grapes.

The Minecrafthall here has unearthed jade of all colors. The difficulty the woodsmiths have with working the mighty hardwoods looks like rush weaving next to the skill needed to carve jade. It is used for many purposes besides that of ornamentation. The translucent jade makes handsome jewelry, but the less attractive opaque jade serves when a smooth, very hard surface is needed. The Healercraft commissions mortars and pestles and plates for measuring powders or molding pills. Cooks who have a light hand for pastry seek to buy rolling pins, bowls, and boards made of jade, which can be chilled to keep delicate dough cool. Skilled carvers can even make belt buckles and liqueur decanters.

Jade is tough enough to take the place of metal in some applications in this ore-poor Hold. The stone is far harder than Lemos's copper, and easier to work than its bauxite.

WOODCRAFTHALL

Woodsmith: On a white field, a forest-green Conifer

Wood has been in scant supply throughout the history of Pern. The only hardwood was brought by the original colonists; with Threadfall decimating the plant life fifty years out of two hundred and fifty, hardwood trees did not evolve. Except for the sky-broom, native Pernese trees are softwoods. Sky-brooms are giants, standing many dragonlengths high over the Lemosan forest. The abnormally tall trunks terminate in bushy crowns of tufted needles, much like the growth on Earth cedars. The wood of the sky-broom is dense and metal-hard, covered with a rough mat-like material protection from Threadfall. It is difficult to work, though it is much prized in the Woodcraft. Until the carefully fostered oak forests mature, sky-broom is the wood of choice for supporting the roofs of freestanding buildings.

Asgenar's father propagated the forests in Lemos Hold in an effort to bring up the supply of usable wood. He was fond of whittling and wood carving and understood the importance of the different types of trees, knowledge that he shared with his son. He and Asgenar permitted their holders to cut wood free to heat their homes during the long cold season. Pine, deal, and spongewood grew quickly, increasing the availabil-

ity over the long Interval. Asgenar innovated the hardwood and fruitwood stands while still his father's heir, a little over five Turns ago. Unfortunately, these trees take a long time to mature, and he fears it will be many Turns before his investment pays off.

Wooden furniture, a mark of wealth elsewhere, is plentiful in Lemos. Popular items are upholstered chairs and settees, chairs made with wooden frameworks and leather slings, canopy beds, and pigeonhole desks. Styles vary widely, depending on the imagination and skill of the woodworker.

Lemos and Bitra also ship wood to the Harper Hall for instrument making, and to the Smithcraft for use as tool handles where a nonslip grip is required and hide will not serve. As F'lar explained to Lord Asgenar, wood is a flexible and important commodity, and the Pernese are just relearning its uses. The Crafthall also provides the wood blanks for marks and formulates varnishes and oils for the care of wood, as well as stains and dyes for tinting it. The Woodcraft is young and has a lot of potential into which it may expand.

Cards for Dragon Poker

BITRA HOLD

Bitra Hold: On a dusty red field, four white Eight-Pointed Stars

Bitra was named for Avril Bitra, an original colonist and the group's only experienced and qualified astrogator. She is believed to have been heroically martyred for the sake of the colonists of Pern when she single-handedly piloted a small ship with faulty controls head-on into the wandering planet, the colonists' name for the Red Star.

The original founders of Bitra left Benden Hold because of disagreements they had over Bitra's role in the foundation of Pern. Their view was that Admiral Benden and Governor Boll stood by to let Pern fall to the terrible menace while only Bitra and her colleagues tried to save it. Bitra was called the champion of the lost cause, who was failed not by her skills but by a sabotaged starship. In the end, despite the opposition, the Hold was named as a memorial to Avril Bitra.

Bitra was beholden to Benden Weyr and is responsible for tithing a third of the Weyr's support. During Intervals, most notably the recent Long Interval of 450 Turns, Bitra and Lemos Holds, urged by the powerful Lord Holder of Benden Hold, remained loyal to the Weyr. Situated as it is, nestled in its mountain valley in the far northeast corner of the Northern Continent, Bitra is the closest major Hold to the Weyr except for Benden Hold itself, ensuring that it has a constant reminder of its debt to dragonkind.

Bitra has a reputation among those who like to gamble for having the highest concentration of card manipulators and sharpers of Hold or Weyr on Pern. If anybody is looking for a cutthroat game of dragon poker or polydice, Bitra is the best place to look. With one another, Bitrans play mah-jongg and other games at which it is difficult or impossible to cheat, but outsiders are fair game for all Bitra's skills.

To be fair, they have also kept alive many other games of skill and strategy brought to Pern by the Ancient Timers, although a stranger had better make sure he knows all the rules before play begins. Tarok, chess, pinochle, chase board games, backgammon, go, and a hundred others are mentioned in the copious records kept by generations of Bitran Lord Holders.

Dragon poker cards

There are three suits of seventeen cards, with four face cards apiece: Ace to 13, F1, F2, F3, F4. The ace of each suit is a large dragon in the color appropriate to the suit. Weyr suit has the gold queen on its ace, and its symbol is the dragon. Hold suit has the bronze, and its symbol is the sheaf. Craft suit has the brown, and uses the hammer. The traditional deck has a repeating pattern of intertwined blue and green dragons on the backs of the cards. The face cards of Sheaves are Lord Holder, Lady Holder, Steward, and holder. The face cards of Dragons are Weyrwoman, Weyrleader, Wingsecond, weyrling. And the face cards of Hammers are Craftmaster, journeyman, apprentice, student. There are three Harper cards, of which none, one, two, or all three may be included in the game and act as wild cards or picture blanks as needed.

Certain cards have their own meanings. A hand containing all three elevens is bad luck. Legend says a man died suddenly while holding those cards. Whether he died as a result of having angered someone he cheated or of more natural causes is unrecorded. The thirteen of Hammers is called the Bakers' card. The five of the Dragons is known as the Clutch, for the five colors of dragons.

Designers of the decks find their work more popular if they paint the faces of the local Lord Holder, Craftmasters, and Weyrleaders on a dragon poker deck. The decks are good barter items at Gathers. A handsomely marked set may be worth more than four marks, depending on the level of artistic skill that went into its design. Cheap ones can be had for a good deal less.

It is often a matter of politics to see whose faces are on the most popular decks. Anyone wishing to sell a Present Pass deck by Journeyman Larin of the Weaverhall, a skilled artist, bearing the faces of Lessa, F'lar, and Wingsecond F'nor of Benden; Lord Jaxom of Ruatha; and Mastersmith Fandarel; with Harper cards Robinton, Sebell, and Menolly, will probably be able to ask and *get* whatever price he likes. But even the sharpers in Bitra cannot remember a single deck being designed with the face of Oldtimer Weyrwoman Mardra or Weyrleader T'ron. There is no market for them. Unpopular faces on face cards are considered to be unlucky.

GREYSTONES HOLD

Greystones Hold: On a violet or purple field, four medium blue Roundels

Greystones Hold is so named simply because of the gray stones found there. The Hold's predominant type of stone is a heavy granite with sparkling fragments of mica scattered throughout. It is popular as a building material in the Northern Continent and is transported by sea on the many trading vessels that ply their way along the east coast from Valley Hold southward around Nerat Tip, though few ships are equipped to take very many blocks at a time. If a Holder or Lord Holder is erecting a building using only Greystones granite, he had better be a patient man.

The stonemasonhall in Greystones is an offshoot of the Minecrafthall in Crom. As the granite is more plentiful here in Benden than anywhere else, apprentices in masonry are frequently sent here to learn to quarry and work it. As a result, the Hold has more than its share of stone benches, tables, ornamental pillars, troughs, and unrecognizable apprentice carvings left behind by the minecrafters. Many a beastfold wall near some of the stone cots is built out of the profusion of discarded carved blocks.

NERAT HOLD

Nerat Hold: Per Bend Sinister, bright orange and golden yellow

Nerat lies on the southern curve of the tail of the Northern Continent. Its fertile fields and thick forests support thousands of people up and down the coast.

The name Nerat came from the initials of its original settlers. Men and women from Ierne Island others far from the earthquake epicenters in the Southern Continent came at last to Nerat, abandoning their stakeholds. Most of them continued north to Benden Hold, but some came back in the Interval to found Nerat Hold.

The land is fertile and the climate is warm, providing the best possible site for the Masterfarmhall. Saving the land for crops leaves less room for beastfolds. Nerat eats mostly fish, chickens, and wherries, and trades with other Holds for red meat. Free-range hen eggs provide another source of protein, and the calcium-rich shells make a high-quality fertilizer and mulch.

The presence of the Farmcrafthall means that Nerat has access to the most varied selection of high-quality fruits, vegetables, grain, and woods of any other Hold but Southern. Lord Holder Vincet has done much to protect a hardwood tree similar to teak. The stumpy trees have a broad central trunk well suited to hand-carving. Lord Vincet has a few carved statues of the teakwood on display in the Hold, which some stuffier Lord Holders consider blatant ostentation.

The Hold is surrounded by small cotholds hewn out of rough rock lining the road from the dock. Nerat's wharf supports a busy fleet of fishing boats and trading vessels. All the buildings on the slope close to the wharf stand on pilings of stone like thick legs.

The Nerat seaholders like hearty Benden red wines and fruit liquors, which they distill themselves from the abundance of fruits and nuts growing around the Hold. Good wine grapes grow on ancient, carefully tended vines in arbors fenced to keep the herdbeasts out. It is not uncommon at Gathers to see competitions going on to judge who makes the finest brandies and liquors. Nerat also distinguishes itself by holding singing competitions at Turnover, based on an old seamen's custom. Nerat sends almost as many men to sea as High Reaches does.

A bamboolike grassoid that can be braided and twisted like wicker grows in plenty in the marshy land between Nerat Hold and the Tip. It is triangular in cross-section, like all of Pern's native plants. Much of the Hold's furniture is made from this light, surprisingly strong material, either woven in strips or cut in short lengths and bound together with dried vines that are tough yet flexible.

FARMCRAFTHALL

Farmcrafter: On a white field, a golden yellow Plowshare

Masterfarmer Andemon looks like the epitome of the dour farmer. If a reproduction of Grant Wood's *American Gothic* had survived to this day, cynics might find in it a family resemblance to this Craftmaster.

Holders find Andemon difficult to get along with, but they have to admit that his advice is always sound. He is more inflexible in his relations with other people than with matters relating to his Craft. It was with his influence that F'lar was able to convince some of the Lord Holders that the grubs they had been destroying through the Turns were what saved the Southern Continent from Thread burrows. What convinced the Masterfarmer that the grubs were not inimical to plant life was the fact that the plants grown in grub-enriched soil grew larger and stronger than the ones that did not. To him, that was reason enough to endorse their use.

Andemon is always seeking to make every acre of land count, and has journeymen out combing the land for the best of every kind of plant. The Farmcraft experiments with high-yield grains and superior vegetables. They also understand the importance of conservation of the soil, feeding it so it can continue to feed them. With so many humans and animals to feed and good land as scarce as it is, food propagation is a serious matter. The Holders who come for his advice may not like the way in which it is presented, but they cannot fault him on fact.

Like the Beastcraft, Tannercraft, Weavercraft, and Bakercraft, the Farmcraft is the science for the average farmer. It provides the holder with the fruit of Turns of experience and the results of experiments to which the holder does not have to sacrifice precious dragonlengths of land.

The Farmcraft is aware of the uses of cross-pollination to produce larger and healthier root vegetables, sweeter redroots, or bigger tubers, and it understands the need for fertilization to keep the soil from becoming exhausted. The Masterfarmer himself takes on the task of negotiating with Nerat fishermen for fish heads and bones to enrich the soil. His journeymen travel through the farmlands advising small holders on matters of healthy soil, suggesting where to plant what for superior yield, and acting as arbiters on when to plant certain crops. Small cotholders often refuse, as a matter of pride, to follow the journeymen's directions, but eventually common sense wins out. One

Trundlebugs

162

problem that has never been solved is the difficulty the holders have with propagating broad roots.

The bee was one species that did not survive the transition from Earth to Pern. Besides having to rely upon vegetable sweetening for cooking, the Pernese also had to make use of the pollinating insects that existed on the planet already. The chief pollinator is the trundlebug.

Trundlebugs cannot fly, but they live long and crawl far. Their bodies are round and black, and when they reproduce, the young trundlebugs attach themselves to the back of the mother like a chain of bobbles. When they grow to adulthood, they detach, and the females form their own chains.

There are several other flying insects that scatter pollen, so the Farmcraft has had to develop a substitute for plastic sheeting that allows a plant to develop without letting pollinators near them. One of the specialties that a journeyman can follow is that of a seedling or nursery master, crossing hybrids and keeping close watch on the results. Others go around and about Pern, gathering seeds, cuttings, and saplings, or raising experimental crops in remote patches.

HALF-CIRCLE SEA HOLD

Half-Circle Sea Hold: On a white field, four medium blue Half Lozenges

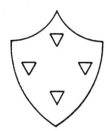

Half-Circle Sea Hold, on the west side of the Nerat peninsula, houses 350 people in the Hold itself and in the family holds to the north along the cliff face. Half-Circle gets its name from the shape of the cove in which it lies. Seen from above, the harbor is perfectly hemispheric.

A curious volcanic overhang provides a sheltered Docking Cavern into which tall ships can sail without taking down their masts, and in which the entire fishing fleet

Half-Circle Sea Hold

can dock. There is room on the deep shelf for dray carts to haul away the catch to the drying caverns or to build or repair fishing boats.

A causeway leading from the Docking Cavern to the Hold overlooks a curving sandy beach thirty dragonlengths long. The road that leads to the east from the center of the beach, and the palisade road toward the north, provide access for beachfront cliff dwellers to reach cropland where the seaholders grow grain, tubers, and fruit, and gather wild greens along the shore.

The Sea Hold is virtually isolated through most seasons of the Turn except during Gathers and when a ship docks or a party of traders comes through. Until recently, the Sea Holder had no exchange of fosterlings to draw Half-Circle closer to any other Hold and to bring new ideas. The coming of the new journeyman harper, Elgion, precipiated many changes that would prove beneficial to Half-Circle including preparing the

Sea Holder for his daughter Menolly's new status as a journeywoman of the Harper Hall. Half-Circle is an excellent example of a Hold's autonomy; it is so far from any other Hold that in times of Threadfall or other disaster, no one but a dragonrider could reach it with any speed. It must be completely self-sufficient to survive. But it need not be so isolated.

SOUTHERN HOLD

Southern Hold: On a light green field, four emerald-green Spades

This province overlaps the ancient stakeholds of Cathay, Macedonia, Delta, and part of Dorado. The area that is now inhabited as Southern Hold was established by F'nor of Benden going back *between* times to ten years before the beginning of the Ninth Pass.

The Hold Cavern is along the eastern face of the sea cliff that shelters the harbor. Everyone in the Southern Continent learns to swim. Otherwise, it is impossible to stay cool unless one remains inside all the time.

The Hold has a sheer white stone face that is somewhat imposing from below. Those inside the caves can easily see approaching ships from a great distance. The

Menolly and Fire-Lizards

Halfway Lookout is at the hairpin bend of the steep path leading up from the beach to the caverns.

Southerners live outside more than their counterparts do. The forested plateau above the cavern is thick with cotholds. Giant local native trees out of which harpers could easily cut a full-sized message drum are similar to Earth sequoias. The boles are formed of many triangular stems fused together into one massive trunk. They are inimical to fire but tend to rot out into hollow shells of trees, still with healthy leaves growing on the branches high above the forest floor. Bamboo grasses grow so swiftly that in the afternoon a kitchen auntie has to cut down stalks she planted in the morning, or they will be too tough to eat at dinner.

The tropical rain forest was invaded by wind-borne kernels from the maturing forests planted by the original settlers at Boca settlement, so there are as many Earth and Centauri plants as there are native Pernese flora on the high, flat plateau.

The Hold was established by the healers and Weyr support staff who accompanied the riders from Benden and the seaholders from Ista. Even after abandoning the project to raise more dragons in doubled time, ten Turns before the Ninth Pass began, the Southern Hold continued. Riders who were badly injured riding against Thread were usually sent to the healers at Southern to recuperate. After the duel between F'lar and T'ron, the Oldtimer dragonriders who did not wish to follow Benden's lead were exiled to the Southern Weyr.

A young Holder with a large family and a great deal of ambition, Toric of Ista took Hold in Southern over the turns. At first he was friendly to the Benden Weyrleaders, sneaking new holders in and information out, right under the Oldtimers' noses. But as he explored farther into the new continent and observed its size and richness, his character changed from one of bluff heartiness to one of closer cunning and greed. He demanded to be confirmed in his Holding of land bounded by the sea to the Western Barrier Range south of Drake's Lake, and ranging from the Great Bay in the west to the Black Rock River in the east, with more than a hundred families looking to him.

The Benden Weyrleaders had in the meantime learned the true extent of the continent and allowed Toric to think that he was duping them, all the while securing for themselves a larger, more lush expanse of the land than he had. Toric was confirmed as Lord Holder before he learned the truth about Southern's size.

Southern Hold broke many of the accepted traditions of the North. For example, instead of the rainbow sails that most Sea Holds use to declare their port of origin, Southern Sails are uninterrupted spans of bright red. Southern imports wine and cloth and exports pelts, craft items, medicinal plants, and fruit. Plants in Southern grow bigger and healthier than any in the North.

As the Oldtimers decline and Benden's influence allows more and more holders to go south, more small holds are being established in Lord Toric's Hold. The new holders tend to be more independent because there is less need to rely upon dragonriders. The land is fully grubbed, and Toric only accepts men and women with sense and daring into the Hold. They have to be willing to fend for themselves, even in the most pressing emergencies, since the Oldtimers fly Threadfall only infrequently. Toric employed the traders to enlist younger sons of the Blood, who would otherwise be landless when their older brothers took Hold on the death of their Fathers.

Since it is easier to exist Holdless, southerners can explore and establish new Holds even during a Pass. More Holds have been built near the Great Delta south of the main hold and on the island to the east. Independent hunters and trappers live in the jungle, bringing back any unusual animals they can catch or kill, and pelts to sell or trade at Gathers. The beastcrafters have a difficult task determining what are sports and what are natural animals among the peculiar beasts found in the jungle.

Toric was excited by the reports of some strange ruins of a mine near the new Delta holding. The shafts piqued his curiosity because the beams used to shore them up appeared to be made of a substance harder than stone or metal, but light and showing no signs of rust.

He has been trying to get a Masterminer to investigate the ruins for him. Not just anyone will do. Toric wants a tamable or blackmailable man who will give him the findings without reporting them back to the Masterminer in the North. His demands that any discoveries of Ancient Timer artifacts be shared by all appears to apply only to others. Toric argues that Southern is his jurisdiction, but every miner he has approached has argued back that all matters having to do with mines are in Nicat's province. He fears that Nicat will bring the matter up in full Council before he has had a chance to learn all he can about the ruins.

Moreover, under the jungle vegetation in the land south of the Island Hold, there are numerous buildings, left over from ancient settlements that are smooth and melted together as if they had been formed of one piece. Something cut the stones perfectly square. Toric believes that they date from the Ancient days, but he will not reveal their discovery until he finds out how they were made. All explorers report privately to him, and he makes it worth their while to keep the news under wraps.

Farther south of his Hold, there are traces of other Ancient settlements. Most of the metal implements brought back are so badly corroded that no one can tell what they were, but there is the occasional find of a curious tool wrapped against the tropical weather in a clear envelope. Toric considers these artifacts of the Ancient Timers his reward for patience and good management of his Hold, and refuses to share them.

Toric was angry when Jaxom and Lessa uncovered the Plateau and the Ship Meadow, feeling that he should have reached those sites first.

SOUTHERN WEYR

Southern Weyr: Bend Sinister in light green and emerald-green, separated in black

After twenty-four hundred years during which no one crossed back to the South, the dragonriders were surprised by their first view of the Southern Continent. The lush tropical forest, thicker than any in Southern Boll or Ista, was fruitful and healthy, exceeding the hopes of the Bendan Weyrleaders that it would be merely *safe* to live in. A grassy headland with a small freshwater lake that proved to be a plateau without exit suggested itself as an ideal Weyr, though without

Southern Weyr

wallows for the dragons, who were not as upset to be sleeping in the open air as their riders were.

The Southern Weyr began as a desperate venture by the sole remaining Weyr on Pern to build up their numbers of dragons before the Pass began. T'bor and N'ton, bronze riders, and Kylara, Weyrwoman for Ramoth's first daughter, Prideth, were sent down with F'nor to breed as many dragons as possible *between* times.

Because of Lessa's discovery of "timing it" four hundred Turns, and because of the effect such a long period being doubled up in time had on men and dragons, the Southern venture became obsolete, but the Weyr continued. The main Weyr and the west Weyr, honorary names for buildings and sand wallows instead of the volcanic homes to which the northern dragonriders were accustomed,

the usual cavern complex. The Hatching Grounds were situated in a small extinct volcano sloping down onto the beach between the main Weyr complex and the Hold. Plenty of rocky hollows would provide comfortable

F'nor and Grall

Hatching Fire-Lizard

became the infirmary for any rider who was badly injured. It was while convalescing here that F'nor, napping on the beach, rediscovered fire lizards and learned that they were Impressable.

Southern Weyr changed leadership frequently, reflecting the political situation up north. First Kylara and T'bor were the Weyrleaders, then T'ron and Mardra after they were banished by F'lar from the North, and finally D'ram of Ista, who leads the Weyr alone, sadly waiting for most of the Oldtimers to die before requesting a Weyrwoman and queen from another Weyr.

The Southern holders, immune to most ravages of Threadfall in a thoroughly grubbed land and adequate stone buildings for protection, have a different attitude toward dragonriders than those in the North. They are used to protecting themselves by stowing beasts and humans under cover and flaming any remaining Thread with flamethrowers and agenothree. They do not need the dragons to fight for them. Nowhere else on Pern are the Weyrs considered expendable.

The Weyr's relationship with Hold and craft runs cyclically, depending on the phase of the Red Star. Before and during the early part of a Pass, Holders and craftsmen are so afraid of Threadfall that they will go so far as to bribe dragonriders to save them. Unscrupulous riders can extort nearly anything they want in this phase. As the Pass progresses, the three parts of the society fall into a mutual interdependence in which the Weyr is supplied by the other two groups it is protecting. When the Pass is near its end, the Weyr becomes the supplicant. While the dragonriders are still entitled to a tithe of the harvests and goods from each Hold and Hall, the immediate need for their services is ended.

It is this third part of the cycle that Lessa and F'lar of Benden are working on changing by opening up the eastern half of the Southern Continent as dragonrider land. In the Present Past there is still a need for dragons and riders to sear Thread from the skies, but once grubs are established in the North, the Weyr's job will be limited. When that happens there will likely be new disillusionment with the concept of the Weyrs, and the dragonriders want to be prepared.

COVE HOLD

Cove Hold: On a light green field, a rich blue Harp

Cove Hold is the newest of the modern-day holds. It was discovered by Masterharper Robinton on a reconnaissance journey to the Southern Continent. He described it as "... the most beautiful place I've ever seen, a perfect semicircle of a white sanded beach, with this huge cone-shaped mountain far, far, in the distance, right in the center of the cove..." (*The White Dragon*). When he suffered a heart attack and made the decision to turn over the responsibility of the Harper Hall to Sebell, the Holds, Weyrs, and crafts chose to honor him by building a new, comfortable Hold where he could retire. The resultant building and grounds were designed, built, and furnished with love.

In only eleven days, hundreds of men and women constructed a Hold in the South-

Apprentice Robinton's First Experiment

BUBBLY PIES

Every Hold has its own special method for making bubbly pies. The traditional fruit used in this special dessert is Terran blueberries, though any berry can be substituted. This recipe makes half a dozen dessert-sized pies or a dozen hand-sized snacks.

Crust:

½ cup butter or margarine
2 tablespoons granulated
   sweetening
2½ cups flour
½ teaspoon salt
½ cup ice water

Cut the butter into chunks. Combine the dry ingredients in a bowl. Work the butter gently into the dry mixture with a fork until pieces the size of peas form. Sprinkle the water over and work it in. (Do not overwork the dough.) Form the dough into a ball.

Filling:

5 cups blueberries (or one 20-ounce
   package, frozen)
1 cup granulated sweetening
¼ teaspoon powdered klah bark
   (cinnamon)
2 teaspoons citrus juice
1–2 tablespoons butter or
   margarine

Gently toss berries with sweetening and klah bark in a large bowl. Sprinkle citrus juice over mixture. Spoon berries into crust and dot with butter.

ern fashion, suspended off the ground on pillars of black reef rock to allow cool air to pass below the floors. The corridor runs right through the building from end to end to act as a breezeway, and the sliding door that leads into the main hall is situated to form other breezeways, at crossing angles to the first, with the windows in the main hall and those in two of the guest rooms.

In order to prevent Master Robinton's concentration from being interrupted by the clatter of food preparation, the kitchen is at the far end of the Hold from the study. The entire building is surrounded by a wide veranda shaded by a wide, tiled roof. The house is designed for comfort. In addition, special gifts add to Master Robinton's pleasure: a wooden chair from Masterwoodsmith Bendarek made to the Masterharper's measure, a full set of the Traditional teaching tunes, and most important, a supply of Benden white wines. Robinton's favorite bubbly pies are always available in the kitchen.

Master Robinton's personal harp was a gift given to him by Harper Evarel and Weyr Harper C'gan on behalf of Hold and Weyr when Robinton, then journeyman, was made assistant to Evarel in Benden Hold. It is said to be there that he perfected his virtuosity in identifying Benden wines by taste alone.

The harp, crafted in the Harper Hall by Mastercraftsman Liesult, Master Sharmut, and Journeyman Joilin, was constructed of two layers of white honey-wood sandwiching a layer of the same wood dyed harper blue, a deep, rich color associated with that craft. In the outer curve of the sound bow is carved a pattern of dragons in flight taken from the tapestry entitled *Threadfall Over Bitra,* woven early in the last Interval by Masterweaver Wikvalen. The dragon pattern is repeated around the top and bottom rims of the pillar. The harp is otherwise unadorned. The sounding board, which is rounded in-of the archaeological investigation, employing the talents of the Smithcraft, the Minecraft, volunteer dragonriders from every Weyr, and workers from Southern Hold, all of whom are eager to help uncover the mysteries of Pern's past.

Cove Hold's peace and quiet are also broken by the arrival of the occasional traveler on his way to or from Southern Hold, or

For Six Tarts:

1 crust recipe
1 filling recipe

Divide the ball into two pieces. Work with one at a time. Form each into a ball and press out into a circle. Divide each circle into six. Roll each piece into a ball. Flatten to ⅛-inch, cut into 5-inch circles, and fit six into the tart pans. Fill with berry mixture. Moisten the edge of each tart and top with second circle of dough. Seal and flute the edges. Cut slits in the top of each tart with a knife. Cover edge of each tart with foil.

Bake at 375° for ten minutes. Remove foil. Bake for 8–12 minutes more, or until crust is golden. Serve hot.

For Twelve Gather-Pies:

1 crust recipe
1 beaten egg
½ filling recipe

Roll out dough on a floured surface to a 1/8-inch thickness. Using a 3-inch cookie cutter, cut out 24 circles. Lay out 12 on a lightly greased cookie sheet. Divide filling among circles, spooning approximately 2–3 tablespoons into the center of each, leaving a 1/4-inch border.

Brush the border with egg. Lay the second circle on top of each pie, and press edges together with a fork all the way around. (Stretch the top crust gently to fit if necessary.) If desired, mix together 1/4 cup water with 1½ tablespoons sweetening; brush top of each pie with mixture for a sugary glaze. With a knife, cut three or four short slits in the top of each pie.

Bake at 400° for 20–25 minutes, until crust is golden. Slide gently off cookie sheet with spatula. Serve hot.

stead of squared, produces a mellow, almost introspective sound when the harp is played.

The harp, like all of Master Robinton's personal instruments, resides permanently in Cove Hold on the Southern Continent, but it may be lent to Instrument-Craftmaster Jerint for journeyman instruction in the crafting of lute-back style harps.

Cove Hold acts as a base of operations while the Ancient Timers' Plateau and the Ship Meadow are being excavated. The Masterharper's quiet retirement Hall became a center of activity when Lord Lytol left Ruatha for a fresh challenge, leaving Lord Jaxom and Lady Sharra to be confirmed in their rank. Lytol chose to act as administrator students from the Harper Hall who have come to learn techniques and tunes only Robinton can teach them. Dragonriders from Benden fly Threadfall over the Hold, and Robinton has a housekeeper to look after him, so his retirement is not a lonely one.

THE ANCIENT TIMERS' PLATEAU (LANDING)

The Plateau was the site on which the shuttles landed. There is not much to find of Landing's original beauty in the present Pass, but it was once very handsome.

Under the regular mounds preserved by the volcanic ash lie the hemispheric and half-cylindrical buildings that were set around squares instead of streets for a cozier neighborhood feel, not to mention more efficient use of space. It is clear from an aerial view that the mounds are not natural. Like the archaeologists who discovered the Incan and Mayan ruins buried deep in the Central American jungle, the curious Pernese investi-

gators would not know where to look if they had not seen the site from above.

The buildings were intended to be functional but not beautiful. The engineers put them up quickly from extruded silicon-and carbon-based plastics and galvanized metal. They are not unlike Quonset huts. The roofs are half-dome shaped for most efficient distribution of heat.

When the earthquakes began, there was time to move out nearly all of the personal effects of those living in Landing. But some things were deliberately left behind, and were vacuum-sealed in the Catherine Caves all around the perimeter of the Plateau. One of the items that remained was the voice-activated computer, which was in a protected room in Landing's main administration building. As the volcanic ash has preserved and protected it from time and dirt, it is very likely operational and needs only a voice to ask it questions—in the right language, of course.

As Lessa and F'lar began to discover when they started the excavation at Landing, under the regular mounds preserved by the volcanic ash lie hundreds of hemispheric and half-cylindrical buildings.

Landing

The first buildings constructed on Pern were the landing grids and the three-story-high landing control tower for the meteorologists and the flight coordinator. A field was laid out, providing room for all six shuttles plus the atmospheric transport sleds and the Admiral's own gig, the delta-winged *Mariposa*. An experimental farm site was scouted at once, and an emergency infirmary erected.

Housing and work areas were erected daily for successive waves of arriving colonists. The buildings were designed to be functional but not beautiful. The engineers put them up quickly from extruded silicon- and carbon-based plastics and galvanized metal. In shape, they were not unlike Quonset huts, with half-dome-shaped roofs for most efficient distribution of heat. The domiciles were set around squares instead of streets for a cozier neighborhood feel, not to mention more efficient use of space. In the center of the residential area was a bonfire square, for assembly at night. The seats from the shuttles were off-loaded and placed around the open square.

Living quarters offered only basic comforts. Typically, a family domicile would have one large and two small bedrooms, a large all-purpose room with a food preparation section at one end, and a sanitary unit.

A main administration complex was constructed at one side of the plateau under the looming shoulders of the volcanoes. Governor Boll, Admiral Benden, and their staff set up office here to coordinate the equitable distribution of stakeholds. A central government seat was always intended to be temporary; Pern's settlers were to have the autonomy for independent action, with the Charter to guide them.

All around the perimeter of the plateau was an extensive system of dry caverns, named the Catherine Caves after their discoverer. They were used for emergency living quarters in the Ancient times. The first dragons and their riders lived in them for a time, as did people left homeless by the first Threadfall. Most of the time they were used for storage. When the earthquakes began and Mount Garben showed signs of eruption, the buildings were evacuated. There was time to move out nearly all of the personal effects of those living in Landing. But some things were deliberately left behind, vacuum-sealed in the Catherine Caves.

When the seal was broken on the cave entrance in the Ninth Pass, the caves were found to be full of cutlery, kitchen utensils, boots, furniture, and office supplies, much of which was still usable. Also of interest to the explorers were the records of the Dunkirk evacuation, with the manifests of goods color-coded according to importance. There was also a quantity of computer equipment and loose data storage disks, wheels, crates of tools, implements smeared in petroleum jelly for protection, and plenty of the plastic printout sheets. All of these items were of use either as new goods, templates for new manufacture, or curiosities. The buildings that remained intact after excavation served as temporary living quarters for the archaeological teams and as storage for their finds.

Landing continues to be of paramount

The Pern Colony Flag

importance as a link between the founders of the colony and their descendants and as an ongoing resource. No one authority holds sway at Landing. Instead, a consortium from Hold, Hall, and Weyr govern, following the example of Lord Warder Lytol, retired Weyrleader D'ram, and, until his death, Masterharper Emeritus Robinton. Landing is now intended to be a center for education for all Pern.

XI.

The End of Thread

When Weyrleader F'lar vowed at the beginning of the Ninth Pass to try and put an end to Thread for good, he had no idea that he would one day have help from his own ancestors, the original Pern colonists.

Harper tales of mysterious riddle-asking statues and ancient spirits who could work wonders seemed to come to life in the seventeenth Turn of the Ninth Pass, on the day searchers unearthed the small building at Landing that contained the Aivas, the Pern colony's Artificial Intelligence Voice Address System computer, Mark 47A.

The searchers investigating the Landing site had been curious about the mysterious designation "aivas" on the Ancient Timers' maps of the settlement. When Journeyman Piemur, Journeywoman Smith Jancis, Masterharper Robinton, and Mastersmith Fandarel managed to get into the "aivas" room, they found intact and running machinery that spoke to them. It had a marked personality and a compelling, rich, authoritative, baritone voice, but was clearly not a human being.

Function had already been restored to the main computer when the solar panels that powered it were uncovered. The heat-resistant mortar and ceramic tiles that had protected it from the lava flow that damaged so much of Landing had kept it completely intact. The Aivas annex to the Administration building had

double-thick walls and no direct access from the rest of the complex. The ventilation ducts at the top of the walls were the only form of natural light in the chamber. A window was cut on the second day to provide better air circulation.

At first, the words "*panel charging*" showed on the main screen, followed by "AIVAS FUNCTION RESTORED." It then asked for ID and access code in a deep humanlike voice. When there was no appropriate response to its query, the AI initiated an emergency communication program.

There were initial difficulties in communication because of lingual shift. The Pernese language had acquired consonantal slurring, and

Voice Activated Computer Bank in the Main Administration Building

there was some alteration of vowels from the original language of the colonists. The complex semantics program in Aivas recognized these as natural linguistic evolution, and altered its programming to respond. A sampling taken from the first series of visitors to speak to Aivas enabled it to become fully up-to-date on word usage and pronunciation. It also changed the vocabulary of the modern Pernese. The word "year" came into use, for example, and began to supersede the word "Turn," which had been in common use for centuries.

Aivas opened up worlds of questions in its listeners with every new sentence, offering unfamiliar words and concepts, such as "artificial" and "spaceships." The only thing that the discoverers could do was begin to ask it questions. Answering them was Aivas's primary function.

State-of-the-art for the colony ship, the "wall that talks" was a wonder for people who had only in the present generation rediscovered electricity.

The first information it recited to its rapt audience was the history of the first years of the Pern colonization. Aivas showed video and diagrams on a screen, the likes of which had never been seen or dreamed of by modern Smithcrafters. Over the following several hours it narrated the history of the Great Crossing, the landing on Pern, and what came after in the life of the colony until the day that volcanic ash covered its facility and cut off its exterior optic receptors. Its final message received was from Captain Ezra Keroon, informing Aivas that Fort Hold was operational, on the fourth day of the tenth month in the eleventh year after Landing.

PROCESS INITIATED

Before the captains departed from the Landing facility, they had programmed Aivas to give pri-

ority status to a means to destroy the organism known as Thread. Now it told its rapt listeners that, with a willing workforce and the reintroduction of lost skills, Thread could indeed be stopped.

Aivas displayed to his visitors data gathered by the colony astronomer Xi Chi Yuen, who had observed the Red Star's eccentric orbit from space. Although his listeners did not have the working vocabulary to comprehend the explanation, Aivas proved to them that the source of Thread was definitely the Oort cloud that surrounded the Rukbat system. The computer mapping program used by the colony ship showed that the wanderer came in farther than the usual fourth planet penetration and intruded on the Oort cloud at aphelion. Xi reported that he had actually observed the rogue planet exiting the Oort cloud, trailing cloud matter behind it. He gave it as his opinion that the dust would produce spectacular meteor showers on Pern eight years after landing.

The frozen matter in the Oort cloud was originally observed by Admiral Paul Benden, but Ezra Keroon, captain of the *Bahrain* and fleet astrogator, told him to ignore it as an "astronomical curiosity." The original EEC team had reported the cloud in the initial survey of Pern but hadn't mentioned any meteorite strike sites. Scuttlebug probes deployed before landing showed no signs of dangerous conditions. The mysterious polka dot effect of the landscape spotted by the EEC team could not be attributed to a meteorite storm since there were no impacts, and they were largely overgrown by vegetation by the time of Landing.

Next, Aivas showed a recording of original observations of the Thread that fell first in year eight of the colony. After some experience, scientists determined that Thread travels in a pod that burns away when it hits atmosphere, leaving an inner capsule. At approximately fifteen thousand feet up, it opens into long, thin, gray ribbons. Some burn up during entry, but the rest fall as Thread. As the Weyrleaders knew, the corridors of Threadfall proved to be fifty kilometers wide per fall. Threadfall takes ten to fifteen minutes to overfly a stationary point. Aivas retained visual images of the first captured specimens of mature Thread.

The period of roughly two hundred years between each Fall was determined with the help of the star charting program. The Falls themselves varied in length. Aivas's calculations showed that the Ninth Pass would be only forty-seven years long. The Red Star's orbit and transit through the Oort cloud actually varied by up to ten percent, so a Pass might be as short as forty-six years or as long as fifty-two. It did not have accurate data at first as to why there had been two Long Intervals when no Thread fell.

Construction of a New Computer Workstation

WINDOW OF OPPORTUNITY

According to Aivas's calculations, there were just over four years and ten months to a window of opportunity during which it would be possible to destroy Thread forever. In order for the Pernese to implement any of its plans for removing the threat of Thread, they would have to learn a fair amount of scientific language and be conversant with advanced technology. Aivas offered remedial teaching in all branches of science to close the enormous knowledge gap. It also insisted that it was vital to obtain access to the main databanks aboard the *Yokohama* for star and asteroid positions.

Aivas began by requesting full records from the Harper Hall, the Smithcrafthall, the Healer Hall, and every Hold. Each hide page was scanned into memory, correcting faded and illegible letters by picking up traces of the chemicals in the inks embedded in the hide and surface impressions. During this research, Aivas freely answered questions and provided clear copies of documents. It was able instantly to correlate hundreds of Turns' worth of records and make clear charts of lineal descent.

In answer to a query by Mastersmith Fandarel, Aivas informed them that it had in its memory banks Planetary Engineering and Colonization data, and multicultural and historical files considered relevant by the colony administrators. Seismic activity had been monitored actively by Aivas since the occupation of the Landing facility.

In order to be able to disseminate information more widely, Aivas immediately suggested that twelve extra "computer workstations" be assembled from components in the Catherine Caves. Lists and diagrams were provided, plus a plan of how to redesign the building to hold them. Its printer was adapted to take plastic rolls, of which there was a limited supply in the caves, or paper, to be provided by Master Woodsmith Bendarek. The large conference chamber in the complex was to be used for seminars that Aivas would conduct. Numerous small rooms in the center would be used for the workstations. The main computer room was expanded on both sides overnight to allow many more listeners to hear Aivas speak.

Two workstations were constructed at first. Master Glass-smith Norist was sent for to replace two of the glass screens on the "monitors" from the Catherine Caves. Mastersmiths Jancis and Terry, Journeyman smith Benelek, and Journeyman harper Piemur were assigned to assemble the computer boards; replace the damaged chips, resistors, transistors, and capacitors; and wire the connections, which were designed to be larger than their Earth counterparts, to allow for easy visual inspection. When that was done, a course of study to learn keyboard configuration and basic commands was begun.

RESTORING POWER TO PERN

Increased power was the first requirement of the facility. Aivas learned that water wheels were already in use on Pern; thus the first step had already been taken toward the hydroelectric plants that would augment the solar power supply to run the auxiliary workstations.

Journeyman smith Facenden brought to Landing the primitive nickel-cadmium batteries that the Smithcraft had developed, to augment Aivas's own solar power system until such time as the hydroelectric plant could be completed. The batteries would be attached to auxiliary power points that Aivas indicated.

New Power Plant

Master Fandarel flew on dragonback to inspect a manmade lake formed by damming a long narrow mountain valley. The dam was made of a substance unknown since the earliest days of the colony: plascrete. It was impervious to Threadfall, pressure, and all but the heaviest impact. The remains of the Ancients' power station lay to one side of the lip of the dam. There, a power wheel was built. The generator that would power the system was first made in miniature, then in full scale.

LEARNING NEW SKILLS

Space travel was but one of the skills that Aivas hinted might be used by the dragonriders to alter the course of the Red Star. Many of the other subjects would have seemed mundane to the Ancient Timers, but were new and fascinating to their descendants.

Among the remedial courses that Aivas felt were vital to the success of his plan for the eradication of Thread were chemistry, physics, and biology. The large Administration facility, now almost entirely unearthed, was divided into several chambers for lectures, including one for concentrated courses, such as the manufacture of plastic. Students came from Hold, Hall, and Weyr. Laboratory experiments were conducted in superconductivity, electromagnetism, the properties of liquid gas, and refrigeration; workshops were held in glasswork (creating thermos flasks, mirrors, lenses, light bulbs), smithcraft, and woodcraft; navigational mathematics and spatial relationships were taught. The subjects appeared to have little connection to one another, but Aivas assured the students that all the areas of study were relevant to the main task. Other subjects, such as the use of antimatter, he would only direct, not explain.

Those who were interested in knowing more could research those topics later, if they chose, once the crisis was past.

PLASTICS

On the second day after the computer complex was discovered, Mastersmith Hamian approached Aivas for information on the production of silicate-based plastics. He was curious to know how his ancestors had made the imperishable struts and beams that shored up the mine adits he had been exploring in the south. Aivas's explanation was full of incomprehensible and unfamiliar vocabulary, but Hamian came away with directions to a cave containing a pair of polymerizing units that could be used as templates for new machinery. He would also have to learn chemistry and physics to make his new craft functional. Aivas offered instruction in all facets of plastic-making, including information on how to keep the new industry from polluting its environment.

OPPOSITION ARISES

Not everyone accepted the information from the talking wall as a boon to Pern. "Unbelievers" such as Master Glass-smith Norist did not see how Aivas could benefit his craft and refused to have anything more to do with "the Abomination"; he abandoned glasscrafting in Landing to a Master Morilton and his journeymen and apprentices.

Master Norist was only the first of the nonbelievers who felt that Aivas was a threat to life on Pern instead of a miracle. An attack was made upon the storage batteries, but only five were smashed. A further attack, which penetrated into the Aivas chamber itself, resulted in the assailants being rendered unconscious and deaf by a sonic barrage from Aivas itself.

The cultural upheaval brought on by so much new information caused outbreaks of violence, mostly out of fear and ignorance. There were further attacks on the materials being accumulated in the fight against Thread at its source. Microscope lenses and barrels were destroyed in two different locations. Luckily, the vandals seemed to be unaware of the truly important components Aivas felt were vital to the success of its venture.

THE PROJECT BEGINS

The two most important stages of the project were set in motion in the nineteenth year of the Pass, two years after the discovery of Aivas. Both involved dragonkind and their riders.

Aivas had determined that only the presence of dragons and fire lizards made it possible for the endeavor to succeed. At first it tried to have dragons or fire lizards teleport a solid object from one place to another, but the experiment was unsuccessful. The concept confused both the large and small creatures. When that failed, Aivas altered that part of the plan.

Aivas then assigned exercises for those who had Impressed fire lizards, and who had trained them to a high standard, to instruct them to go physically *between* to the bridge of the orbiting spaceship *Yokohama* and perform certain tasks. Farli, Journeyman Piemur's queen lizard, as the most intelligent of the small beasts, was given more complex exercises than most, although in the end she wasn't imaginative enough to differentiate between an image on Aivas's screen and the place itself. She couldn't go *between* to a place she had never seen. The white dragon Ruth, understanding the concept and the need, went *between* on his own to the *Yokohama*.

Once Ruth had made the jump *between* the first time, Farli could follow and do the jobs she had been trained for: to activate the life-support systems on the long-dormant ship, and to transmit a report on the ship's condition to Aivas. Once that was done, the astronavigational computer could be programmed to take telescopic sequences to give Aivas accurate data on the locations of Rukbat's planets and the Red Star. More fire lizards accompanied Jaxom, Ruth, and Piemur so they would understand the long transfer *between* to the spaceship.

The body of Sallah Telgar was retrieved and brought back to the surface of Pern for an honorable burial at Telgar Hold. Her spacesuit was used as a prototype for others, since that, too, was part of Aivas's plan. Suit fabric was the product of a collaborative enterprise between Masterweaver Zurg and Mastersmith Hamian's plastic makers.

Fire lizards were trained to go *between* to the bridge and return on their own to fetch objects needed by anyone working up there. Aivas wanted as many as possible accustomed to the transference. Such training would also make the fire lizards useful messengers on Pern when the mission was over.

Aivas called for the largest bronze dragons and the smallest green dragons to be trained for the plan, requesting the largest pool of candidates possible for success, plus a full complement of backup flyers. Hundreds volunteered, eager to help. Few of the dragonriders who were recruited for training came from the Old Time. Most were young, more able to pick up the new jargon and technology.

For the green riders, those with greatest aptitude for the work who had Impressed the smallest mature dragons were chosen. The four main pairs were Mirrim and Path, L'zan and Beerth, G'rannat and Sulath, and S'len and Bigath.

In addition, Aivas insisted on the involvement of Lord Jaxom and the white dragon Ruth. The education process was long and tediously repetitive, but Aivas insisted that every phase of it was necessary and must be learned exhaustively.

The four green riders were instructed in making the transfer *between* to the bridge, to continue the research begun by Piemur and Jaxom on Ruth, and to complete other objectives. It still remained to reestablish oxygen-producing algae in the hydroponics tanks in the Environment section, to freshen the air shipwide.

Aivas tried to determine how much weight a dragon could take *between*. The answer seemed to be that dragons could take as much as they thought they could. How did dragons know where to go? Their riders told them. Aivas was not satisfied with the answer, and could not really comprehend why, when teleportation was possible, telekinesis was not.

The green dragons were needed to go outside the *Yokohama* and help alter the ship's telescope for Aivas's scan of the system. Starcraftmasters and artists went up to the *Yokohama* in teams to map the Red Star through the newly readjusted telescopes. A team of Mastersmiths familiarized themselves with the cargo bays and engine rooms of all three star ships. They examined how the ships were constructed, and where the engines were attached to the body of each ship. Master Fandarel was curious about construction in space, and how each part of the ship related to the others. Only certain parts of the ship were heavily shielded. Aivas kept only a few of those parts in life support, to conserve limited supplies of fuel and oxygen.

Eighteen more usable space suits were discovered in the *Yokohama* EVA ready room. The cargo bays were warmed and flooded with fresh atmosphere so all the able dragons and riders could practice moving in free fall.

Mastersmith Hamian used his new plastics to manufacture protective clothing for the dragonriders, as well as gloves for dragon paws to protect them from ice-cold metal in space. The outer shell of the space suits was a flexible plastic cloth filled with a heat-retaining fiber from the Southern Continent, and lined with cotton fabric. These suits needed to be glue-bonded; sewing them would have damaged suit integrity. Because of the difficulty in creating a glue that would hold, the Smithcraft was unable to make more than two hundred suits by Aivas's deadline. Aivas assured the anxious Pernese that the number would be sufficient. The Smithcraft managed to complete three hundred pairs of dragon gloves, more than enough to carry out the mission.

As soon as there were enough space suits to go around, Aivas also insisted that the dragonriders practice EVA (Extra Vehicular Activities). Having discovered that dragons could exist in the freezing cold of *between* without harm, Aivas determined that dragons could probably sustain themselves without harm in the cold of outer space. The plan required that dragons be able to function in the airless vacuum of space for up to fifteen minutes, with twelve as the absolute useful minimum. Though they were accustomed to *between*, they did not remain in it for longer than ten seconds during a normal transference. Aivas had to be sure they and their riders would not be harmed by it.

Since dragons could carry *between* any amount of material that they *thought* they could move, Aivas's intention was that the dragons should move the engine sections of the spaceships to the Red Star. Each engine block alone was five dragonlengths wide by twenty long, held in a framework of spars as long as the rim of a Weyr. In order to breach the containment field, Aivas directed the Smithcraft to make gigantic agenothree (HNO_3) tanks, two to a ship. They were to be attached to the flat tops of the engines with suction cups, which would hold until a cold-resistant glue had set. Once the acid began to drip onto the engine couplings from the tanks' plastic nozzles, covered by black

EVA Practice

solar panels to prevent solar boil-off of acid, it would be only a matter of time until the casings were eaten through and the engines exploded.

2 for 10,000, 3.6 for 100,000, 4.8 for 1 million, and 7 to 10 seconds for 10 million kilometers distance.

THE FACE OF THE RED STAR

On a visit to the Red Star, Lessa, F'lar, and Jaxom made note of an immense rift canyon with stone pillars like jagged teeth around its rim. The surface was thickly littered with inert Thread ovoids, but showed bare rock wherever the solar winds had swept the slagged and torn terrain. The chasm reached to the horizon in both directions from where the three dragons had landed. In the canyon were three protruding ledges of stone broad and strong enough for the massed dragonriders to rest the engine frameworks.

To their surprise, the Red Star was free of the roiling clouds that F'nor and Canth had encountered on their heroic attempt on the ancient enemy. When asked later, Aivas explained that the planet's surface could vary depending on its position in space, distance traveled from the Oort cloud, and proximity to Rukbat itself. The clouds must have subsided because the planet was now far enough from the sun for its surface to have cooled to the temperature of space.

Each engine section would be placed in a strategic point along the great rift. When all three were successfully deployed, the explosions would sufficiently alter the Red Star's path so that it would never again pass within Pern's orbit. The calculation of how long it would take to move the engines *between* to the Red Star was based on a logarithmic formula Aivas devised. Travel *between*, leaving out actual time for picturing references and actually taking off from the ground, took 1 second for 1,600 kilometers,

"PROJECT OVERKILL"

The attack on Thread was to be two-pronged: to alter the orbit of the Red Star so that it could never again drop its lethal load on Pern, and to completely destroy Thread at its source. Toward the latter goal, Aivas wanted a sample of Thread capsules captured from the Oort cloud or from the tail of the Red Star. Pre-Fall Thread had never been successfully analyzed by the colonists.

The first sample of a Thread ovoid was captured by a fire lizard and placed in an airlock, where it remained frozen and dormant until it could be examined. In order to accomplish an exhaustive scientific analysis of the Thread matter, Aivas had to instruct the examiners in a variety of scientific methods. The shell of the Thread capsule was almost impossible to penetrate. The job was finally accomplished using a black diamond cutter. A waldo chamber was used to protect the investigators from direct contact with the Thread organism.

Thread appeared to be a very disorganized life form. "Rings that wrap round and round . . . tubes and patches of bubbling stuff," were found, plus a curious, fluid gel; some yellow liquid; yellow, gray, and white pastes; and some unknown substances that changed color during observation. The investigators were able to guess that the yellow liquid was probably helium.

The first cross-section of the capsule showed row upon row of layered, springy filaments; the next showed them twisted up. These were likely to be strands of Thread in their dormant state. Toroidal rings found in the organism

Thread Dissection

that sprang away from an experimental prod might be parasites or a means of reproduction. The job of the investigators was to find a parasite that they could alter into a predator.

The appropriate vector was found to be a springlike component Aivas called a "zebedee." The investigators were to use it as the base material to tailor a parasite virus that would leap from one Thread ovoid to another, infecting all it came in contact with. The team had only months left to culture enough for spreading among living Thread.

THE WINDOW OPENS

A key element to Aivas's plan was the white dragon, Ruth, and his special talent of always knowing where and when he was in time. Aivas had already noted that a temporal anomaly was at work. The project to destroy Thread would succeed, because it had already begun centuries before Aivas was ever found. The Red Star's orbit had already altered significantly from the norm charted by the settlers during the first Fall. Bright flashes had been observed on the surface of the Red Star during the Fourth and Eighth Passes, both immediately prior to a Long Interval. Obviously Aivas's plan *would* be put into operation—and it *would* succeed. To ensure that success, Jaxom and Ruth would have to guide two of the engines into the past.

Over six hundred dragonriders had been trained to take part in the mission to the Red Star. Three teams of two hundred dragons each would move an engine from the Dawn Sisters to prechosen points on the rogue planet. Three more teams of three dragons, all greens, would accompany them, to scatter "disimproved" Thread ovoids over the surface of the Red Star and orbiting matter nearby, while the engines were being set in place.

Three teams of Mastersmiths led by Master Fandarel detached the great engine shafts from the main sphere of the ships. After a brief delay while the long-unused clamps were lubricated with liquid gases and silicon fluid, the dragons moved in to grasp their burden. First to go was the engine from the *Bahrain,* carried *between* by Jaxom and Ruth, accompanied by two hundred dragons from Eastern, Southern, and Ista Weyrs. They were to take it to one end of the great Rift observed by the advance party. Thirty-two breaths later, having taken their cues from Ruth, they were hovering above the surface of the Red Star, eighteen hundred Turns in their past, at the end of the Fourth Pass.

T'gellan and bronze Monarth directed the set-down. Mirrim and two more green riders sowed infected Thread into the clouds and masses of frozen ovoids. That first explosion set off the first recorded Long Interval.

The *Yokohama*'s engine was the next to be deployed. F'lar and bronze Mnementh led that team of dragons from Benden, Igen, and Telgar Weyrs to the center of the great Rift of the Ninth Pass Red Star.

Jaxom then joined the *Buenos Aires* team to control placement of the third engine in Eighth Pass Pernese skies. That explosion set off the second Long Interval; the riders jumped back home, never knowing that they had jumped over six hundred Turns into the past and back again in the space of twelve minutes.

Several days later, a fireball was visible on the surface of the Red Star from the *Yokohama*'s control room and, more faintly, from the Southern Continent. It was widely believed that all three engines detonated simultaneously. Master Menolly composed a ballad on the suc-

Dragons Setting an Engine on the Red Star

cess of the heroic venture, led by Aivas, but carried out by hard work and all the Weyrs of Pern. One more mission remained: for safety's sake, the fuelless hulks of the *Bahrain* and the *Buenos Aires* had to be sent spinning toward the sun by brown, blue, and green dragons who hadn't participated in the assault on the Red Star.

Within a week after the three engines were carried to their destination, the Aivas program decided that its mission was complete and turned itself off. It intended never to be reactivated, in hopes of allowing the people of Pern to regain their self-reliance. At the same time, Pern mourned the death of Masterharper Robinton, who was found with the body of his fire lizard, Zair, in the master computer chamber and was believed to have been present at the time Aivas discontinued itself.

A single line of type showed on the main screen in the computer chamber: "And a time to every purpose under heaven." Later research, probably by Lord Warder Lytol, who wrote the account of the historic destruction of Thread, traced the quote to its source: a most important book in the cultural library database.

XII.

Life After Thread

Since it was now assured that the Ninth Pass would be the last, there was much concern over the future of Pern. Students of the history that Aivas had poured out for them noticed a pattern: new demands had often brought on an erosion of values and the subversion of tradition. Many felt the technology revealed by Aivas would overwhelm traditional lifestyles. Most of the question of what happened when Thread no longer fell concerned the dragonriders. What would happen when dragons were no longer needed to perform the function for which they had been created?

Masterharper Robinton had expressed his hope that the new sciences would occupy Hold and Hall and allow the Weyrs to create a new lifestyle on their own. He knew that the Weyrleaders, led by Benden, wanted to lay claim to lands in the south, so they would be self-sufficient forever.

To those who studied history, the answer was for Pern to reclaim the future that its colonist ancestors had always intended it to have. Aivas had explained that the settlers had wanted to remain at the lowest possible level of technology, but that did not mean that comforts should be unknown to them, nor that they should go without machinery that was useful. Among the improvements introduced by Aivas were cloth made on the new power looms, reliable clocks, refrigerators, irrigation systems,

weather reports, ink pens, pads of paper, portable stoves and orchard heaters, and new surgical techniques. In order for the new skills not to be lost, new crafthalls were initiated to teach them.

COMPUTERERS HALL

Computerer:
On a white field,
a bright red Computer Chip

The informal genesis of the Computerers Hall came when Aivas initiated the construction of remote computer terminals using the components left behind by the Ancient Timers in the Catherine Caves. The new craft was formed, under the aegis of the Smithcraft, to pass on that knowledge to as many apt pupils as possible so that the Ancients' precious knowledge wouldn't be lost again.

As soon as more materials were available, the Computerers constructed terminals for the Healercraft classrooms in the Harper Hall. When the Smithcraft was able to duplicate the components, the Computerers intended to place terminals wherever one was wanted. Harper Piemur was placed in charge of teaching in the Crafthall, aided by his mate, Mastersmith Jancis.

TECHNICIANS HALL

Technician: On a white field, a bright red Cog

Loosely allied with the Smithcraft, the Technicians took over repairing and improving the new technology. The main crafthall was to be at Landing, in order to be in close proximity to the main Aivas terminal and its extensive database. A second crafthall would be located near the Smithcrafthall in Telgar. Benelek was named the first Craftmaster.

The technicians experimented with the new forms of technology, making useful gadgets and constructing machines from plans in Aivas's database. Not all of the diagrams in the files could be used because some of the materials were not available on Pern, but the Technicians fiddled with the designs to achieve similar ends. They learned new applications for the principles given to them by Aivas, such as using ultrasound as an analysis device on a molecular level. Among the inventions of particular use were a more effective wheel/axle grease, and cotter pins that neither bent nor snapped, earning them the thanks of every cart and wagon owner on Pern.

The Technicians provided the Pernese with reliable timepieces for the first time in thousands of years. Barometers were a new tool of use to sea men and women, as well as land-dwellers whose livelihood was affected by the weather. A transmitter/receiver project resulted in a communication system that could attain greater distance and clarity than radios could. Each would have a code number that could be tapped out on buttons on the units, like telephones on Earth.

PRINTERS HALL

Printer: On a white field, a rich blue Printing and Binding Press

As part of the Thread elimination project, Aivas had already had the Harper Hall build a printing press. The first was made at Landing; subsequent units were produced in the Harper Hall and elsewhere, but remained under the auspice of the Harpercraft.

The technology was simple, and the presses could be run by any number of power sources already available: hand, animal power, water, wind, or electricity. Rolls of paper, provided by Bendarek and the Woodcrafthall, would feed the press.

Lead type, handset in line-forms, was eagerly adopted by the Harpers. It was durable, easily repaired, cleaned, and changed. More importantly, it was easy to read. And the ancient printers' jargon delighted the harpers.

The Printers Hall is allied with the Harpercraft but independent and autonomous. The main crafthall is at Landing, under the direction of Harper Tagetarl; another is at Ruatha, giving that ancient hold its first crafthall since the Beastcraft and Farmcraft moved out once Keroon was established; a third is at Lemos, to oversee the papermaking branch of the Woodcraft, under Master Bendarek, for its needs.

PAPERCRAFT HALL

Papermaker: On a white field, forest green Print Rollers

Papermaking is a sub-branch of the Woodcraft and allied to the Smithcraft. One of the early techniques given by Aivas to Master Wood-

smith-turned-Papersmith Bendarek to improve his papermaking was the introduction of a quantity of rag in pulp. A new source of fiber, a swift-growing plant discovered in the Southern Continent, helped to eke out the supply when the new forests were quickly threatened by the hunger for the printed word. That fibrous plant was also used in the production of thermos bottles, a joint project of the Glasscraft, the Woodcraft, and the Plastic-craft.

NEW HEALERCRAFT HALL

The Healercraft maintained its traditional structure, but the technological advances revealed by Aivas provoked much thought and discussion, and many necessary changes were made in diagnosis and treatment.

At any time, Threadfall injuries affect less than 5 percent of the population of Pern. Other ailments are far more universal. The condition known as joint-ail affects most adults from the sixth decade onward. Aivas displayed a file showing therapy for extreme cases that could restore a stiff-jointed patient from pain and immobility to productivity. Another chronic condition is brittle-bone. Pernese stock tends toward healthy bones, but poor nutrition and care might leave an old auntie or uncle too frail to move. Ancient files showed modern healers how patients should consume basic daily requirements of vitamins and minerals.

With Aivas's aid, it became possible to combat most bacterial infections. Master Oldive learned about the uses of a microscope to examine blood and tissue samples for bacterial and viral invasion. Oldive also championed the return of the use of surgery, but he was deterred both by the centuries-old Pernese taboo against invasive procedures, and by his own and others' lack of training. Only repair surgery, cesarean sections, and appendectomies were widely done by healers. Oldive hoped to be able to do more comprehensive procedures in the future.

Oldive also investigated the unique abilities of dolphins as diagnosticians in a cooperative project with the Dolphineers Halls at Kahrain, Monaco Bay, Ista, Igen, Nerat, and Fort Sea Hold. Dolphins were able to use their sonar to see minute changes in body mass. They were able to make accurate assessments of infections, tumors, or growths, and could also spot pregnancies even in the earliest stages. Such nonintrusive scans made it possible to treat ailments before they became serious, and to protect women from going *between* in the early stages of pregnancy, when they might otherwise abort. Dolphins could also spot badly healed fractures even when the wound was very old. The sea mammals made a better than adequate substitute for the x-ray machines mentioned in the Aivas databanks. The greatest drawback in dolphin diagnostics was that though they could identify tissue masses, they couldn't tell what they were nor how to treat the ailment. Treatment was left up to the human healer.

PLASTIC-CRAFT HALL

Plastic-maker:
On a white field,
three bright red Roundels

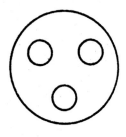

Master Hamian, who was made a mastersmith in the eleventh Turn of the Ninth Pass, became interested in the lightweight beams and supports that he found in ancient mines and stakeholds throughout the south. Quizzing Aivas led him to learn to make this fabulous new substance—plastic. The plastic-crafthall is a sub-branch of the Smithcrafthall; the plastic-craftsmen are generalists in making and using all forms of plastic.

One of the first uses of the new plastic was to build new wharves in and reinforce the piers of Tillek harbor.

SCHOOL AT LANDING

The last legacy of Master Robinton was a center for education established in the Ancients' complex three buildings over from the Admin building. Twenty-five students, chosen for their unusual aptitude, were to be taught in special classes using the terminals in the Aivas complex. The pupils either came in daily by dragonback or lived in temporary accommodations in Landing until a dormitory could be prepared for them.

Each Turn thereafter, the classes have increased in size and number. By the twenty-fourth year of the Pass, there were four hundred pupils at Landing, studying the science behind and the uses of the new technology. Games and sports such as baseball, soccer, and water polo, revived from information in the Aivas database, also occupy students' time. And Eastern Weyr helps out with field trips, conveying the students to places like Honshu, to see the fascinating workmanship of their ancestors, proudly maintained by Dragonholder F'lessan.

Other school facilities were opened in other holds to supplement the Landing school. At the Harper Hall, changes in the apprentice system were inaugurated by Masterharper

Sebell, acting on a suggestion once given him by Master Robinton. The main concern of the Harper Hall is no longer musicianship but the future of Pern.

NEW HOLDS IN OLD PLACES

ISLAND RIVER HOLD

Island River Hold: On a light green field, per pale a blue wavy Fret

HIGH PALISADES HOLD

High Palisades: On a red field, three steel-gray Bends sinister

On the biggest of the five small islands to the southwest of Ista, this fishing hold has as its most distinctive feature the high ridge of land overlooking the harbor. High Palisades is famous as the birthplace of Lord Toric, Lady Sharra, Mastersmith Hamian, and their other nine siblings. Most of Lord Toric's family came to play significant roles in settling the vast Southern Continent.

Inevitably, many of the places newcomers to the Southern Continent found desirable to live in were discovered to have been occupied by the Ancient Timers.

One new hold established in an old stakehold was at the mouth of the Island River. Island River Hold was built on the foundations of Boca Stakehold, established at the colony's inception by Admiral Paul Benden and his family. Mastersmith Hamian wanted to form a hold there because the river, once called the Boca, east of Southern Hold, was so much more navigable than the Lagoon River west of Southern. Also, he saw an easy overland passage from Southern to the Island River. He built a hold and a pier there on the foundations of the stone buildings and using the plastic pilings in the river which had not perished away in 2,500 Turns.

Hamian's cousins slated the damaged roof and rebuilt the wide porches that surrounded the strong stone building full of high-ceilinged rooms. This spacious holding has a large new

191

THE DRAGONLOVER'S GUIDE TO PERN

wharf, intended as a transshipment point for vessels on their way to the north. Piemur stayed there once on his trek across the Southern Continent to map on behalf of Master Robinton and Lord Toric.

ROMA HOLD

Master Hamian also wanted to establish a hold just beyond the conjunction of the Island River and an east-flowing tributary north of Drake's Lake. This location coincided with Roma Stakehold, claimed originally by the Galliani family. The remains of their sturdy stone buildings still exist in the junction between the Island River and the Sparta River. Hamian also had people opening the old mines at Karachi Camp.

CENTRAL HOLD

Central Hold: On a light green field, centered, a white Lozenge

Another Southern hold established by a member of Lord Toric's family, Central was governed by

Kevelon, one of Toric's younger brothers. It is located approximately in the center of Toric's Southern Hold.

BIG LAGOON HOLD

Big Lagoon Hold: On a sea-blue field, an open Roundel of light green, centered in sea-blue

This fishing port was settled by Toric's holders. The curve of the lagoon, on the western side of Toric's holding and opposite Big Island/Ierne, makes an excellent natural haven for fishing ships.

GREAT BAY HOLD

Great Bay Hold: Per pale bright red and sea-blue, with a half circle of sea-blue centered and adjacent to the sea-blue

Another hold founded by Toric, Great Bay lies upon the shore of the bay across from the ancient Ierne Island.

PARADISE RIVER HOLD

Paradise River Hold: Chequy of bright red and dark brown, per fess a steel-gray Wave

Paradise River Hold was first settled in the earliest days of the colony. In the Ninth Pass, Jayge Lilcamp, a trader and a linear descendant of the storesmaster Joel Liliencamp, was shipwrecked there with his wife Aramina while on a legitimate trading run to Southern Hold. "Shipfish" buoyed them up and brought them ashore in the gale. The castaways took advantage of the still-intact shelter they found, and, within a few Turns, turned it into a thriving hold.

Paradise River Hold had been well-designed. The main building was a large structure faced with stone, with a wide, plastic-slab roof that covered an equally wide porch on all four sides. Steps led up from the salt grass to the porches on at least two sides. The building was set several steps above ground level so storm-tossed waves wouldn't wash into the building. The wide windows and louvers on the inside, being made of plastic, had survived intact from the Ancient Time. The walls inside had been made in a cool green-blue. There were twelve rooms in the house.

There were several other large and small buildings nearby, all of them clad in stone and roofed with the fingerlength-thick plastic sheets. The Lilcamps discovered that there had once been a decent-sized pier, and found good fishing off the sea coast to the north. Colored nets left behind, also of an imperishable plastic, were still strong enough to be of use to the castaways.

The largest building must have been a storehouse. It had vents along the roof but no windows. All the buildings were shaded by huge trees, including enormous fellis trees more than eighteen feet in circumference.

Strewn about in this place were dozens of containers left at Paradise Cove during the "Dunkirk crossing," when rough weather had required that many personal and nonessential possessions be left behind. The gifts of their ancestors were of tremendous use to the destitute newcomers, who had lost everything when their ship sank. Plastic containers kept foodstuffs fresh and free of vermin.

Paradise River has deposits of unusually fine and pure white sands, suitable for technical and laboratory glass, so a Glassmaster from the Smithcrafthall has set up a small foundry there. Jayge Lilcamp requested a harper to teach the children, and built an individual three-room hold for the harper's exclusive use.

PARADISE RIVER SEA HOLD

SOUTH BEND HOLD

Paradise River Sea Hold: On a sea-blue field, a steel-gray Wave, and a steel-gray half-circle beneath

South Bend Hold: A field divided per fess by a wavy Fret, golden yellow, white, and peridot green

Nearer the coast, this smaller holding is held by Alemi, formerly of Half-Circle Sea Hold and Master Menolly's brother. He and his crew trawl for fish in the yawl *Fair Winds* among the huge schools that run in the deep waters just off the coast. Redfin, a large game fish, is a favorite for its succulent flesh, tasty fresh or smoked. Shipfish were frequently seen leaping in the waters of the bay, and accompanying the fishing vessels. After establishing contact with dolphins in Monaco Bay, Alemi erected a bell in the harbor of Paradise Cove. He reinstated the custom of rewarding the dolphins with small treats of fish for responding to the bell or for other favors, and demonstrated the bell-response system to Master Idarolan, who saw the sense of using it on all ships. He also built a dolphin marina with a bell at Tillek Sea Hold where he could receive reports as the "pod leader" of all ship captains, and where injured and sick dolphins could come to be treated. Alemi continues to send regular reports to the Fishcraft.

This fertile farmhold shares its northern boundary with Paradise River. Surveyed by Jayge Lilcamp, his trader kin, and dragonriders, the new hold ran along the eastern bank of the river from the bend that marked the end of Paradise River to the stream's origin. The new holders, a large extended family group, came from Keroon. They brought with them a harper and other crafthall journeymen to help create a viable, thriving hold.

Another hold was surveyed across the river, to the southwest of South Bend, for future occupation.

MONACO BAY HOLD

The deep, perfect crescent of Monaco Bay was the main harbor for Landing. Master Idarolan wanted to reestablish it as a major Sea Hold for passage between the Northern and Southern Continents. During Landing's first occupation it was a thriving center for trade. The new wharf is in much the same location as the original, situated at the eastern tip of the crescent.

The dolphin's main sea bell and pier was originally located here. The bell and its plinth were brought up from the sea floor and descaled so it could be put to its proper use. The bell is four hand-spans wide across the mouth, with a good carrying tone.

XIII.

Dolphineers

"Nature's born humorists," Captain James Tillek called the twenty-five blue and bottle-nosed dolphins who came with humans to Pern in special cryogenic tanks aboard the *Bahrain*. All the dolphins had been volunteers, eager to leave the badly polluted waters of Earth for the clean seas of a new world. Like the human settlers, each dolphin had to be given a clean genetic bill of health so that though their gene pool was small, future generations would have the best possible chance of avoiding birth defects and certain kinds of illness.

Like the dragons later developed by Kitti Ping Yung, the dolphins had been mentasynth-enhanced, the effects of which are transmitted genetically. They were good candidates, being naturally intelligent, curious, resilient, and empathetic.

The senior dolphin, a blue, was named Theresa, and her pod included Kibby, Amadeus, Aphrodite, China, Captiva, Sandman, Oregon, Cass, Olga, Pha, Aleta, Tory, Maximillian, and a dozen others. There had been ten males and fifteen females on the colony vessel, but by the eighth year they had multiplied until there were hundreds in the seas of Pern.

The pods, ranged geographically, operated autonomously. They consisted of extended family units with one senior female dolphin at its head. As their numbers began to increase,

seventy dolphins remained in Theresa's pod near Monaco Bay, and Cass moved a subsidiary pod eastward toward Young Mountain. All adults protected the calves, helping to birth them and teach them how to survive. The pods established friendly competitions among themselves to help keep them sharp.

THE DOLPHIN CONTRACT

Negotiations that had begun on Earth on the Dolphin Contract were finalized on Pern. Dolphins were free to explore the seas, but they owed several duties to the human beings who had brought them on the fifteen-year journey. Dolphins must answer the call of the sea-bell situated at Monaco Bay. They must guard human beings on or near the water, to the best of their abilities, even to the cost of their own lives. They must assist in all sea rescues of humans. They must inform humans of on-coming weather conditions, and warn them of sea hazards, including the presence of dangerous sea creatures. Dolphins must aid humans with their abilities to detect earthquakes and track tsunami waves. When asked, they were also to spot schools of food fish and inform fishing boats where they were to be found. Fortunately, work for humans was play to them. In an honorary capacity, dolphins also escorted the bodies of the human dead, buried at sea, to their final resting place.

In exchange, humans agreed to teach and talk to any dolphin, to rescue any who were in distress, to restore to the sea any that accidentally beached themselves, to cure sickness and mend wounds, and to remove all bloodfish that attached themselves to dolphin flesh.

The first dolphineers, or marine rangers, had been trained on Earth with their respective dolphin partners. Jan Regan was the senior dolphineer; her companion Theresa was considered the head dolphin of all the pods. Not every dolphineer had a permanent partner from the dolphin pods, but most dolphins who paired with a human chose to work exclusively with that person. Among the first dolphin/human pairs in the rescue teams were Theo Force and Dart, Ben Byrne and Amadeus, Claire Byrne and Tory, Efram Zarkius and Kibby, Gunnar Schultz and Pha, and Toby Duff and Oregon. Other dolphineers, such as Gus, Bernard Shattuck, and Ann Gabri, worked closely with the pods but not necessarily with a specific dolphin.

The experienced rescue teams took apprentices and trained them at the beautiful, deep harbor off Monaco Wharf, center of marine activities for Landing. In order to be a dolphineer, a student needed to be able to swim well and be at home in the water. A high empathy factor helped in cooperating with the dolphins, as did a reverence for sea life-forms and the biosphere.

The apprentices went through full lifeguard training, CPR and other life-saving techniques, basic paramedic skills, and SCUBA training. For shallow rescues, the dolphineer might need no more gear than a shortie suit, a mask, fins, and a dive knife; she or he had to know how to wear, repair, and use the whole kit. For deeper dives, they required SCUBA apparatus. Rescues from the hulks of foundered ships couldn't be undertaken by a dolphin alone. They lack hands to pull aside wreckage and open hatches. But dolphins could convey wounded humans or vital cargo to the surface, and buoy them up tirelessly until they could get their charges to shore or a ship came to their aid. Together, a dolphin and a diver with an air tank proved to be an unbeatable team.

Dolphineers needed a working knowledge of meteorology, so they could learn by rote what dolphins knew by instinct. Seamanship and care of boats were also in their curriculum. They had to learn the hand signals and bell signals, in order to communicate with dolphins at a distance and under water.

After an apprentice had been in the teams for a while, s/he might strike up a friendship with a particular dolphin, but the choice, like the Impression of a dragon, was always the dolphin's.

COMMUNICATION

Dolphins had several ways of communicating among themselves or with humans. They are a talkative species normally, venting their natural enthusiasm in a range of sophisticated high-pitched and supersonic noises. Their spoken language was readily learned by humans. (Commander Zi Ongola had been a student of dolphin speech on Earth, but was too claustrophobic to tolerate being under water or in a diving suit.) They sang their own songs about their history, fish, people they had met, daring deeds, games, humans they had rescued and ships they had escorted, or anything else that caught their interest. Like the harper tradition, dolphin song was meant to entertain as well as inform.

Dolphin Bell

Dolphins use a natural form of long-distance communication between themselves called "sounding." They are able to send complex messages by undersea sound waves. In such a manner, a dolphin off the coast of the Southern Continent can receive word within minutes from another off the coast of Tillek Head, by sounding to the next pod hundreds of dragonlengths distant. That pod will repeat the sounding until it reaches its destination, and pick up the reply when it arrives. Sounding is a most efficient way for a dolphin to communicate with entire pods at once.

Though their palates and tongues were not identical to those of land mammals, they had adequate faculties to adapt for human speech. In fact, empathy enhancement done on dragonets was inspired by the good experience that human scientists had had from similar work on dolphins, using the advanced biogenetic techniques invented by the Beltrae of Eridani.

Once mentasynth had been introduced and altered the dolphins' genetic makeup, they were capable of learning, understanding, and using the human speech. Mentasynth also enhanced their memories. For the first time dolphins understood the concept of history and time, and had a coherent way of recalling events.

They also acquired names. Before dolphin intelligence was enhanced, they did recognize words as recurring patterns of sound which they came to associate with instructions or commands, a specific object, or one of them. After mentasynth, dolphins adopted the names they had been given, and formed a tradition of passing them on to their offspring. The name "Tillek," for Captain Jim Tillek, came to mean the leader of all dolphins. The source of the name has been handed down in their verbal tradition.

A large bell was erected atop a six-by-six pylon at the end of the pier in Monaco Bay for use by dolphins to summon humans to hear their reports, or for humans in need to call the pods. A floating platform tethered beside it was for mariners to use in speaking with dolphins. Both species were instructed in the sequences and signals for report, emergency, and the red alert recall sequence that summoned all dolphins within range to the site.

The dolphins established a rite of passage in which young dolphins attempted to swim the Great Subsidence, an undersea feature in the arctic waters to the northwest of High Reaches Head. Challenging, exhilarating, and dangerous, the ritual had never been witnessed by any human. It took place around Turnover, when the pods gathered to exchange news. First the Name Song was sung in its entirety, honoring the dolphins who had made the Great Crossing to Pern. Then the young dolphins had to swim many kilometers across a vicious undertow without letting it yank them down into the swirling depths and away from lifegiving air. It required strength, timing, and daring. Not every one who tried it survived.

THE DUNKIRK CROSSING

When the explosion of the volcano Mount Garben above Landing became imminent, a planned evacuation was set into motion to move all its population and goods northward, eventually to Fort Hold. There were too few sleds and shuttles left to transport everything and everyone quickly. The administration at Landing, aided by storesmaster Joel Liliencamp and his assistant Desi Artheid, oversaw the evacuation, but it was run by the shipmasters, because most of the transshipment was to be accomplished by sea.

Every one of the siliplex vessels that could haul cargo was pressed into service. The flotilla, led by Captain James Tillek in his forty-foot sloop *Southern Cross,* was intended to take goods from Landing via Monaco Bay, around Kahrain Head, where it was believed it would be temporarily safe from the volcanic ashfall. The larger ships would go as far as Paradise River Hold.

Gale-force winds following the catastrophic eruption caused many of the boats to founder. Much of the cargo was blown off ships into the water. Dolphins rounded it up and helped move most of the urgently needed and delicate red- and orange-tagged containers safely to their destination. It was the last major undertaking for humans and dolphins working together for many centuries to come.

Although humans failed to maintain contact with the dolphins after the migration to the north and a subsequent plague, the sea mammals kept their side of the Dolphin Contract, accompanying ships, and saving drowning humans. It came to be considered lucky for "shipfish" to swim beside a fishing vessel. The dolphins push their hard triangular dorsal fins into the hands of shipwrecked people and drag them as close to shore as they can without beaching themselves. Men who fall overboard from fishing vessels are often lifted up by dolphins who swim under their bellies or between their legs.

The passage of time separated the Pernese from the origins of the practice of dolphin rescue. Though the shipfish tried to speak with men, humans believed that any resemblance the sounds bore to human speech was accidental, an illusion or, at worst, a hallucination. For their part, dolphins missed interaction with the sea captains and mariners at the ports.

Dolphin society continued to prosper. Though each pod was autonomous, the traditions and the naming song were taught to each new generation by the Tillek, the traditional leader of all dolphins. Usually the senior female, the Tillek maintains the standard of spoken human language and sees that the young are taught their history and responsibilities.

The Tillek also comes down firmly upon dolphins who use disrespectful terms for humans. "Long-foot" or "finless" have always been considered rude language.

RUBICON RIVER HOLD

Rubicon River Hold: On a white field, per bend a dark blue wavy Fret

In the deep cove on the Rubicon River, Readis Lilcamp rediscovered communication with the pod of dolphins that lived in that part of the sea. He created by himself a rough hold that became the kernel of a new Crafthall.

DOLPHINEERS HALL

Dolphineer: On a white field, a sea-blue Dolphin

By the time interest in communication with dolphins was resumed in the Ninth Pass, humans' speech had suffered linguistic slippage, but the dolphins' speech pattern was still that of the first settlers. Humans believed that the smiling, finned creatures called themselves "doll-fins," a pronunciation that was speedily corrected once humans started listening properly once again. Charts of hand signals and a lexicon of human words used by dolphins were provided by Aivas. People began interacting more closely with dolphins, getting reports of schools of fish and using pod intelligence to avoid undersea hazards. Hauls of fish increased two- to fivefold where the dolphins' advice was taken, and accidents at sea decreased. There were several dolphin halls, but no official Dolphincrafthall, and no Dolphineer.

The Tillek herself, Theresa, brought Readis out into the Great Western Current and swam him to where Master Idarolan's ship *Dawn Sisters* was waiting. In the presence of Masterfisherman Idarolan, the Benden Weyrleaders, and Lord Holder Oterel of Tillek Hold, Theresa named Readis the Dolphineer. He established the new Hall at Rubicon, to coordinate among dolphineers already at work in Eastern Weyr, Monaco Bay, Paradise River Sea Hold, Southern Hold, Ista (Cetus Hall), Tillek, Fort Sea Hold, and Nerat Bay, among others. Theresa herself would instruct him in dolphin history, tradition, and knowledge as part of his duties as a Craftmaster; he, in turn, would teach others who came to him.

Thanks to the technology revived by Aivas so that the dragonriders could breathe in the void of space, compressed air was available for the resumption of SCUBA diving. Face masks,

with their flexible straps and sealed glass eye plates, were the biggest snag. Master Hamian worked on the puzzle of what plastic would work until he found the correct formula. Another link with the colony's past was reforged.

DOLPHIN MEDICINE

With the exception of one Ancient Timer dolphin, Maximillian, who went on record saying he thought that it lacked substance, dolphins love to eat the Thread that drowns in the sea. They are largely immune to the devastation of Threadfall, since they can submerge for up to fifteen minutes on a single breath of air, long enough for Threadfall to pass over an area. If Thread lands on a dolphin's back, he dives, and the strand drowns.

Dolphins tend to heal quickly, due to the effect of salt water and their own speedy metabolisms, but as in the treatment of humans, the use of numbweed helps speed the cure.

It is possible for dolphins to sustain grievous wounds, during storms or ship rescues, or attacks by native Pernese sea creatures. Surgical repair is difficult because dolphins are slippery and have tough skins, but they are good patients, who are intelligent enough to follow orders for their care. Beyond surgical intervention and antibiotic injections, dolphins need relatively little help from humans.

The most prevalent threat to their health is the bloodfish, a native Pernese parasite. It attaches itself to any open wound with a suction-cuplike mouth. Through it, a sucker penetrates scratches and wounds and burrows deep into the host's flesh. Although the puncture itself is very small, it goes deep enough to endanger internal organs. It is occasionally necessary to make a larger incision to remove the whole sucker. Part of the Dolphin Contract agreed to on Pern requires dolphineers to remove bloodfish from dolphins. The most common procedure when the parasite has fastened onto a human involves touching a burning ember to the bloodfish's head. However, it is less injurious to the dolphin to scrape the parasite off with a sharp-bladed knife. More skillful healers can cut off the bloodfish's head and extract the sucker, thereby keeping intrusive surgery to a minimum.

In return, dolphins assist in healing humans (see *New Healercraft*).

XIV.

New Life for the Dragons

HONSHU WEYRHOLD

Honshu Weyrhold: On a bright red field, a white Roundel and Radial Lines outlined in black

Honshu had been mentioned in old records that tantalized the curiosity of the Benden Weyrleaders. It lay in the foothills of the Western Barrier Range.

F'lessan, their son, and his bronze dragon Golanth, managed to uncover the narrow entrance to the hold that had been abandoned since Stev Kimmer's clan left it in the fifty-eighth year of the settlement. The original home of Kenjo Fusaiyuki and his wife held many marvels for new explorers: interesting personal belongings, an aircraft, and sacks of a light, odd-smelling liquid.

Overgrown over 2,500 Turns, the cliff-hold was almost hidden from view. A sheer face rose straight up from the river flowing near the entranceway, above a path worn smooth by wild beasts hiding from predators and Thread-fall. The beasthold was on the lowest level.

The wide doorway and window slits gave little light into the interior, suggesting that the primary light source had come from somewhere other than the sun. The hold door slid aside and fit into a neat niche in the front wall. It had been left open by the last people to leave Honshu.

Hidden in another chamber whose lock crumbled into dust with age was a large sled, one of the atmospheric shuttle craft employed by the settlers for carrying personnel and goods, and for fighting Thread in the early falls. The room had been cut out of the rock expressly to contain the small craft. Unfortunately, no power packs remained to power the shuttle, so it was graceful arch of surprising size, and into a vast room with ten shuttered windows. The admirable skills of the ancients allowed the shutters to turn easily upon their long-unused hinges, letting in the sunlight to show off the glory of the main hall of Honshu: brilliantly colored and accurately rendered murals depicting Pern's Ancient times. They included scenes of the landing of the shuttles in the Ship Meadow, people working the land, the first experience of Threadfall, settlers in sleds and shuttles fighting Thread with HNO_3 and flamethrower, and a beautiful space scene of Rukbat with all its planets.

Dragonholder F'lessan planned to settle Honshu, making it the first Weyrhold. He duly extended living space to holders, farmcrafters, and herders, who cleared the debris and overgrowth out of the stone-bordered fields and put herds and crops where their ancestors had once kept them. They also cleared the terraces on the face of the cliff, where on a fine day one may have a clear view of the Barrier Range.

Golanth Discovering Honshu

The Murals of Honshu

an object of curiosity rather than a new tool for the current occupants.

In another part of the hold was a great workroom, obviously used for fine craftwork. In it were a kiln and a large forge, plus extensive workbenches.

Up one level from the workroom was the hold's great hall. The main entry led through a

EASTERN WEYR

Eastern Weyr/Monaco Bay: On a midnight blue field, three silver Roundels

Eastern Weyr, in the volcanic range just above Landing, is administered by Weyrleader T'gellan and bronze Monarth, and his weyrmate Mirrim and green Path.

Most of the dragons and riders at Eastern are young. Quite a few of them studied in the Aivas complex and helped with the excavation of Landing.

Here, dragons and riders do not live in a dormant volcano caldera as they do in the north. Instead, dragons who are old enough to move out of the weyrling barracks sleep in sandy wallows. Riders have small accommodations suited to their needs in and around the common Weyr facilities. The kitchens are substantial, but most of the cooking takes place in the open air.

A rider might have a single room hold with a hammock and a clothes press or chest to hold his riding gear and repair tools. Because the entire continent is grubbed, one might live right in the jungle without fear of Thread infestation or burrows.

Near the sea strand at the mouth of the river that runs along the Weyr, rider T'lion hung a small bell in the branches of a large tree for calling dolphins.

THE NINTH WEYR/XANADU

At the time of the mission to destroy Thread, a ninth Weyr was proposed to relieve the overcrowding in every one of the older Weyrs. A favored site was examined at the eastern end of the Western Barrier Range.

On the western shore of the Caspian Lake, at the confluence between the edge of the wide Rubicon River and the small inner sea, a small body of water full of tiny upthrust islands, stands the high palisade of granite cliffs that once housed Xanadu stakehold. Wide stone steps were cut in the granite leading down to the lake shore.

The dwelling itself had been built of the native stone. Its chimney stack still stood into the Ninth Pass. The impressive vista in the sheltered valley and the broad lake with the interesting chimneylike islets would make a good weyr when Thread no longer fell.

Breda, a journeywoman weaver from Crom, and her dragon Amaranth, were thought to be good candidates for Weyrwoman and chief queen for the ninth Weyr when it should be founded. Amaranth was Ramoth's last daughter, clutched before the mission to end Thread.

THE FUTURE OF DRAGONKIND

At the end of the Ninth and Last Pass, dragons, no longer Weyrbound by Thread, will have the freedom to live anywhere they choose. Most people agree that, after centuries of service, often unthanked, the dragonriders deserve to have first choice of the rich lands of the Southern Continent once their duties as protectors of Pern end. The Weyrs expect to have substantial holdings in the Southern Continent, to avoid ever being dependent upon the northern Holds as they were in the past.

Naturally, dragons will not die out just because Thread did. They will simply turn their talents to other endeavors. Hatching and weyrling training will remain as it has been, because eggs are vulnerable, and each new Impressed pair needs to be protected and educated to ensure the survival of the hatchling. Weyrlings will continue to live in the barracks until the dragon is able to fly and go *between*.

The huge numbers of dragons normally used to fight Thread will no longer be needed, so queens and bronzes may keep their mating flights shorter and produce fewer eggs. But the species, well established and respected on Pern, will never die out.

Advanced education will help to make the transition easier. Since the days of the first colonists, the Pernese have always been of an independent turn of mind. Every man and woman will need to make a suitable decision for the future based upon personal needs and ambitions. By custom, a third of the places at the Landing school are set aside for Weyr pupils.

Older dragons and riders should reason-

ably be allowed to take their retirement with honor, but for the younger riders, jobs would help to put the odd mark in one's pocket. Every rider has a craft-based sideline, and a journeyman with his own infallible transportation would be a boon to any Hall. The urge to know what else exists on Pern will send many dragon and rider pairs on flights of discovery around the planet. Exploration already occupies many during the times they are not required to fight Thread. Until every length of Pern is mapped, overflying the land and sea to find good land and safe passages will be the job of the Weyrs. Dragons will continue to be unsurpassed in transporting people, messages, and even goods from place to place instantly and safely. Dragons excel at heavy lifting and surface excavation, rescue operations, and getting into and out of places that are inaccessible on the ground. Some dragonriders have expressed interest in moving out among the holders, taking employment as couriers or members of mountain rescue teams.

The Weyrs may also be needed, occasionally, as the guardians of order and peace. Dragons and their Impressed riders will always be symbols of aspiration, ambition, and freedom on Pern.

XV.

Pronunciation Guide to Names on Pern

Most two-syllable names are emphasized on the first syllable (*Des*dra, *Tal*mor). Three-syllable names can be emphasized on either the first or second. Four-syllable names are almost invariably stressed soft on the first syllable and hard on the third (Rato*shi*gan).

Dragonriders' honorifics are slurred, pronouncing the initial letter as though it were followed by a schwa (ə), as in Sh'gall or N'ton, or ignored completely, as in F'lar. The purpose of shortening the name in this fashion is to make it easier to pronounce in haste.

Alessan (ă lĕs' ən) Lord Holder of Ruatha, Sixth Pass

B'greal (ba grēl') weyrling, Fort Weyr, Sixth Pass

B'lerion (ba lĕr' ē ən) Wingleader, rider of bronze Nabeth, High Reaches, Sixth Pass

Belior (bé lē' ōr) Pern's larger moon

Berchar (bĕr' chaär) Masterhealer, Fort Weyr, Sixth Pass

Bitra (bĭt' rä) major Hold in the Northern Continent, named for Avril Bitra

Brekke (brĕ' kē) queen rider of Wirenth (deceased), Benden Weyr, Ninth Pass

Briaret (brī' ă rĕt') Masterherder, Keroon Hold, Ninth Pass

Burdion (bĕr' dē ŏn) healer, Igen Sea Hold, Sixth Pass

C'gan (sgăn) Weyrsinger, deceased, blue dragon Tagath, Benden Weyr, Ninth Pass

C'ver (kvĕr) brown rider of Hogarth, Telgar Weyr, Sixth Pass

Campen (kăm' pən) heir to Tolocamp, Lord Holder of Fort, Sixth Pass

Cr'not (kr' nŏt') Weyrlingmaster, High Reaches, bronze Caith, Sixth Pass

Crom (krōm) major Hold in the Northern Continent

Dalova (dă lōv' ă) Weyrwoman for golden Allaneth, Igen Weyr, Sixth Pass

Declan (dĕk' lăn) Candidate, Fort Weyr, Sixth Pass

Desdra (dĕz' drə) journeywoman healer, Fort Hold, Sixth Pass

Domick (dŏ'mĭk) composition master, Harper Hall, Ninth Pass

Elgion (ĕl' jē ŏn) journeyman harper, Half-Circle Sea Hold

F'lar (flăr) Weyrleader, Benden Weyr, bronze Mnementh, Ninth Pass

F'neldril (fnĕl' drĭl) Weyrlingmaster, Fort Weyr, brown Mnanth, Sixth Pass

F'nor (fnōr) Wingleader, Benden Weyr, brown dragon Canth, Ninth Pass

Falga (fŏl'gă) Weyrwoman for Tamianth, High Reaches Weyr, Ninth Pass

Fandarel (făn' də rĕl) Mastersmith, Telgar Hold, Ninth Pass

Fergal (fĕr' găl) runner handler at Ruatha Hold, Sixth Pass

Fortine (fŏr tīn') Master of Archives, Harper Hall, Sixth Pass

Gemma (jĕm' ă) mother of Jaxom of Ruatha Hold, deceased

Gianarth (jă närth') bronze dragon of S'ligar, High Reaches, Sixth Pass

Groghe (grō' gē) Lord Holder of Fort Hold, Ninth Pass

Idarolan (īd' ă rōl' ăn) Masterfisherman, Tillek Hold, Ninth Pass

Igen (ĭg' ən) desert Hold in Northern Continent

Jancis (jăn sĭs') Mastersmith, Landing, Ninth Pass

Jaxom (jăks' ŏm) Lord Holder of Ruatha, rider of white Ruth, Ninth Pass

K'lon (klŏn) blue rider of Rogeth, Fort Weyr, Sixth Pass

Keroon (kĕr ōōn') plateau Hold in Northern Continent; founder of Hold, Ezra Keroon

klah (klä) popular drink brewed from fragrant bark of klah tree

Kylara (kĭ lăr' ă) queen rider for Prideth (deceased), Southern Hold, Ninth Pass

Laudey (loud' ē) Lord Holder of Igen Hold, Ninth Pass

Leef (lēf) Lord Holder of Ruatha, Alessan's father, Sixth Pass

Lemos (lē' mŏs) major Hold in North, known for its forests, named for Bart Lemos

Leri (lĕ' rē) Weyrwoman for Holth, Fort Weyr, Sixth Pass

Lessa (lĕs' ă) Weyrwoman for Ramoth, Benden Weyr, Ninth Pass

Ligand (li gand') journeyman tanner, Fort Hold, Ninth Pass

Lytol (lī' tōl) Lord Steward of Ruatha, deceased dragon brown Larth, Ninth Pass

M'barak (mĭ bär' ăk) weyrling, Fort Weyr, blue dragon Arith, Sixth Pass

M'ray (mĭ rā') son of Moreta and D'say, dragon brown Quoarth

M'tani (mĭ tă' nē) Weyrleader, bronze Hogarth, Telgar Weyr, Sixth Pass

Manora (mă nōr' ă) mother of F'nor, head-woman of Lower Caverns, Benden Weyr, Ninth Pass

Menolly (mĕn' ōl' lē) journeywoman harper, Harper Hall, Ninth Pass

Merelan (mĕ' rĕ lən) mother of Robinton, Harper Hall, Ninth Pass

Meron (mĕr' ən) Lord Holder of Nabol Hold, Ninth Pass

Mnementh (nĕ mĕnth') bronze dragon of F'lar, Benden Weyr, Ninth Pass

Moreta (mō rĕ' tə) Weyrwoman for Orlith, Fort Weyr, Sixth Pass

N'ton (nə tŏn') Wingleader, Benden Weyr, bronze dragon Lioth, Ninth Pass

Nabol (nā' bōl) major Hold in Northern Continent

Nerilka (nĕ rĭl' kə) daughter of Tolocamp, wife of Alessan, and Lady Holder of Ruatha, Sixth Pass

Nicat (nĭ' kat) Masterminer, Minecrafthall, Ninth Pass

Oklina (ōk lē' nă) sister to Alessan, Weyrwoman for Hannath

Oldive (ōl' dīv) Masterhealer, Healercraft Hall, Ninth Pass

Oterel (ōt' ĕr ĕl) Lord Holder of Tillek, Ninth Pass

Petiron (pĕtch' rŏn) harper, Half-Circle Sea Hold, Ninth Pass

Piemur (pī' mer) journeyman harper, Southern Hold, Ninth Pass

Pressen (prĕs' ĕn) healer, High Reaches Weyr, Sixth Pass

Raid (rād) Lord Holder of Benden Hold, Ninth Pass

Ramoth (ră' mŏth) senior queen dragon, Benden Weyr, Ninth Pass

Ratoshigan (ră tō' shē' gən) Lord Holder of Southern Boll Hold, Sixth Pass

Robinton (rô' bĭn tŏn') Masterharper, Ninth Pass

Robse (rŏb' sĕ) eldest son of Menolly and Sebell of the Harper Hall

Ruatha (rōō ă' thă) second oldest Hold in the Northern Continent

Rukbat (rŭk' băt) blue-white star around which Pern revolves

Sangel (săn' jĕl) Lord Holder of Southern Boll, Ninth Pass

Sebell (sē' bĕl) journeyman harper, then Master-harper, Harper Hall, Ninth Pass

Sh'gall (shĭ găl') Weyrleader, Fort Weyr, bronze Kadith, Sixth Pass

Shonagar (shō' nă găr') Voicecraftmaster, Harper Hall, Ninth Pass

Silvina (sĭl vē' nă) headwoman of the Harper Hall, Ninth Pass

Suriana (sōō rē ăn' ă) deceased wife of Alessan of Ruatha, Ninth Pass

T'gellan (tgĕ' lăn) rider of bronze Monarth, Benden Weyr, Ninth Pass

T'ron (trŏn) Oldtimer Weyrleader at Fort Weyr, dragon Fidranth, originally Eighth Pass

Tagetarl (tăg' ĕ tărl') journeyman harper, Harper Hall, Ninth Pass

Tamianth (tăm' ē ănth') queen dragon of Falga, High Reaches Weyr, Ninth Pass

Telgar (tĕl' găr) major grain-producing Hold in Northern Continent, named for Sallah Telgar

Timor (tĭ' mōr) Pern's smaller moon

Tirone (tē rōn') Masterharper, Sixth Pass

Toronas (tō rŏ' năs) Lord Holder of Benden Hold succeeding Lord Raid, Ninth Pass

Tuero (twĕ' rō) journeyman harper, Ruatha Hold, Sixth Pass

weyr (wēr) any place in which a dragon lives

wher (hwĕr') Impressable creatures bioengineered by Wind Blossom Ping

XVI.
Dragons and
Their Riders

ABBREVIATIONS

D'F = Dragonflight
D'Q = Dragonquest
WD = The White Dragon
D'Song = Dragonsong
D'Sing = Dragonsinger
D'Drums = Dragondrums
D'Dawn = Dragonsdawn
ATWoP = All the Weyrs of Pern
CoP = The Chronicles of Pern: First Fall
DoP = The Dolphins of Pern
MOR = Moreta, Dragonlady of Pern
NER = Nerilka's Story
RoP = The Renegades of Pern

D'E = Dragonseye

H'Reaches = High Reaches
H = Hold
W = Weyr
o.a.a. = out and about (no fixed address)
Moncobay = dolphin for Monaco Bay
Paradriv = dolphin for Paradise River
en route = aka o.a.a.
d. = deceased before novel but mentioned
Jrym/Jryw = Journeyman or Journeywoman
Ob-gyn = obstetrics-gynecology
joat = jack of all trades

THE COMPLETE CAST

Name	Dragon	Color	Rank	Book	Hold/Weyr/Hall
A'dan	Tigrath	green	rider	MOR	Fort Weyr
A'murry	Granth	green	rider	MOR	Igen Weyr
A'ton				RoP	
Abuna			kitchen staff	D'Sing	Harper Hall
Adjai, Ju			biologist	D'Dawn	Boca
Adrea	Belgjeth	gold	Weyrwoman	RoP	Southern Weyr
Afo			dolphin	DoP	Moncobay
AIVAS			computer	RoP	Landing

Dragons and Their Riders

Name	Dragon	Color	Rank	Book	Hold/Weyr/Hall
Ajay			dolphin	DoP	Fort waters
Akamoto, Jiro			copilot	D'Dawn	
Alda			trader	RoP	Lilcamp Train
Aldrin, John			pilot	D'Dawn	Jordan
Aleki			Alemi's son	DoP	Paradise River Hold
Alemi			seaman	D'Song	Half-Circle Sea Hold
Alessan			Lord Holder	MOR	Ruatha Hold
Aleta			dolphin	CoP	
Alhinwa, Cobber			miner	D'Dawn	Karachi
Alianne Chereth		gold	queen rider	D'Dawn	Landing
Almie			Jayge's daughter	DoP	Paradise River
Alta			dolphin	DoP	Moncobay
Alta (2nd of that name)			dolphin	DoP	Eastern waters
Amadeus			dolphin	CoP	
Amania			student	D'Sing	Harper Hall
Amilla			Fort daughter	NER	Fort Hold
Ampris			herbalist	ATWoP	Healer Hall
Anama			holder girl	RoP	Nerat Hold
Andemon			Masterfarmer	D'Q	Nerat Hold
Ander			holder	RoP	Benden Hold
Andiyar, Ben			child	D'Dawn	Karachi
Andiyar, Cara			child	D'Dawn	Karachi
Andiyar, Dena			child	D'Dawn	Karachi
Andiyar, Ram Da			child	D'Dawn	Karachi
Andiyar, Tarvi			geologist	D'Dawn	Karachi
Andriades, Akis			physician	CoP	Ruatha Hold
Andriades, Tim				D'Dawn	Paradise River
Anella			Fort 2nd wife	NER	Fort Hold
Angie			dolphin calf	DoP	Paradriv
Angie		green	rider	D'E	Telgar Weyr
Anskono			child	DoP	Paradise River Hold
Aphro			dolphin	CoP	
Aramina			hears dragons	RoP	o.a.a.
Aranya			Jayge's daughter	DoP	Paradise River
Armald			trader	RoP	Lilcamp Train
Arnor			Craftmaster	D'Sing	Harper Hall
Arthied, Desi			commissary	D'Dawn	Jordan
Arthied, Emthal			engineer	D'Dawn	
Asgenar			Lord Holder	D'F	Lemos Hold
Athpathis			rice farmer	D'Dawn	Sadrid

Name	Dragon	Color	Rank	Book	Hold/Weyr/Hall
Atlanta			dolphin calf	CoP	en route
Audiva			student	D'Sing	Harper Hall
Auster, Louise			ob-gyn nurse	D'Dawn	Jordan
Azury			Lord Holder	D'E	Southern Boll
B'dor		bronze	rider	D'Q	Ista Weyr
B'fol	Gereth	green	rider	D'F	Benden Weyr
B'greal			weyrling	MOR	Fort Weyr
B'irto	Cabenth	bronze	rider	D'Q	Benden Weyr
B'lerion	Nabeth	bronze	Wingleader	MOR	H'Reaches Weyr
B'naj	Seventh	brown	rider	D'Q	Fort Weyr
B'ner-	Miginth			D'E	Telgar Weyr
B'nurrin	Ianath	bronze	Weyrleader	D'E	Igen Weyr
B'rant	Fanth	brown	rider	D'Q	Benden Weyr
B'ref				CoP	
B'refli	Joruth	brown	rider	WD	Benden Weyr
B'ris	Gesilith	bronze	Wingleader	CoP	New Benden
B'zon	Ranilth	bronze	rider	WD	Southern Weyr
Baid			cropholder	MOR	Ruatha Hold
Baldor			harper	WD	Ista Weyr
Balfor			Beastmaster	MOR	Keroon Beasthold
Banak			head stockman	D'Drums	Harper Hall
Banger			Lord Holder	D'F	Igen Hold
Bantur			harper	D'Sing	Igen Hold
Bargen			Lord Holder	D'F	H'Reaches Hold
Barla			Dowell's wife	RoP	Ruatha Hold
Barly			healer	MOR	H'Reaches Hold
Barndy			Hold Bailiff	NER	Fort Hold
Bastom			Lord Holder	D'E	Tillek
Bedda (aunt)			trader	RoP	Lilcamp Train
Bedella	Solth	gold	Weyrwoman	D'Q	Telgar Weyr
Begamon			Lord Holder 2	WD	Nerat Hold
Beldona, d.			pilot/ archaeologist	CoP	EEC Vessel
Belesdan			Mastertanner	D'Q	Igen Hold
Bell, O			physician	D'Dawn	Landing
Beltara			Mastersmith	ATWoP	Telgar Smith Hall
Belterac			Mastersmith	ATWoP	Landing
Bendarek			woodsmith	D'Q	Lemos Hold
Benden, Paul			admiral	D'Dawn	Boca/Landing
Benden, Ross Vaclav			lt. s.g.	CoP	*Amherst*
Benelek			Jrym Smith	D'Q	Smith Hall

Dragons and Their Riders

Name	Dragon	Color	Rank	Book	Hold/Weyr/Hall
Bengel			student	ATWoP	Landing
Benis			younger son	D'Sing	Fort Hold
Berchar			Masterhealer	MOR	Fort Weyr
Berdine			Jrym Healer	D'Drums	Nabol Hold
Besel			drudge	D'Drums	Nabol Hold
Bessel			beastman	MOR	Beastmasterhold
Bessera	Odioth	gold	queenrider	MOR	H'Reaches Weyr
Bessie			dolphin	D'Dawn	Jordan
Bestrum			smallholder	NER	High Hill hold
Bethany			teacher	D'E	Fort College
Bilwil			Debera's horse	D'E	
Birsan			renegade	RoP	holdless
Biswy			schemer	ATWoP	holdless
Bitra, Avril			pilot	D'Dawn	Bitkim Island
Bitty	f-l	bronze	Aramina's	DoP	Paradise River
Biz			dolphin	DoP	Moncobay
Blaze	f-l	bronze	Sean's	D'Dawn	
Blesserel			holder son	ATWoP	Tillek Hold
Bloors			renegade	RoP	holdless
Boll, Emily			Governor	D'Dawn	Jordan
Bonna			Larad's daughter/artist	ATWoP	Telgar Hold
Bonneau, Drake			pilot	D'Dawn	Drake's Lake
Bonneau, Frank			rider	CoP	Fort Weyr
Bonneau, Svenda			miner	CoP	Benden Weyr
Bonz			apprentice	D'Sing	Harper Hall
Boojie			Alta's calf	DoP	Eastern waters
Boranda			healer	MOR	Healer Hall
Borel (uncle)			driver	RoP	Lilcamp Train
Borgald			carter	RoP	Amhold Train
Boris			holder	D'E	Telgar Hold
Boskoney			Jrym Harper	DoP	Paradise River
Brace			Masterharper	NER	Harper Hall
Brand	f-l	blue	steward	WD	Ruatha Hold
Brare			fisherman	RoP	Keroon Port
Breda	Amaranth	gold	queenrider	ATWoP	Crom Hold
Bregard			healer	MOR	Peyton Hold
Breide			steward	RoP	Landing
Brekke	Wirenth	gold	weyrwoman	D'Q	Benden/ Southern
Brennans			family	D'dawn	o.a.a.
Brennans – 2			fosterlings	CoP	Ruatha Hold
Brestolli			driver	ATWoP	Nurevin Train

Name	Dragon	Color	Rank	Book	Hold/Weyr/Hall
Brever			Toric's brother	RoP	High Palisades Hold
Briala			student	D'Sing	Harper Hall
Briaret			Masterherder	WD	Keroon Hold
Bridgely			Lord Holder	D'E	Benden Hold
Brindel, d.			guard	RoP	Benden Hold
Briskin			holder child	D'E	Bitra Hold
Brolly			apprentice	D'Sing	Harper Hall
Brooks, Jack			joat	D'Dawn	
Brooks, Sara			joat	D'Dawn	
	Rimbeth	brown	rider	RoP	Benden Weyr
Brudegan			Jrym Harper	D'Q	Harper Hall
Burdion			healer	MOR	Igen Sea Hold
Byrne, Ben			dolphineer	CoP	Monaco Bay
Byrne, Claire			dolphineer	CoP	Monaco Bay
C'gan	Tagath	blue	rider	D'F	Benden Weyr
C'tarel			rider	D'Song	Benden Weyr
C'ver	Hogarth	brown	rider	MOR	Telgar Weyr
Cal			dolphin	DoP	Kahrain waters
Camo			half-wit	D'Sing	Harper Hall
Campen			Fort son	MOR	Fort Hold
Campila			healer	ATWoP	Ruatha Hold
Candler			harper	D'Drums	Nabol Hold
Capiam			Masterhealer	MOR	Fort Hold
Captiva			dolphin	CoP	
Carolina			dolphin	CoP	en route
Carter, Cabot Francis			Legist	D'Dawn	Cambridge
Caselon			apprentice glass-smith	ATWoP	Landing
Casmodian			harper	NER	Fort Hold
Cass			dolphin	CoP	
Castor			capt. EEC	CoP	EEC Vessel
Catarel, David	Polenth		bronze	D'Dawn	Landing
Celewis			Masterhealer	ATWoP	Bitra Hold
Celina	Lamanth	gold	queenrider	D'Q	Benden Weyr
Cervantes, Angelo			ob-gyn	D'Dawn	Jordan
Cervantes, Corazon			farmer	CoP	en route
Cervanteses - 2			fosterlings	CoP	Ruatha Hold
Chad			harper	D'Q	Telgar Hold
Ch'mon	Helith	bronze	rider	MOR	Igen Weyr
Chaldon			holder child	D'E	Bitra Hold
Challer			driver	RoP	Lilcamp Train
Chalkin			Lord Holder	D'E	Bitra Hold

Dragons and Their Riders

Name	Dragon	Color	Rank	Book	Hold/Weyr/Hall
Chernoff, Dasha			worker	D'Dawn	Bitkim
Chernoff, Ivan			miner	CoP	Karachi
Chernoff, Jacob			child/smith	D'Dawn	Seminole
Chernoff, Jake			com. tech	D'Dawn	
Chernoff, Martha			com. tech	D'Dawn	
Chernoff, Peter				CoP	
Chernoff, Tarrie	Porth	gold	queenrider	D'Dawn	Landing
Cherry			wife to Kizan	D'E	Tillek Hold
Childon			holder	RoP	Kimmage Hold
China			dolphin	CoP	
Chink			black dog	RoP	Paradise River
Chomas			woodworker	D'E	Hall Domaize
Chrislee			head chef	D'E	Fort Hold
Chung			child	D'Dawn	
Ciottis, d.			family	D'Dawn	Milan
Ciparis			Lord Holder Begamon's brother	ATWoP	Nerat Hold
Clargesh			Master Glass-smith	MOR	Tillek Hold
Clell			app. drummer	D'Drums	Harper Hall
Clisser			college head	D'E	Fort College
Clissmann, Dieter			computer spec.	D'Dawn	Jordan
Clissmann, Nyassa	Milath	gold	queenrider	D'Dawn	Landing
Coatls - 3			fosterlings	CoP	Ruatha Hold
Cona			candidate	ATWoP	Nerat Hold
Connell, Bridey			traveler	D'Dawn	o.a.a.
Connell, Porrig			traveler	D'Dawn	o.a.a.
Connell, Sean	Carenath	bronze	rider	D'Dawn	Landing
Connell, Mick				D'Dawn	
Connell, Sinead			traveler	D'Dawn	o.a.a.
Conwy			Beastmaster	RoP	Benden Hold
Corana			holder girl	WD	Plateau Hold
Corey			dolphin	DoP	The Sea
Corey			head medic	D'E	Fort
Cori			dolphin calf	DoP	Paradriv
Corman			Lord Holder	D'F	Keroon Hold
Cosira	Caylith	gold	queenrider	WD	Ista Weyr
Cr'not	Caith	bronze	Weyrlingmaster	MOR	H'Reaches Weyr
Crenden			trader	RoP	Lilcamp Train
Cricket			Sean's grey	D'Dawn	Landing
Curmir			harper	MOR	Fort Hold
Curran			Masterfisherman	DoP	Fort Hold Port

Name	Dragon	Color	Rank	Book	Hold/Weyr/Hall
D'clan	Pranith	brown	rider	ATWoP	Landing
D'fio	Drenth	brown	rider	WD	Ista Weyr
D'ltan			weyrling	MOR	Fort Weyr
D'miel	Ronelth	bronze	Weyrleader	D'E	Ista Weyr
D'nek	Zagenth	bronze	rider	D'Q	Fort Weyr
D'nol	Valenth	bronze	wingsecond	D'F	Benden Weyr
D'ram	Tiroth	bronze	Weyrleader	D'Q	Ista Weyr
D'say	Kritith	bronze	wingleader	MOR	Ista Weyr
D'vid	Wieth	bronze	rider	CoP	Fort Weyr
D'wer	Trebeth	blue	rider	D'Q	Benden Weyr
Dag			herdsman	MOR	Ruatha Hold
Dalova	Allaneth	gold	Weyrwoman	MOR	Igen Weyr
Dangel			Alessan's bro.	MOR	Ruatha Hold
Danja			violinist		
Dannell			candidate	MOR	Benden Weyr
Dar			dolphin	DoP	Moncobay
Dar, Eba			agronomist	CoP	
Dart			dolphin	CoP	Monaco Bay
de Broglie, Maurice			miner	CoP	Ruatha Hold
de Broglie, Patrice			vulcanologist	D'Dawn	Young Mountain
de Curci, Pierre			caterer	D'Dawn	Jordan/Fort
de Poel, Corte			app. dolphin.	D'Dawn	Jordan
Debera	Morath	green	rider	D'E	Telgar Weyr
Deckter			Lord Holder 3	D'Drums	Nabol Hold
Declan			candidate	MOR	Fort Weyr
Deece			Jrym Harper	D'Drums	Harper Hall
Deefer			holder	MOR	Ruatha Hold
Deegan			apprentice archivist	ATWoP	Landing
Deelan			nurse	WD	Ruatha Hold
Delfi			dolphin	DoP	Kahrain waters
Delky			pony	DoP	Paradise River
Denol			steward	RoP	Southern Boll
Derabal			minor holder	RoP	Hilltop Hold
Dermently			Jrym Harper	D'Sing	Harper Hall
Desdra			Jryw Healer	MOR	Fort Hold
Diatis			Lord Holder	MOR	Tillek Hold
Dik			dolphin	DoP	Eastern waters
Diona	Kilanath	gold	Weyrwoman	MOR	H'Reaches Weyr
Dirzan			Jrym Drummer	D'Drums	Harper Hall
Disana			Lady Holder	RoP	Far Cry Hold
Domaize			artist/master	D'E	Hall Domaize
Domick			Craftmaster	D'Sing	Harper Hall

Dragons and Their Riders

Name	Dragon	Color	Rank	Book	Hold/Weyr/Hall
Dook, Kes			agronomist	CoP	Ruatha Hold
Dook, Licia			chef	CoP	Ruatha Hold
Dook, Mar			agronomist	D'Dawn	
Doove			Sorka's mare	D'Dawn	Landing
Doral			Fort son	NER	Fort Hold
Doris			Lady Holder	RoP	Igen Hold
Dorse			foster brother	WD	Ruatha Hold
Dowell			woodsmith	RoP	Ruatha Hold
Doyle, Mercy				D'Dawn	
Du Vieux, d.			family	D'Dawn	Amsterdam
Duff, Bill			zoologist	D'Dawn	Ierne Island
Duff, Cherry			historian	D'Dawn	Jordan
Duff, Evvie			com. tech	D'Dawn	Landing
Duff, Helga			dolphineer	CoP	Monaco Bay
Duff, Kathy	Amalanth	gold	queenrider	D'Dawn	Landing
Duff, Steve			sailor	CoP	en route
Duff, Toby			dolphineer	CoP	Monaco Bay
Duff-Vassaloe, Carol				D'Dawn	Ierne Island
Duke	f-l		bronze	D'Dawn	
Dulkan			engraver	ATWoP	Harper Hall
Dulsay			Lady Holder	RoP	Telgar Hold
Dunca			cotholder	D'Sing	Harper Hall
Duquesnes			family	D'Dawn	Bavaria
Durack			healer	ATWoP	Healer Hall
Durras			Weyrwoman	DoP	Eastern Weyr
Dushik			trooper	RoP	Tillek Hold
Eagles, Beth			physician	CoP	en route
Eddik			herdsman	RoP	Telgar Hold
Efram			dolphineer	CoP	
Elgion			harper	D'Song	Half-Circle Sea Hold
Elimona			harper	ATWoP	Harper Hall
Emmet	f-l		bronze	D'Dawn	
Empie	Dulchenth	gold	queenrider	MOR	Igen Weyr
Emun			Jrym Harper	MOR	Benden
Enyart				D'E	
Esselin			Masterminer	RoP	Landing
Estes, Leland			plastologist	D'Dawn	
Evan			Jrym Design	ATWoP	Landing
Ezremil			second son	CoP	Landing
F'duril	Dilenth	blue	rider	MOR	Fort Weyr
F'gal	Sanalth	bronze	Weyrleader	MOR	Ista Weyr
F'lar	Mnementh	bronze	Weyrleader	D'F	Benden

Name	Dragon	Color	Rank	Book	Hold/Weyr/Hall
F'lessan	Golanth	bronze	Wingleader	D'Q	Ruatha Hold
F'lon, d.		bronze	Weyrleader	D'F	Benden
F'mar	Tallith	bronze	rider	CoP	Landing
F'neldril	Mnanth	brown	Weyrlingmaster	MOR	Fort Weyr
F'nor	Canth	brown	Wingleader	D'F	Benden Weyr
F'rad	Telorth	green	rider	D'Q	Benden Weyr
F'tol		bronze	Wingleader	D'E	Telgar Weyr
Fabry			healer	DoP	Healer Hall
Facenden			Mastersmith	ATWoP	Landing
Fairex			pony	RoP	Lilcamp Train
Falga	Tamianth	gold	Weyrwoman	MOR	H'Reaches Weyr
Famira			Lady Holder	D'F	Lemos Hold
Fancy	f-l			D'Dawn	
Fandarel			Mastersmith	D'F	Smith Hall
Fanna	Mirath	gold	Weyrwoman	D'Q	Ista Weyr
Farelly			harper	MOR	Ruatha Hold
Fargoe, Anise			Captain	CoP	*Amherst*
Farley			minor holder	D'E	Fort Hold
Farli	f-l	gold	Piemur's	D'Drums	Southern Hold
Fax			Lord Holder	D'F	High Reaches Hold
Federen			Master Glass-smith	ATWoP	Bitra Hold
Feldon			apprentice	D'Sing	Harper Hall
Felena			asst. Headwoman	D'F	Benden Weyr
Felim			head cook	NER	Fort Hold
Felldool			healer	MOR	Hold Brum
Felleck			holder	RoP	Lemos Hold
Fendler			woodsman	D'E	Bitra Hold
Feng			colonist	D'Dawn	
Ferfar			smallholder	RoP	Kadross Hold
Fergal			Dag's gr.son	MOR	Ruatha Hold
Ferina			smallholder	D'E	Bitra Hold
Fesnal			apprentice	D'Sing	Harper Hall
Fessi			dolphin	DoP	Eastern waters
Festa			castaway	RoP	Southern Continent
Fidello			holder	WD	Plateau Hold
Finder			harper	WD	Ruatha Hold
Fira			Lady Holder	RoP	Telgar Hold
Fitatric			Lord Holder	MOR	Ista Hold
Flip			dolphin	DoP	Fort waters
Flo			dolphin	DoP	Moncobay

Dragons and Their Riders

Name	Dragon	Color	Rank	Book	Hold/Weyr/Hall
Foley, Deccie			horsehandler	CoP	Ruatha Hold
Foley, Denzil			Power Resource	D'Dawn	
Foleys			family	D'Dawn	o.a.a.
Follen			Jrym Healer	MOR	Ruatha Hold
Force, Theo			dolphineer	D'Dawn	
Forris			holder	RoP	Benden Hold
Fortine			Masterhealer	NER	Healer Hall
Fortine			Master Archive	MOR	Fort Hold
Fosdak			apprentice smith	ATWoP	Landing
Franco			Lord Holder	D'E	Nerat Hold
Fransman			harper	D'Sing	Bitra Hold
Fredig			designer/weaver	D'E	
Fremlich, Fritz			miner	D'Dawn	Karachi
Frenkal			medic	D'E	Tillek
Fusaiyuki, Alun			survivor	CoP	Honshu
Fusaiyuki, Chio			survivor	CoP	Honshu
Fusaiyuki, Ita			colonist	D'Dawn	Honshu
Fusaiyuki, Jiro			survivor	CoP	Honshu
Fusaiyuki, Kenjo			pilot	D'Dawn	Honshu
Fusaiyuki, Kimo			survivor	CoP	Honshu
Fusaiyuki, Meishun			survivor	CoP	Honshu
Fusaiyuki, Pat			survivor	CoP	Honshu
Fusaiyuki, Shensu			survivor	CoP	Honshu
G'dened	Barnath	bronze	Weyrleader-2	WD	Ista Weyr
G'don	Chakath	bronze	Weyrleader	D'E	H'Reaches Weyr
G'drel	Dorianth	bronze		NER	Fort Weyr
G'lanar	Lamoth	bronze	watchrider	ATWoP	Ruatha Hold
G'nag	Nelanth	bronze	rider	D'Q	Southern Weyr
G'narish	Gyarmath	bronze	Weyrleader	D'Q	Igen Weyr
G'rannat		green	rider	ATWoP	
G'sel		green	rider	D'Q	Southern Weyr
Gabin			Fort son	NER	Fort Hold
Gabred			Masterfarmer	RoP	Southern Hold
Gabri, Ann			dolphineer	D'Dawn	
Gale			healer	MOR	Big Bay Hold
Gale, Tony			worker	D'Dawn	Bitkim
Gallardy			healer	MOR	Healer Hall
Gallen			Fort son	NER	Fort Hold
Gallian			Holder son	D'E	H'Reaches
Galliani, Caesar			cattleman	D'Dawn	Roma
Galliani, Marco	Duluth	brown		D'Dawn	Landing
Galliani, Ramona			meteorologist	D'Dawn	Roma
Galliani, Stefano			sheepman	D'Dawn	Roma

Name	Dragon	Color	Rank	Book	Hold/Weyr/Hall
Galliani, Terry			horsewoman	CoP	en route
Galnish			healer	MOR	Hold Gar
Gana			wife to Bestrum	NER	High Hill hold
Gandidan			child	D'Q	Benden Weyr
Ganmar			Debera's suitor	D'E	Telgar Hold
Gar			dolphin	DoP	Eastern waters
Garben			Nerilka's suitor	NER	Fort Hold
Gardilfon			holder	RoP	Benden Hold
Gardrow			holder lad	RoP	Kimmage Hold
Garm			ship master	RoP	
Gayton			guard	ATWoP	Landing
Gedenase			Lord Holder	RoP	Lemos Hold
Gemma			Lady of Crom	D'F	H'Reaches
Genjon			Master Glass-smith	MOR	Tillek Hold
Genteely			student	D'Song	Harper Hall
Giri			brindle dog	RoP	Paradise River
Giron			dragonless	RoP	ex-Telgar Weyr
Gisa			Debera's stepmother		
Glay			renegade	RoP	holdless
Gledia			Jayge's mother	RoP	Lilcamp Train
Gollagee			tenor	D'E	
Gomalsi			son of Holder	ATWoP	Bitra Hold
Gomez, Andi			plastician	CoP	Landing
Gorby			healer	MOR	Keroon/runner Hold
Gorta			app. headwoman	MOR	Fort Weyr
Gram			Lord Holder	MOR	Nerat Hold
Grant, Felicia			biologist	D'Dawn	Landing
Grant van Toorns, d.			family	D'Dawn	Oslo Harbor
Grasella		green	rider	D'E	Telgar Weyr
Greene, John			marine sgt.	CoP	*Amherst*
Greene, Johnny			engineer	D'Dawn	Landing
Groghe			Lord Holder	D'F	Fort Hold
Gustavson, Gus			sailor	D'Dawn	Oslo Harbor
H'ages	Kerth	bronze	Wingsecond	D'Q	Telgar Weyr
H'grave	Hallath	green	rider	MOR	Benden Weyr
H'mar	Janereth	bronze	Weyrlingmaster	DoP	Eastern Weyr
H'nalt			Weyrlingmaster	ATWoP	Fort Weyr
Halefor			abductor	ATWoP	holdless
Hally			apprentice harper	DoP	Harper Hall
Hamian			Mastersmith	RoP	Southern Hold

Dragons and Their Riders

Name	Dragon	Color	Rank	Book	Hold/Weyr/Hall
Hamil, Barr			copilot	D'Dawn	Cardiff
Hamil, Jess			farmer	D'Dawn	Cardiff
Hanrahan, Brian			engineer	D'Dawn	Jordan/Fort
Hanrahan, Jair			Brian's wife	CoP	
Hanrahan, Mairi			nursery	D'Dawn	Jordan/Fort
Hanrahan, Michael (M'hall)	Brianth	bronze	rider	CoP	aka Mihall/New Benden Weyr
Hanrahan, Red (Peter OP)			veterinarian	D'Dawn	Jordan/Ruatha
Hanrahan, Ryan			youngest of 9	CoP	Ruatha Hold
Hanrahan, Sorka	Faranth	gold	Weyrwoman	D'Dawn	Jordan
Harkenon, Bay			micro-bio	D'Dawn	Jordan
Haura	Werth	gold	queenrider	MOR	Fort Weyr
Havers, Chuck			zoologist	D'Dawn	
Havers, Sue				D'Dawn	
Hedelman			guard	RoP	Benden Hold
Hegelman, Bernard			vintner	D'Dawn	
Hegelman, Eric, d.			child	D'Dawn	
Hegelman, Otto	Shoth	brown	rider	D'Dawn	
Hegmon			vintner	EE	Benden Hold
Heinrich				D'Dawn	Jordan
Helly			race rider	MOR	Ruatha Hold
Hemlet			marine	CoP	
Hempenstall, Aisling				D'dawn	Bordeaux
Hempenstall, Pat			botanist	D'Dawn	Bordeaux
Hittet			holder son	D'Drums	Nabol Hold
Holstroms, d.			family	D'Dawn	Amsterdam
Horon			son	DoP	Fort Hold
Hosbon			holder son	DoP	H'Reaches Hold
I Bit			dolphin	DoP	Fort waters
Iantine			portraitist	D'E	Benden/Telgar Weyr
Idarolan			Masterfisherman	D'Q	*Dawn Sisters*
Iggie			dolphin	DoP	Southern waters
Ind			Healer	MOR	Ista Weyr
Inka			dolphin	DoP	Fort waters
Irene	Maruth	gold	Weyrwoman	D'E	Benden Weyr
Irtine			holder lad	RoP	Kimmage Hold
Issony			teacher	D'E	ex-Bitra
Italia			dolphin	CoP	en route
J'dar		bronze	Wingleader	D'E	Telgar Weyr
J'ralt	Palanth	green	rider	D'F	Benden Weyr
J'tan	Sharth	bronze	rider	MOR	H'Reaches Weyr
Jacobsen, David			engineer	CoP	Ruatha Hold

Name	Dragon	Color	Rank	Book	Hold/Weyr/Hall
Jallora			Jryw Healer	MOR	Fort Weyr
Jamson			Lord Holder	D'E	H'Reaches Hold
Jancis			Jryw Smith	RoP	Smith Hall
Jane			Lady Holder	D'E	Benden Hold
Jarrol			child	RoP	Sharra/Jaxom
Jassap			holder	RoP	Benden Hold
Jaxom	Ruth	white	Lord Holder	D'Q	Ruatha Hold
Jean	Greteth	gold	rider	CoP	New Benden Weyr
Jemmy			composer/joat	D'E	Fort College
Jenette			queenrider	CoP	
Jepson, Arnold			colonist	D'Dawn	Landing
Jepson, Ben			child/pilot	D'Dawn	Landing
Jepson, Bob			child/pilot	D'Dawn	Landing
Jepson, Elizabeth			colonist	D'Dawn	Mexico
Jerint			Craftmaster	D'Sing	Harper Hall
Jess			Fort son	NER	Fort Hold
Jim			dolphin	DoP	Moncobay
Jissamy			Lady Holder 2	ATWoP	Telgar Hold
Joanson			medic	D'E	South Boll
Jora, d.	Nemorth	gold	Weyrwoman	D'F	Benden Weyr
Jorgenson, Simone				D'Dawn	
Josi			dolphin	DoP	Kahrain waters
Jule	Plath	green	rider	D'E	Telgar Weyr
Julie	Rementh	gold	queenrider	CoP	New Benden Weyr
K'dall	Teelarth	blue	rider	MOR	Telgar Weyr
K'der	Warth	blue	rider	D'Q	Ista Weyr
K'din	Buleth	brown	rider	DoP	Eastern waters
K'dren	Kuzuth	bronze	Weyrleader	MOR	Benden Weyr
K'irnety	Fidrith	bronze		D'Q	Telgar
K'lon	Rogeth	blue	rider	MOR	Fort Weyr
K'nebel	Firth	bronze	Weyrlingmaster	WD	Fort Weyr
K'net	Piyanth	bronze	Wingleader	D'F	Benden Weyr
K'van	Heth	bronze	Wingleader	WD	Benden Weyr
K'vin	Charanth	bronze	Weyrleader	D'E	Telgar Weyr
Kaarvan			captain	CoP	*Pernese Venturer*
Kaiden, Jess	Hallath	bronze		CoP	Benden Weyr
Kale			Lord Holder	RoP	Ruatha Hold
Kaljan			Masterminer	D'Drums	Harper Hall
Kalvi			engineer	D'E	Telgar Mines
Kami			Alemi's daughter	DoP	Paradise River
Kamiana	Pelianth	gold	queenrider	MOR	Fort Weyr

Dragons and Their Riders

Name	Dragon	Color	Rank	Book	Hold/Weyr/Hall
Kashima, Ebon			colonist	CoP	en route
Kashima, Ika			plasticist	CoP	en route
Kayla			kitchen staff	D'Sing	Harper Hall
Keating, Greg			worker	D'Dawn	
Keita			holder	RoP	Greystones Hold
Kenalas			weyrperson	D'Q	Benden Weyr
Ker			guard	ATWoP	Landing
Kern			son	DoP	Crom Hold
Keroon, Ezra			Capt./*Bahrain*	D'Dawn	Jordan
Ketrin			steward	RoP	Telgar Hold
Kevelon			holder	RoP	Central Hold/ Southern Continent
Kib			dolphin	DoP	Paradriv
Kibbe (2)			dolphin	DoP	The Sea
Kibby			dolphin	CoP	
Kiersey, Andrew			farmer	D'Dawn	Ierne Island
Kiersey, Jennifer			farmer	D'Dawn	Ierne Island
Kiffin, Saki			metallurgist	D'Dawn	
Kilamon			Jrym Harper	MOR	Ruatha Hold
Kimi	f-l	bronze	Sebell's	D'Sing	Harper Hall
Kimmage, Chuck			farmer/orchard	D'Dawn	Malay River
Kimmer, Charity			survivor	CoP	Honshu
Kimmer, Faith			survivor	CoP	Honshu
Kimmer, Hope			survivor	CoP	Honshu
Kimmer, Stev			miner	D'Dawn	Bitkim Island
King			bay stallion	CoP	Ruatha Hold
Kinver			Lord Holder	D'E	ex-Bitra
Kista			Fort daughter	NER	Fort Hold
Kitrin			Alemi's wife	DoP	Paradise River
Kizan			shipmaster	D'E	Tillek Hold
Kulan			smallholder	MOR	Ruatha Hold
Kung			guard	D'Dawn	Landing
Kung, Ashok			rider		Fort Weyr
Kurt				D'Dawn	Jordan
Kylara	Prideth	gold	queenrider	D'F	Southern Weyr
Kylos			healer	MOR	Sea Cliff Seahold
L'bol	Timenth	bronze	Weyrleader	MOR	Igen Weyr
L'mal, d.	Clinnith	bronze	Weyrleader	MOR	Fort Weyr
L'rad			rider	D'F	Benden Weyr
L'rayl	Sorth	brown	rider	MOR	Fort Weyr
L'ren			rider	CoP	New Benden
L'ser	Vuroth	bronze	rider	D'E	Telgar Weyr

Name	Dragon	Color	Rank	Book	Hold/Weyr/Hall
L'trel	Falgrenth	blue	rider	D'Q	Southern Weyr
L'vin	Jith	bronze	rider	MOR	Benden Weyr
L'zal	Beerth	green	rider	ATWoP	Eastern Weyr
Lady Tela			Fax's woman	D'F	H'Reaches Hold
Langsam, Ilsa			teacher	CoP	Ruatha Hold
Lao, Shih	Firth	bronze	rider	D'Dawn	Landing
Larad			Lord Holder	D'F	Telgar Hold
Laradian			holder son	ATWoP	Telgar Hold
Laudey			Lord Holder	D'Q	Igen Hold
Laura	Jemath	gold	Weyrwoman	D'E	Ista Weyr
Lavel			holder	D'E	Telgar Hold
Layrence			teacher	D'E	Fort College
Leef, d.			Lord Holder	MOR	Ruatha Hold
Lemos, Bart			pilot	D'Dawn	Yukon
Lemsia			Menolly and Sebell's daughter	ATWoP	Harper Hall
Lensdale			purser	D'Dawn	
Leopol			helper lad	D'E	Telgar Weyr
Leri	Holth	gold	ex-Weyrwoman	MOR	Fort Weyr
Lessa	Ramoth	gold	Weyrwoman	D'F	Ruatha
Lesselam			harp. cand.	DoP	Harper Hall
Leta			dolphin	DoP	Kahrain waters
Levalla	Oribeth	gold	Weyrwoman	MOR	Benden Weyr
	Lidith	gold	queen		
Lidora	Ilith	gold	queenrider	MOR	Fort Weyr
Lieb, Valli			geologist	D'Dawn	Drake's Lake
Ligand			Jrym Tanner	D'Sing	Fort Gather
Lilcamp, Jayge			trader	RoP	Lilcamp Train
Liliencamp, Buck			engineer	CoP	Ruatha Hold
Liliencamp, Joel			commissary	D'Dawn	Jordan
Lilla			Fort daughter	NER	Fort Hold
Liu, Mo Tan			nexialist EEC	CoP	
Logorides, Gygorg			agronomist	D'Dawn	Thessaly
Logorides, Kolya			ob-gyn	CoP	Ruatha Hold
Logorides, Paul		brown	rider	D'Dawn	
Loki			dolphin	DoP	Kahrain waters
Lonada			holder girl	D'E	Bitra Hold
Loreana			healer	MOR	Bay Head Seahold
Lorenzo, Wade			musician	D'Dawn	Sadrid
Losacot			Masterfarmer	ATWoP	Nerat Hold
Lottie			dolphin	D'Dawn	Jordan
Lozell			harpist	D'E	Fort College

Dragons and Their Riders

Name	Dragon	Color	Rank	Book	Hold/Weyr/Hall
Luccha			holder girl	D'E	Bitra Hold
Lucil			nursery auntie	NER	Fort Hold
Lur			holder	DoP	Paradise River
Lytol (L'tol)	Larth	brown	rider	D'F	Benden Weyr
M'barak	Arith	blue	weyrling	MOR	Fort Weyr
M'dam	Kessuth	bronze	Weyrlingmaster	D'E	Telgar Weyr
M'gent	Ith	bronze	Wingleader	MOR	Benden Weyr
M'leng	Sith	green	rider	D'E	Telgar Weyr
M'rak	Canith	bronze	rider	D'E	Telgar Weyr
M'rand	Tileth	bronze	rider	ATWoP	H'Reaches Weyr
M'ray	Quoarth	brown	Moreta's son	MOR	Ista Weyr
M'rek	Zigeth	bronze	wingsecond	D'Q	Telgar Weyr
M'shall	Craigath	bronze	Weyrleader	D'E	Benden Weyr
M'sur		brown		DoP	Eastern Weyr
M'tani	Hogarth	bronze	Weyrleader	MOR	Telgar Weyr
M'tok	Litorth	bronze	rider	WD	Benden Weyr
MacArdle-Cooney, Chris			child-carer	D'Dawn	Jordan
Macabir			healer	NER	internment camp
Macartor			painter	D'E	
Maindy			herdsman	RoP	Southern Hold
Maindy II			holder	RoP	Far Cry Hold
Makfar			Alessan's bro.	MOR	Ruatha Hold
Malawi			dolphin	CoP	en route
Mallibeau, Rene			vintner	D'Dawn	
Manora			Headwoman	D'F	Benden Weyr
Manotti			Jrym Smith	ATWoP	Telgar Smithhall
Mara			Fort daughter	NER	Fort Hold
Maranis			medic	D'E	Telgar Weyr
Marceau, Kwan			zoologist	D'Dawn	Bordeaux
Marchane, Ziv			physician	D'Dawn	
Mardra	Loranth	gold	Weyrwoman	D'F	Fort Weyr
Marella			Lady Holder	RoP	Southern Boll Hold
Margatta	Ludeth	gold	queenrider	D'Q	Fort Weyr
Mari	Susuth	gold	Weyrwoman	D'E	High Reaches
Mariah	f-l	gold		D'Dawn	
Marl			Beastmaster	MOR	Ruatha Hold
Martin	Dagmath	blue	rider	CoP	Fort Weyr
Masdek			Jrym Harper	MOR	Fort Hold
Mattew			holder son	D'E	Fort Hold
Mavi			Lady Holder	D'Song	Half-Circle Sea Hold
Maxmillian			dolphin	D'Dawn	Jordan

Name	Dragon	Color	Rank	Book	Hold/Weyr/Hall
Maylone			candidate	MOR	Fort Weyr
Mechalla			holder	RoP	Southern Hold
Medaman			holder	RoP	Lemos Hold
Meer	f-l	bronze	Sharra's	D'Drums	Southern Hold
Mel			dolphin	DoP	Moncobay
Mellor	Dalgeth	gold	Weyrwoman	MOR	Telgar Weyr
Melvinah, Cos			psychologist	CoP	Seminole
Mendir			healer	MOR	Ground Hold
Menolly	10 f-l		harper	D'Song	Half-Circle Sea Hold
Mercer, Jerry	Manooth	brown	rider	D'Dawn	
Mercia & Merin (twins)			Fort	NER	Fort Hold
Merika		gold	Weyrwoman	D'Q	H'Reaches Weyr
Merelan			singer	D'Sing	Harper Hall
Meron			Lord Holder	D'F	Nabol
Mesla		green	rider	D'E	Telgar Weyr
Messurier, Madeleine			chatelaine	CoP	Ruatha Hold
Mibbut			healer	MOR	Keroon Beasthold
Mihall	Brianth	bronze	Weyrleader	CoP	New Benden
Milan, George			farmer	D'Dawn	Calusa
Milan, Joe, d.			child	D'Dawn	
Milla			dead mother	D'E	
Miridan	Sutanith	gold	queenrider	MOR	Telgar Weyr
Mirrim	Path	green	rider/healer	D'Q	Southern/Benden Weyr
Miskin			guard	ATWoP	Landing
Mislue			patient	DoP	Healer Hall
Moorhouse			family	D'Dawn	o.a.a.
Moorhouse, Lally			traveler	D'Dawn	o.a.a.
Moreno, Dino				D'Dawn	
Moreta	Orlith	gold	Weyrwoman	MOR	Fort Weyr
Morilton			Master Glass-smith	ATWoP	Landing
Morinst			border guard	D'E	Bitra Hold
Morshal			Craftmaster	D'Sing	Harper Hall
Mostar			Holder son	MOR	Fort Hold
Mott, Amy		gold	queenrider	CoP	
Mott, Purdee			miner	D'Dawn	Bitkim
Muhammed, Dos			plastician	D'Dawn	
Mul			dolphin	DoP	Moncobay
Munchaun			Nerilka's uncle	NER	Fort Hold
Munson, Ozzie			miner	D'Dawn	Karachi
Murda			fisher	RoP	Big Lagoon

Dragons and Their Riders

Name	Dragon	Color	Rank	Book	Hold/Weyr/Hall
Musgrave-Blake, Betty				D'Dawn	
N'klas	Petrath	bronze	rider	CoP	Fort Weyr
N'men	Jelth	blue	rider	MOR	Fort Weyr
N'mool	Bidorth	bronze	rider	MOR	H'Reaches Weyr
N'ran	Galath	brown	medic/ animal doctor	D'E	Fort Weyr
N'tar	Melath	bronze	rider	MOR	H'Reaches Weyr
N'ton	Lioth	bronze	Weyrleader	D'F	Benden/Fort
Nabol, Nabhi			pilot	D'Dawn	Landing
Nadira		gold	Weyrwoman	WD	Igen Weyr
Nadona			Lady Holder	D'E	Bitra Hold
Namurra	Jilith	gold	Weyrwoman	MOR	Igen Weyr
Nataly			candidate	ATWoP	Fort Hold
Nattal			Headwoman	MOR	H'Reaches Weyr
Natua			dolphin	DoP	Eastern waters
Nazer			trader	RoP	Lilcamp Train
Nemekke			child	RoP	Brekke/F'nor
Nerilka			Lady	MOR	Fort Hold
Nessel			Lord Holder	D'F	Crom Hold
Nesso			Headwoman	MOR	Fort Weyr
Nev, Cahill Bralin			ensign	CoP	*Amherst*
Nevesham, Flora, d.			zoo-bot	CoP	EEC Vessel
Nexa			youngster	GWHD	o.a.a.
Ni Morgana, Saraidh			lt. sci.	CoP	*Amherst*
Nia			Fort daughter	NER	Fort Hold
Nicat			Masterminer	D'F	Crom Hold
Nielsen, Becky			worker	D'Dawn	Bitkim
Nietro, Pol			biologist	D'Dawn	Jordan
Nik (aunt)			driver	RoP	Lilcamp Train
Nilwan, Bart			mechanic	D'Dawn	
Nilwan, Blackie			joat	D'Dawn	
Norist			Master Glass-smith	ATWoP	
Norman			Course Mgr.	MOR	Ruatha Hold
Nurein			trader	ATWoP	o.a.a.
Nyadezda, Roma			musician	D'Dawn	
Nyassa	Milath	gold	queenrider	D'Dawn	Landing
O'Hara, Sue			physician	D'Dawn	
O'ney	Queth	bronze	Wingleader	D'E	Telgar Weyr
Obrin, Limpy			fisherman	D'Dawn	Oslo Harbor
Oharan			harper	D'Song	Benden Weyr
Oklina	Hannath	gold	Lady, sister	MOR	Fort Weyr
Oldive			Masterhealer	D'Sing	Healer Hall

Name	Dragon	Color	Rank	Book	Hold/Weyr/Hall
Olga			dolphin	D'Dawn	Jordan
Olivine, Bruce			mechanic	CoP	
Olodkey			Drummaster	D'Drums	Harper Hall
Olos			Menolly 2 son	DoP	Harper Hall
Olubushtu, Svenda			geologist	D'Dawn	Drake's Lake
Oma			Alessan's mom	MOR	Ruatha Hold
Ongola, Shuvin			child	D'Dawn	
Ongola, Zi			Commander	D'Dawn	Jordan
Oregon			dolphin	CoP	
Osemore			fisherman	RoP	Southern Hold
Ostrovsky, Sonja			miner	CoP	Telgar Hold
Ostrovsky, Volodya			miner	CoP	Telgar Hold
Oterel			Lord Holder	D'Q	Tillek Hold
P'leen	Aaith	bronze	rider	MOR	Igen Weyr
P'llomar	Kadarth	green	rider	WD	Benden
P'nine	Ixth	bronze	rider	MOR	Fort Weyr
P'ratan	Poranth	green	rider	RoP	Southern Weyr
P'ter	Siwith	blue	rider	CoP	Fort Weyr
P'tero	Ormonth	blue	rider	D'E	Telgar Weyr
P'zar	Roth	bronze	Wingsecond	D'Q	Fort Weyr
Pagnesjo, Per			Captain	CoP	*Perseus*
Pahlevi, Boris			Engineer	D'Dawn	
Palim			Jrym Baker	D'Sing	Fort Hold
Paramundi, Jivan			Ob-gyn	D'Dawn	Jordan
Pardure			holder lad	DoP	Paradise River Hold
Parren			Jrym weaver	DoP	Paradise River Hold
Patrick, Bjorn			teacher	D'Dawn	Ierne Island
Patrick, Jess				CoP	Ruatha Hold
Patrick, Tom			psychologist	D'Dawn	Longwood, I. I.
Paulin			Lord Holder	D'E	Fort Hold
Pell			youngster	RoP	o.a.a.
Pendora (married)			Fort daughter	NER	Fort Hold
Pendra			Lady Holder	MOR	Fort Hold
Pergamol			journeyman	D'Sing	Smith Hall
Perschar			harper/artist	RoP	o.a.a.
Persellan			Jrym Healer	DoP	Eastern Weyr
Peterpar			herdsman	MOR	Fort Weyr
Peth			Fort son	NER	Fort Hold
Petiron, d.			harper	D'Song	Half-Circle Sea Hold
Petter			Jrym	RoP	Bitra Hold

Dragons and Their Riders

Name	Dragon	Color	Rank	Book	Hold/Weyr/Hall
Pha			dolphin	CoP	
Piemur			singer/harper	D'Sing	Harper Hall
Pilgra	Segrith	gold	Weyrwoman	D'Q	H'Reaches Weyr
Pol			holder	RoP	Benden Hold
Pol			runnerhandler	NER	High Hill Hold
Pollan			healer	MOR	Big Bay Hold
Pona			student	D'Sing	Southern Boll
Pressen			healer	MOR	H'Reaches Weyr
Prilla	Selianth	gold	queenrider	WD	Fort Weyr
Putsch, Caleb			Meteorologist	D'Dawn	
Quitrin			healer	MOR	Southern Boll Hold
R'bert	Jenoth	brown	rider	CoP	Fort Weyr
R'gul	Hath	bronze	Weyrleader	D'F	Benden
R'len	Ponteth	bronze	rider	MOR	H'Reaches Weyr
R'limeak	Gionth	blue	rider	MOR	Fort Weyr
R'mart	Branth	bronze	Weyrleader	D'Q	Telgar Weyr
R'mel	Sorenth	brown	rider	D'Q	Benden Weyr
R'nor	Virianth	brown	rider	D'Q	Benden Weyr
Radamanth, Phas			zoologist	D'Dawn	Cathay
Radelin-Doyle, Cathy	Singlath	gold	queenrider	D'Dawn	Landing
Radelins, d.			family	D'Dawn	Bavaria
Rado, Cecilia				CoP	
Raghir, Egend			engineer	CoP	Ruatha Hold
Raid			Lord Holder	D'F	Benden Hold
Ramala			Lady Holder	RoP	Southern Hold
Rampesi			Ship master	RoP	*Bay Lady*
Ranly			apprentice	D'Sing	Harper Hall
Rannelly			nurse	D'Q	Southern Weyr
Ranrel			Lord Holder	ATWoP	Tillek Hold
Rapal			healer	MOR	Campbell's Field
Ratoshigan			Lord Holder	MOR	Southern Boll
Readis			trader	RoP	Lilcamp Train
Readis—2			holder boy	RoP	Paradise River Hold
Regan, Jan			dolphineer	D'Dawn	Jordan
Rena			dolphin	DoP	Kahrain waters
Richud			Lord Holder	D'E	Ista Hold
Robina			fisherman wife	DoP	Fort Hold Port
Robinton			Masterharper	D'F	Harper Hall
Robse			child	RoP	Menolly/Sebell
Rokayas			Jrym Drummer	D'Drums	Harper Hall
Rom			dolphin	DoP	Eastern waters

Name	Dragon	Color	Rank	Book	Hold/Weyr/Hall
Rona			apprentice	ATWoP	Landing
Runel			eidetic	MOR	Ruatha Hold
S'gar	Dunluth		watchrider	ATWoP	Ruatha Hold
S'gor	Malth	green	rider	MOR	Fort Weyr
S'goral	Betunth	green	rider	D'Q	Southern Weyr
S'kedel	Adath	brown	rider	MOR	Fort Weyr
S'lan	Binth	bronze	rider	D'F	Benden Weyr
S'lel	Tuenth	bronze	Wingleader	D'F	Benden Weyr
S'len	Bigath	green	rider	ATWoP	Fort Weyr
S'ligar	Gianarth	bronze	Weyrleader	MOR	H'Reaches Weyr
S'mon	Tiabeth	bronze	rider	D'E	Telgar Weyr
S'nan	Magrith	bronze	Weyrleader	D'E	Fort Weyr
S'peren	Clioth	bronze	Wingleader	MOR	Fort Weyr
S'rond			rider	ATWoP	Southern Weyr
Sal			Pol's bro.	NER	High Hill Hold
Salda			Lady Holder	D'E	Telgar Hold
Sallisha			teacher	D'E	traveling
Samvel			schoolmaster	DoP	Landing School
Sandi			dolphin	DoP	Kahrain waters
Sandman			dolphin	CoP	
Saneter			harper	D'Drums	Southern Hold
Sangel			Lord Holder	D'Q	Southern Boll
Sanra			child nurse	D'Song	Benden Weyr
Sara			child	RoP	Southern Hold
Sarai	Lanath	gold	Weyrwoman	D'E	Fort Weyr
Sarra		green	rider	D'E	Telgar Weyr
Scag			marine	CoP	
Scallak			castaway	RoP	Southern Continent
Scand			Masterhealer	MOR	Ruatha Hold
Schultz, Anna			dolphineer	CoP	en route
Schultz, Emily			fosterling	CoP	Ruatha Hold
Schultz, Gunnar			dolphineer	CoP	Maori Lake
Schultz, Max			fosterling	CoP	Ruatha Hold
Sebell			harper	D'Q	Harper Hall
Sefal			healer	ATWoP	Healer Hall
Sejby, Anders			shipmaster	CoP	*Mayflower*
Sejby, Nora	Tenneth		queenrider	D'Dawn	Landing
Sella			daughter	D'Song	Half-Circle Sea Hold
Semling, Hans			teacher	D'Dawn	Landing
Semling, Peter	Gilgath		bronze	D'Dawn	Landing

Name	Dragon	Color	Rank	Book	Hold/Weyr/Hall
Semment			healer	MOR	Great Reach Hold
Sevya	Butoth	gold	queenrider	CoP	New Benden Weyr
Shadder			Lord Holder	MOR	Benden Hold
Sh'gall	Kadith	bronze	Weyrleader	MOR	Fort Weyr
Shanna	Haralth	gold	Weyrwoman	D'E	Igen Weyr
Sharra			healer	WD	Southern Hold
Shattuck, Bernard			Captain	CoP	*Mayflower*
Shavva			nav-scout EEC	CoP	EEC Vessel
Shawan			2nd son/Jaxom	ATWoP	Ruatha Hold
Sheledon			composer	D'E	Fort College
Sherris			apprentice	D'Sing	Harper Hall
Shonagar			Craftmaster	D'Sing	Harper Hall
Shulse			mathematician	D'E	Fort College
Shwartz, Rudi			head teacher	D'Dawn	
Sidny			nephew	D'E	Fort Hold
Sifer			Lord Holder	D'F	Bitra Hold
Sifuentes, Bessie			child-carer	D'Dawn	
Sifuentes, Ramon			ind. tech.	D'Dawn	
Sigomal			Lord Holder	ATWoP	Bitra Hold
Silfar			apprentice archivist	ATWoP	Landing
Silga			candidate	ATWoP	
Silga	Brixth	gold	Weyrwoman	MOR	Igen Weyr
Silma			Fort daughter	NER	Fort Hold
Silon			child	D'Sing	Benden Weyr
Silton			Jrym, Smith	ATWoP	Landing
Silvina			Headwoman	D'Sing	Harper Hall
Sim			drudge	MOR	Fort Hold
Sira			weaver auntie	NER	Fort Hold
Smithlad	Braneth	bronze	candidate	ATWoP	Igen Smith Hall
Sneel			healer	MOR	Greenfields Hold
Sograny			Masterherder	D'Q	Keroon Hold
Soover			smallholder	MOR	Southern Boll Hold
Sopers, A. C.			xenobio	D'Dawn	Zanadu
Sopers, Betty				CoP	Ruatha Hold
Soreel			woman	D'Song	Half-Circle Sea Hold
Sousmal			Lord Warder	ATWoP	Bitra Hold
Squealer			runnerbeast	MOR	Ruatha Hold

Name	Dragon	Color	Rank	Book	Hold/Weyr/Hall
St. John, Persis			pediatrician	D'Dawn	
Stein, Sabra			colonist	D'Dawn	Landing
Stone, Fulmar			Flight Officer	D'Dawn	Landing
Stupid			runnerbeast	D'Drums	Piemur's steed
Sturt, Arkady				CoP	Jordan
Sufur			Masterherdsman	MOR	Keroon Beasthold
Suriana, d.			Alessan's wife	MOR	Ruatha Hold
Swacky			trooper	RoP	o.a.a.
Swann, Patsy, d.			child	D'Dawn	
Sydra			teacher/sopr.	D'E	Fort College
T'bor	Orth	bronze	Weyrleader	D'F	Benden/Southern Weyr
T'gellan	Monarth	bronze	Wingleader	D'Q	Benden Weyr
T'gor	Relth	blue	rider	D'F	Benden Weyr
T'gran	Branth	brown	rider	D'F	Benden Weyr
T'grel	Raylinth	bronze	Wingleader	MOR	Telgar Weyr
T'kul	Salth	bronze	rider	WD	H'Reaches Weyr/ Southern Weyr
T'lan		brown	rider	D'E	Telgar
T'ledon	Serith	blue	rider	D'Q	Fort Hold/Weyr
T'lel	Banuth	brown	rider	D'E	Telgar Weyr
T'lion	Gadareth	bronze	rider	DoP	Eastern Weyr
T'lonneg	Jalerth	bronze	Wingleader	MOR	Ista Weyr
T'mas			rider	CoP	New Benden Weyr
T'nure	Tapeth	green	rider	MOR	Fort Weyr
T'ragel	Keranth	blue	weyrling	MOR	Fort Weyr
T'ral	Maneth	brown	rider	MOR	Fort Weyr
T'ran	Rederth	bronze	rider	WD	Igen Weyr
T'reb	Beth	green	rider	D'Q	Fort Weyr
T'red		brown	rider	D'E	Telgar Weyr
T'ron	Fidranth	bronze	Weyrleader	D'F	Fort Weyr
T'sel	Trenth	green	rider	D'Q	Benden Weyr
T'sen		green	rider	D'E	Telgar Weyr
T'sum			rider	D'F	Benden
Tagetarl			Jrym Harper	D'Q	Harper Hall
Talina			queenrider	D'Q	Benden Weyr
Talla	f-1	brown	Sharra's	D'Drums	Southern Hold
Talmor			Jrym Harper	D'Q	Harper Hall
Talpan			vet. healer	MOR	Keroon Beasthold
Tana			dolphin	DoP	Eastern waters
Tarathel, d.			Lord Holder	RoP	Telgar

Dragons and Their Riders

Name	Dragon	Color	Rank	Book	Hold/Weyr/Hall
Tashkovich				D'Dawn	
Tashvi			Lord Holder	D'E	Telgar Hold
Tawkin			oarsman	RoP	Southern Hold
Tegger			holder	WD	Ruatha Hold
Telgar, Sallah			pilot	D'Dawn	Karachi
Tellani			woman	MOR	Fort Weyr
Temma (aunt)			driver	RoP	Lilcamp Train
Temp			dolphin	DoP	Moncobay
Terbo, d.			zoo-chem	CoP	EEC Vessel
Terentel			Holder son	ATWoP	Tillek Hold
Teres			dolphin	DoP	Moncobay
Teresa			dolphin	D'Dawn	Jordan
Terry			Craftmaster	D'Q	Smith Hall
Texur			first mate	DoP	Fort Hold Port
Thea			Lady Holder	D'E	H'Reaches Hold
Thella			Lady	RoP	Telgar Hold
Theng			guardleader	MOR	Fort Hold
Theskin			Fort son	NER	Fort Hold
Tikini			child	DoP	
Tilarek			wagonman	D'F	Ruatha Hold
Tilgin			apprentice	D'Drums	Harper Hall
Tillek, James			Capt./B.Aires	D'Dawn	Monaco Bay
Tillek, The			Dolphin Sage	DoP	Whirlpool
Timareen			Weaver Craftmaster		D'Sing Telgar Hold
Timiny			apprentice	D'Sing	Harper Hall
Timore			engineer	D'E	Telgar Mines
Ting, Pei Pei			pharmacist	D'Dawn	Ierne Island
Tini			dolphin	DoP	Kahrain waters
Tino			trader	RoP	Lilcamp Train
Tirone			Masterharper	MOR	Harper Hall
Tisha			headwoman	D'E	Telgar Weyr
Tobin, Joe			Engineer	D'Dawn	Ierne Island
Tolocamp			Lord Holder	MOR	Fort Hold
Tom			dolphin	DoP	Eastern waters
Tomlinson, Basil			Chief Med. Off.	CoP	
Tomlinson, Greta			midwife	D'Dawn	
Tomol			harp. cand.	DoP	Harper Hall
Tonia			healer	MOR	Igen Seahold
Tordril			fosterling	WD	Igen/Ruath Hold
Torene	Alaranth	gold	Weyrwoman	CoP	New Benden Weyr

Name	Dragon	Color	Rank	Book	Hold/Weyr/Hall
Toric			Lord Holder	D'Q	Southern Hold
Tork	f-l	bronze	Jayge's	DoP	Paradise River
Toronas			Lord Holder	ATWoP	Benden Hold
Torsten			tanner	RoP	Southern Hold
Tory			dolphin	CoP	Monaco Bay
Tosikin			Jrym Joiner	ATWoP	Bitra Hold
Trader Jol			Lilcamp train	D'E	o.a.a.
Tragger			troop leader	RoP	Ruatha Hold
Trelbin			healer	NER	High Hill Hold
Trestan			apprentice	ATWoP	Landing
Trig	f-l	bronze	Jancis's	ATWoP	Landing
Trume			Masterherdsman	MOR	H'Reaches Hold
Trury, Emma			meteorologist	D'Dawn	
Tubberman, Lucy, d.				D'Dawn	Calusa
Tubberman, Mary			farmer	D'Dawn	
Tubberman, Ned			pilot	D'Dawn	
Tubberman, Petey			child	D'Dawn	Calusa
Tubberman, Ted			botanist	D'Dawn	Calusa
Tubridy			weyrman	RoP	Benden Weyr
Tuero			Jrym Harper	MOR	Ruatha Hold
Tumara			candidate	ATWoP	Ista Hold
Turnien, Ben			geologist, EEC	CoP	EEC Vessel
Tursi			dolphin	DoP	Kahrain waters
Turvine			cropholder	MOR	Ruatha Hold
Turving			smallholder	MOR	Ruatha Hold
	Tuzuth	bronze		MOR	Benden Weyr
Uloa	Elliath	gold	rider	CoP	Fort Weyr
Ussie			decorator	D'E	Hall Domaize
Usuai				D'Dawn	
Uvor			Beastmaster	RoP	Keroon Hold
V'last	Collith	bronze	wingleader	D'E	Telgar Weyr
V'line	Clarinath	bronze	rider	RoP	Eastern Weyr
V'mal	Koth	brown	rider	MOR	H'Reaches Weyr
V'mul	Tellath	brown	rider	MOR	Benden Weyr
Vandentine			student	ATWoP	Landing
Vander			smallholder	MOR	Ruatha Hold
Vanira		gold	queenrider	D'Q	Southern Weyr
Varena	Ralenth	gold	queenrider	WD	Southern Weyr
Varney			Masterfisherman	MOR	*Windtoss*
Vartry			marine	CoP	Honshu
Vassaloe, Francesco			technician	CoP	Jordan

Name	Dragon	Color	Rank	Book	Hold/Weyr/Hall
Veranera, Pete			shipmaster	CoP	*Maid*
Vergerin			Lord Holder	D'E	Bitra 2
Viderian			fosterling	D'Sing	Fort Hold
Vina			dolphin	DoP	Paradis
Vincet			Lord Holder	RoP	Nerat
W'ter	Taventh	bronze	rider	MOR	Benden Weyr
W'ven	Balgeth	green	rider	MOR	Fort Weyr
Waine			painter/joat	D'E	Telgar Weyr
Wangs, Sal & other			fosterlings	CoP	Ruatha Hold
Wansor			Glass-smith	D'Q	Smith Hall
Warbret			Lord Holder	D'Q	Ista Hold
Warder				D'F	Ruatha Hold
Wilcox			vet	D'Dawn	
Wimmia	Torenth	gold	Weyrwoman	MOR	Ista Weyr
Wind Blossom			geneticist	D'Dawn	Jordan
Worlain			healer	DoP	Healer Hall
Xavior-Kimmage, Chaila				D'Dawn	Malay
Yanus			Sea Holder	D'Song	Half-Circle Sea Hold
Yoritomo, Chio-Chio			colonist	D'Dawn	
Yuen, Xi Chi			astronomer	D'Dawn	Xanadu
Yung, Kitti Ping			bio-geneticist	D'Dawn	Jordan
Z'gal	Tracath	blue	rider	D'E	Telgar Weyr
Z'ran		brown	rider	D'E	Telgar Weyr
Zair	f-l	bronze	Robinton's	D'Q	Harper Hall
Zane, Rezmar Dooley			lt. nav.	CoP	*Amherst*
Zulaya	Meranath	gold	Weyrwoman	D'E	Telgar Weyr
Zulieta, Yashma			chef	CoP	Fort Weyr
Zulueta, Alianne	Chereth		queenrider	D'Dawn	Landing
Zurg			Masterweaver	D'F	Southern Boll Hold

NOTABLE FIRELIZARDS
AND THOSE THEY LOOK TO

Name	Color	Firelizard	Name	Color	Firelizard
Menolly	queen	Beauty	Menolly,		Diver
	bronze	Rocky	cont'd		Poll

Name	Color	Firelizard	Name	Color	Firelizard
Menolly, cont'd	brown	Brownie	Mirrim	green	Reppa
		Lazybones			Lok
		Mimic		brown	Tolly
	blue	Uncle	Sharra	bronze	Meer
	green	Auntie One		brown	Talla
		Auntie Two	Robinton	bronze	Zair
Piemur	gold	Farli	Sebell	gold	Kimi
Lord Groghe	gold	Merga	Brekke	bronze	Berd
N'ton	brown	Tris	F'nor	gold	Grall
Sorka	bronze	Duke	Asgenar	brown	Rial
	gold	Kundy	Sean	bronze	Blaze
			Bay Harkenon	gold	Mariah

FIRST DRAGONRIDERS OF PERN

Name	Dragon	Color	Name	Dragon	Color
David Catarel	Polenth	bronze	Kathy Duff	Amalath	queen
Tarrie Chernoff	Porth	queen	Nora Sejby	Tenneth	queen
Shih Lao	Firth	bronze	Catherine R–Doyle	Singlath	queen
Peter Semling	Gilgath	bronze	Alianne Zulueta	Chereth	queen
Nyassa Clissmann	Milath	queen	Sean Connell	Carenath	bronze
Marco Galliani	Duluth	brown	Sorka Hanrahan	Faranth	queen

2nd Hatching

Name	Dragon	Color	Name	Dragon	Color
Paul Logorides		brown	Jerry Mercer	Manooth	brown
Nicolas	Petrath	bronze	Boris Pahlevi	Gesilith	bronze
Otto Hegelman	Shoth	brown	Robert	Jenoth	brown

DRAGON LISTINGS

Dragon Name	Color	Rider	Book	Weyr
Aaith	bronze	P'leen	MOR	Igen
Adath	brown	S'kedel	MOR	Fort
Alaranth	gold	Torene	CoP	New Benden
Allaneth	gold	Dalova	MOR	Igen
Amalath	gold	Kathy Duff	D'Dawn	Landing
Amaranth	gold	Breda	ATWoP	Benden
Arith	blue	M'barak	MOR	Fort
Balgeth	green	W'ven	MOR	Fort
Banuth	brown	T'lel	D'E	Telgar
Barnath	bronze	G'dened	D'Q	Ista
Beerth	green	L'zal	ATWoP	Eastern
Beljeth	gold	Adrea	RoP	Southern
Beth	green	T'reb	D'Q	Fort
Betunth	green	S'goral	D'Q	Southern
Bidorth	bronze	N'mool	MOR	High Reaches
Bigath	green	S'len	ATWoP	Fort
Binth	bronze	S'lan	D'F	Benden
	blue	K'lon	MOR	Fort
Braneth	bronze	smithlad	ATWoP	Igen
Branth	bronze	R'mart	D'Q	Telgar
Branth	brown	T'gran	D'F	Benden
Brianth	bronze	M'hall	CoP	New Benden
Brixth	gold	Silga	MOR	Igen
	bronze	J'dar	D'E	Telgar
	bronze	S'mon	D'E	Telgar
	brown	T'lan	D'E	Telgar
	brown	Z'ran	D'E	Telgar
	brown	Paul	D'Dawn	Landing
	brown	T'red	D'E	Telgar
Buleth	brown	K'din	DoP	Eastern
Butoth	gold	Sevya	CoP	New Benden
Cabenth	bronze	B'irto	D'Q	Benden
Caith	bronze	Cr'not	MOR	High Reaches
Canith	bronze	M'rak	D'E	Telgar
Canth	brown	F'nor	D'F	Benden
Carenath	bronze	Sean Connell	D'Dawn	Landing
Caylith	gold	Cosira	D'Q	Ista
Chakath	bronze	G'don	D'E	High Reaches
Charanth	bronze	K'vin	D'E	Telgar
Chereth	gold	Alianne	D'Dawn	Landing
Clarinath	bronze	V'line	RoP	Southern

237

Dragon Name	Color	Rider	Book	Weyr
Clinnith	bronze	L'mal	MOR	Fort
Clioth	bronze	S'peren	MOR	Fort
Collith	bronze	V'last	D'E	Telgar
Craigath	bronze	M'shall	D'E	Benden
Dagmath	blue	Martin	CoP	Fort
Dalgeth	gold	Mellor	MOR	Telgar
Dilenth	blue	F'duril	MOR	Fort
Dorianth	bronze	G'drel	NER	Fort
Drenth	brown	D'fio	WD	Ista
Dulchenth	gold	Empie	MOR	Igen
Duluth	brown	Marco	D'Dawn	Landing
Dunluth		S'gar	ATWoP	Ruatha Hold
Elliath	gold	Uloa	CoP	Fort
Falgrenth	blue	L'trel	D'Q	Southern
Fanth	brown	B'rant	D'Q	Benden
Faranth	gold	Torene	D'F	Benden
Faranth	gold	Sorka	D'Dawn	Landing
Fidranth	bronze	T'ron	D'F	old Fort
Fidrith	bronze	K'irnety	D'Q	Telgar
Firth	bronze	Shih Lao	D'Dawn	Landing
Firth	bronze	K'nebel	WD	Benden
Folrath	brown		ATWoP	
Gadareth	bronze	T'lion	DoP	Eastern
Galath	brown	N'ran	D'E	Fort
Gereth	green	B'fol	D'F	Benden
Gesilith	bronze	B'ris	CoP	Fort
Gianarth	bronze	S'ligar	MOR	High Reaches
Gilgath	bronze	Peter Semling	D'Dawn	Landing
Gionth	blue	R'limeak	MOR	Fort
Golanth	bronze	F'lessan	D'Q	Benden
	gold	Kathy Duff	D'Dawn	Landing
Gorianth	bronze		D'E	Telgar
Granth	green	A'murry	MOR	Igen
	green	Sarra	D'E	Telgar
	green	T'sen	D'E	Telgar
	green	T'sum	D'F	Benden
Greteth	gold	Jean	CoP	New Benden
Gyarmath	bronze	G'narish	D'Q	Igen
Hallath	green	H'grave	MOR	Benden
Hallath	bronze	Jess Kaiden	CoP	Benden
Hannath	gold	Oklina	MOR	Ruatha Hold
Haralth	gold	Shanna	D'E	Igen
Hath	bronze	R'gul	D'F	Benden

Dragons and Their Riders

Dragon Name	Color	Rider	Book	Weyr
Helith	bronze	Ch'mon	MOR	Igen
Heth	bronze	K'van	WD	Benden/Southern
Hogarth	brown	C'ver	MOR	Telgar
Hogarth	bronze	M'tani	MOR	Telgar
Holth	gold	Leri	MOR	Fort
Ianath	bronze	B'nurrin	D'E	Igen
Ilith	gold	Lidora	MOR	Fort
Ith	bronze	M'gent	MOR	Benden
Ixth	bronze	P'nine	MOR	Fort
Jalerth	bronze	T'lonneg	MOR	Ista
Janereth	bronze	H'mar	DoP	Eastern
Jelth	blue	N'men	MOR	Fort
Jemath	gold	Laura	D'E	Ista
Jenoth	brown	R'bert	CoP	Fort
Jilith	gold	Namurra	MOR	Igen
Jith	bronze	L'vin	MOR	Benden
Joruth	brown	B'refli	D'Q	Benden
Kadarth	green	P'llomar	WD	Benden
Kadith	bronze	Sh'gall	MOR	Fort
Keranth	blue	T'ragel	MOR	Fort
Kerth	bronze	H'ages	D'Q	Telgar
Kessuth	bronze	M'dam	D'E	Telgar
Kilanath	gold	Diona	MOR	High Reaches
Koth	brown	V'mal	MOR	High Reaches
Kritith	bronze	D'say	MOR	Ista
Kuzuth	bronze	K'dren	MOR	Benden
Lamanth	gold	Celina	D'Q	Benden
Lamoth	bronze	G'lanar	ATWoP	Ruatha Hold
Lanath	gold	Sarai	D'E	Fort
Larth	brown	L'tol/Lytol	D'F	Benden
Lidith	gold		D'F	
Lioth	bronze	N'ton	D'Q	Benden/Fort
Litorth	bronze	M'tok	WD	Benden
Loranth	gold	Mardra	D'F	Fort
Ludeth	gold	Margatta	D'Q	Fort
Magrith	bronze	S'nan	D'E	Fort
Malth	green	S'gor	MOR	Fort
Maneth	brown	T'ral	MOR	Fort
Manooth	brown	Jerry Mercer	D'Dawn	
Maruth	gold	Irene	D'E	Benden
Melath	bronze	N'tar	MOR	High Reaches
Meranath	gold	Zulaya	D'E	Telgar
Miginth	bronze	B'ner	D'E	Telgar

Dragon Name	Color	Rider	Book	Weyr
Milath	gold	Nyassa	D'Dawn	Landing
Minath	green	Jule	D'E	Telgar
Mirath	gold	Fanna	D'Q	Ista
Mnanth	brown	F'neldril	MOR	Fort
Mnementh	bronze	F'lar	D'F	Benden
Monarth	bronze	T'gellan	D'Q	Benden/Eastern
Morath	green	Debera	D'E	Telgar
Nabeth	bronze	B'lerion	MOR	High Reaches
Nelanth	bronze	G'nag	D'Q	Southern
Nemorth	gold	Jora	D'F	Ruatha
Odioth	gold	Bessera	MOR	High Reaches
Oribeth	gold	Levalla	MOR	Benden
Orlith	gold	Moreta	MOR	Fort
Ormonth	blue	P'tero	D'E	Telgar
Orth	bronze	T'bor	D'F	Fort/Southern
Palanth	green	J'ralt	D'F	Benden
Path	green	Mirrim	D'Q	Southern/Eastern
Pelianth	gold	Kamiana	MOR	Fort
Petrath	bronze	N'klas	CoP	Fort Weyr
Piyanth	bronze	K'net	D'F	Benden
Pirith	gold		WD	Ista Weyr
Polenth	bronze	David Catarel	D'Dawn	Landing
Ponteth	bronze	R'len	MOR	High Reaches
Poranth	green	P'ratan	RoP	Southern
Porth	gold	Tarrie	D'Dawn	Landing
Pranith	brown	D'clan	ATWoP	Landing
Prath	green	Angie	D'E	Telgar
Prideth	gold	Kylara	D'Q	Benden/Southern
Queth	bronze	O'ney	D'E	Telgar
Quoarth	brown	M'ray	MOR	Ista
Ralenth	gold	Varena	WD	Southern
Ramoth	gold	Lessa	D'F	Benden
Ranilth	bronze	B'zon	WD	Southern
Raylinth	bronze	T'grel	MOR	Telgar
Rederth	bronze	T'ran	WD	Igen
Rementh	gold	Julie	CoP	Benden
Relth	blue	T'gor	D'F	Benden
Rimbeth	brown		RoP	Benden
Rogeth	blue	K'lon	MOR	Fort
Ronelth	bronze	D'miel	D'E	Ista
Roth	bronze	P'zar	D'Q	Southern
Ruth	white	Jaxom	D'Q	Ruatha Hold
Salth	bronze	T'kul	D'F	Benden

Dragons and Their Riders

Dragon Name	Color	Rider	Book	Weyr
Sanalth	bronze	F'gal	MOR	Ista
Segrith	gold	Pilgra	D'Q	High Reaches
Selianth	gold	Prilla	WD	Fort
Serith	blue	T'ledon	D'Q	Fort
Seventh	brown	B'naj	D'Q	Fort
Sharth	bronze	J'tan	MOR	High Reaches
Shoth	brown	Otto Hegelman	D'Dawn	
Singlath	gold	Cathy R-Doyle	D'Dawn	Landing
Sith	green	M'leng	D'E	Telgar
Siwith	blue	P'ter	CoP	Fort
Solth	gold	Bedella	D'Q	Telgar
Sorenth	brown	R'mel	D'Q	Benden
Sorth	brown	L'rayl	MOR	Fort
Spelth	bronze		D'E	Telgar
Susuth	gold	Mari	D'E	High Reaches
Sutanith	gold	Miridan	MOR	Telgar
Tagath	blue	C'gan	D'F	Benden
Tallith	bronze	F'mar	CoP	Fort
Tamianth	gold	Falga	MOR	High Reaches
Tapeth	green	T'nure	MOR	Fort
Taventh	bronze	W'ter	MOR	Benden
Teelarth	blue	K'dall	MOR	Telgar
Tellath	brown	V'mul	MOR	Benden
Telorth	green	F'rad	D'Q	Benden
Tenneth	gold	Nora Sejby	D'Dawn	Landing
Tiabeth	bronze	S'mon	D'E	Telgar
Tigrath	green	A'dan	MOR	Fort
Tileth	bronze	M'rand	ATWoP	High Reaches
Timenth	bronze	L'bol	MOR	Igen
Tiroth	bronze	D'ram	D'Q	Ista
Torenth	gold	Wimmia	MOR	Ista
Tracath	blue	Z'gal	D'E	Telgar
Trebeth	blue	D'wer	D'Q	Benden
Trenth	green	T'sel	D'Q	Benden
Tuenth	bronze	S'lel	D'F	Benden
Tuzuth	bronze		MOR	Benden
Valenth	bronze	D'nol	D'F	Benden
Virianth	brown	R'nor	D'Q	Benden
Vuroth	bronze	L'ser	D'E	Telgar
Warth	blue	K'der	D'Q	Ista
Werth	gold	Haura	MOR	Fort
Wieth	bronze	D'vid	CoP	Fort
Wirenth	gold	Brekke	D'Q	Southern

Dragon Name	Color	Rider	Book	Weyr
Zagenth	bronze	D'nek	D'Q	Fort Weyr
Zigeth	bronze	M'rek	D'Q	Telgar

RIDER LISTINGS

Rider	Dragon	Color	Book	Weyr
A'dan	Tigrath	green	MOR	Fort
A'murry	Granth	green	MOR	Igen
A'ton			RoP	
Adrea	Beljeth	gold	RoP	Southern
Alianne	Chereth	gold	D'Dawn	Landing
Angie	Plath	green	D'E	Telgar
B'dor		bronze	WD	Ista
B'fol	Gereth	green	D'F	Benden
B'greal			MOR	Fort
B'irto	Cabenth	bronze	D'Q	Benden
B'lerion	Nabeth	bronze	MOR	High Reaches
B'naj	Seventh	green	D'Q	Fort
B'ner	Miginth	bronze	D'E	Telgar
B'nurrin	Ianath	bronze	D'E	Igen
B'rant	Fanth	brown	D'Q	Benden
B'ref			CoP	
B'refli	Joruth	brown	WD	Benden
B'ris	Gesilith	bronze	CoP	New Benden
B'zon	Ranilth	bronze	RoP	Southern
Bedella	Solth	gold	D'Q	Telgar
Bessera	Odioth	gold	MOR	High Reaches
	Braneth	bronze	ATWoP	Benden
Breda	Amaranth	gold	ATWoP	Benden
Brekke	Wirenth	gold	D'Q	Benden/Southern
C'gan	Tagath	blue	D'F	Benden
C'tarel			D'Song	Benden
C'ver	Hogarth	brown	MOR	Telgar
Cathy	Singlath	gold	D'Dawn	Landing
Celina	Lamanth	gold	D'Q	Benden
Ch'mon	Helith	bronze	MOR	Igen
Connell, Sean	Carenath	bronze	D'Dawn	Landing
Cosira	Caylith	gold	D'Q	Ista

Dragons and Their Riders

Rider	Dragon	Color	Book	Weyr
Cr'not	Caith	bronze	MOR	High Reaches
D'fio	Drenth	brown	WD	Ista
D'clan	Pranith	brown	ATWoP	Landing
D'ltan	weyrling		MOR	Fort
D'miel	Ronelth	bronze	D'E	Ista
D'nek	Zagenth	bronze	D'Q	Fort
D'nol	Valenth	bronze	D'F	Benden
D'ram	Tiroth	bronze	D'Q	Ista
D'say	Kritith	bronze	MOR	Ista
D'vid	Wieth	bronze	CoP	Fort
D'wer	Trebeth	blue	D'Q	Benden
Dalova	Allaneth	gold	MOR	Igen
Debera	Morath	green	D'E	Telgar
Diona	Kilanath	gold	MOR	High Reaches
Empie	Dulchenth	gold	MOR	Igen
F'duril	Dilenth	blue	MOR	Fort
F'gal	Sanalth	bronze	MOR	Ista
			MOR	Fort
F'lar	Mnementh	bronze	D'F	Benden
F'lessan	Golanth	bronze	D'Q	Benden
F'mar	Tallith	bronze	CoP	Fort
F'lon		bronze	D'F	Benden
F'neldrin	Mnanth	brown	MOR	Fort
F'nor	Canth	brown	D'F	Benden
F'rad	Telorth	green	D'Q	Benden
F'tol		bronze	D'E	Telgar
Falga	Tamianth	gold	MOR	High Reaches
Fanna	Mirath	gold	D'Q	Ista
G'dened	Barnath	bronze	D'Q	Ista
G'don	Chakath	bronze	D'E	High Reaches
G'drel	Dorianth	bronze	NER	Fort
G'lanar	Lamoth	bronze	ATWoP	Southern
G'nag	Nelanth	bronze	D'Q	Southern
G'narish	Gyarmath	bronze	D'Q	Igen
G'rannat		green	ATWoP	
G'sel		green	D'Q	Southern
	Gorianth	bronze	D'E	Telgar
Galliani, Marco	Duluth	brown	D'Dawn	Landing
Grasella		green	D'E	Telgar
H'ages	Kerth	bronze	D'Q	Telgar
H'grave	Hallath	green	MOR	Benden
H'mar	Janereth	bronze	DoP	Eastern
Haura	Werth	gold	MOR	Fort

Rider	Dragon	Color	Book	Weyr
Irene	Maruth	gold	D'E	Benden
J'dar		bronze	D'E	Telgar
J'ralt	Palanth	green	D'F	Benden
J'tan	Sharth	bronze	MOR	High Reaches
Jaxom	Ruth	white	D'Q	Ruatha Hold
Jean	Greteth	gold	CoP	New Benden
Jora	Nemorth	gold	D'F	Benden
Jule	Alanth	green	D'E	Telgar
Julie	Rementh	gold	CoP	New Benden
K'dall	Teelarth	blue	MOR	Telgar
K'der	Warth	blue	D'Q	Ista
K'din	Buleth	brown	DoP	Eastern
K'dren	Kuzuth	bronze	MOR	Benden
K'irnety	Fidrith	bronze	D'Q	Telgar
K'lon	Rogeth	blue	MOR	Fort
K'nebel	Firth	bronze	D'F	Benden
K'net	Piyanth	bronze	D'F	Benden
K'van	Heth	bronze	WD	Benden/Southern
K'vin	Charanth	bronze	D'E	Telgar
Kaiden, Jess	Hallath	bronze	CoP	Benden
Kamiana	Pelianth	gold	MOR	Fort
Kathy	Amalath	gold	D'Dawn	Landing
Kylara	Prideth	gold	D'F	Southern
L'bol	Timenth	bronze	MOR	Igen
L'mal	Clinnith	bronze	MOR	Fort
L'rad			D'F	Benden
L'rayl	Sorth	brown	MOR	Fort
L'ren			CoP	New Benden
L'ser	Vuroth	bronze	D'E	Telgar
L'tol	Larth	brown	D'F	ex–Benden
L'trel	Falgrenth	blue	D'Q	Southern
L'vin	Jith	bronze	MOR	Benden
L'zal	Beerth	green	ATWoP	Eastern
Lao, Shih	Firth	bronze	D'Dawn	Landing
Laura	Jemath	gold	D'E	Ista
Leri	Holth	gold	MOR	Fort
Lessa	Ramoth	gold	D'F	Benden
Levalla	Oribeth	gold	MOR	Benden
Lidora	Ilith	gold	MOR	Fort
M'barak	Arith	blue	MOR	Fort
M'dam	Kessuth	bronze	D'E	Telgar
M'gent	Ith	bronze	MOR	Benden
M'hall	Brianth	bronze	CoP	New Benden

Dragons and Their Riders

Rider	Dragon	Color	Book	Weyr
M'leng	Sith	green	D'E	Telgar
M'rak	Canith	bronze	D'E	Telgar
M'rand	Tileth	bronze	ATWoP	High Reaches
M'ray	Quoarth	brown	MOR	Ista
M'rek	Zigeth	bronze	D'Q	Telgar
M'shall	Craigath	bronze	D'E	Benden
M'sur		brown	DoP	Eastern
M'tani	Hogarth	bronze	MOR	Telgar
M'tok	Litorth	bronze	WD	Benden
Mardra	Loranth	gold	D'F	Fort
Margatta	Ludeth	gold	D'Q	Fort
Mari	Susuth	gold	D'E	High Reaches
Martin	Dagmath	blue	CoP	Fort
Mellor	Dalgeth	gold	MOR	Telgar
Merika		gold	D'Q	High Reaches
Mesla		green	D'E	Telgar
Miridan	Sutanith	gold	MOR	Telgar
Mirrim	Path	green	D'Q	Southern/Eastern
Moreta	Orlith	gold	MOR	Fort
N'klas	Petrath	bronze	CoP	Fort
N'men	Jelth	blue	MOR	Fort
N'mool	Bidorth	bronze	MOR	High Reaches
N'ran	Galath	brown	D'E	Fort
N'tar	Melath	bronze	MOR	High Reaches
N'ton	Lioth	bronze	D'F	Benden/Fort
Namurra	Jilith	gold	MOR	Igen
Nora	Tenneth	gold	D'Dawn	Landing
Nyassa	Milath	gold	D'Dawn	Landing
O'ney	Queth	bronze	D'E	Telgar
Oklina	Hannath	gold	NER	Fort
P'leen	Aaith	bronze	MOR	Igen
P'llomar	Kadarth	green	WD	Benden
P'nine	Ixth	bronze	MOR	High Reaches
P'ratan	Poranth	green	D'Q	Benden
P'ter	Siwith	blue	CoP	Fort
P'tero	Ormonth	blue	D'E	Telgar
P'zar	Roth	bronze	D'Q	Fort
Peter	Gilgath	brown	D'Dawn	Landing
Pilgra	Segrith	gold	D'Q	High Reaches
Prilla	Selianth	gold	WD	Fort
R'bert	Jenoth	brown	CoP	Fort
R'gul	Hath	bronze	D'F	Benden
R'len	Ponteth	bronze	MOR	High Reaches

Rider	Dragon	Color	Book	Weyr
R'limeak	Gionth	blue	MOR	Fort
R'mart	Branth	bronze	D'Q	Telgar
R'mel	Sorenth	brown	D'Q	Benden
R'nor	Virianth	brown	D'Q	Benden
	Rimbeth	brown	RoP	Benden
S'gar	Dunluth		ATWoP	Ruatha Hold
S'gor	Malth	green	MOR	Fort
S'goral	Betunth	green	D'Q	Southern
S'kedel	Adath	bronze	MOR	Fort
S'lan	Binth	bronze	D'F	Benden
S'lel	Tuenth	bronze	D'F	Benden
S'len	Bigath	green	ATWoP	Fort
S'ligar	Gianarth	bronze	MOR	High Reaches
S'mon	Tiabeth	bronze	D'E	Telgar
S'nan	Magrith	bronze	D'E	Fort
S'peren	Clioth	bronze	MOR	Fort
S'rond			ATWoP	Southern
Sarai	Lanath	gold	D'E	Fort
Sarra		green	D'E	Telgar
Sevya	Butoth	gold	CoP	Fort
Sh'gall	Kadith	bronze	MOR	Fort
Shanna	Haralth	gold	D'E	Igen
Silga	Brixth	gold	MOR	Igen
Sorka	Faranth	gold	D'Dawn	Landing
	Spelth	bronze	D'E	Telgar
T'bor	Orth	bronze	D'F	Benden/Southern
T'gellan	Monarth	bronze	D'Q	Benden
T'gor	Relth	blue	D'F	Benden
T'gran	Branth	brown	D'F	Benden
T'grel	Raylinth	bronze	MOR	Telgar
T'kul	Salth	bronze	WD	High Reaches/ Southern
T'lan		brown	D'E	Telgar
T'ledon	Serith	blue	D'Q	Fort
T'lel	Banuth	brown	D'E	Telgar
T'lion	Gadareth	bronze	CoP	Eastern
T'lonneg	Jalerth	bronze	MOR	Ista
T'mas			CoP	New Benden
T'nure	Tapeth	green	MOR	Fort
T'ragel	Keranth	blue	MOR	Fort
T'ral	Maneth	brown	MOR	Fort
T'ran	Rederth	bronze	WD	Igen
T'reb	Beth	green	D'Q	Fort

Dragons and Their Riders

Rider	Dragon	Color	Book	Weyr
T'red		brown	D'E	Telgar
T'ron	Fidranth	bronze	D'F	Fort
T'sel	Trenth	green	D'Q	Benden
T'sen		green	D'E	Telgar
T'sum			D'F	Benden
Tarrie	Porth	gold	D'Dawn	Landing
Torene		gold	D'F	Benden
Torene	Alaranth	gold	CoP	New Benden
	Tuzuth	bronze	MOR	Benden
Uloa	Elliath	gold	CoP	Fort
V'last	Collith	bronze	D'E	Telgar
V'line	Clarinath	bronze	RoP	Southern
V'mal	Koth	brown	MOR	High Reaches
V'mul	Tellath	brown	MOR	Benden
Varena	Ralenth	gold	WD	Southern
W'ter	Taventh	bronze	MOR	Benden
W'ven	Balgeth	green	MOR	Fort
Wimmia	Torenth	gold	MOR	Ista
Z'gal	Tracath	blue	D'E	Telgar
Z'ran		brown	D'E	Telgar
Zulaya	Meranath	gold	D'E	Telgar

Sources

BIBLIOGRAPHY

Allen, Richard Hinckley. *Star Names, Their Lore and Meaning.* New York: Dover, 1963, p. 357 (originally published by G. E. Stechert as *Star-Names and Their Meanings,* 1899).

Brown, Tom, Jr. *Tom Brown's Guide to Wild Edible and Medicinal Plants.* New York: Berkley, 1985.

Cox, Beverly, with Joan Whitman. *Cooking Techniques.* Boston/Toronto: Little Brown, 1981.

Fonstad, Karen Wynn. *The Atlas of Pern.* New York: Del Rey Books, 1984.

Lust, John. *The Herb Book.* New York: Bantam Books, 1974.

Matthews, Anne. *Vogue Dictionary of Knitting Stitches.* New York: Quill, 1984.

McCaffrey, Anne. *All the Weyrs of Pern.* New York: Del Rey Books, 1991.

———. *The Chronicles of Pern: First Fall.* New York: Del Rey Books, 1993.

———. *The Dolphins' Bell.* Newark, N.J.: Wildside Press, 1993.

———. *The Dolphins of Pern.* New York: Del Rey Books, 1994.

———. *Dragondrums.* New York: Atheneum, 1979.

———. *Dragonflight.* New York: Del Rey Books, 1968.

———. *Dragonquest.* New York: Del Rey Books, 1971.

———. "Dragonrider." *Analog Science Fiction/Science Fact,* December 1967 and January 1968.

———. *Dragonsdawn.* New York: Del Rey Books, 1988.

———. *Dragonseye.* New York: Del Rey Books, 1997.

———. *Dragonsinger.* New York: Atheneum, 1977.

———. *Dragonsong.* New York: Atheneum, 1976.

———. "The Smallest Dragonboy." In *Get Off the Unicorn.* New York: Del Rey Books, 1977.

———. *The Girl Who Heard Dragons.* New Castle, Va.: Cheap Street, 1985.

———. *Moreta, Dragonlady of Pern.* New York: Del Rey Books, 1983.

———. *Nerilka's Story.* New York: Del Rey Books, 1986.

———. *The Renegades of Pern.* New York: Del Rey Books, 1989.

———. *Rescue Run.* Newark, N.J.: Wildside Press, 1991.

———. "Weyr Search." *Analog Science Fiction/Science Fact,* October 1967.

———. *The White Dragon.* New York: Del Rey Books, 1978.

McGregor, Sheila. *Traditional Knitting.* London: B. T. Batsford, Ltd., 1983.

Middle Eastern Cooking. Time/Life Foods of the World Series. New York: Time-Life Books, 1976.

Nye, Jody Lynn. *Dragonfire.* New York: Tor Books, 1988.

————. *Dragonharper.* New York: Tor Books, 1987.

Thompson, Gladys. *Patterns for Guernseys, Jerseys & Arans; Fishermen's Sweaters from the British Isles.* 2d ed. New York: Dover, 1971.

OTHER SOURCES

The Adler Planetarium, Chicago, Illinois.

Alm, Marilyn and Harry, et al. *The Weyr Book of Isia.* New Orleans, 1994.

————. "Weyrwords" no. 42, New Orleans, 1985.

The Dragonriders of Pern game. Mayfair Games. Chicago, 1983.

Ecklar, Julia. "Brekke's Lament." In *The Traveller.* Waukegan, Ill., 1981.

Erickson, Niels, Threadfall Charts, 1987.

Hold, Hall & Weyr Badges, designed by Marilyn Alm, 1996.

Interviews, Anne McCaffrey, 3–11 October 1987, and assorted letters and conversations. 1987–1988.

Interview, Anne McCaffrey, 10 January 1996, and assorted faxes and letters, 1995–1996.

Correspondence, Christine V. Power, 1987, 1988.

Index

Page numbers in italic refer to illustrations.

Index